Praise for Victoria Laurie and
TO COACH A KILLER

"Enjoyable . . . Fans of superior cozies will be
well satisfied."
—*Publisher Weekly*

"A principled main character; well-drawn secondary
characters; satisfying plot twists; and a smattering of
humor distinguish this engaging mystery."
—*Booklist*

"A fun read that gets by on its characters' charm."
—*Kirkus Reviews*

Books by Victoria Laurie

COACHED TO DEATH

TO COACH A KILLER

COACHED IN THE ACT

Published by Kensington Publishing Corp.

To Coach a Killer

VICTORIA LAURIE

KENSINGTON
PUBLISHING CORP.

www.kensingtonbooks.com

KENSINGTON BOOKS are published by

Kensington Publishing Corp.
119 West 40th Street
New York, NY 10018

All Kensington titles, imprints, and distributed lines are available at special quantity discounts for bulk purchases for sales promotion, premiums, fund-raising, educational, or institutional use. Special book excerpts or customized printings can also be created to fit specific needs. For details, write or phone the office of the Kensington Special Sales Manager: Attn. Special Sales Department. Kensington Publishing Corp., 119 West 40th Street, New York, NY 10018. Phone: 1-800-221-2647.

The K logo is a trademark of Kensington Publishing Corp.

ISBN-13: 978-1-4967-2036-8
ISBN-10: 1-4967-2036-9
First Kensington Hardcover Edition: September 2020
First Kensington Mass Market Edition: August 2021

ISBN-13: 978-1-4967-2038-2 (ebook)
ISBN-10: 1-4967-2038-5 (ebook)

10 9 8 7 6 5 4 3 2 1

Printed in the United States of America

Chapter 1

Gilley wiped his eyes as he stepped into the office. I pretended not to notice. Fluffing a pillow on the love seat opposite my chair, I worked to appear busy while he pulled himself together.

Finally, Gilley cleared his throat and said, "You look nice."

I glanced up and saw the pain in his eyes and it made my own eyes mist. Still, I forced a smile to my lips and said, "Thank you, lovey. You're looking pretty smokin' hot yourself."

Gilley swiveled his torso in a way that told me he was pleased I'd noticed his layered sweater ensemble and skinny jeans, but then an awkward silence fell between us.

I decided to call out the elephant in the room. "Did Michel get to the airport on time?"

Gil swallowed hard. "He did."

I walked over and took up his hand. "A month isn't *that* long, you know."

Gil's chin dropped to his chest and he shrugged. "I know. It's just hard watching him get on *another* flight for *another* far-off destination when he was only home for two and a half months."

I squeezed his hand. "I know, sweetie. What can I do for you?"

Gil shook his head sadly. "Nothing, Cat. But thank you."

I tilted my head sideways to try and make eye contact. "Really? Nothing? Not even a little retail therapy?"

Gilley sighed. "Maybe later. Right now I only want to sit at my desk and work on that e-mail blast for you."

Gilley was helping me with a marketing campaign for the life-coaching business I'd started shortly after selling off my own mega-successful marketing firm, finalizing a divorce, and relocating to the Hamptons from Andover, Massachusetts, to be closer to my twin sons, Matt and Mike—who'd chosen boarding school over joint custody. A decision on their part that continues to break my heart. But I'd never tell them that.

Still, relocating to East Hampton had been a good decision, even if it had gotten off to a rather difficult start. I'd built myself a big, beautiful house—nicknamed Chez Cat, and a charming guesthouse, Chez Kitty—where two of my dearest friends in the world, Gilley Gillespie and his husband, Michel, had moved in after selling their ridiculously expensive place in Manhattan.

Initially, Gilley and Michel had only planned on staying a few months while they searched for a more affordable apartment in the city, but as time wore on, and Michel's reputation for being an outstanding fashion photographer took off—he's in high demand from *Vogue*, *Elle*, and *Harper's Bazaar*—it became clear that Gilley and I needed each other to combat the loneliness of my empty nest, and his constantly traveling husband.

So we settled into a routine; Gilley became my assistant and helped me launch my newfound purpose of becoming East Hampton's premiere life coach . . . which was getting off to a much slower start than I'd originally anticipated five months earlier when I'd first hung out my new professional shingle.

"How's that coming along, Gilley?" I asked, referring to the e-mail blast, which I hoped might spark up some business.

"Good," he replied. "I should have some copy for you to look at by the time you finish with your client this morning."

I rubbed my hands together eagerly. Finally! After nearly a month of radio silence I had a brand new client to focus on and parcel out some of my sage direction for the lost soul who needed it.

With a glance at my watch, I noted that said client—Willem Entwistle—would be here any minute.

"Perfect," I told Gil, and turned toward my chair, which was set in the middle of a large, open space in what served as my office.

I'd first decided to hang my shingle in an older building with a ton of character, but not a lot of commercial appeal, until I'd purchased the building and subsequently poured a ton of money into renovating it. Luckily, the renovations had turned out fabulously, and the entire building was fully rented with professional tenants who paid their rents on time and seemed to keep mostly to themselves.

It's probably what I liked most about the building, in fact; it was superbly quiet. Especially the third floor, where an accountant and an import/export merchant worked.

Of course, that could be due to the fact that the import/export merchant was rarely in residence. In fact, he hadn't been to his office in the Hamptons—at least as near as I could tell—in over three months. Something that troubled me quite a bit, actually, but, like Gilley, I was trying hard this morning not to dwell on topics that made me feel sad.

As I sat down in the chair opposite the couch, I inhaled deeply, held it for a moment, then let it out very slowly. I did that two more times and felt ready to face any challenge.

In hindsight, perhaps I should've taken a few more deep breaths.

Like fifty.

At promptly ten a.m., the main door to my office opened, and over the top of Gilley's desk I saw someone enter who almost appeared to be walking in on his knees, he was so low to the ground.

It took me a full minute to realize that the person wasn't on his knees. He was walking. At full height.

Gilley looked up from his computer and did a double take. He then shoved the heel of his hand into his mouth and tried to stifle a startled giggle.

He failed, miserably.

I stood up and rushed over to the desk. "Hello," I said, subconsciously bending at the waist toward the stranger, who was all of four and a half feet tall, and trying to ignore Gilley. "May I help you?"

The stranger squared his shoulders, but a sheen of perspiration glinted off his forehead. Taking my outstretched hand, he said, "Hello. I'm Willem. I have an appointment for ten a.m."

His palm was quite sweaty, and I felt my face flush, both at the embarrassment of having my assistant lose it in front of Willem, and for the fact that I'd once hired a crew of little people to dress up like cupids and dangle out of two pear trees at my sister's wedding (which, not coincidentally, had ended in disaster). The shame I'd felt these few years later at my insensitivity caught up with me as I shook Willem's sweaty palm.

"Wonderful to meet you, Willem," I gushed, perhaps a bit too enthusiastically. "I'm Catherine Cooper. Your life coach."

By this time, Gilley had recovered himself enough to look quite contrite, but I'd still have words with him later. I was furious that he'd so obviously insulted my client.

Willem shook my hand, and his gaze nervously darted around the room. I felt terrible that he'd come into my office for his first session and had been made to feel uncomfortable. "Can I offer you coffee, water, or another beverage?" I asked, waving my hand to indicate the seating area.

"Do you have any herbal tea?"

I nodded toward Gilley and narrowed my eyes to let him know that he was in trouble. "Gilley, would you please prepare a cup of herbal tea for Mr. Entwistle?"

"Right away!" Gilley said, trying to cover for his earlier insult. Jumping up from his chair and hurrying over to the counter where we kept our beverage selection, he pulled out the drawer for the tea and said, "We have chai, cinnamon, ginger, and . . ."

Gilley paused while he rooted around in the tray looking for other flavors.

"Any chamomile?" Willem asked.

Gil frowned. "No, sorry, we're a little short."

My eyes widened.

So did Gilley's. He rushed to fill in the sudden awkward silence. "I . . . I . . . I mean we don't have any. Not that you're short—*we're* short. . . . Out. We're out. Of chamomile."

Gilley's face was flushed bright red, and probably mirrored my own.

Willem, however, seemed to find Gil's sudden embarrassment funny. He cracked a tiny smile and said, "Cinnamon."

Gilley nodded like an overly enthused bobblehead before turning away to make the tea.

Meanwhile, Willem and I sat down opposite each other, giving me the chance to fully take him in.

He was an interesting character, which had nothing to do with his being a little person, although, perhaps that did make him a tad more compelling. His face was quite handsome, fairly square with a prominent jaw, which was covered by a well-trimmed dark brown beard and mustache, but his forehead—which was also quite prominent—revealed that he spent a good deal of time with a furrowed brow as there were lines etched into his forehead. Overall I'd put him in his early-to-midthirties. And, while his head and torso were normal size, his legs and arms were shortened, which likely meant that he was born with a form of disproportionate dwarfism.

Still, sitting across from me, his height was far less noticeable and I focused on other features, like his brown hair, parted on the side, and the perfectly tailored charcoal-colored wool blazer, crisp white silk dress shirt, black slacks, and Italian leather shoes he wore, suggesting that he'd spent quite a bit of money on his attire.

And if that weren't a big enough clue, the gold Rolex on his wrist and the diamond-studded cufflinks were dead giveaways.

The most striking thing about him, however, were his eyes. Large and colored a deep chestnut brown, they were framed by impossibly long lashes, giving him an innocent quality I found endearing.

"So tell me why you're here, Willem," I said, reaching for a pen and pad that I kept on a table next to my chair.

Willem sat on the couch and folded his hands, his feet dangling above the floor. "Wow, where do I even begin?" he asked.

I smiled. "Start anywhere. We can piece together what we need to later. For now, just tell me what impulse led you to my door?"

"Um . . . okay. I guess it's because of my grandmother."

"Your grandmother?"

"Yes. I live with her. And I'm not some loser who can't earn a living. I handle my grandmother's portfolio and do some freelancing for several luxury car magazines, so I do okay."

I jotted myself a note. He was intelligent, educated, and obviously a self-motivated worker. That was a relief. It'd be one less problem to solve.

Willem continued. "Grandmother and I live together because, for the most part, she raised me from the age of four, and we look after each other."

"Your parents . . . ?" I inquired.

"Dead to me."

I nodded. "Ah. Yes, I've got parents in that category as well."

Willem cocked his head, but a small hint of a smile

touched his lips. We in the dysfunctional childhood club feel especially reassured when meeting other members.

Gilley approached us with a steaming cup of tea and a dispenser of honey. "Here you are, Mr. Entwistle," he said, setting down the cup and the honey.

"Thank you, you're too kind," Willem said. And it was a genuine statement, and one, I noted, which made Gilley's face flush. I could see he was beginning to feel really bad about laughing at Willem when he'd first appeared. Perhaps I didn't need to lecture him after all.

Gilley then turned to me, dipped his chin as if to apologize to me personally. I nodded slightly and there was peace between us once again. He then scurried over to his desk to get focused on my newsletter.

"You know, I haven't spoken to my parents in many years either," I said, getting back to Willem's point.

Willem picked up the steaming mug next to him and hovered his lips over the brim while looking at me with raised brow. "Are they divorced or still together?"

"They're still together. Making each other miserable for nearly fifty years, now."

Willem smiled and nodded knowingly. "My parents have been divorced from each other since I was three. They've each been married and divorced from four other people throughout the years too, but I remain their only child, which, I suppose, is a blessing considering . . ."

I bit my lip. I hoped that Willem wasn't referring to his dwarfism as something that should never be replicated. True, the condition came with its setbacks, but Willem seemed to be a perfectly lovely young man.

To get us back on track I said, "You had said that your grandmother is the reason you're here?"

"Oh, yes, almost forgot. Grandmother has requested I

get out into the world and explore it. She wants me to go places and meet people—you know, socialize and all of that—but I'm reluctant."

I nodded. I could only imagine how difficult it might be for him as a little person. The stares. The ridicule. The inappropriate giggling . . .

"Is it really so bad?"

Willem shifted slightly. "Well, yes," he said. "It's pretty much a disaster anytime I step foot into a new setting."

"People can be so cruel," I agreed.

Willem stared at me oddly. "Oh, you think it's the reaction to this that I'm concerned with?" He made a sweeping motion down the length of his body.

I was caught off guard. I mean, *wasn't* it? "Well . . . I . . . I didn't want to assume, but you did say . . ." I let out a sigh and gave up. "Willem, I apologize. Please continue to tell me why you'd like to employ my help."

Willem bit his lip, as if suddenly nervous about speaking to me. He then glanced over his shoulder at Gilley, who sat typing away on his computer.

I looked over too, and, although I couldn't say for sure that Gilley wasn't listening, it didn't seem like he was. "Whatever you have to say will remain private," I encouraged. "It will never leave this office."

Willem folded his hands together and straightened his shoulders as if gathering his resolve. "I need your help, because I believe—very strongly—that I'm cursed."

I blinked.

Then blinked again.

Then I leaned in a little and cocked my head. "You believe you're . . . what now?"

Somewhere in the background, I heard the steady

clicking of keys on Gilley's keyboard come to an abrupt stop.

Willem leaned toward me too, mirroring my stance. "I'm cursed. Hexed. Damned. Doomed. Jinxed. Vexed. Pick your synonym, it's all the same affliction."

I sat straight again and found myself smiling. It wasn't that I found Willem's confession funny; it was simply that I didn't quite know how to react. So, seeing that he was obviously an intelligent person, I tried stating the obvious. "Willem, curses aren't real. They're something roadside fortune-tellers level at gullible patrons."

"Oh, they're real, Cat," Gilley called out.

I shifted my gaze to send him the most smoldering look I could muster. But Gil merely ignored my warning glare and got up from his seat and came over to perch on the arm of the couch at the opposite end of where Willem sat. "Who cursed you?" Gil asked.

"Directly? No one I know," Willem said.

Gilley and I exchanged a confused glance before I addressed Willem again. "Then why do you believe that you're cursed?"

"My mother inherited a series of run-down apartment complexes in the Bronx. While pregnant with me she wanted to evict a woman from one of her buildings based solely on the fact that other tenants had complained that the woman was a gypsy who'd been setting curses on people in the building. The building's super was too afraid to confront the woman and tell her to get out, so, in a show of bravado—which my mother is famous for— she went down to the building herself with two thugs in tow and personally evicted the woman, throwing all of her meager belongings onto the street.

"On her way out the door, the woman issued a curse. Allegedly, she pointed to my mother's belly and said that the son born to her would become the source of her greatest shame and bring nothing but disaster to any new environment wherever he would go. Five weeks later I was born like this," he said, waving to himself again. "And disaster *has* followed me wherever I've gone."

I stared at Willem with widened eyes, and then pulled my gaze away to look at Gilley. We exchanged an unspoken *Yikes!*

"Willem," I said calmly, focusing back on him, "I'm quite sure your dwarfism isn't due to any curse. From the little that I know about it, it's a condition that's caused by genetics, correct?"

"Typically," Willem agreed. "But there're no other little people on either side of my family. I'm the anomaly, and when I was born, I was indeed the source of my mother's greatest shame. She detested the fact that I wasn't perfect, and that I drew stares and pitying looks from others. She sent me to live with my paternal grandmother early on, thank God. My grandmother has never shown me anything but unconditional love."

I took that in and then tried another, reasonable tactic. "Well, when you moved in with your grandmother, that was a new environment for you, correct? No destruction or chaos followed you, did it?"

"On the contrary," Willem said. "The day I went to live with her a freak storm struck and caused major destruction to her estate. She and my grandfather spent months and a fortune repairing it."

Gilley and I exchanged another unspoken, *Yikes!*

Willem continued, as if he really wanted to convince

us. "When I was five and attended my first day of kinder-garten, a pipe burst in the building, flooding the entire school. When I was six, Gran treated me to a vacation in Montauk. The day we arrived the hotel's parking lot de-veloped a sinkhole that swallowed up three cars, includ-ing the hotel's shuttle van. On the first day of middle school, a construction crew hit a gas line and the resulting explosion caused the gymnasium's ceiling to cave in. My first day of high school, the bus I was supposed to ride to school in, crashed into a pickup truck twenty feet from my bus stop. And on and on it goes. The only silver lining is that no one has ever been seriously hurt, but I have lit-erally dozens of these stories, Catherine. They all end in some kind of disaster."

I could feel my heart rate tick up a tiny notch as a seed of doubt crept into my mind. All I knew about curses was what my sister, a world-renowned psychic, had told me; and that was that they weren't real—just a gimmick the corrupt played upon the vulnerable.

But Gilley's insistence to the contrary had rattled me. Gilley had spent a decade as a professional ghostbuster in partnership with two very gifted psychic mediums, M.J. and Heath Whitefeather.

Out of the corner of my eye, I'd watched Gilley nod his head while Willem had recounted some of the chaos and destruction that had followed him throughout life and I began to think that perhaps my sister had been mis-taken. I mean, Gilley would know better than anyone if there was some credence to the idea.

Still, perhaps because I was scared, I tried pushing back against the notion one more time. "But, Willem, you've been here . . . what? Fifteen minutes already, and nothing even remotely unusual or destructive has happened."

The second that last word left my mouth the building's fire alarm went off.

All three of us jumped at the ear-piercing sound, and Gilley let out a high-pitched squeal.

I lifted my chin and began sniffing the air. Sure enough, the smell of something burning wafted faintly to my nose. "Call nine-one-one!" I yelled at Gilley before turning to run out the interior door, which placed me in the central hallway leading to the stairs and the upper floors.

Dashing up to the second-story landing, I shouted to the wide-eyed tenants standing in their doorways, "Get out of the building! Everyone, clear out!"

The tenants and their staff began to rush for the stairs, and I did too, but instead of going down, I went up.

I know it was stupid, but my first obligation as landlord was to make sure that everyone got out of the building, so, against all common sense, I rushed up the stairs to a now thickening haze of smoke and, upon reaching the landing, I was picked right up off my feet and carried back down the steps.

The move was so sudden and unexpected that I didn't take in who'd lifted me into his arms until we reached the second-floor landing. It was as I was shifted slightly in those strong arms that I realized I was staring right into the handsome face of Maks Grinkov, my former . . . or maybe current . . . flame. (No pun intended.)

"Maks!" I exclaimed. "What're you doing here?"

Maks rounded the landing and began to fast-track us down to the first floor. And even though he was exerting himself, he was still able to offer me a crooked smile. "Currently, I'm earning my hero badge by saving a beautiful woman from a burning building."

I held on to Maks and said nothing more until we reached the exterior door; he turned and pushed on it with his back. Once outside I felt the bite of the early spring cold and shuddered.

Maks held me tighter. "It's all right, Catherine," he said soothingly, obviously misinterpreting my reaction to the cold. "You're safe."

I eyed him skeptically. "Am I?"

His smile widened. "Of course," he said, easing me to my feet again.

Gilley appeared next to me, his phone in his hand and a desperate look on his face. *"What were you thinking?!"* he shouted.

I took a step back. Gilley had never screamed at me like that.

"You could have died!" he went on, and then I understood.

"Oh, Gil," I said, placing a hand on his shoulder. "I'm perfectly fine."

"Gilley has a point," Maks said.

I narrowed my eyes. "You're not helping."

"Catherine, when a building's on fire, you find the nearest exit, not the nearest way to the top floor."

"I was trying to warn my tenants."

Maks pointed up into the air, where the sound of the smoke alarm and now approaching sirens were becoming far too loud to ignore along with the ever present smell of smoke. "I think we would've figured it out," he said.

I stared up at the top floor as if expecting to see the

glow of orange flames, but only a thin sliver of smoke eked out the top right window.

Just then Martin Wallace came running down the street toward us. He was the tenant in that section of the building. Holding a cup of coffee and pale as a ghost, he came to a stop next to us and said, "Oh, God! I think that might be my toaster!"

Turning to me as if he needed to explain himself, he said, "I put my English muffin in, and that's when I noticed I was out of coffee, so I went down the street to grab a cup. I've only been gone a few minutes!"

A fire truck pulled to a stop in front of the curb and three firemen jumped out. They were all looking up at the window leaking smoke. "Is the building manager here?" one of them asked.

I stepped forward. "Yes, sir. I'm the owner of the building."

He took his eyes off the building, waved to the two others, and they dashed inside. "Can you take a head count for me, please?" he asked, motioning to the gathering crowd. "We need to know if there's anyone still inside."

"Yes, of course," I said.

Moving through the crowd, I silently counted all of my tenants, including Maks, but I then approached the dentist, Dr. Strickland, and because I wasn't familiar with his entire staff, I had to ask if all of his employees and patients were accounted for. He pointed to the small group surrounding him and confirmed that everyone had made it out safely.

At that moment, the two firemen who'd dashed into the building appeared again, one holding a smoking toaster, which he set down on the sidewalk and then blasted with a fire extinguisher. It made a huge mess, but I wasn't about to complain.

I then headed back over to the man in charge. "Everyone made it out of the building safely."

The fireman nodded and pointed to the toaster. "That seems to be your culprit. My guys are still gonna do a suite-by-suite check just to be thorough. We had to break down the door to the suite to get to the toaster, but it'd be a good thing if we didn't have to repeat that process for all the others. Do you have a set of master keys handy?"

I motioned over my shoulder toward the building. "They're in my office."

He waved us forward. "I'll escort you in."

Once inside, I headed straight to Gilley's desk, quickly rummaging through the top drawer to locate the master key ring. After handing that over to the chief, he then escorted me out of the building. Luckily, I was able to grab both my coat and Gilley's on the way out.

Everyone waited in the cold for about twenty minutes as the firemen went floor to floor and suite to suite. At last we were able to move back inside, and Martin followed me, Maks, and Gilley into my office. "Catherine, I'm so, so sorry," Martin said. He looked absolutely beside himself.

"Martin," I said calmly, "Please, don't worry too much about this. The building has insurance, and, if you could cover the cost to repair the door of your suite, and promise that you'll never leave a toaster unattended in your office again, then I think we can put this whole matter behind us."

Martin nodded vigorously, thanked me profusely, and left.

Once he was gone I collapsed onto the sofa. The morning had been quite eventful on a number of counts. Sitting up again, I looked around. "Where's Willem?" I asked Gilley.

"He ran to his car and drove away the moment we got outside."

My jaw dropped. "And you just . . . *let* him go?"

"What did you want me to do, Cat?" Gilley snapped. "Hang up with nine-one-one to give him a comforting hug and beg him to stay right before something big, like a meteor, fell out of the sky to kill me?"

I stared at Gilley wondering if he'd lost his mind. "What *on earth* are you talking about?"

"You heard him," Gil said, positioning his hand on his hip to show me he wasn't about to back down. "The boy is cursed! I'm not cuddling up to that. In fact, I should get some holy water and spritz this whole office just to flush out any bad juju."

I put a palm to my forehead, feeling the first painful twinges of a stress headache. "Gil," I sighed.

"What's this about a curse?" Maks asked. He'd been hovering near us, listening to our conversation, and he seemed genuinely concerned.

Before I could tell him that it wasn't anything I could discuss—I'd meant it when I'd promised Willem that our conversation would be private—Gilley said, "Cat's new client is cursed. It's why the building caught fire."

"Gilley!"

"Well, it's true!"

"It is *not*!" I yelled, my temper getting the best of me. "The building *didn't* catch fire, a toaster did, and Willem had nothing to do with that!"

Gilley pursed his lips and eyed me skeptically. "So it's

just a *coincidence* that he walks in at ten this morning, confesses that a gypsy cast a spell on him in utero, and that he's had a string of catastrophes follow him his *entire* life and by ten-twenty all the smoke alarms are going off?"

I stared incredulously at Gilley. Was he kidding? "*Of course* it's a coincidence!"

Gilley crossed his arms, his lips still pursed. "I think not."

Meanwhile Maks had taken up a corner of Gilley's desk to perch himself on and watch our back and forth like taking in a tennis match. To Gilley he said, "Was he really cursed by a gypsy?"

"Yes," Gil said.

"No!" I yelled.

Gilley turned again to me. "Cat, I know you don't believe in curses, but they're real, okay? Just ask M.J. or Heath. We've dealt with them before, and their aftermath, and they were never anything to take lightly or dismiss."

I sighed heavily. It wasn't even eleven a.m. and already the day felt long. "My sister says they're a bunch of hooey, and I'll take her word for it."

"Really?" Gilley said, tapping his foot. "And Abby's handled exactly how many demons in her time?"

I frowned. "Well . . . none that I know of, but I think she'd know if any of that was real."

"Would she?" Gilley asked, then he lowered his voice another octave and dipped his chin. "*Would* she?"

"I can't even believe I'm having this conversation," I said, completely exasperated. "Gilley, get me Willem's phone number. I want to call him and see how he's doing."

"Why call when we could probably just turn on the

news and follow the path of destruction all the way back to his house?" Gil muttered, but he did head around his desk to peck at his computer for a moment. He then jotted down the number on a sticky note and handed it to me. "Here. Please *don't* encourage him to come back here."

I took the note and offered him a withering look. He simply squinted at me and pursed his lips again.

We were at our version of a standoff.

Maks interrupted the uncomfortable silence by sliding off Gilley's desk and coming around to stand in front of me. Lifting my chin with his finger, he said, "Can we talk later?"

I softened, but a part of me was still a tiny bit hurt that he'd disappeared on me nearly four months earlier and I hadn't seen or heard from him since. "During this talk will you be planning to explain why, after everything that went down around here, you chose to simply disappear like a thief in the night? And for that matter, why I haven't heard from you since before Christmas?"

"I will," he promised. "But first allow me to apologize for that, Catherine. It wasn't what I wanted, and I had every intention of getting in touch with you, but you have to trust me that circumstances dictated that I stay away for a time."

"That's cryptic," I mused.

"Yes, I know. But I'll explain everything tonight, if you're willing to hear me out."

"Tonight is pretty short notice," I said, feeling a blush touch my cheeks. Maks unsettled me in a way that I found both vexing and intoxicating. I couldn't quite figure out his power over me, well, other than—for a man— he was simply breathtaking.

"You have other plans?" Maks asked. I liked it that he sounded a tiny bit jealous.

"No," Gilley said. "She's got nothing on her agenda other than another night of Hallmark movies and Skinny-girl popcorn."

I turned and gave Gilley an absolutely murderous look. He shrank in his seat and held his hands up in surrender.

Turning back to Maks, I said, "What time were you thinking of getting together?"

Maks lifted my hand and stroked it ever so lightly with the fingers of his free hand. The move sent a delicious shiver up my spine. "Seven o'clock?"

"Seven could work," I said.

"Please, she'll be ready at six-thirty," Gilley assured him.

If Maks weren't holding my hand I would've used it to smack Gilley. As it was, my smile tightened and I reiterated, "Seven o'clock will be fine."

Maks winked at me, kissed the top of my hand, nodded to Gilley, and left the office. The second the door closed I rounded on Gilley. "I know that you're quite upset that Michel left this morning, which is why I'm not going to fire you on the spot, but, Gilley Gillespie, if you *ever* leak another client's personal confession from this office again, I swear to God, friendship or no friendship, your butt will be out that door faster than you can say Candy Darling!"

Gilley gasped and put a hand to his mouth. He knew how serious I was, because I only invoked the name of his favorite icon when I really meant what I said.

"You'd . . . *fire* me? *Me*, Cat?"

I crossed my arms and glared at him. "In a minute, Gilley. That was unconscionable!"

Gilley's eyes watered slightly and his lower lip trembled.

Inwardly I groaned. He looked like a sad puppy and I felt my conviction soften. Still, he needed to understand that, without the sacred trust that exists between all life coaches and their clients, the system simply couldn't work. So I stood my ground. "I mean it, Gilley. What's revealed within these four walls *stays* within these four walls."

"But it was just Maks," Gilley said hoarsely. "I mean, wouldn't you have told him over dinner all about your crazy client who thinks he's cursed?"

"No," I said, and I meant it. "It's none of Maks's business. And it's none of *yours* either. You don't get to repeat the intimate details of someone's life for your own amusement."

Gilley's gaze dropped to his lap. After a moment, he nodded. "Okay. I get it. I'm sorry, Cat."

I inhaled deeply and let it out in a measured exhale. "Good. Thank you. And now that we're on the same page, please get Willem on the phone for me. I want to make sure he knows that I don't think he had anything to do with this morning's events."

Gilley sat in his chair looking at me with an uncomfortable expression. I couldn't tell if he was feeling contrite for having been reprimanded, or if there was something else triggering his expression.

"What?" I finally asked.

"Curses are real, Cat. They are. And if Willem is under one, then that could mean trouble for us."

I considered that for a moment.

See, I believed that Gilley was more knowledgeable in this area than I was, but I still found the whole thing a bit far-fetched. Still, didn't I at least owe it to Willem to consider the possibility that the life he was describing was some giant series of coincidences?

So, I asked Gilley, "Do you think M.J. or Heath would be willing to talk to me about it?"

"Sure. But let's ask Heath and keep M.J. out of it. I don't want her to worry about us."

I nodded. "Good. Yes, we don't want to upset M.J. so early in her pregnancy."

Gilley smiled at me, looking genuinely relieved, and just like that we were back to being on good terms again. He then turned to ring Willem and I headed to my chair where I could pick up the extension.

In the few moments that Gilley took to place the call, I reflected on the sudden reappearance of Maks Grinkov, and while I was thrilled to see him back in town—and in the building no less—I was also a bit nervous about all that came with that.

Maks was involved with something that frightened me—namely, the Chechen mafia. Weeks earlier, I'd had a nasty encounter with one of their paid assassins who'd also tried to frame me for murder. Maks knew the assassin. Hell, he'd had dinner with her on the night she'd tried to murder me. And she'd shot someone else I was developing feelings for—a local police detective who, if not as sophisticated and cosmopolitan as Maks, still managed to hold his own in the captivating department.

And I wondered if Maks being back in town also meant that I'd have to make some sort of emotional decision about which man I preferred.

That'd be difficult, because I had strong feelings for both, and, frustratingly, both men had been elusive of late. Maks had been tied up with his mafia connections, and Detective Shepherd had been busy obsessing over his ex-wife's murder. Both of the men's endeavors had kept them out of circulation these past four months, which'd been fine because my sons had come home for the holidays, and I'd been busy with all of that, but now that I had a little more free time on my hands, it was nice to see that at least one of the two men was making an effort to see me.

Gilley jolted me out of thought when he waved to get my attention and said, "Willem's on line one."

"Right," I said, reaching for the receiver. "Best to focus on the task at hand and worry about the rest later."

"What's that?" Gilley asked.

"Nothing," I assured him, even though I was hardly sure of anything in that moment.

Chapter 2

"Willem?" I said when I picked up line one.

"Hi, Ms. Cooper."

I relaxed a little. He hardly sounded traumatized. "Please," I said. "Call me Catherine."

"Okay. Hi, Catherine. If you're inquiring about your fee for today, I've already sent you payment via Venmo."

That took me by surprise. I wasn't even thinking about charging for the session, mostly because it hadn't really even been a session, just fifteen minutes of tea and a little background. "Thank you," I said, "but I wasn't calling you about that."

"Then what can I do for you?"

"Well, you ran out of here so quickly, I didn't have a chance to apologize for the chaos of the morning."

"Why would you apologize?" he said, his voice sounding weary. "It was my fault."

"Nonsense. Willem, all blame rests firmly on the shoulders of one of my tenants. He left a toaster unattended and it was something so minor in the end. Truly, there was no harm done and none of it was your fault."

"I brought the curse with me when I came to your office. It was me. And I wouldn't have done that, but you insisted on meeting face to face for our first session, and I . . . well . . . I suppose I was a little desperate for someone to help me."

My heart went out to this poor man. "Willem, I want you to listen to me. I understand that you believe this curse is real, so I want you to know that—if you're right, if in fact this curse and other curses are real—I can recommend someone who might be able to help."

"Who?"

"A friend of mine and a former associate of Gilley's. A very gifted spirit medium who's had extensive experience in the realm of the paranormal. I'd like to give him a call and speak to him about this, if you're all right with me discussing your personal business with another professional, that is."

"Of course," he said quickly. "If you think it might help, by all means, do it."

"Excellent," I said. "Give me a day or two to get in touch with him, and I'll get back to you as soon as I can, all right?"

"That's fine," he said. "I'm open to anything at this point."

After hanging up with Willem, I headed toward the stairs, intent on checking in on Martin, but as I entered the central hallway the exterior building door opened and in rushed Detective Steve Shepherd.

He took one look at me and blew out a sigh of relief. "Hey," he said.

"Hi," I replied, startled by his sudden appearance. "I'm surprised to see you. Is something wrong?"

He looked up toward the stairs and then all around the hallway. "I heard there was a fire here this morning."

I laughed and waved my hand. "Oh, that. It was nothing. Just a toaster left on too high in one of the office suites. Really, it was a lot of commotion for nothing."

Shepherd nodded, but there was something in his eyes that still held a bit of concern.

To reassure him I reached out and squeezed his arm. "Hey . . . I'm fine."

He looked at my hand on his arm and something small and intimate passed between us. Just like the last time we were together, which was oh, three months ago now.

"Good," he said softly, covering my hand with his. "That's good."

The door behind Shepherd opened and a man walked in, startling us both. I let my hand fall away and Shepherd cleared his throat uncomfortably.

We both stared at the stranger, who eyed us with curiosity before he pointed to the stairs and asked, "Doctor Strickland's office?"

"Second floor," I told him, with a nod toward the stairs.

The man moved past us and carried on his way.

"I better let you get on with your day," Shepherd said, turning to leave.

"Detective," I said.

He turned back. "Yeah?"

I shook my head and forced a smile. "Nothing. Thanks for checking on me."

He tipped an imaginary hat, headed out, and I was left to ponder the meaning of his sudden appearance.

"Cat?" Gilley said.

I jumped, realizing Gil was poking his head out of the entrance to our suite. "Yes?"

"Heath's on the line. He's got a few minutes if you'd like to talk to him."

"Oh, yes. Yes, that'd be great. Thank you, Gilley."

Abandoning my earlier mission to check on Martin, I followed Gilley back into my office and picked up the line at my chair. "Heath?"

"Cat!" he said sweetly. "Good to hear your voice. How've you been?"

I knew Heath mainly through my friendship with Gilley, who, along with Heath and his wife, M.J., had once led incredibly adventurous lives as psychic mediums who hosted a weekly cable TV series called *Ghoul Getters*. It'd been a ratings hit for years, but several location shoots had also proven to be quite dangerous and at one point or another, M.J., Gilley, and Heath had almost died at the hands of evil spirits.

When M.J. became pregnant with their first child, the couple had decided to retire from ghostbusting, and they both now lived very quiet, peaceful lives in Santa Fe, New Mexico, surrounded by Heath's family and raising their daughter while also preparing for another two bundles of joy arriving about five months from now.

"I'm fine, my friend, thank you," I said, replying to his inquiry. "And I don't think I've had a chance to congratulate you and M.J. yet! Such wonderful news!"

Heath chuckled, clearly happy to talk about his expanding family. "Yeah, can you believe it? Twins!"

"You both must be so thrilled," I said. "And if you need any advice about how to get through the first few months with the babies, just give me a call. I have plenty of experience to draw from should you need some help."

"Oh, yeah, you have twin sons, right?"

"I do. Matthew and Michael. They're fourteen going on thirty."

Heath chuckled. "We'll definitely look forward to picking your brain, Cat, although, M.J. thinks she can handle everything on her own. She keeps reminding me that she was once a badass demon buster, and handling twin babies and a toddler should be child's play."

"Those are the hormones talking," I said with a laugh. "Don't believe her. She'll need plenty of help."

"Agreed. Lucky for her, I'm not an idiot, and I'll be ready for the handoff when it comes. So, Gilley tells me that you've got a new client who says he's been cursed, is that right?"

"It is. But it's just so hard for me to believe, Heath. I was hoping you could help shed some light on its validity or offer me some advice about how to convince him that it's all in his head."

"For sure. But first tell me why he thinks he's cursed."

I detailed for Heath everything that Willem had said to us, and Heath listened silently throughout the lengthy explanation. When I was through, he said, "Wow. That's some interesting anecdotal evidence."

"It is, but like I said, I just have a hard time believing some gypsy could've cast a spell on poor Willem before he was even born."

"Actually, that's the time when a curse might form the most powerful attachment," Heath said.

"It is?"

"Absolutely. If this woman really did wield some energetic, manipulative prowess—and mind you that's an extremely rare psychic talent to have—then pointing a curse at a pregnant woman's unborn child would be the easiest way to get revenge. Babies in utero have no aura—no field of electromagnetic energy yet. They don't get that until they're born, so they're totally defenseless for the entire time they're in the womb."

"Wouldn't they be protected by their mother's aura?" I asked.

"Yes and no. There's a point at which the aura protecting the mother and child would thin for the baby, and that happens usually around the third trimester, a few weeks before the baby's born. It's a tricky time, energetically speaking, for the child. So, if Willem's mother was near the later end of her pregnancy, then it's entirely possible that he could really be cursed."

"How can we know for sure?"

Heath sighed. "Well, you could set him up for a quick session with me, and I could take a look."

I brightened. "You'd do that?"

"Sure. If it'll help you and him, I'm all for it."

"I would so appreciate it," I told him, but then I thought of another question. "Heath, if Willem is actually cursed, what should he do? Get an exorcism?"

"No, nothing so crazy as that," Heath said. "I think the place to start is for me to connect with your client and see if I can pick up anything. Once I know what we're dealing with, I might be able to come up with a plan."

"I can't tell you how grateful I'd be for your help," I

told him. I hated the thought of this poor man being confined in his home due to something that happened to him before he was even born.

"It's no problem, Cat. I'm happy to help. Have Gilley send me a text with Willem's info and I'll look at my schedule for a good time for us to talk."

After hanging up with Heath I glanced at Gilley, who was pretending to be immersed in my marketing campaign. "Will you please text Heath Willem's phone number? Oh, and please call Willem and let him know who Heath is and why he'll be in touch, okay?"

"Heath is going to help lift the curse?" Gilley asked.

"I don't know about that," I said. "But he's at least going to use his talents to try and determine if one is in fact attached to Willem."

"Got it," Gil said, reaching for his cell phone to text Willem and Heath.

I got up and walked to the closet to grab my coat and purse. "I'm heading out for the rest of the afternoon. Text me if you need me, Gilley."

"Where're you off to?"

"The twins are flying out with their father to Aruba next week for spring break and I want to do a little shopping and send them each a care package in time for them to leave."

"Care package?"

"Yes. Nothing major, just some sunscreen, swim trunks, new sunglasses, a few outfits for dinners out . . . you know . . . the essentials."

Gilley smirked at me. "Your kids have *big* first-world problems, huh?"

I rolled my eyes, gave Gilley a casual wave, and headed for the door.

Much of the rest of the day was spent gathering all the items I planned to send to the boys. I had no doubt their father would forget the sunscreen, and they'd both had a growth spurt this year, so new swim trunks and casual wear for all the places they'd go besides the beach were in order.

My last stop was at the post office to send off the care package, and while I stood in line, I couldn't help but reflect moodily over the fact that Tom—my ex-husband— got to take the boys on a vacation that used to be a family tradition.

Deep down I had to admit that it hurt to be excluded from all the fun, but the divorce agreement was very strict when it came to assigning not only an equitable number of vacation days between the two of us, but also what holidays were assigned to whom. Tom got spring break, I got an extra week during the summer. And, truthfully, unless I wanted Tom to protest where I spent my vacations with the boys, I pretty much had to keep my mouth shut about wherever he ventured with them.

Still, it irked me that he'd chosen to take Matt and Mike to the very same hotel resort that we'd always visited for spring break as a family, but then the man was never very good at coming up with new adventures, preferring to stick with the old.

God, my ex was dull.

Just as I finished paying the clerk at the counter for the shipping fee, my cell rang. "Hello, Gilley," I said.

"Are you done with your errands yet? I'm home and I'm bored."

I sighed tiredly. It'd been a whirlwind of a day. "Yes, love. On my way back. I should be there in less than fifteen minutes."

"Perfect!" he said. "I'll have some baked treats for you to try out, because I doubt you stopped to eat lunch."

I smiled. "It's like you know me."

"Mmmhmmm," Gilley said smugly. "See you in a few."

Ten minutes later, I pulled into the circular driveway and, instead of parking in the garage, I opted to park right at the front door. I had several packages I'd picked up for myself while I was out, and depositing them at the stairs from the front foyer was easier than lugging them from the garage, through the kitchen, family room, and front hallway.

Moving to the front door, I looked directly into the small peephole and said, "Sebastian, open the door, please."

The door clicked open and a soothing voice with a British accent said, "Welcome home, Lady Catherine. Would you like to hear some music?"

Sebastian was my AI butler. An eye scan at the front door allowed him to recognize me and open the door on command. It was wonderfully convenient. "Music would be lovely," I told him. "Something soothing, please."

The speakers located throughout the house immediately began kicking out the sound of a harmonious melody. I deposited the shopping bags at the foot of the stairs and headed into my favorite rooms in the house, the kitchen and family rooms.

My interior designer had suggested the colors of my cabinets, which were a gorgeous Prussian blue on the lower level and bright white upper, all with burnished gold pulls and topped by a marvelous bright white marble countertop that also served as a backsplash. The kitchen itself faced my front garden, or what would become my front garden once I had the landscapers install one in the next few weeks. I couldn't wait to spend my first spring and summer at Chez Cat, admiring the colorful array of blooms I'd planned while I did the dishes at the sink.

Separating the kitchen from the family room was a large kitchen island, which allowed unfettered food prep on one side, and on the other side, up to six people to sit comfortably in the high-backed, upholstered, peacock-blue bar stools with gold rivets rimming the seams.

The family room off the kitchen was also a cozy, welcoming space, with a large, impossibly soft, L-shaped modular couch upholstered in a pearl-white velvet with powder-blue and soft violet throw pillows. Sheepskin rugs adorned the dark wood floors, giving the entire ensemble an inviting appeal.

A painting by the artist Daniel Bilmes that reminded me of my sister hung above the mantel of the large white-stone fireplace, and bookshelves filled with my favorite books lined the walls.

All in all, Chez Cat had nineteen rooms, but this area was where I spent the bulk of my time, constantly drawn to its comforting essence.

I sighed as I entered, and Gilley looked up from the oven where he was just removing a tray of meringues, no doubt working on his homework project for the pastry chef class he was taking.

Setting the tray of white confections trimmed in green food coloring on the counter, he said, "Well, don't you look worn slap out!"

I tossed my purse on the counter, frowned, and sent Gil a hefty dose of side eye, unsure if that was one of his quaint southern phrases or some kind of insult.

"Relax," he cooed. "It's what we say in the South when we're dog-tired."

"Oh, well then, yes, consider me slapped out."

Gilley chuckled, came around the counter at a trot, hugged me, then patted the top of my head. "You're adorable. Now, sit your fanny down and I'll get you some tea and cookies."

I plodded to the middle chair and plopped my butt into the seat. Meanwhile, Gilley retraced his steps over to the stove area and turned the burner on for the teakettle. After setting the kettle on the flame, he opened the door to the microwave, removing a bowl of melted dark chocolate, which he stirred thoroughly before moving that to the counter. Next, he uncovered a bowl of chopped Andes mint chocolates.

While I watched him dip the meringues first into the melted chocolate, then the chopped thin mint candies, he said, "The benefit of this snack is that it'll keep your breath minty fresh."

"They look spectacular," I said.

Gilley smiled, pleased by the compliment. "So! What'd you buy?"

I sighed and got up because the kettle was starting to whistle and Gilley's hands were covered in chocolate.

"Too much. The boys will have plenty of choices for beach, pool, and restaurant attire, let me tell you."

"No, not for them," Gilley said as I poured the hot water over the tea infuser, already filled with loose tea and resting in my favorite teapot.

"I might've picked up one or two things for myself," I admitted.

Gilley paused his methodical confection process to

turn and stare at me over his shoulder. "Only one or two things?"

I rolled my eyes and brought over the teapot, setting it on the island counter to steep. "Fine. Maybe more than one or two."

Gilley's brow arched. "Anything . . . *fancy*?"

I shrugged casually and walked back to my stool. "Not overly fancy."

"Something gorgeous, though, right?"

I grinned. He knew me too well. "Well, there *was* a little number that I simply *had* to have."

Gilley pursed his lips like he'd known it all along, and made a trotting motion with his fingers before pointing toward the stairs. "You know the drill. If one of us buys something fabulous away from the supervision of the other, then a runway walk is mandatory."

I sighed again. "Can I at least have some tea and a meringue first?"

"Of course," Gilley said. "I wouldn't want you to get chocolate on the outfit you'll be wearing on your hot date with Maks."

I stared at Gilley. "You think it's a date?"

"Isn't it?"

"That's not the impression I had. I thought he just wanted to talk to me about where he's been the past few months."

Gilley shook his head a little. "Ah, you heteros and your flirty mischief. You should all take a page out of our bible. We're direct about our passions. It's what makes us the superior sex."

"Orientation," I corrected.

"That too," he agreed.

I poured us each a cup of tea and spooned a little sugar into mine. "You really think we're going on a date?" I asked him again.

"You really think you're *not*?"

"I can't be sure, but now I'm glad I have a new outfit to wear. Truthfully, I bought it thinking that, if Shepherd ever asked me out again, I'd wear it then."

Gilley made a face. "*That* man is a lost cause. I mean, he's *clearly* into you, but he's wandering around town obsessed with his ex-wife. It's pathetic."

"He's obsessed with her murder, Gilley. Not her."

Gil shrugged. "Tomato-tamurder. What's the damn difference? He's still obsessed."

I frowned. The truth was, Shepherd *had* been completely focused on trying to hunt down leads to not just the woman who'd killed his wife, but any evidence leading to a motive.

Lenny—Shepherd's ex-wife—was a Realtor, and one day while hosting an open house in an upscale area of town, she'd been shot point blank and killed instantly. Thanks to a murder case that Gilley and I had helped solve a few months earlier, we now knew who'd pulled the trigger but we didn't know the motive.

In fact, the biggest outstanding question remaining in Lenny Shepherd's murder case, besides where her assassin was hiding, was the fact that said assassin, better known as the Angel of Death, had seemingly killed Lenny for no good reason. Just a random act of unspeakable violence, and it was the random part that Shepherd didn't believe.

Truthfully, neither did I.

I decided to change the subject. "Did you make contact with Willem?"

"I did," Gilley said. "He and Heath are speaking at one o'clock tomorrow."

"Good. I'll be anxious to hear what Heath has to say about Willem."

Gilley handed me a plate of two of his creations. "That boy is definitely cursed."

"It might be all in his head," I said. "Today *could* have been a coincidence, you know."

Gil crossed his arms stubbornly and looked at me like I was slow on the uptake.

Not wanting to argue, I bit into the beautiful little confection and moaned. The meringues were light, delicate, and full of flavor. "Oh, my God, Gil. These are heaven!"

Gilley sipped demurely at his tea. "Chef Alvario doesn't give out grades, but I think he'd give these an A all the same."

"Is your class tonight?"

"It is. We're all bringing in our final projects."

"Well, these are the clear winner," I said, polishing off the meringue. It was then that I noticed the time and jumped off the bar stool. "I need to get ready," I said. "Maks is going to be here at seven."

I started to take my teacup and remaining cookie with me toward the stairs, but then I remembered that I had several packages to take up with me. Standing indecisive for a moment, I was relieved when Gilley came to my rescue. "Shoo," he said, wiping his hands on a towel and waving at me to be on my way. "I'll follow behind you and grab whatever loot you can't manage to get up the stairs."

With Gilley's help we got all the bags up the stairs and set them down next to the bed. Gilley then began to exit the room and called over his shoulder, "I'll be back up in a while to check on you and take a look at this hot little number you bought today." Pausing at the door, he added, "For now, enjoy your shower, and don't forget to shave your legs. After all, nobody wants to cuddle up next to a cactus."

With that he left me to consider what *that* might mean.

Chapter 3

An hour later I exited my closet and brought my arms slowly up over my head in a "Ta-da!" fashion.

Gilley, clad in the tiara I wore on my wedding day, and a very expensive faux mink stole, clapped wildly from his perch on one of my wing chairs. "Gorgeous!"

I lowered my hands and looked at him demurely. "I loved this suit the moment I saw it. It feels amazing."

"And it fits you like a glove."

I ran my hand along one of the sleeves, delighting in the feel of velvet fabric against my fingertips. The black Versace suit was a spectacular find. I'm petite by nature, only a hint above five foot one, but in this slim-fitting number I looked taller, my legs longer, and the flared pant bottoms gave my walk a sassy kick.

Under the blazer I wore a black silk shirt—Gilley's recommendation as I'd wanted to go white—open at the neck to the third button down, which I was still a little unsure about, but every time I tried to button it Gilley would shout, "NO!" so I let it be.

Moving to the mirror on the far wall, I admired myself. I looked *good* for an old broad with two tween sons.

"Dahling," Gilley said as he too stared at my reflection. "In that outfit you're like *liquid sex*. Temptation personified . . . sinfully delicious!" He then giggled and giggled like a young man tickled by dirty thoughts.

I giggled too. "What should I wear for jewelry?" I asked him.

Gilley pressed a finger to his lips. "We'd need something long, that can dip in and out of the décolletage."

"I think I have just the thing!"

I hurried back to my closet and pushed on one of the shelves, which rose in the air revealing a wall safe. I spent the next few moments turning the dial to the right, then the left, then right again.

"I didn't know you had a wall safe," Gilley said from right behind me.

I jumped. I hadn't realized he'd come into the closet. "Of course I have a wall safe," I said, opening the safe door.

"Whatcha hiding in there?" he asked.

I sighed, rooting around for the particular piece of jewelry to go with my outfit. "Valuables."

"Aren't you worried you'll get robbed with all that in there?"

I turned to look at him. "Who would know, besides you and me?"

Gil shrugged. "Dunno. Maybe the guy who installed it?"

I waved the thought away. "It was installed by a very

reputable company. Besides, no one but me knows the combination."

"I bet it's the twins' birthday."

"It's *not* the twins' birthday," I said, adding a mental note to change the safe's combination to something other than the twins' birthday. "Ah, here it is!"

Extracting a long gold chain with a teardrop aquamarine stone dangling from it, I draped the necklace around my neck and smiled gamely at Gilley. "What do you think?"

"Whoa. How many carats is that?"

"A smidge under thirty," I said, bouncing my brows. I'd bought it many years ago when I'd been vacationing in Brazil. "And there's a ring in here that could go with it!"

I dug back inside the safe and found the ring made of a thick gold band and a gleaming blue gemstone in the middle. Donning both, I put my hands on my hips and shimmied a little.

Gilley clapped his hands. "Perfection!"

"You think?"

"Honey, if I wasn't married, even *I'd* be tempted."

Gil and I looked at each other and laughed uproariously. He sobered first. "Ah well, it was worth saying."

I giggled anew. "I appreciate the compliment. But do I really want to be this tempting?"

Gilley put his chin in his hand to consider me. "Why *wouldn't* you?"

"Well, I haven't seen Maks in about four months. And he's mixed up in this whole mafia mess with Greta the Angel of Death. I'm just wondering suddenly if it's wise to have accepted his invitation out."

"Your sister vouched for him, though, right?"

I nodded. My sister, Abby, had some sort of history with Maks that she absolutely refused to speak about. She would only tell me that it involved some top secret government business and that at one point during that escapade, Maks had saved her life and the life of her husband. Heady stuff to believe, no doubt, but Abby wouldn't lie about something like that and so I took it as a fairly powerful recommendation for Maks's character. "Abby says I can trust him."

"Well, then I think you owe it to him to hear him out."

Just then the doorbell rang.

I gasped. "What time is it?"

"Ten to," Gilley said.

"Ack! He's early!"

I rushed around the room for a moment gathering up my clutch and tossing in the bright red lipstick I'd chosen to wear that evening. Hurrying down the stairs with Gilley in tow, I got to the front door and took a breath before opening it. "You're early—"

"I'm early?" Shepherd said. And then he stepped back and took me in. "Whoa. Catherine, you look . . ."

"Sinfully delicious?" Gilley asked, peeking over my shoulder.

I swatted at Gilley and recovered myself. "Detective! I . . . I wasn't expecting you."

Shepherd looked me up and down again. "Obviously."

Playing at the collar of my silk blouse, suddenly *very* aware of how open it was, I said, "What can I do for you?"

Shepherd adopted a crooked smile and took a long time to answer. The longer he took, the redder my face got. "I . . . uh . . . I wanted to talk to you about a new development."

"What kind of development?" I asked.

The driveway behind Shepherd lit up with approaching headlights. Shepherd turned and I felt my back stiffen as a pearl-white Maserati Gran Turismo pulled up alongside Shepherd's Buick sedan.

No one said a word as the engine cut, the door opened, and out of the car came Maks, dressed in a charcoal-gray suit, white silk dress shirt, bourbon-colored pocket square, and ruby cuff links. Pausing outside the car to shoot the cuffs, he regarded the car next to his and then his gaze took in the scene at my front door.

His expression, upon seeing me and Shepherd, was mixed, I thought, but he didn't give a whole lot away as he approached us. As he did so I felt my pulse quicken, both in anticipation and maybe a little dread.

"Good evening, Catherine," he said warmly before addressing Shepherd with an abruptly icier tone. "Detective."

"Grinkov," Shepherd said, his voice hard. "I heard you were back in town."

"Who tattled?" Maks asked, adopting a bemused smile.

It was immediately clear to me that these two men didn't care for one another. And I doubted that I was the only reason why. Something more than simple jealousy was coursing between them, although I had no doubt that the two of them finding the other at my front door hadn't exactly been a welcome surprise.

"A little birdie told me," Shepherd said.

"Ah," said Maks, now standing next to Shepherd on my front porch. "You're not here to arrest my date again, are you?"

I bit my lip. My last night out with Maks had ended in

a total disaster, no thanks to Shepherd, but that was back when the detective and I weren't exactly on good terms.

A lot had changed since that night four and a half months before.

"No, I won't be arresting *her* this time," Shepherd said with a not-so-subtle warning. "You two have a terrific evening, though."

Shepherd then glanced at me with a tight smile. For a moment, something flashed in his eyes . . . something like hurt, but it was gone before I was certain I'd seen it. Then, he pivoted on his heel and walked casually to his car.

We watched as he got in, turned the engine over, and backed out of my driveway. He was gone before I even had a chance to ask him more about the development he'd come here to talk to me about.

"Oh, my," Gilley said. I realized he'd been standing behind me the whole time. "That was intense!"

"The detective isn't still harassing you, is he?" Maks asked me.

"No," I said quickly. "Not at all. We're on good terms, actually."

Maks's brow rose in surprise. "Oh?"

I felt another blush touch my cheeks and tried to cover that by rubbing my arms. "You know it's quite chilly out here. Maks, would you like to come in?"

Maks bowed slightly and offered me his arm. "Or, we could get in my car and get on with our evening. We have lots to talk about. Apparently."

"Ruh, roh," Gilley whispered in my ear.

I pushed up the wattage of my smile and took Maks's arm. "Perfect," I said.

He walked me to the passenger side door and paused

after opening it for me. "You look incredible, by the way."

"Thank you," I said, so pleased that he'd noticed.

As we backed out of the drive, I waved to Gilley, who then fiddled with his phone. A moment later my own phone pinged, and a text from Gilley indicated that he wouldn't wait up, but he'd have breakfast ready for me at Chez Kitty the next morning.

"So!" I said, putting away the phone. "How're things?"

Maks smiled but kept his eyes on the road. "Things are well. How're things with you?"

"Equally well." There was a bit of an awkward silence that filled the car after that, but then I thought of something I could talk about. "I'd probably be better though if my ex-husband weren't taking my sons to Aruba next week for spring break. I'll miss knowing they're just three hours away."

"Ah," Maks said with a tisk of sympathy. "I know how difficult it is to be away from your children. Remind me again, how old are they?"

"They're fourteen going on thirty."

Maks chuckled. "Yes, all young men believe they're much too old to be parented once they reach that age. Will they be gone long?"

I sighed sadly. "Ten days. But they've promised to come home the following weekend so that I can pamper them and cook their favorite meals."

Maks turned to me. "Pizza?"

I laughed. "No, would you believe beef Wellington?"

"You know how to make beef Wellington?"

"I do," I said. "And it's delicious."

"You should make that for me sometime."

I felt yet another blush touch my cheeks. "Should I now?"

"I'm sorry, did that sound too demanding?"

"No. I'd love to cook for you."

"Good," Maks said.

All of the sudden his gaze turned to the rearview mirror. "Uh oh," he said.

I craned my neck to look behind us. His rear window was lit up with red strobe lights. "Is that for us?"

"Yes, I think so," Maks said, already pulling over.

An officer appeared at Maks's window while he fidgeted to fish out his license. Lowering the window, Maks spoke politely to the officer, who was curt and unpleasant and asked him all sorts of questions about where we were headed and if he'd been drinking. Maks answered every question, but the officer seemed to want to escalate the matter. Opening Maks's door, he told him to step out of the car. Maks complied. The officer continued to drill him about where he'd been, what he'd been doing, where he was going, and if he'd been drinking. Maks answered all of those questions politely but each time he did so, the officer's voice just got angrier.

He then took Maks to the back of the car and pointed the flashlight right in his face and sternly told him to walk forward along the white line in the road. Maks complied, but the officer wasn't satisfied and he began taking him through all of the physical tests for determining if someone might be impaired.

I couldn't understand what Maks had done to set the patrol officer off; Maks hadn't even been going that fast when we'd been pulled over, and he most certainly hadn't been weaving or driving erratically.

There was no reason for the third degree . . . unless . . .

And then I angrily pulled out my cell phone and placed a call

"Hello, Catherine," Shepherd said easily. "I'm surprised to hear from you. I thought you'd be out on the town by now."

"*You* did this!" I snapped, knowing for certain he'd had a hand in interrupting our evening.

"Don't know what you're talking about. Could you be a little more specific?"

"You don't know what I'm talking about? How about the fact that Maks is currently being grilled by a patrol officer and is also being threatened with a Breathalyzer test!"

Shepherd let out a snicker but quickly tried to cover it. "A Breathalyzer test, huh? Wow. That's thorough. Was Grinkov drinking before he showed up to take you out?"

"Steve," I said evenly, "you know very well he wasn't. This was mean, even for you!"

Shepherd cleared his throat but he didn't offer anything else, not even an apology.

And that just made me angrier. So I lit into him again. "This is the second time you've attempted to ruin a lovely night out for me, and I'm *over* your little games! When you want to grow up, you call me, okay? Until then, go take a long leap off a short pier, you . . . you . . . *jackass*!"

I hung up angrily and waited with bated breath to see how far the patrol officer would escalate things, suddenly worried if my terse send-off to Shepherd would actually make things worse.

And just when I thought for certain that Maks was likely to be arrested there was a garbled call on the officer's shoulder mic and he abruptly stopped his lecture. Instead, the officer spoke a 10-4 into his mic, handed

Maks back his license, then went back to his patrol car without issuing so much as a ticket.

Maks got into the Maserati and stared at me in disbelief. "That was very strange," he said. "For a minute there, I thought the man was going to put me in cuffs and take me on a ride to the station, but then he just let me go."

"Very strange indeed," I said, but I knew that my call to Shepherd had done the trick. He'd relented and sent a message through dispatch to have the officer stand down. "Should we be on our way?"

"We should," Maks said, and within moments we were once again back on the road.

We arrived a few minutes later at a lovely eatery in Northampton and I walked in on Maks's arm feeling like a movie star.

As we entered, we turned heads and sent lips quietly murmuring. It was a sinfully scrumptious feeling to know that we were causing a stir.

The hostess seated us in a cozy booth and presented us with menus and a wine list.

"So," I said after she had departed.

"So," he repeated.

"You said you wanted to talk to me," I began. "And here I am. . . ."

Maks dropped his gaze to the table and covered my hand with his. "Yes," he said. "I should get on with it."

"It?"

"The hard part."

"I don't know that I like the sound of that."

Maks's gaze lifted and I felt that special thrilling shiver that only came when he looked at me with those gorgeous smoldering eyes. When he spoke, he did so in barely above a whisper. "Catherine, what I'm about to tell you can never be repeated. If it were repeated, it could cost both of us our lives."

He had my full attention. "This is about Greta, isn't it?"

"In part," he said. "As you know, Greta was an assassin, working primarily for Boris Basayev."

"Basayev was the guy that Heather double-crossed, right?" Heather Holland was a former neighbor. She'd been murdered four and a half months earlier, and for a while there, I'd been the primary suspect.

"Yes," Maks said. "And, as you probably also know, Boris runs a powerful branch of the Chechen mafia."

"I did know that," I said. "Although, I kind of wish I didn't."

"I understand," Maks said, squeezing my hand. "I wish you didn't either."

"What I want to know is how do *you* know all this, Maks?"

"Because I work for them," he said, so casually you'd have thought I'd asked him about the weather.

My breath caught, and it was a moment before I could ask him about *that* because our server appeared at the table and asked if we were ready to order.

I ordered the sea bass and Maks ordered the short rib and then we were once again alone and I had a chance to speak privately again. "What do you mean you work for *them*?"

"I'm a liaison between two of the most powerful branches of the family," Maks said. "One branch is rooted in Toronto, the other is rooted in New York City. I make sure peace is kept between the branches by representing both interests and negotiating deals when they need to be made."

I stared at Maks in stunned silence for a long minute.

Just knowing this about him was something I was quite sure I could be murdered for, and it frightened me to the core. "So . . . you're a member of *the mafia*?" I whispered.

"Yes and no," he answered, rubbing his thumb along my fingers. "And, this is the part that you must never, ever repeat to *anyone*, Catherine."

"I won't." And then I recalled what Abby always told me about Maks, which, other than nothing, was that she couldn't tell me or anyone else, for that matter, anything about him other than he could be trusted. Completely. I sucked in another breath as I at last connected the dots. "You're an informant."

Maks's eyes twinkled. "Yes."

"For the Feds?"

Maks gave a one-shoulder shrug. "More or less."

"How is that more or less?"

"Officially, I work for CSIS—"

"CSI—like crime scene investigators?"

Maks chuckled. "No. Not them. CSIS, which stands for Canadian Security Intelligence Services. Your equivalent is the CIA."

"Ahhhhhh," I said, understanding fully. "So you're . . . a spy?"

"Not exactly," he said. "I'm like an informant for the CSIS, but on loan whenever I'm in the US to the FBI."

I blinked rapidly and reached for my water glass. This was a lot to take in. "That's the business you had with my sister," I said, to let him know I'd already put a little of it together.

"I can't talk about that," Maks said, but his eyes told me that I was right.

"Because it's classified?" I asked almost as a joke.

Maks shrugged noncommittally and pulled my hand to his lips to kiss my fingers. I didn't know if I was terrified or turned on. . . . Maybe both.

Our server came back with the bottle of wine that Maks had ordered, and we were both silent as our glasses were filled and our server departed.

Lifting my wineglass and, taking a tentative sip, I nodded to Maks. He'd chosen a beautifully smooth cabernet for the table. "So, you're not *really* a bad guy, right?" I asked, setting the glass down and running my finger around the rim.

"Oh, I'm bad. But I'm reformed bad."

"What does that mean?"

Maks inhaled deeply. "It means that once upon a time, I was a bad man. And I lost some people I loved because of my actions. It made me reevaluate my entire existence, and not wanting their lives to be given in vain, I reformed and sought out the good guys, knowing I could be of service. Now, here I am a decade later, still atoning and still of service."

I stared at Maks and it was as if, in that confession, he'd opened himself up totally to me. It was like a window to a lovely home that was normally kept shuttered had just opened up, and I got to peek at the decor, which was beautiful, but a mess; as if someone had gone in and displaced all the furnishings.

"You lost your family, didn't you?"

Maks pushed a smile onto his lips, and just like that the shutters closed. "There are things I can't talk about, Catherine, and things I won't talk about. That loss is a little bit of both."

I nodded and wrapped my hand around his, feeling very close to him all of the sudden. I'd been through an awful divorce after which my own sons had declined the invitation to live with me full time, so I understood on at least a small level how devastating it was not to come home to your children every night. "I'm so sorry, Maks."

"It's the past," he replied. "I prefer to focus on the future. Which we must also talk about."

"The future? You mean *our* future?" (Was he kidding? We'd barely just met!)

"Of sorts," he said. "I need your help. And I wish that I didn't because I'd rather not involve you directly. I want nothing more than to keep you out of this business, but things have changed since the last time we saw each other and I find I'm beginning to attract some unwelcome attention."

"Whoa," I said, reaching again for my wineglass. "This is a lot, Maks."

"I know. I'm sorry. Maybe I shouldn't have mentioned any of it."

"No, I'm glad you did. It's better to know whom I'm getting involved with. And, my sister says I can trust you. Abby wouldn't lie to me about something like this."

At that moment Maks's phone buzzed from the inside pocket of his suit coat, and he retrieved it quickly to look at the display. He looked at me a bit pained when he said, "Catherine, I apologize, but I must take this. I'll make it short and be right back."

"Of course," I said.

Maks made a quick exit out of the booth and I was left with my thoughts, which tumbled over one another until he returned just a few minutes later.

"Again, I apologize for that."

"It's fine," I said. "I understand."

Our dinners arrived then and Maks took up his fork

and knife but didn't cut into his dinner while I simply stared at my entrée, not really sure if I was hungry.

Finally, I picked up my fork and a bit of my courage as I got back to the topic at hand. "What do you need my help with?"

Maks exhaled, as if he'd been waiting to see if I'd want to continue the thread of our conversation before the interruption of his phone call. "I have a handler," he began. "He's part of your government and he relays messages to the men in my government. I've recently become aware that my movements are being tracked, along with anyone I associate with."

I stiffened. "Anyone?"

"Yes. Even you. But you'll check out, Catherine. There's no need for someone in the organization to suspect you of being anyone other than who you are."

"And who am I?"

"A wealthy local businesswoman. Completely legit and completely outside anything to do with the organization."

"Except for the fact that the Angel of Death attempted to murder me after she also tried to frame me for Heather Holland's murder."

"Yes, but all of that has already been explained to Boris. You're clear."

"Good to know," I said, thinking I would've rather not known that Boris Basayev knew anything about me.

"Anyway, as I was saying, I have a handler. Occasionally I need to pass a flash drive on to him, but with this new scrutiny, it's become quite difficult to be seen in the company of someone my business associates don't recognize as being part of the organization."

"Don't tell me," I interrupted, lowering the bite of sea

bass back to my plate. "You want to pass the flash drives on to me and have me give them to your handler, right?"

"Yes."

"Oh, my God, this is like something out of a spy novel."

"It is a bit, I agree," Maks said.

I shook my head, thinking it through. "Where would I meet your handler?" I finally asked, thinking that perhaps it wouldn't be so terribly risky if it was simply making a drop for Maks now and then.

"Your office," he said.

"*My* office?"

"Yes. You have the perfect cover, you see. You're a life coach and my handler would be a new client for you. You could meet in your office, deliver the flash drive, and he would be on his way at the end of the hour."

"Is everything satisfactory?" our server said. He'd come up behind me and I jumped at the sound of his voice.

"We're fine," Maks said to him. "Thank you. If we need anything more, we'll wave."

The server bowed and backed away.

When I looked again at my plate, I realized my hands were shaking. "Do you think he overheard us?"

"Probably."

My eyes widened. "Aren't you worried about that?"

"No," Maks said. "He's fine."

"How do you know?" I asked, turning to look toward our server, who was busy talking to another table.

"Because he's my handler."

I gasped and quickly looked back toward Maks. "Come on!" I whispered. "You're joking!"

"No, actually. He's the reason I feel free to talk to you here in this setting."

I took another quick peek at the server. He was about average height, maybe five eleven at the tallest, with sandy brown hair and skin that looked as if it'd seen the sun recently. He wore a sport watch, white shirt, black pants, maroon apron, and matching bow tie. His silhouette was trim and athletic—he was built like a runner, and given the watch, I'd bet that was how he kept so fit.

"What's his name?" I asked, wondering if Maks would really tell me.

"Sam. Sam Dancer."

"Sam Dancer," I repeated. "Is that made up?"

Maks glanced curiously over at the server. "I've no idea, actually."

"Huh," I said. "Well, for a name, Sam Dancer sounds completely unremarkable."

"Exactly."

I tapped the tabletop, thinking about what Maks was proposing. "Is there anything else I'd have to do?"

Maks shifted in his seat. It was the first time I'd seen him looking uncomfortable since we'd sat down. "Yes, but perhaps it wouldn't be so terrible."

"What is it?"

"You'd have to continue dating me for a bit."

"Naturally," I said, purposely withholding any reassurance that I'd be happy to do that, although, the thought of continuing our relationship did give me a little thrill. And it also filled me with anxiety.

"And," Maks said, "you'd have to stop seeing Shepherd."

I lowered my chin. "I'd have to what now?"

"The detective. You'd have to put some distance between the two of you."

"Why?" I demanded. I didn't like that part. In fact, of

all the parts that Maks had told me about so far, that was the one I disliked the most.

"Other than the obvious reason that Shepherd is law enforcement and I could hardly excuse my girlfriend cozying up to a member of the police—"

"He saved my life," I said curtly. "And he's my friend, Maks."

Maks put up his hands in a small gesture of surrender. "Be that as it may, Sam and I believe the reason my movements are being so closely monitored is because there's a leak within the East Hampton P.D."

"A leak? What do you mean, a leak?"

"Someone there is reporting back to Boris about what I'm up to."

"Well, that's just ridiculous," I said. "You make it sound like Shepherd is personally keeping close tabs on you."

"Is it so ridiculous, Catherine? Not an hour ago, wasn't I pulled over, even though I was only going five miles over the speed limit? Wasn't I harassed by one of East Hampton's finest shortly after picking you up and crossing paths with Detective Shepherd?"

I bit my lip. I knew that Shepherd had in fact been the one to sic that cop on Maks, but I couldn't readily admit that to Maks *now*.

"He's not the leak," I insisted.

"How do you know?"

"Because I know him. And I know his sister. They're good people."

"Good people do bad things all the time," Maks said easily, and I had to take that in for a moment because he, more than anyone, would probably know.

"Listen," I said at last. "Here's what I'm willing to do. I'm willing to pose as your girlfriend as long as I'm not in any immediate danger—"

"You're not."

"And I'm willing to have Sam come to my office and pose as a client and give him your flash drives, but I'm not willing to give Shepherd the cold shoulder. Not after all he's done for me, and besides, if I were to do that and he *was* the leak, wouldn't he find that pretty suspicious?"

Maks drummed his fingers lightly on the table for a few moments, thinking that over. "You have a point. I agree," he said. Then he took up my hand again. "And thank you. I appreciate your willingness to help me more than you could know."

"Well, you did save my sister's life, and my brother-in-law's to boot. I figure the Coopers owe you at least a little gratitude."

Maks chuckled. "If you knew what I'd done for the two of them, you'd probably think I was owed more than a little."

"Maybe someday you'll tell me?"

Maks ran his thumb along the inside of my palm. "Perhaps . . ." was all he'd commit to.

A bit later as we got up from the table, Maks asked, "Would you care for a nightcap at Chez Maks?"

I wound my arm through his and leaned in against him. With a sigh I said, "Would it be all right with you if I took a rain check? It was an exhausting day."

"Of course," Maks said, patting my hand and kissing the top of my head.

It was a lovely moment, but the truth was that I hadn't declined his offer solely because I was tired. I'd also said no because there'd been a *lot* revealed about Maks at dinner, and I felt the need to take a step back and process it all.

Once we were home, Maks walked me to my door, and when I turned to face him I caught Gilley peeking at us through the window of Chez Kitty, but he ducked out of sight once he realized I was glaring at him.

"We're being watched?" Maks asked, thumbing over his shoulder in the direction of the guesthouse.

"We were."

Maks grinned. "I like Gilley."

"He'll be absolutely thrilled to hear that."

"And I like you," Maks said, lifting my hand to kiss it.

"I'm equally thrilled," I laughed.

"Are you?" Maks asked, and there was this sweet hopefulness in his eyes that sort of undid me.

Leaning in, I cupped his face and kissed him tenderly on the lips. He responded in kind and it was such a lovely, light, promising moment that I could've almost forgotten all the caution I'd felt on the drive home.

Pulling back, I said, "Good night, Maks."

"Good night, Catherine. Until we meet again."

With that, he was gone, and I went inside to sit in the dark and think troubled thoughts.

Chapter 4

I found Gilley in his kitchen at Chez Kitty the next morning, busily putting the finishing touches on a giant fruit bowl that he'd placed in the center of the dining table, already set for two.

"Can I help?" I asked, when he whipped back over to the counter to retrieve a coffee carafe and a bowl of yogurt.

"I got it," he said. "You sit. And talk. And tell me *everything*."

I smiled and wished very much that I could tell Gilley everything. Or even most of everything. Or even really *some*thing, but what could I actually tell him that wouldn't betray my promise to Maks?

"We had a lovely time," I began.

Gilley took his seat and poured me some coffee. "Obviously not too lovely."

I stared at him in confusion.

Gilley waved as if it were obvious. "You were home by ten and went to bed alone," he said. "I mean, how scintillating could the conversation have been to make up for *that*?"

I sipped my coffee. "Actually, scintillating is an apt way to describe our conversation."

"*Do* tell," Gilley said, resting his chin on his hand to stare at me with big, expectant eyes.

"We talked . . . politics," I said. I'd have to be careful if I didn't want to talk myself into a hole I couldn't get out of.

"Boring!" Gilley sang, and began to ladle out some fruit for both of us. "What else?"

"Well . . . um . . . let's see now . . . I talked about the boys, and we talked about the food, which was very good, and . . . um . . . the weather . . . and our plans for the summer . . . and . . ."

I paused because Gilley was eyeing me keenly. "What?" he said.

"What, what?"

"What aren't you telling me?"

Heat flooded my cheeks. "What do you mean? I'm telling you what we talked about."

"Catherine Cooper, I know full well when you're withholding information. You do that, 'um . . . well . . . um' thing every time!"

"What information could I possibly be withholding?"

Gilley wagged a finger at me. "Don't know. But I know I want to know."

I rolled my eyes and waved my own hand dismissively. "Oh, you. Truly, Gilley, it was a very tame evening. We sat, we talked, we got on quite well, and then, like a perfect gentleman, he walked me to my door, gave me a sweet kiss good night, and left me to get some rest."

Gilley nibbled on a bite of melon. "Sure, sure. When you're ready to come clean, you let me know."

"You're impossible."

Gilley smirked. "Am I?"

"Yes. Anyway, how was *your* night? Did your pastry class love the meringues? And did you hear from Michel?"

"They did, and I did, but now you're just changing the subject."

"Oh, really, Gilley, you're being impossible! I'm not hiding anything from you, okay? We had a perfectly lovely if uneventful evening and that's all there is to it."

"When are you seeing him again?"

I smiled. "Soon."

"Hmmm . . . Okay, I buy that at least. And to answer your questions more specifically, my meringues were a total hit, as in I don't even have any leftovers, and Michel called around midnight. He landed safely and he already misses me."

"That's a relief," I said. "It's a long way to Marra-kesh."

Gilley nodded and poured himself more coffee. "What're you going to do about Shepherd?"

I stiffened. It was almost as if Gilley knew that Maks had wanted me to cut off contact with the detective. "What do you mean?"

"He stopped by here last night, didn't he? I assumed you'd want to call him to find out what it was that he wanted."

I put a hand to my forehead. "Oh, my God. I totally forgot about that."

"From what I remember, he said something about a new development. I wonder what *that's* about."

"It could be he has a lead on Greta," I said.

"That'd be good. It really eats at me that this assassin is still out there in the world, enriching herself one contract killing at a time."

I shook my head in disgust. "I know what you mean."

"Did Maks mention her?" Gilley asked. Gilley knew that Maks had some involvement with the people Greta was hired by, but he also knew that Abby had vouched for Maks and that I could trust him.

"He didn't."

"Odd that he wouldn't mention the woman who tried to kill you. Especially since he had dinner with her on the night in question."

"That was months ago."

"True. But that was also the last time you saw Maks. He truly doesn't know where she is?"

"I think if he did, he'd tell me."

"Are you sure of that?"

"What're you getting at?"

Gilley shrugged. "Nothing. I'm just surprised that you seem so willing to trust this man. Especially after you learned about his . . . associations."

"Abby insists I can trust Maks, and that's good enough for me."

"How well does she know him, though?"

"Good enough for her to form an opinion—and a strong opinion at that—about his character."

"Yeah, but you'd never heard of this guy before meeting him when he applied for the open suite in your building, right? What I'm saying is that your sister never mentioned him."

"That's true, but that doesn't mean anything. I'm sure

there are plenty of people in my sister's life whom I haven't met or heard about yet."

"Yes, but how many of *them* have had dinner with an assassin on the very night she tried to murder you?"

I sighed. This conversation was exhausting for all the things I had to keep close to the vest. "What's your point, Gilley?"

"My point is that, even though I like Maks, I think you should be careful. He may be hiding something."

Gilley had no idea how on target his intuition was. "I'll be careful. But to your earlier point, I think it'd be a good idea to pay Detective Shepherd a visit today."

Gilley clapped his hands. "Can I come?"

"No," I said firmly. I didn't want Gilley to know that Shepherd had sent a patrol officer after Maks, and I was definitely going to bring that up when I went to see the detective.

"You're no fun."

"You're just noticing that?" I mocked, but reached out to squeeze his shoulder. "I'm sorry, honey, but it's a little awkward between me and Shepherd now that he knows I'm dating Maks, and I don't think he'd like any witnesses when I show up again at his desk and remind him of that."

Gilley frowned but he nodded too. "Fine. I get it."

I got up from the table and took my dishes to the sink, but then I remembered something else I'd forgotten to ask Gilley about. "How's that e-mail blast coming along?"

"I'll have the rough draft of the copy ready for you to review by eleven."

"Excellent," I said, putting my bowl and coffee cup in the dishwasher. Wiping my hands on a towel, I added, "In the meantime, I'll pay our favorite detective a visit."

Gilley chuckled. "Remember when he *wasn't* our favorite? Like, when he was our *least* favorite?"

"I remember," I said with a laugh, and headed for the door. "I'll be in the office in time to take you to lunch, all right?"

Gilley gave me a peace out and I was on my way.

I found Shepherd at his desk tapping at his keyboard with his hands bound up in fists while his two index fingers darted and poked at the keys. It reminded me of two pigeons, each fighting for birdseed on the pavement.

"Good morning," I said, stepping up behind him.

Shepherd stiffened. "Catherine," he said curtly.

I went around his desk to take a seat in the chair opposite him, offering him a cool expression.

Shepherd's office is toward the back of the East Hampton's police station—which is quite a bit larger than you might expect for a super-affluent, mostly beach-season, coastal town. His desk is next to a window that usually has the blinds drawn, which I find sad, because I know they're drawn due to the fact that the detective thinks the stunning view of the water on the other side of the blinds is nothing more than a distraction for his very serious police work.

"What's up?" he asked casually.

"I believe I asked you the same thing last night."

Shepherd sat forward. "Ah. That."

"Yes. That."

Shepherd got up and moved over to a credenza where a stained coffeepot held the remnants of the tar they thought passed for coffee around these parts. Filling one of the dingy-looking mugs with the brew, he brought it back to his desk and set it down next to him.

He then leaned back in his chair and cupped the back of his head with his hands, staring at me casually. "How was your date?"

It wasn't lost on me that he'd failed to answer my question. "Splendid. Once you finally reined in Officer By-the-Book we had a lovely evening."

Shepherd nodded, but I noticed an involuntary twitch to his lips and knew it for the green-eyed monster it betrayed. Shepherd was jealous, of that I was certain, but as he'd never really gotten around to officially asking me out even once in the past four months, I thought it rather ridiculous.

"Good," Shepherd said. "Good."

"Yes," I replied, still looking at him expectantly.

Shepherd averted his eyes and rocked in his seat for a beat. "So what brings you by?"

I sighed. "Really?"

"What?"

"Are we really going to play this game round and round?"

"What game is that?"

"The one where you pretend that you didn't tell me last night that you had some sort of a new development, and then not update me about it."

"Ah, that."

"Yes. *That.*"

"Are you sure you want to hear it?"

"Why wouldn't I want to hear it?"

This had to be the most unproductive conversation I'd ever had. And I'm the mother of tween sons.

"Because it involves your boy, Grinkov," Shepherd said.

I stiffened slightly, and Maks's warning about Steve came back to my mind. "What's that supposed to mean?"

"It means that his story from the night I got shot—where he insisted that he was sitting in the restaurant alone, minding his own business when our friend Greta approached him for the first time to ask if he was eating alone and could she join him—is totally bogus. He knew her. Hell, he even walked into the place with her."

My heartbeat ticked up. Of course, *I* already knew this, but I didn't know how Shepherd did. "How do you know that?"

"The restaurant finally handed over their video of the parking lot from that night. Grinkov and Greta drove separate—that much is true—but they greeted each other at the door like they were best buds and into the restaurant they went. The hostess was a little fuzzy on remembering if she sat them together, but their server remembers that they were already sitting together when she approached the table."

"Have you talked to Maks about this?"

"Not yet," Shepherd said. "But I plan to."

"I see."

"Something about him doesn't add up, Catherine."

I nodded again, because, what else could I say? I couldn't tip off Shepherd about Maks, and I found it difficult to outright lie to the man who'd saved my life. "Well, I guess you'll have to do what you'll have to do," I said.

"That's all you got?"

"What else can I say?"

Shepherd leaned forward and studied me intently. "How about, 'Gee, Steve, that's a big bad coincidence and maybe my new boyfriend knows more about Greta's where-abouts than he's letting on!'"

Shepherd's face was flushed with anger. I couldn't really blame him. "He's not my new boyfriend," I said. "I barely know the man."

Shepherd made a dismissive sound. "Yeah, right."

"Believe what you want, Detective. You're going to anyway."

"I'll tell you what I believed, Catherine. I believed you and I were friends. I believed that you wanted to bring Greta to justice as much as I did. I mean, after all, she only tried to *murder* you and she actually shot me *and* murdered my wife!"

I bit my lip. In point of fact, Greta had murdered Shepherd's *ex*-wife, and I wondered if he wasn't making this even more personal because he was upset that I was dating Maks. "Of course I want to bring her to justice," I said softly. "And if Maks knows anything that might be helpful to you, all you have to do is ask him."

Shepherd looked at me for a long moment. I don't think he'd expected me to keep my cool and sympathize with him. I think he was looking for a reason to be angry at me, and I'd be damned if I'd make *that* easy for him.

"What about you, Catherine?" he finally asked.

"What about me?"

"Are you going to be helpful?"

"Haven't I always been?"

The hard expression Shepherd had been wearing since I walked in softened. And the corner of his lip quirked. "Not always," he said. "In fact, mostly not."

"That's because you find it so difficult to accept help when it's offered. But I promise you, Steve, I'll help you in any way I can."

"Oh, yeah?"

"Yes."

"Okay. I'll take you up on that."

I blinked. What did that mean?

"The next time you see Grinkov," he continued, "ask him about Greta. He knows more than he's willing to tell us, that's pretty obvious."

"I can do that," I said. I didn't know if I was saying it simply to placate Shepherd or because I too was curious if Maks was perhaps withholding information from me. If he was, I reasoned, it was only to protect me.

"Good," said Shepherd. "Let me know what he says."

"I will," I promised, hoping that I could. "Are you going to question him too?"

Shepherd shuffled some papers on his desk. "Not yet. I want to hear what he tells you first. But don't worry, I won't let on that you were the one who told me anything."

There was something about that statement that I didn't trust, and I had the feeling that when Shepherd spoke to Maks it would be to set him up and try to catch him in a lie, which would accomplish two things: one, it would put Maks on notice that Shepherd was suspicious of him, and two, it would sow some mistrust between Maks and me.

"Great," I said, pushing a smile to my lips before getting up. "Thanks for the update, Detective."

He nodded and attempted to smile back at me, but there was something between us now that was unpleasant and cold, and I was very worried that, if given half a chance, it would grow into suspicion and betrayal. "Have a nice day," he said without even a hint of warmth.

"You too," I replied, then hurried away.

*　*　*

I met Gilley for lunch at our favorite little bistro a block and a half north of my office building. Walking into the restaurant, I'll confess that it was very reassuring to see Gilley's smiling face tucked in our favorite corner booth away from most of the other patrons. At least he was one friend I could always count on.

"Hey," I said.

"Hey yourself!" I noticed immediately that Gilley looked excited about something. "I ordered us both the Caesar salad, no cheese for you, extra croutons for me."

"Perfect," I said, taking a seat and unfolding my napkin just as the server appeared with our food.

The moment he disappeared, Gilley slapped his thighs excitedly and said, "Guess what?!"

Taking up a fork to poke at my salad I said, "The new season of *Big Brother* starts soon?"

Gilley laughed. "I *wish*! That's this summer." (Gilley is a BIG reality TV junkie. And the crazier the contestants, the more he loves them.) "No, *you* got a new client!"

I pulled my head back in surprise. "I did?"

"Yes! And he's quite well spoken, at least on the phone he is."

"Who is it?"

"His name is Sam Dancer."

I felt my eyes widen and for a moment I didn't know what to say.

"You don't look happy," Gilley said.

I shook my head and forced a smile. "No, sorry. That name sounded familiar to me for a moment, but now that I think about it, it doesn't."

I took a sip of water to cover the fact that my nerves were a bit rattled. I hadn't expected for the espionage to start so soon.

"You okay?" Gilley asked.

"Yes. Of course. I think I'm just unnerved by my visit with Shepherd."

"Uh-oh," Gilley said. "He's upset that he found out you're dating Maks, isn't he?"

"He is," I said. At least I was pretty sure that was the truth.

"Ah, well, he'll get over it. But I'm sorry he was a jerk to you."

"It's okay, Gilley, not to worry. I'll rally. So, when is this Sam Dancer coming in for our first meeting?"

"This afternoon at three o'clock," Gilley said. "You had nothing on the books for that time."

"Perfect," I said, making sure to sound perky so that Gilley wouldn't suspect something was off. But something was off. Maks hadn't left me with anything to pass on to Sam, so I wondered what this first meeting would be about.

"Oh, and," Gilley continued, "I wanted to ask you if it's okay if I'm not there when he arrives. He said on the phone that he prefers to have total privacy for his weekly meetings with you. I checked him out on social media just to be sure he's not a serial killer, and he's super normal. Boring even, which is probably why he needs a little life-coaching advice from you. He's a waiter at Chez Mans who loves ultra-running, the classics, and bird-watching. Hello, snore."

I laughed lightly. "He hardly sounds like a snore, Gilley. I'm sure there's more to him than you might think. And of course you can have the afternoon off. Do you have anything special planned?"

Gilley bounced in his seat. "A massage with Reese. He had a cancellation and I snagged it!"

I couldn't help but smile and shake my head. Reese, the masseuse at Woodhouse Spa, was a bone of contention between Michel and Gilley. A gorgeous young man who looked remarkably like a young Christopher Reeve, he was an unapologetic flirt with both the ladies and men. Gilley had a major crush on him, and Michel knew it and didn't like it.

Truthfully, it surprised me that Michel took issue with Gilley's crush on Reese, because Gilley had a crush on most handsome men.

Perhaps it was because there was actual touching going on during Gilley's massages, or perhaps it was that Reese had all the same physical characteristics that Michel had— dark hair, beautiful light-blue eyes, square chin, long, lean frame—however, on Reese the combination was the kind of beautiful that should only exist in heaven, whereas Michel was the kind of beautiful that made you sigh sweetly and enjoy the lovely view. Two beautiful men to be sure, but in the looks alone department, Reese was the clear winner, and maybe that bothered Michel.

"Are we not mentioning this to Michel?" I asked Gilley.

"Only if you want me to get divorced," Gilley said. He knew I wouldn't mention it to his husband, but inwardly I laughed at how nervous it made Gilley to even joke about.

Changing the subject, I said, "Remind me, what time are Heath and Willem talking today?"

Gilley glanced at his phone. "They should be done right about now."

I lifted my wrist and noted the time. It was half past one. "I wonder how it went. . . ."

As if on cue my phone rang. The number was Heath's.

"Well, hello there, Mr. Whitefeather," I said. "Gilley and I are having lunch and I was literally *just* asking him when you'd be done talking to Willem."

Heath chuckled. "I have great timing."

"How'd it go?" I asked.

"Well," he said, seeming to gather his thoughts for a moment. "It was . . . interesting."

"Is that good interesting? Or bad interesting?"

"A little of both. I have to admit I wasn't expecting to actually find a curse on this guy, but, Cat, there is definitely something there."

Gilley was leaning over and pressing up against me, listening to the call. The moment Heath said that, he sat up and bounced his eyebrows knowingly.

"So . . . he really *is* cursed?" I asked, putting the call on speaker.

"I think so," Heath said. "It's faint, but there's definitely some negative energy attached to his aura. It's almost like a cloud that follows him everywhere. And whenever he enters a new space, it rains down some bad juju."

"Is it dangerous?" I asked next.

"Maybe," Heath said. "But probably not overly dangerous."

"What does that mean?"

"It means that the curse doesn't have the ability to start trouble on its own. But if it finds a flaw, it'll enhance that so that little disasters can turn into big disasters pretty quickly."

"And it only affects new situations?"

"Yes. That part didn't surprise me, actually, because if you're going to curse someone, you want them to suffer, you know? And the best way to cause suffering is to lengthen the time of that suffering. So, if the curse were more intense, more . . . deadly, then Willem wouldn't have survived birth let alone growing into his adult years. So, this particular curse is subtle; it sends an initial shock, then it allows him to get comfortable again, but the older he gets the more afraid he is to venture out into the world, making his home his prison."

"Terrible," I said with a tisk. "Is there anything you can do for him?"

Heath sighed. "I can't think of anything that I can do to free him from it, Cat, sorry. But there may still be a way to help him."

"How?" Gilley and I both asked.

There was a startled silence on Heath's end of the call. "Hey, Gil," he said. "Didn't know you were listening."

"Please," Gilley said. "That surprises you?"

Heath laughed. "No. And it's good to know some things never change. Anyway, here's what I'd do if you really want to help this guy. . . ."

"We do," I said.

"Good. Like I said, the curse isn't very strong. It can't actively start trouble on its own, and when Willem enters a new situation, this curse uses some of its own energy to go search for something to mess with—the toaster in one of your office suites being a perfect example."

I was nodding along as I listened to Heath. Gilley looked totally focused too.

"So, what I think you should do is take Willem to places where there's likely to be very little opportunity for the curse to muck with stuff."

"Like where?" Gilley asked.

"Like a wide open field. Or the beach. Places that are *big* without a lot of people nearby. If you push the limits of this curse, then it's likely that, over time, you'll weaken it and it'll let go of Willem."

I tapped the table thoughtfully. "I love it. We'll do it."

"We will?" Gilley asked.

"Of course!" I said. "We'll start with the beach. We can easily take Willem there and not encounter a single soul this early in April."

"Great," Heath said. "Keep me posted on how it's going, okay?"

"We will," I promised.

When I hung up the phone Gilley hardly looked pleased. "What?" I asked.

"I hate that we're messing with some gypsy juju."

"We'll be fine," I assured him, and I was mostly . . . somewhat . . . sort of positive of that.

A bit later, as I was paying the lunch tab, I said, "I'll call Willem and set up the beach excursion. If you can think of other places to take him, that'd be great."

"Will do," Gilley promised, already glancing repeatedly at the time. I knew he was anxious to be on his way. Getting a massage from Reese was a real treat. Or so I've heard.

"Go," I told him, setting some cash in the check holder. "Have a lovely time. But not too lovely."

Gilley bounced his eyebrows again, leaned over to kiss me on the cheek, then hurried out of the restaurant.

I watched him go with a sigh, wishing he could come with me to the office. It wasn't that I was afraid of this meeting with Sam per se. It's just that I was already feeling swept up in something that made me uncomfortable, and nervous.

Still, I managed to square my shoulders, strengthen my resolve, and head out to meet Sam.

When I reached the office, however, I stopped short. At the inner door to my suite was a bouquet of yellow, long-stemmed roses. They were gorgeous.

I unlocked the door and bent to bring them inside. Then I leaned over the blooms and took a good long sniff. They smelled heavenly.

It was as I was backing away again that I noticed something dark against the neck of the vase. Moving one of the rose leaves aside, I tucked two fingers against the glass and retrieved the object, which had been taped to the inside.

I think I was only a little surprised when I realized it was a flash drive. "Maks," I said softly.

As I held the flash drive in my hand, I felt the need to look over my shoulder.

There are two doors to my office. The first—the front door—faces the street, and the other faces the inner hallway of the office building, which also leads to the stairs and the back exit. That's the door where the roses had been left, and it was probably an easy thing for Maks to sneak downstairs after the roses were delivered and tuck the flash drive into the vase without being seen. I had to hand it to him that it was a clever ruse, albeit a bit risky. Anyone could've come along and snatched up the flowers after all.

I put the bouquet on a table next to the front door where I could see them from my chair in the center of the large space. And, even though I knew they were a delivery service for the flash drive, they still made me smile.

After all, Maks could've chosen to send me a pizza but instead he'd chosen flowers.

I then bustled around the office, tidying up a bit. I wanted to call Willem and speak with him, but I was a little nervous about my meeting with Sam and I was afraid I'd be distracted on the call if I did that before my three o'clock with the handler.

At exactly three p.m. the front door opened and in walked a man I hardly recognized from the evening before. He had the same hair color and silhouette, but breezing through my entryway was someone eminently more confident. More powerful. And perhaps, even more dangerous.

As he came through the door he looked immediately to his right, his left, then straight ahead to the exit behind me, and he did all this almost reflexively. I wondered if all agents did that—scoped out every room they entered for available exits.

"Hello, Sam," I said as calmly as I could.

Sam's gaze shifted to me. He nodded as he came forward. "Ms. Cooper," he said. "It's nice to see you again."

He stopped in front of my chair and extended his hand to me. I took it and found his palm dry and relaxed, unlike mine, which I'm sure gave away how nervous I was.

Still, Sam pretended not to notice and he took a seat across from me, spreading his knees wide and cupping his hands between his legs. The posture was probably supposed to look relaxed, but I couldn't help but think that Sam was the kind of man who could pounce on you before you even realized he was in motion.

"The dinner last night was delicious," I said, because I didn't know what else *to* say.

Sam chuckled. "That's not the first time I've waited a table."

That surprised me. "Oh? You mean that wasn't your usual cover?"

"No," he said. "My usual cover is accountant, and we thought about renting a suite here to make it easier on Grinkov, but your building is fully rented, and I'm positive the organization has already thoroughly investigated everyone in the building."

"Ah," I said, feeling goose bumps line my arms at the thought of the Chechen mafia investigating my tenants. Clearing my throat, I said, "How will this work exactly?"

Sam shrugged and sat back against the sofa. "Probably just like you'd operate if I really were your client. I'll come in a couple of days a week for half an hour, we'll sit here like this and talk for a bit so that it looks like we're having a session together, and then you'll walk me to the door. We'll shake hands and you'll slip me the flash drive. Then I'll be on my way."

"Sounds easy enough," I said.

"It should hold up to any scrutiny."

"And *will* there be scrutiny for each of our appointments?"

Again Sam shrugged. "Hard to say, but I expect there will be."

"Am I in danger, Sam?" I asked next.

He shook his head. "If I thought you were in danger, Ms. Cooper, I wouldn't have agreed to this arrangement. No, you'll be checked out, verified, and left largely alone."

"Who's doing the looking, exactly?"

"Any one of a number of henchmen for Boris Basayev. Charming guy."

"And by charming I'm assuming you mean big, bad mafia boss man?"

Sam winked and shot me with a finger gun.

"But I'm not in danger." I said it as a statement rather than a question, because I wanted to be absolutely sure that I wasn't inviting a big heap of trouble into my life.

"No. We've already checked you out. You're exactly the type of person someone like Maks would want to acquaint himself with. You're educated, accomplished, well-traveled, and stable. There's nothing suspicious about you."

"And the fact that my sister and her husband work for the FBI—that won't be a problem?"

"They're based in Texas, right?"

I nodded. "Austin."

"Austin's half a country away from here, and as long as they're not scheduled to come for a visit anytime soon, you'll be fine."

"They're not."

"Good."

I studied Sam for a minute. He was relaxed and there was nothing tense or staged about his words or mannerisms. He could've been a very good liar—in fact, I had no doubt he actually *was*, but I still trusted that what he was telling me was the truth. I didn't feel like I was in danger from Boris Basayev, and as long as I didn't have to accompany Maks to any mafia family shindigs, I thought that this whole handoff of secret flash drive thing might be okay.

And then I had another thought. In hindsight, it was my undoing, but at the time it seemed almost harmless.

"Sam?"

"Yes?"

"How long have you been assigned to this case?"

"Two years, four months, and sixteen days," he said seriously, and then he smiled. "But who's counting?"

"Oh, my. It's been that long? And you've kept track?"

"We're close to the end," he said. "But, to your unspoken point, yes, it's been a long time and I'm ready to end it. Maks is the key to bringing an indictment. With a little more time, we'll have enough to bring in the whole organization."

"Good," I said. "But, can I ask you about someone who used to work for Basayev?"

"Who?"

"I only know her first name. Greta."

Sam's eyes betrayed a hint of surprise. "You got up close and personal to her not too long ago, right?"

"I did."

"You don't know how lucky you are to still be walking around, Ms. Cooper. As far as assassins go, she's one of the best."

"So I've heard. Still, is there anything you can tell me about her?"

"I can tell you what we know, which is very little. She's from Croatia, abandoned by her mother at the age of six, and showed psychopathic tendencies at an early age. She was adopted by a couple here in the States when she was seven. They tried to return her six months later. When they couldn't, they had her committed. She got out when she was eighteen, and within three months the primary psychologist assigned to her was found hanging in his living room. No one believes it was a suicide."

I put a hand to my throat and fiddled with my collar. It was one thing to think that Greta was a cold-blooded killer, and an entirely different thing to learn that she was, in fact, clinically psychotic.

"From there," Sam continued, "it's a little sketchy. We think she mostly took low-level jobs around the city for a few years and began acquiring weapons and methods to murder people. One of her signature moves first appeared ten years ago when a couple was murdered in their Manhattan apartment. They were the landlords of a four-unit apartment in Brooklyn, and we suspect they rented one of the spaces to Greta before trying to evict her because of complaints from her neighbors about loud music and the company she kept. On the day the couple in Manhattan were murdered, witnesses remember hearing a series of gunshots coming from the apartment and they also distinctly remember a woman wearing flashy clothes exiting the unit, but no one remembered what she actually looked like. Some witnesses said she was tall, others said she was short, and the sketch artist assigned to the witnesses developed four completely different profiles for Greta's face."

"The clothes are the distraction," I said. "You end up focusing on her getup rather than on her."

"Yep. From there we can trace eleven more murders to someone with her profile—every time it's the same scenario: woman murders someone in broad daylight, almost always there's at least one witness who can describe the clothing, but not the person."

"When did she start working for Basayev?"

"Five years ago. By then she'd amassed a certain reputation, and we think she gave herself the title of the Angel of Death because, in one of her flashier assassinations, she didn't dress up, she dressed down. She wore a bra and panties and a set of angel wings in the middle of February at the entrance to the subway where she shot a bookie who was skimming a little off the top every month.

"There were over twenty witnesses to that one, and nobody remembered her face. But they all remembered her panty and bra number, and of course the wings."

"She was dressed as a Victoria's Secret model?" I said. "One of the angels?"

"Yes. She's a clever one. At the time of the murder, there was a Victoria's Secret modeling shoot just four blocks away."

"She was *actually* one of the models?"

Sam shook his head. "Nope. But it served as a great cover for her getaway. When cops responded they had to interview twenty gorgeous models and run background checks on all of them. They were distracted for *days*. Meanwhile, Greta floated off into obscurity and adopted the Angel of Death moniker. That's how she got Basayev's attention, actually. He heard about the hit and, being your typical perverted mafia guy, wanted her and only her to do his dirty work."

I sat with all that information for a long moment. I wondered if Shepherd knew any of it. "Have you ever shared this information with the local P.D.?" I asked, mostly out of curiosity.

"Nope," Sam answered.

"Why not? Greta's killed a few people here in East Hampton."

"For two reasons: one, we don't want the local police to know *anything* about our investigation into Basayev, and two, we suspect that there may be an informant on the force."

My palms grew a bit sweaty again. Sam's eyes had

hardened as he spoke—it was obvious that he didn't like the fact that I was chummy with an East Hampton detective. And, of course, I knew that he knew I was chummy with Shepherd, because, if he'd already checked me out, how could he not?

Still, I decided to press on. "Do you know where Greta is now?"

"No clue," Sam said. And for the first time I couldn't tell if he was being honest with me.

"Would you tell me if you did know?"

"Probably not."

"Even though she tried to murder me?"

Sam sighed and dropped the whole casual posture act. Leaning in toward me and resting his elbows on his knees, he said, "We don't have any reason to suspect she's back in the area. Once she botched the Heather Holland job and her cover was blown, Basayev ended his professional relationship with her. By now she's likely off somewhere, trying to find other work on another coast or in another country."

My shoulders relaxed a little. "That's a relief."

Sam nodded and looked around like he was ready to end our discussion and get back to doing what undercover agents like him do.

But I had one more question. "Sam," I said, stopping him.

"Yeah?"

"Do you know why Greta killed Detective Shepherd's ex-wife, Lenny?" It was the one question that I knew haunted Shepherd most of all, and perhaps the only one I might be able to shed some light on for him if I was very careful.

"No," Sam said simply.

"No?"

He shook his head. "Sorry. That one's a mystery to us."

"So Lenny Shepherd didn't work for or double-cross Basayev?"

"Not that we can determine."

I thought of something that Maks had told me a while back. "I've heard that Greta always kills for money or revenge. That she doesn't kill for fun, but maybe Lenny was the exception?"

"That occurred to us too, but it would be highly unusual for Greta to take such a risk for no reason. She's psychotic but she's not crazy, if you get what I mean."

I smiled darkly. "I looked directly into her eyes, Sam. I understand more than you know."

Sam laid his hands on his knees and inched forward on the couch. "That it?"

I nodded. "Yes, thank you."

"Do you have the flash drive on you?"

"It's in my pocket."

"Great. Walk me to the door, please?"

"Of course," I said.

I walked Sam to the door, which had a clear glass insert around a wood frame, so that we were in full view of anyone on the street. He turned and stuck out his hand to me.

"Thank you for doing this, Ms. Cooper."

I took his hand and slipped the flash drive into his palm. "Please, Sam, let's not be so formal. Call me Catherine."

Sam smiled, dipped his chin, pocketed the flash drive, and was gone.

Chapter 5

"Cat?" Gilley said, pulling me from my thoughts.

"Hmm, what now?" I said, trying to cover for the fact that I'd been lost in thought.

Gilley eyed me curiously. "You okay, sugar?"

"Fine!" I said, a bit too forcefully. "Why do you ask?"

"Well, I've asked you three times now if you talked to Willem today."

I shook my head, trying to clear out all the other thoughts clouding my brain. "No. I got his voice mail and left him a message. I haven't heard back."

"Ah," Gil said, still studying me. "So, how about you tell me what's really going on with you?"

"Going on? Nothing's going on, honey. Everything's fine."

"Cat, you've been lost in thought ever since you got home and, incredibly sumptuous as this dinner is, it can't make up for stilted conversation and you moving your fork around your plate like you're trying to figure out the best strategy for herding cats."

I smiled. "*You* made dinner."

"Yes, which is why it's so delicious and should be given the proper attention it deserves."

To humor him I took a bite of the lemon chicken he'd prepared. "Mmmmm!" I said. "Yummy."

He rolled his eyes and set aside his own fork. "Come on, Cat. What gives?"

I sighed and put down my utensil as well. "It's this thing that I heard today about Greta," I confessed before I realized what I'd actually let slip out.

"Greta? You mean you heard something about the Angel of Death?"

"Yes." My mind was racing to think of a plausible explanation for where I'd heard it.

"From who?"

"Maks," I said, settling on a name.

Gilley shivered. "I still can't believe they had dinner together only a few hours after she tried to murder you. It takes a special kind of cold-blooded killer to act so casually mere hours after shooting up a place."

"See, that's just it. There was something he said about Greta's mental state that's been bugging me."

"What'd he say?"

"Well, as only you and I know, Maks had met Greta before—"

"Yeah. She did business with someone he did business with, right?"

"Right."

Gilley's expression turned suddenly troubled. "You don't think Maks is working for . . . for . . ."

"The mafia?"

Gilley nodded.

I waved my hand dismissively, hoping to throw him off track. "Not directly, but he knows a great deal about their organization."

"Hmmm," Gilley said suspiciously. "Maybe you should be careful around him. I mean, if he knows so much, he could become a target, right?"

"Maks is careful," I said. "He knows what he's doing."

"And you're sure he's running a legitimate business?"

"Quite sure," I said. That part at least was true.

"Okay, then. What did he have to say about Greta?"

"Well, I was asking him if, through his connections, he knew anything about the Lenny Shepherd murder."

"Did he?"

"No. But he did say something about it that gave me pause."

"The suspense here is killing me; would you spit it out already?"

"Yes, of course, sorry. I was asking him if it was possible that Greta had murdered Lenny for the thrill of it. Like, maybe she got bored and felt like killing a random stranger, and Maks said that he didn't think that fit her persona. He said that Greta was psychotic, not crazy."

"Huh," Gilley grunted. "That's telling."

"It is, but I'd like to hear what you think it tells."

"Well, it's obvious, right? Lenny must've been a hit. Someone paid to have her killed."

"Yes, that's what I concluded too."

"Did Maks know if Lenny had any connection to . . ." Gilley put a finger on the side of his nose and pushed on it.

"The mob? No. He says that as far as he knows, she didn't."

"Well, there has to be some connection, otherwise, why would Greta kill her?"

And just like that, I understood Shepherd's obsession with the case, other than the obvious, of course, that Lenny was his ex-wife and a part of him still cared for her even if the divorce had been sticky. He had to know that being murdered by the Angel of Death would definitely mark you as someone connected to the mafia, and that had to be eating away at him, especially as she didn't appear to actually be connected.

"So who paid Greta for the hit?" I asked aloud.

"Yeah. That's the real question. As much as Shepherd wants to find Greta and bring her to justice, the *real* person behind Lenny's murder could still get away with it even if Greta was caught because we both know she'd probably refuse to talk."

"She would definitely refuse to talk," I agreed. "We need to know more about Lenny Shepherd and who she dealt with."

"Wait, wait, *wait*!" Gilley said, putting up his hand in a stopping motion. "What do you mean, *we* need to learn more about who she dealt with?"

I set my napkin on the table and looked at Gilley intently. "I think we should dig around a little."

Gilley's jaw dropped. "*Why* would we want to do that?"

Because I was feeling guilty about lying to Shepherd, who was clearly torturing himself with this obsession to solve his ex-wife's murder. And because I was sitting on all this information that could help his case, and perhaps bring him a bit of release, but I wasn't at liberty to tell him any of it. And, if I was being honest (and I was), also because the thought of solving another mystery was somewhat thrilling to me.

Of course I couldn't say any of that to Gilley, so I went with, "Because I think we can help, Gilley. Shepherd's too close to this to be able to really look at it objectively. But you and I could root around a little and maybe come up with a theory that might help him track down the person who paid Greta to murder Lenny."

Gilley crossed his arms and raised one skeptical eyebrow while he looked at me. "You liked playing amateur sleuth in the Heather Holland murder case, didn't you?" he said.

I blushed and got up to pace the floor. "I did a little."

"More than just a little."

"Okay, okay. You got me. I found it thrilling. Way more thrilling than sitting around my office, thinking up e-mail marketing content."

"I thought you really liked being a life coach."

"I do!" I said quickly. "I honestly, honestly do. But even with that new purpose . . . I don't know. I feel like something's still missing."

Gilley shook his head, staring at his lap before lifting his chin again to me, wearing a disapproving frown. I braced for the lecture that was sure to follow.

Instead, his face transformed into a gleeful smile and he shouted, "I *love* that idea!"

I blinked. "You do?"

"Hell yeah!" he said, reaching forward to offer me a high five. I slapped his hand. "Girlfriend, I've been *so* bored. I mean, I love being your assistant and all, but I *miss* the days when M.J., Heath, and I used to do the whole gumshoe thing!"

"I thought you couldn't wait to retire from ghostbusting?"

"*That* gig I couldn't wait to give up for sure. Spooks are *freaky*! Especially the ones we dealt with, but this . . . this whole solving real crimes that don't involve some demon or grounded spirit is like, huzzah! I've found my calling!" I laughed as Gilley flashed me some jazz hands.

"You're crazy," I said, pushing on his shoulder.

"No crazier than you."

"Thank God we're not psychotic," I said with a wink, and we both laughed. I sobered first. "Are you sure though, Gilley? I mean, this could be dangerous."

"That's part of the thrill though, right?"

I nodded. "It is. At least for me."

"I'm in, Cat. Let's do this!"

I nodded again. "Okay!"

And then Gilley and I just stared at each other for a minute, and as the excitement wore off, things felt awkward.

"So, ah, where do we start?" I asked.

Gilley shrugged. "Not sure. Where do *you* think we should start?"

"Well," I said, tapping my lip. "I think we should start . . . with a plan!" I felt so relieved to have struck on the idea.

"Perfect!" Gilley said, getting up while grabbing both of our plates and hustling them to the sink. He then retrieved his laptop and came back to the table.

"Okay, so step one," I said as Gilley opened his laptop and began to type. "Step one is . . ." I tapped some more on my lip, waiting for inspiration to hit me again.

After a looooong pause, Gilley said, "How about instead of step one, two, three, et cetera, we focus on the ways we can get information and work our way backward into the plan?"

"I love that. Yes. Let's do that. So, how can we get information about Lenny?"

"We'll start with her known associates," Gilley said.

"Who are?"

"Well, Shepherd for one," he said as he typed.

"Yeah, but we can't ask Shepherd."

"Why not?"

"Because he'll know we're digging into his case on our own and then he'll want to shut that right down, and, well . . . because he's mad at me."

Gilley eyed me with sympathy. "The Maks thing, huh?"

"Yes."

"He'll get over it," Gilley said, waving his hand dismissively. "But I get it. We won't ask Shepherd. Who else would know about Lenny, though?"

We both thought on that for a moment, and then we turned to each other and at the same time shouted, "Sunny!"

Sunny was Steve's sister, and the total opposite in personality. She was as bright and warm as her name, and I genuinely found her delightful.

"Wait," I said, thinking of an issue almost immediately. "What if she tells her brother that we're snooping around in Lenny's business?"

"We'll ask her not to say anything," Gilley said easily.

"Do you think she'll actually do that?"

Gil shrugged. "She might. I mean, she didn't share with him anything about our snooping around into Heather Holland's background way back when."

"But that was different. Heather wasn't family. Lenny was."

"All we can do is ask, Cat, and let the chips fall where they may."

"Good point. Okay. So we start with Sunny. Who's next?"

"I have no idea, so maybe our plan should just be to talk to Sunny and see what shakes out?"

"Good," I said. "I like that. When?"

Gilley eyed the clock. "It's only seven o'clock and Sunny's husband's still on the road, right?"

"He is, that jerk." Sunny was about thirty-eight weeks along in her pregnancy and her record producer husband had been away for most of that time. It made me angry because I remember how anxious and worried I'd been when I was near the end of my pregnancy with the twins. It'd been a torturous time and even though Tom had turned out to be a lying, cheating jerk at the end of our marriage, he'd been an absolute prince to me back when I was pregnant and for several years afterward when the twins were little.

"Maybe going to see her would make her feel less lonely," Gilley suggested. He then pointed to a delicious-smelling cherry coffee cake he'd pulled out of the oven right before I'd arrived. "We could take that over as a gift for disturbing her."

"You didn't want to save that for breakfast?"

"I can bake another one tomorrow," he said easily. "I still have leftover ingredients."

"Let's do it," I said, with a clap of my hands.

Gilley and I hurried through cleaning up the dinner dishes before we scurried out of Chez Kitty. Before leaving the guesthouse, Gil had found a red bit of ribbon that he wrapped around the coffee cake to make it look more festive.

We rolled down Sunny's driveway not even three minutes later—she lives just two streets over from Chez Cat—and sat in the car for a moment after I parked. "What's our story?" Gilley asked as we looked out the window at the warmly lit, blue colonial with bright white trim.

My eyes widened. I hadn't even thought about what we'd say to Sunny for dropping in unannounced. "Maybe we should just start with the truth," I said.

"Which is?"

"We're digging into Lenny's murder."

"Should we say why?"

"Hmmm," I said, thinking.

"Uh oh," Gilley said, looking over my shoulder.

I stiffened. "What's uh oh?"

"Sunny just peeked out of the curtains. She knows someone's in her driveway."

"Rats. Okay, I'll have to think of something on the fly. Let's go in before we alarm her."

We got out of the car and approached the house. As we came up to the steps the front door opened and there stood Sunny. Beyond her enlarged belly, Shepherd's twin sister was tall, thin, and Hollywood beautiful. She had lightly bronzed golden skin, very long blond hair, and a radiant smile she beamed at us. "Catherine! Gilley! How great to see you!"

"Hi, Sunny!" I said, coming up the stairs quickly.

Gilley also made his way up hastily and immediately offered her the coffee cake. "We brought goodies."

Sunny clapped her hands happily. "Ohmigod! You two are *not* going to believe this, but about ten minutes ago I started craving coffee cake!"

"Do tell," Gilley said, clearly pleased as we followed her through the door and inside her lovely home.

"It's true," she said, waving her hand for us to continue following her to the kitchen. "I wouldn't believe it myself except that I've always been a little bit psychic."

Gilley and I traded conspiratorial smiles. "Yeah, we've also got one of those in my family," I said.

"Mine too," Gilley added, winking at me.

Sunny set the coffee cake on the large marble island in the center of her kitchen and reached for the teakettle. "They say there's one in every family," she said.

I took a seat on one of the bar stools set along the island and Gilley sat next to me. "I believe that," I told her.

"Tea?" she asked us.

"Please," we both said.

Sunny puttered around in the kitchen fetching cups, saucers, cream, and sugar while the water heated. "So what do I owe the pleasure of this lovely little drop-in?" she asked. "Is my brother being a jackass again?"

I chuckled. "No. Well, maybe a little."

Sunny paused. "Need me to deck him for you? I will, you know."

Gilley and I both laughed at how serious she seemed, and of course the picture of a profoundly pregnant twig like Sunny throwing a solid punch at her much bigger, more muscled brother was somewhat hilarious to think about too.

Still, to quell her fighting spirit, I put up my hand and said, "No need. It's under control."

Sunny pointed at me. "All right, but you let me know if he's due to have a can of whoop-ass opened up in his face, you hear?"

"Noted," I said, stifling another giggle. "We are here in part about him, though."

Sunny waddled her feet back two steps, bent awkwardly, and put her elbows on the island before resting her face in her open palms and rocking her hips slightly from side to side. "What's up?"

I smiled a bit at her posture. My back had ached something terrible when I was that pregnant, and I knew that she was trying to find a little relief in any position she could dream up. "I came across some information about Greta," I said.

Sunny's brow lifted and the teakettle began to whistle. She moved to pour the boiling water into the teapot and set a timer on her Apple watch, then focused again on me. "You heard something about the Angel of Death?"

"Yes."

"What?"

"It was something someone said—"

"Who?" she asked.

"Someone who's familiar with Greta," I said vaguely.

"Who?" Sunny pressed.

I looked at Gilley and he shrugged as if to say, *You might as well tell her.*

I took a deep breath and started in on my lie. "There's a man I'm acquainted with who has met Greta, but didn't know until after learning that your brother was shot that she was actually an assassin. After doing a little digging on his own, he said that Greta never killed for pleasure. She killed for a paycheck or out of revenge."

Gilley nodded. "Yeah, we saw that firsthand. Oh, and she'll also kill to cover her tracks. Remember the priest?"

"Yes," I said. "But that brings me to my larger point—that Greta is definitely psychotic, but maybe not serial-killer crazy. There seems to always be a reason for her taking someone else's life."

Sunny's watch beeped and she jerked at the sound. "Ha!" she said, catching herself. "That scared me. Of course, any discussion about the Angel of Death freaks me out, you know."

"I can only imagine," I said.

Sunny began to pour tea into three cups, and she scooted two toward us when she was done pouring. Then she moved over to the coffee cake and lifted the plastic wrap to take a whiff. "This smells amazing."

Gilley grinned, clearly happy with his call to bring the coffee cake. "I made it from scratch," he told her. "It's a recipe from my pastry class."

Sunny smiled eagerly and moved to the cupboards to grab three dessert plates and a knife. We waited while she portioned out a piece for all of us and then handed out forks. I had a sneaking suspicion she was stalling a little because the topic of conversation frightened her, and I felt bad for bringing this to her, but I also knew she might be the key to developing a pool of suspects.

After waiting for her to take a bite (and roll her eyes up with an appreciative moan, which pleased Gilley no end), I got us back on track.

"So, as I was saying, Greta kills for a reason. Not for pleasure or sport. So what I'm wondering is: what was the reason she had for killing Lenny?" I asked Sunny.

She opened her eyes again as she chewed her bite of coffee cake and stared at me with concern. "I have no idea."

I believed her. I also believed that Lenny had had a hit put out on her, and maybe there was someone in this town who'd gotten away with murder.

"Sunny, I want to ask you something and I'm hoping you'll be totally honest with me, and also, maybe you'll do us a kindness and not tell your brother that we were asking about his ex-wife's murder," I said next.

"If you need me to keep this conversation from him, I have no problem with that," Sunny reassured me. "He'd only get all worked up about it anyway. And of course I'll be honest, Cat. Go ahead, ask me your question."

I reached out and squeezed her hand in gratitude. I genuinely adored Sunny. "Thank you. What I wanted to ask is do you think it's possible that Lenny had an enemy who was willing to pay to have her murdered?"

Sunny's jaw fell open. "Seriously?"

"Seriously," Gilley said.

Sunny's eyes blinked rapidly. "I . . . I can't imagine it," she said. "Lenny was such a well-liked, gentle soul. She didn't have any enemies that I know of. And I can't even fathom why anyone would want to hurt her, much less kill her."

"Okay," I said. "Thank you for that. Now let me ask another hard question. Do you think Lenny could've had *some* connection to organized crime?"

Sunny barked out a laugh. "You're joking, right?"

"No. I'm not. Greta worked for the Chechen mafia. She was their contract killer, and we know she was responsible for Tony Holland's death and she was also awarded the contract for Heather Holland too. All that's to say that the work she did here in East Hampton was mostly for money."

"You think someone put a hit out on Lenny?" Sunny said, her eyes wide and disbelieving.

I looked her in the eye as I answered. "I'm saying it's possible. But, you were her sister-in-law, and besides your brother, probably one of the closest people to her. Was there ever a time when you might've thought there was something off about her business?"

Sunny bent at the waist again and set her elbows on the counter to rock her hips side to side while she thought about my question. "No," she said at last. "Lenny was on the level. She was an honest person. In fact, I'd known her since we were all eighteen, and I'd never known Lenny to lie. Like, not even a white lie. She'd tell you the truth to your face and if that made you upset, she was okay with that because she liked to live her truth every day of her life. Which is also why she and Steve broke up when they did."

"What do you mean?" Gilley asked.

"Well, Lenny was super honest with herself. And, when things started getting rough between the two of them, she told him she was having doubts about their compatibility. He took it a little too personally, and instead of trying to work through the issue, he told her to go if she wasn't happy. So she did."

"Yikes," Gilley said, mirroring my thoughts. Tom and I had at least attempted to work through our issues, but I just couldn't get past his affair with the bartender from his country club.

Sunny held her palms up like, *what're you gonna do?* "In the end, Steve was offered up a valuable lesson, I think. Even if he chose not to learn it then, he was still given a chance to understand what it means to hang in there and fight for a relationship."

I suddenly understood why Sunny was hanging on to her own dysfunctional marriage so determinedly. She'd seen what'd happened between her brother and Lenny, and she'd be damned if she'd make the same mistake of quitting before giving it everything she had. It made me feel even more sympathetic to her, and I was, in that moment, very glad we'd dropped by for the visit. Even if we did have an ulterior motive.

"So you genuinely don't believe that Lenny had any connections to anyone nefarious or suspicious in their business dealings?" I asked again.

"No way. Lenny was married to a cop for fifteen years. She definitely wouldn't have entangled herself in anything like that."

"Was she dating anybody else when she was murdered?" Gilley asked.

Sunny sighed. It was a sad sound. "No. She was totally focused on her career. I tried to encourage her to get back out there—that was around the time that Darius and I were thinking about having kids, but Lenny was hesitant to start a new relationship, and at the time she was murdered, I couldn't help but feel she was at the loneliest point of her life."

"Oh," Gilley said. "That's so sad."

"It was," Sunny agreed.

"Was there anything else going on in Lenny's life that maybe hit you as strange?" I asked next.

Sunny stood up and put a hand on her lower back while she stretched and rubbed her belly with her free hand. "Not really. Lenny was just living her life, Cat. I swear. She'd recently opened up her own realty practice, and she was putting a ton of effort into making that work."

Then I thought of something. "Real estate commissions around here can be worth a pretty penny, Sunny. Do you think Lenny could've been murdered because someone saw her as the competition?"

Lenny shrugged and shook her head. "Anything's possible. Especially in the Hamptons' real estate market, which is pretty cutthroat from what I hear."

Following up on that statement, I asked, "Did she ever mention any issues with other real estate agents?"

"Oh, yeah, all the time!" Sunny said. "I mean, those bitches were *bitches* if you get my drift. Lenny had a dozen stories about the unprofessionalism of other agents, but to my recollection, nothing that seemed threatening or even overly alarming."

"So, nothing bad or suspicious was going on in her life at the time of her murder, huh?" I said.

"Nope. Just the opposite, actually. She'd just moved into a really cool new condo on the ocean and she was getting ready to close a huge sale that was going to bring her a commission big enough to completely cover the cost of the major renovation project she had planned."

"Huh," Gilley said. "What happens to the sale on your house when your agent suddenly passes away?"

I looked at Gilley in surprise. What kind of a question was *that*?

"In Lenny's case, her partner took over and the Reynolds sale went through, which was fortunate, because the buyers' agent was an idiot and nearly bungled the whole thing."

"How do you know all that?" Gilley asked curiously.

"Cordelia Reynolds is Darius's cousin." Darius D'Angelo was Sunny's husband. "I actually put Lenny and Cordelia together when she told me that she was thinking of selling her home."

"So, Lenny had a partner?" I asked. This was the first time I'd heard that.

"Yes. Chanel Downey."

Gilley made a note in his iPhone, while Sunny moved over to cut another piece of coffee cake, offering the slice to us. I declined but Gilley nodded.

"Chanel's a sweet girl. You'd like her," Sunny said, heading back over to the coffee cake to slice another sliver for herself.

"How long had they been partners?" I asked.

"Only two years. Chanel was Lenny's protégée when they were at the other realty office. Lenny knew she could hold onto her entire commission if she started her own office, so she and Chanel got their brokerage license at the same time and became partners."

"Is Chanel still selling real estate around here?"

Sunny shook her head. "She moved back to Connecticut right after closing on Cordelia's house to be closer to her family . . . her grandmother lives there, I think."

Gilley made a face. "Hard to believe the sale went through when someone was murdered in that home. You couldn't pay me to buy a house where someone was murdered."

Sunny shook her head. "Lenny wasn't shot in the Reynolds place. She was murdered in another house in Apaquogue. She was there to host an open house that day so she was there alone when she was murdered."

"I'm assuming your brother checked out the people who owned that home?" I said.

"You mean to make sure they didn't have any mafia connections and Lenny's murder was simply a case of mistaken identity? Yes, he checked out that lead, but that house was owned by an elderly woman whose husband had recently passed away from natural causes. And as much as Steve wanted to find something suspicious about them to maybe point to a motive or a reason why the

Angel of Death had gone there, he found nothing. The old man had been a prominent heart surgeon with no known mafia connections, and the wife, who was in her eighties, had never held a job."

"Another dead end," Gilley said, smirking at his own pun.

"Now you see why Steve has been so haunted by Lenny's murder," Sunny said, ignoring Gilley's gallows humor. "He's looked at every angle, considered every possibility for a motive, and he keeps coming back to square one. As far as he can tell, Lenny was murdered for no reason."

But I didn't buy it. And I don't really know why, other than I'd looked into Greta's eyes and I'd seen the calculating, cold-blooded killer, but I hadn't seen that discernable glint that was in the eyes of every serial killer I'd ever seen interviewed on TV.

No, there was a reason Lenny had died; we just didn't know what it was yet.

I set my paper napkin on the now empty dessert plate and took note of the time via the brightly colored clock on the wall. It was getting late and we'd imposed on Sunny long enough. "We should be on our way," I said.

Gilley got up too, making sure to scoop up both our plates and bring them over to the sink for Sunny. "Thank you, sugar. You make a delicious pot of tea."

Sunny grinned and rubbed his shoulder in a friendly gesture. "Thanks, Gilley. And *you* make a delicious coffee cake."

We saw ourselves out and as we got into the car, Sunny waved at us through the kitchen window.

Gilley waved back and said, "Do you think she'll tell her brother about our visit?"

"No," I said, starting the car. "Sunny's trustworthy. She'll honor our request to keep the conversation on the down-low."

"She was a good resource at least," Gil said.

"She was. Almost too good. I mean, where do we even start?"

"I think we should start at the scene of the crime, Cat."

"You mean the house where Lenny was murdered?"

"Yeah. Maybe something will jump out at us."

"But we don't even know where that is. I mean, Sunny only said it was up in Apaquogue."

Gilley wiggled his phone. "I could find it."

I glanced over at him. "How quickly?"

Gilley began to tap at the device. "Give me two minutes."

I drove out of Sunny's driveway, down the street and parked on the side of the road while Gilley conducted his search. He took the two minutes plus just one minute more. "Found it," he said. "There was a news article about Lenny's murder and it listed the address. It's about ten minutes from here."

"Navigate me," I said, getting back on the road.

We wound our way through East Hampton, heading east toward Apaquogue—a small, very expensive section of the Hamptons, with breathtaking views and real estate prices that start in the low millions but can get up into the tens of millions depending on the lot size.

"There," Gilley said, pointing through the windshield at a three-story structure painted a steel gray with black shutters.

I looked through the glass. "That's it?"

"Yeah."

Easing the car over to the curb across the street from

the house, I stared up at it, as Gilley did the same. It was dark save for one lit room above the garage. The window there had no curtain, and we could both see a bright light hanging from the ceiling, and the top of an easel with a canvas propped on it.

The easel was facing away from the window, so it was impossible to say what image it held, and there was no movement in the room that we could see, so it was hard to tell if the artist was at the easel painting or not.

"I wonder if anyone's home," I said.

"Hard to say. Someone could be up there and behind the easel, though," Gilley said, pointing to the room above the garage.

"Makes you wonder what he or she is painting, huh?"

"My guess—it's a fruit bowl."

I laughed. He was probably right. "Hey," I said to Gil. "Could you track down who lives here now?"

"I could but I'd need my laptop."

"Good. Do that."

"Can I ask why?" he said.

"No reason other than I'd like to be thorough. And maybe I'm a little curious about who buys a house where there was a cold-blooded murder?"

Gilley shuddered. "Someone who doesn't believe in ghosts, that's for sure."

I sucked in a breath. "You don't think that Lenny's spirit is now haunting that house, do you?"

Gilley shrugged. "Probably not, but don't order me to find out. I left that life behind for good."

"How would we know, though?" I asked him.

"You'd know," he said with another shudder.

"What if we asked Heath?"

Gilley shifted in his seat. "If Lenny were grounded, I'm

not sure what Heath could do about it being all the way out in Santa Fe."

"Could he make a connection to her if she *wasn't* grounded?" I asked, suddenly getting a big idea.

Gilley jumped right onto my train of thought. "You're thinking you want to ask her about her own murder, don't you?"

"Well, obviously."

"Yeah, good luck with that, Cat. M.J. used to get a ton of requests to talk to the dead to find out the circumstances of their deaths, and in just about every case, the victim was foggy on the details of their crossing."

"Huh," I said. "I wonder why?"

"M.J. used to say it was because the actual method of crossing wasn't important to them. It only mattered that they'd crossed over."

"But what if their life had been cut short, like Lenny's?"

Gilley shrugged. "See, that's the part that's tricky to explain. The other side is *heaven*, Cat. Like, it's awesome. There's no sickness, no old age, no stress, no heartbreak, no anger, no violence, no hunger, no loss, no want, and no need. It's free of all the stuff that we stress out about down here, so when spirits move home—to the other side— they're actually *happy* about it."

"Even if they were murdered in cold blood?"

"Mostly yeah. Weird, huh?"

"Very," I said, a bit unsettled by that notion. I doubted that, if I were to die before seeing my sons grow into men, I'd be "happy" to be away from them. In fact, I couldn't imagine a worse scenario.

"Still, could you ask Heath anyway?"

Gilley nodded. "I'll call him when we get home."

"Thank you," I said. I was about to pull away from the

curb, but I took a moment to look all around the street. "There're some nice homes in this area, no?"

"That's the understatement of the evening."

Ignoring the sarcasm, I said, "A sale's commission on a house over here would be worth, what? Anywhere from the low hundred-thousands to a million bucks?"

Gilley whistled appreciatively. "That's a *lot* of money for an agent to make for one transaction."

"It is," I agreed. And then something else occurred to me. "Gunshots in this neighborhood would've likely been heard too. There aren't any woodlands or hills to muffle the sound."

"Yeah, but Greta's used a silencer before, so not necessarily," Gilley said, reminding me about that particular detail.

"Did the article you read mention any witness statements?"

Gilley lifted his phone and began to read. The light cast by his phone gave his face an eerie glow. "No mention of gunshots heard. Lenny's body was discovered by a couple who came to the open house. They passed a woman exiting the house, wearing a pink, yellow, and lime-green dress with white go-go boots."

"Greta," I said. "The go-go boots are the dead giveaway—no pun intended."

"Yep," Gilley agreed.

"What time of day was it again?"

Gilley scrolled through the article. "A little after ten a.m. On a Saturday."

I looked up and down the street again. "Lenny would've thought it was totally safe to host an open house around here at ten a.m. on a Saturday."

"I'm sure she did. I'm sure anyone would."

"So what was the reason *she* was murdered?" I wondered.

"Don't know. But if we answer that question, I bet we figure out who hired Greta."

"Okay," I said, moving the car away from the curb again. "Tomorrow, let's tackle the leads Sunny identified for us and figure out what was really going on."

With that, we headed home.

Chapter 6

We heard from Willem early the next day. "Good morning!" I sang, when Gilley patched him through to my line. "How are you, Willem?"

"I'm fine, Catherine, thank you," he said. But he didn't sound fine. He sounded stilted and stubborn.

"Did you have a nice chat with Heath?" I tried.

There was a pause, then, "He was amazing. He picked up on my grandfather. It freaked me out at first but it was also really, really cool."

I relaxed, hearing Willem ease into a more casual conversational tone. Mentioning Heath had been the right move. "So, I also talked to Heath, and he says that he was able to detect that something has definitely attached itself to you, Willem."

"He told me that too. It's a relief to know that someone else can validate it for me."

"I'm sure. Did Heath also mention the plan he came up with to break the curse?"

There was a pause, then, "No. No he didn't. What plan?"

"Heath thinks that the curse attached to you isn't especially powerful. And because it's not strong enough to incite its own trouble, it has to go looking for things to muck with. So, when you came here to my office, it probably had to search the whole building before it found the unattended toaster."

"Again, I'm so sorry about that. I should have given you fair warning before coming to meet you."

"Willem, please don't continue to feel guilty about my tenant's irresponsible actions—who's to say that his toaster wouldn't have started smoking on some other day that you weren't here and he went for coffee. There was no lasting damage, and he learned a valuable lesson."

Willem sighed. "It's never my intention to cause harm," he said.

My heart went out to him. "Which is why we need to mount a campaign against this curse. You should be able to get out in the world without fear of causing or exacerbating havoc. Which is also why Heath's solution is actually quite brilliant."

"What is that specifically?" he asked.

"He suggested that we push the limits of your curse by getting you out into the world, to places you've never been, but also places that are wide open, away from crowds or big buildings where there're ample opportunities for this curse to wreak its havoc."

"Like . . . where, exactly?"

"Well," I said, taking a moment to think. "Have you ever gone to the public beach?"

"My grandparents dragged me to the beach when I was little. It was during a heat wave."

"Did anything happen?"

"Plenty. Two surfers collided right in front of us, one of them almost drowned, and the ambulance that came to take away the victim crashed into another car."

"Oh, my," I said. "Which beach was that?"

"I think it was the one here in Amagansett near our home. The one next to the tennis courts."

I pictured the area that Willem was describing and, as I'd taken the boys on a Hamptons' beach tour the previous summer, I was fairly familiar with all the beaches in the area. "I believe you're talking about the Ocean Colony beach," I said.

"That's the one."

"All right, so we won't go there, because the curse has already been there and done that. You say you live in Amagansett?"

"Yes."

Amagansett was to the east. It was an extremely pricey part of the Hamptons. "Have you ever been to Indian Wells beach?" On my tour with the boys, that had been a particular favorite of mine.

"No," he said. "But, Catherine, didn't you hear what I said? The last time I went to a public beach a man nearly drowned and the curse caused a car crash. It was madness."

"And you also said it'd been during a heat wave. Willem, it's the second of April. No one's going to be at the beach right now. Well, maybe an odd jogger or two, but no one will be swimming in the forty-two-degree water. It's hard enough to dip one's toe in even when it's early August and the water temp peaks at sixty-eight degrees." And I knew *that* from experience. "Trust me. The beach will be all but abandoned, and we'll frustrate that curse right off you!"

I felt far less enthusiastic than I sounded, but that's part of being an effective life coach.

Willem took a moment to consider my argument. Finally, he said, "All right. I'll give it a shot. But if anyone gets hurt, don't say I didn't warn you."

"I'm sure it'll be fine," I said, ignoring the sinking feeling resonating in my gut. My sister would've chastised me for ignoring that visceral feeling, but she'd been known to ignore her own intuition on an occasion . . . or twenty.

"When did you want to do this?" Willem asked.

"Let's say tomorrow at one o'clock. We'll meet at the east end of Indian Wells beach, parking area B." That was a section that was smaller than the main part of the beach, and if I remembered correctly, there was a lovely picnic table setup at the top of a fairly steep hill where we could sit in a large, open area and drive the curse mad.

After hanging up with Willem, I filled Gilley in on the details of the call.

"Hold on," he said. "Willem's been to a public beach and his curse caused a man to almost *drown* and the ambulance on scene to then *crash*?"

I waved dismissively. "It didn't sound like there was any lasting damage. Besides, Willem went with his grandparents when the beach was super crowded. I'm sure no one will even be there tomorrow."

"*I'll* be there tomorrow!" Gilley protested.

I frowned at him. "We both need to go to support Willem, Gilley. Especially since I'm sure it's a terrifying prospect for him."

"He's not the only one who'll be terrified," he muttered.

I growled, audibly, crossed my arms, and glared hard at Gilley. I wouldn't stand for having him bring these pesky concerns with him to the beach tomorrow.

For his part, Gilley visibly shrank in his seat. "It's just that . . ."

I cocked an eyebrow.

"I mean, why do *we* have to . . . ?"

I started tapping my arm with my forefinger.

Gilley sighed dramatically. "*Fine*. But if I get dragged out to sea tomorrow by some random rogue wave, I hope you at least feel guilty."

"I'll try," I said, rolling my eyes and unfolding my arms. Deciding to change the subject, I asked, "How's it going with the lead generation on Lenny's case?"

Gilley perked up a bit. "I found Lenny's partner, Chanel Downey."

"What do you mean you found her? Isn't she in Connecticut?"

"She is, but that's a big state and Chanel hasn't exactly been active on social media since Lenny's murder. Tracking her down was a pain in the butt."

I smirked. "Isn't she still in real estate?"

"Not as far as I can tell, which is what made finding her so hard. I can't seem to find any employment for her at all. So, if she's earning money, it's off the books."

That made me frown. "Why would Chanel be living off the books?"

"Beats me. I'm just happy I found her. She's living with her grandaunt."

"How *did* you find her?" I asked next.

Gilley got up and brought over his laptop. Swiveling

the screen to me, he showed me what looked like newspaper copy. "It's an obituary for Erma Janssen, Chanel's grandmother. She passed away six months ago, and she's survived by her daughter, Iris Downey, who lives in Singapore with her husband, Jack Downey, Erma's granddaughter, Chanel Downey, and Erma's sister, Miranda, who, and I quote, '. . . provided a lovely home for the final years of Erma's life.'"

My brow furrowed. "Okay," I said. "How does that suggest that Chanel is living with her grandaunt?"

"I found an address for Miranda. She lives in a four-bed, five-bath home in New Canaan worth just under a million."

"Go, Miranda," I said. "Still, the obituary mentions that Miranda lived with Erma. It doesn't mention that she lives with Chanel."

Gilley wiggled his finger along the mouse pad and clicked to a different window, displaying the Facebook page of an elderly woman with tight curly white hair. Her cover photo was a snapshot of four bright white West Highland terriers. "Miranda breeds Westies. Her Facebook page has forty-two public posts, forty-one of which are about the pups, but the forty-second from three months ago says, and I quote, 'Still so heartbroken over losing Erma. Thank goodness my grandniece is here to offer me good company and good comfort in these sad times.'"

My brow rose. "Chanel's there."

"That'd be my guess."

I squeezed Gilley's arm. "Good sleuthing, Detective Gillespie!"

Gil blushed, and then he curtsied. "It's what I does,"

he said with a wink. He then went over to his desk and came back with a slip of paper that he handed me. "All the numbers that were listed under Chanel's name when she lived here in East Hampton have been disconnected, but I *did* manage to track down the home phone for Miss Miranda. Maybe you could call her and ask to speak to her grandniece."

I took the paper. "What would I say, exactly?"

"To Chanel?"

"No, Miranda. How do I introduce myself?"

"Good question. You could say that you're looking to list your house and you need a Realtor."

"But you said Chanel isn't practicing real estate anymore."

Gilley frowned and pursed his lips. "Hmmm, okay, how about you're a friend from college?"

"I like that," I said. "Yes, I could pass myself off as her roommate or something."

"I wouldn't make it so personal," Gilley said. "Maybe you're just a *friend* from college, trying to locate people for a reunion or something like that."

"Oooo, that's better. Okay, I'll go with that story. Now help me decide what to say to Chanel once I get her on the phone."

"Ugh," Gilley said, making a face. "That is definitely the harder nut to crack."

We both thought in silence for a few moments before Gilley said, "How about you simply go with the truth?"

"That I'm sticking my nose into an open police investigation?"

"Maybe not *that* directly, but not far off from that either. Just tell her that you're a friend of Shepherd's and you're trying to dig up a new angle to solve his ex-wife's murder. She might appreciate your honesty and tell you anything she knows."

"As long as she didn't have a hand in it," I said.

"Yes. As long as she didn't hire Greta to kill Lenny."

"Okay, I'll go for the honest route."

"Great. While you're going with that, mind if I go for coffee?"

"Knock yourself out," I said.

Gilley bent to air-kiss my cheek, then he bounced his way over to the door like Tigger. "The usual for you?" he asked as he was halfway through the door.

"Yes, please."

Gilley left and I took a deep breath, hovered my finger over the touch pad of my phone for a moment, then punched in the number he'd given me and held the phone to my ear.

A woman answered on the third ring—and I couldn't tell initially if the voice sounded old or young. "Hello?"

"Hello! Is this Chanel?"

"No. This is her Auntie Miranda. Who's calling, please?" The elderly woman sounded guarded. "Hello, Miranda, my name is Catherine. I'm a former classmate of Chanel's."

"At Brown?"

My brow rose. Chanel went to Brown? That meant she was smart. "Yes! At Brown."

"Oh! Were you two in the Kappa Gama together?"

And Chanel was a sorority girl . . . interesting. "You got me," I said with a laugh. "I'm a Gama girl all the way. Anyway, I was in the area on business and I was hoping to connect with Chanel. You wouldn't happen to know how I could reach her, would you?"

"Well, I could give you her cell number, but she's moved out of state again."

I was about to ask where when a doorbell chimed in the background, and what sounded like a whole pack of yappy dogs began making a lot of noise. "Oh, drat. Someone's at the door. Can you call back?"

"Uh . . . of course. Yes. Absolutely," I said. "When would be a good time to—"

"Bye-bye," she said abruptly, and all but hung up on me.

I put the phone down and drummed my fingers on the arm of the sofa. I waited five minutes, then tried the number. It rang, and rang, and rang. It never went to voice mail or an answering machine, and I assumed Miranda was still busy with whomever was at the door.

With a sigh I resigned myself to call her in an hour or so, and set aside my phone just as Gilley showed up at the front door with a coffee cup in each hand and a pastry bag dangling from his mouth.

I got up quickly to rush over to the door to let him in, lest he spill the coffee all over himself with the effort of getting in the door. I also took the pastry bag from him and set it on his desk.

"How'd it go?" he asked as he entered.

"You mean with the call?" Gilley nodded and handed me one of the coffees. "Miranda answered. She bought my story of being one of Chanel's sorority friends, but she had to answer the door and told me to call back."

"Did you?" Gil asked, taking a seat at his desk and pulling his laptop close.

"Yes, but now she's not answering my call. I think she's busy with whoever's at the door."

"Could be . . ." Gilley said, but he didn't look convinced.

"What?" I asked.

"Or, it could be that she's figured out you're not Chanel's friend but some snoop like a bill collector and she's now dodging your call."

"A bill collector?"

Gilley shrugged one shoulder as he took a sip of his coffee. "Chanel isn't working, as far as I can tell. She might have money trouble."

"Darn it," I said. "Let's hope it's not that. Oh! But Miranda did tell me that Chanel had moved out of state again."

"She did?"

I nodded.

Gilley frowned. He'd done such a good job of sleuthing that it obviously annoyed him to be thrown a new curve. "If you can't get ahold of the aunt again, let me know and I'll keep digging to try and find Chanel."

"I will, thank you, Gilley. I know you've been working hard on locating her all morning."

"That's not all I've been digging up," he said. "I also found out who bought the murder house."

"Where Lenny was killed?"

"Yep."

"Who?"

"It's a couple. Paul and Jason Sutton. They own an art gallery that used to be in the city, but they moved it here to East Hampton shortly after buying that house."

"Hmmm," I said. "That explains the easel we saw in the window."

"It does."

And then I had another thought. "They own a gallery here in town?"

Gilley pointed out the large picture window and to his left. "The Eastwater Gallery. It's around the corner from the Starbucks on Newtown. We could walk there."

I looked in the direction he was pointing, thinking I'd probably driven past that gallery dozens of times. "You know, I have a friend who's an art dealer in Boston. His gallery is where I got most of the artwork for Chez Cat. He's been very frank with me over how difficult it is to make a living selling art, because it's so competitive among gallery owners. I remember how surprised I was that he owned such a seemingly successful gallery, and yet lived in a very modest house."

"What's your point?" Gilley asked me.

I stared out the window in the direction of the East-water Gallery. "The murder house couldn't have been a modest purchase. Not in that neighborhood. And the property taxes every year . . . also not cheap."

"Huh," Gil said. "Still, I bet they might do better than most gallery owners—their art sells to the one percent of the one percent club."

"True," I agreed. "Lots of massive homes around here with lots of wall space for expensive art." And then something else occurred to me. "You know, I read an article in the *Post* not too long ago that art sales are a fairly easy and effective way for the mob to launder money."

Gilley nodded. "I could see that. It'd be no different than hiding money through renovation costs. I mean, what auditor is going to argue about whether you spent twenty thousand on a piece of artwork or two million? Both are feasible."

"Exactly," I said. "And you know what else I heard?"

"What?"

"I heard that East Hampton has more than its fair share of mafia personnel in residence."

Gilley stared at me, squinting his eyes suspiciously. "Where'd you hear *that*?"

I avoided eye contact, pinning my gaze on the lid of my coffee. "Around."

"By 'around' are you talking Maks Grinkov?"

I looked up again. "Does it really matter?"

Gilley shrugged. "I suppose that, overall, it doesn't, but what hurts me is that I *know* you're hiding something from me about Maks's involvement in all this, Cat, and you don't trust me enough to let me in on it."

I bit my lip. Keeping secrets from Gilley was very hard. There were times when I knew I *couldn't* trust him to keep his mouth shut, and other times when I believed he'd take the information to his grave, but it was difficult to know when I could trust him with absolute secrecy, and when I couldn't.

Still, looking at his pained expression, I gave in, but only a little. "Maks has connections that could be considered . . . sticky, Gilley. He knows things that, if they were to reach the wrong ears, could put him in a dangerous situation, and he's asked me to keep his trust, and I told him I would."

"Maks works for the mob," Gilley said flatly, and there was such a note of disappointment in his voice.

"No," I replied, making sure to look Gilley in the eye so that he'd know I was telling the truth. "His work is more like . . . mob *adjacent*."

"Well, I hope that when the indictments come down, a jury sees *adjacent* as *separate*."

"He'll be fine. He's protected," I said firmly. "You have to trust me on that."

And then something seemed to click for Gilley, and understanding blossomed in his expression. He looked like he was about to comment when I cut him off.

Clearing my throat, I pointed to Gilley's computer. "These two men, the Suttons. Is there a way to find out anything more about them? Like, if they were in town the day Lenny was murdered?"

"You think one of them may have been the target?"

"Lots of art selling to the one percent of the one percent club, so who would really look too closely at receipts? It all sounds like a convenient way to funnel money through a gallery, so, yes, I think it's possible."

"But they bought the house after Lenny was murdered," Gilley said. "I checked. Lenny was murdered in late June, and the house sold in early September. Plus, Lenny wasn't hosting a private showing, she was hosting an open house, which means the house was still looking for an offer at the time that she was murdered."

I nodded, conceding the point to him. "That's true. And that day, even if the Suttons were scheduled to attend the open house, Greta would've been met with possible traffic from other interested buyers. Still, I am a little surprised the house sold so quickly. I mean, can you *imagine* buying a house where someone was murdered so randomly only a few weeks before?"

"Maybe they got a deal," Gilley said. Going back to his computer, he clicked a few keys and said, "Aw, man! There's no sold price listed, which means they probably paid cash for it."

"What's the appraised value?"

Gilley glanced at his screen. "Two-point-two million."

I bounced my eyebrows.

Gilley nodded. "Yeah. I know. Where would a pair of gallery owners get that kind of liquid cash? But they could've sold their apartment in the city or something."

I shook my head. "How much did you and Michel clear from the sale of your place?"

"One twenty," he said proudly. "We made a killing."

"That's my whole point, Gil. You guys cleared only a hundred and twenty thousand for your place in Manhattan. What're the odds that Joseph and Peter—"

"Jason and Paul . . ."

I waved my hand. "Whatever. What're the odds that the Suttons would've cleared at least two million?"

"I'm still not following the thread here, Cat. What's it matter where the money came from?"

I sighed. "I suppose it's that article I read in the *Post*, Gil. I clearly remember that the article noted that the FBI was looking specifically at galleries in New York City, D.C., and L.A. So I'm suspicious about the timing. These guys just so happen to move their gallery to the Hamptons, where we already know there's a Chechen mafia presence, *and* they move into really swanky new digs where an assassin for said Chechen mafia kills the listing agent? I think it may be one too many coincidences for me."

"Okay," Gilley said with a nod. "I'll concede that, circumstantially speaking, it is a teensy suspicious, but it still doesn't explain *why* Lenny was murdered."

I scowled. "Well, that I don't know. Yet. But we should definitely keep digging in this direction. Somebody knows something."

Gilley wiggled his index finger at me. "Call Miranda again. See if she knows something."

"Good idea," I said.

After placing the call, I hit the speaker function and Gilley and I both listened to the phone ring, and ring, and ring without answer.

"It's been forty minutes since Miranda and I talked," I said.

"Hmm, she could be dodging you, or she could be a sweet old lady who forgot you even called, answered the door to get what was probably a package from UPS, then headed off to the market, or her knitting group, or some other crucial errand. Try her back tonight around eight, and if it rings without being answered, then she's definitely dodging you."

I set down the phone and frowned. "I really wanted to talk to Chanel."

"I *could* try hacking into Miranda's Facebook account, you know. . . ."

"No!" I said immediately. "We're *not* hacking anyone's social media account again. Remember the last time and it led to disaster?"

"I do, and that just makes me ask you in return, what're the odds that that would happen *again*?"

"They could be a zillion to one and still not long enough," I said, shuddering. "No, we're going to figure this out the right way. I'll try Miranda again tonight, and hopefully she'll give up her grandniece's phone number and we'll be off to the races."

"And in the meantime" I continued, "I say we visit the Eastwater Gallery and see if it's the kind of place that could support the purchase of a multimillion-dollar home in the Hamptons."

Gilley got up quickly and offered me his arm. "Oooo, an *excursion*. I does lurve me some midday adventure!"

I laughed as we walked out the door together. "I'm glad we're doing this."

He eyed me slyly. "You mean, conducting a gumshoe investigation we have no business sticking our noses into?"

"Yes. Exactly that."

"Me too!"

We arrived at the Eastwater Gallery just a few minutes later. The place was only five blocks from my office. I'd been hoping that the gallery itself was something small and unimpressive to further cement my theory about the place being an obvious front for the mob, however, when we walked through the door, I couldn't help but be immediately impressed.

A spacious, open area greeted us and the brightness of the all-white walls, floor, and ceiling made me feel like I'd walked into a cloud. The artwork on display was large, designed to be hung in the sizable homes of the super wealthy, and the absence of a price listing on the nameplates on each of the pieces gave a not-so-subtle message that, if you had to ask, you couldn't afford it.

The gallery itself was further divided by large white panels hung from the ceiling by piano wire. It was an effective way to showcase the best pieces by putting the canvases on canvases so to speak, and bringing them all enticingly down to eye level.

As I took in the gallery my gaze immediately went to a painting nearby that I recognized right away. There was no mistaking the work of Daniel Bilmes, the same artist who painted my favorite work of art in Chez Cat, and I couldn't resist the temptation to walk over and marvel at the portrait of a breathtaking young lady, maybe no older than twenty, peeking through both the tangles of her wild

hair and the petals of a flower. Gilley followed me leaning over my shoulder to view the art too.

"That looks very similar to the painting hanging above
your mantel," he said.

"It's the same artist," I told him. That painting in my
home, which so much reminded me of my sister, depicted
a young woman, glancing over her shoulder; her chin
dipped low . . . almost demurely, but there was nothing
demure about her gaze. Her eyes conveyed this keen, almost crafty intelligence, and perhaps it was simply the
way her gaze was so knowing, so . . . sharply sardonic,
that reminded me of Abby.

My sister is arguably one of the world's most talented
psychics, and it's nearly impossible to get one over on
her. There were days I envied her ability to see right
through someone's lies and hidden agendas.

And days when I didn't.

"This one is beautiful too," Gilley said, motioning to
the piece in front of us.

"Indeed," I agreed.

"It's quite fetching; don't you think?" a voice behind
us asked.

We both turned to see a tall, thin, bald man in a blue
and pink plaid blazer, with a matching pink dress shirt
and paisley ascot, standing there with his own chin
dipped and a knowing smile on his lips.

I disliked him immediately.

Gilley, however, seemed unfazed. "It's lovely," he said.
"How much?"

I stiffened. It was considered gauche in these circles to
start the conversation about an art piece with the price.

Baldy's lip quirked down ever so slightly to show his
displeasure, which made me dislike him all the more.

"Twenty-two," he said, his eyes narrowing to see if Gilley would balk at the price.

But Gil didn't balk; instead he turned to me and said, "It *would* be beautiful next to the Shkola in the library, don't you think?"

Baldy's brow rose. "You have a Sasha Shkola?"

"Oh, yes," I said easily. I had no idea who she was, but Gilley seemed to know, and Baldy's interest was piqued, so I went with it.

Gilley turned to Baldy, while looping an arm through mine. "She's being modest," he began. "We don't just *have* a Sasha Shkola, we're dear friends of hers."

Baldy's jaw fell open a fraction. "You don't say? You know she's impossible to get ahold of. And *very* selective about where she exhibits."

Gilley laughed lightly and shook his head. "Ahh, that's our Sasha for you! Truthfully, she's confessed to me that she finds dealing with the art world very distracting. She'd rather hole up in her studio and paint, sketch, and sculpt the days and weeks away without having to deal with any of the people who handle the sales of her incredible works."

Baldy cleared his throat. "So . . . how do you know Ms. Shkola?"

Gilley turned to me and I shrugged slightly. I couldn't think as fast on my feet as he could. He turned back to Baldy and said, "Well, we've known her for *ages*. In fact, we were fans of Sasha's back when she was living in a four-floor walk-up in Soho with six roommates and a cat named Turnip. Everyone but Turnip was practically starving!"

Gilley chuckled, and then I chuckled, and then Baldy started chuckling too. We were all expending considerable effort making it appear we thought the topic at hand was *de*lightful.

Gilley was the first to sober. "Back then Sasha sold most of her work at flea markets, which is where we discovered her. Can you *believe* we picked up a few of her early sketches for a pittance just because we felt sorry for her? We couldn't make out much of what she was attempting to sketch back then, but now we see the genius."

Baldy forced a shaky smile to his lips and fiddled with his ascot. "You knew her before she was discovered? And you have some of her earlier sketches?"

Gilley hung on my arm like we were the best of chums. "Oh, yes. We have how many, Cat?" Gil turned to me again and I held up five fingers. He nodded as if that was the correct number. "Yes, five of her earlier works. They're very raw, very moody, but I actually like them better than some of her more recent creations."

"Me too," I agreed.

"Anyway," Gilley continued, "like I said, we met her at the flea market, became friendly, and even had her over for dinner a few times just to help put some meat on those skinny bones of hers. Of course now she only comes over once every couple of months, you know—she's *so* busy these days with all her exhibitions—but whenever her schedule allows for it, we still cook up a storm and send her packing with the leftovers because sometimes she forgets to eat and she's still far too skinny."

Gilley turned to me and I nodded as if that's exactly what we did for this obviously famous artist I'd never heard of. And I didn't quite know how or even *if* Gilley knew her, but I was very happy he was spinning this current tale because he was definitely causing some interest from the man in front of us, and I believed that he would tell us anything we wanted to know simply for the off chance of connecting with the famous Sasha Shkola.

Baldy reached into his side pocket and produced a card. "You know, I would be willing to lower the price of that Bilmes painting if, in turn, you were willing to make an introduction for me to Ms. Shkola."

Gilley accepted the card and showed it to me. I realized then that we were speaking to Jason Sutton himself. "How much of a discount would you be willing to offer?" I asked. His answer would tell me a lot about how much of a markup there was on the Bilmes painting. I'd only paid eight thousand for mine, but that was a few years ago, and it might've been the case where the artist's work simply appreciated a great deal since he'd started to become more widely known.

"I can go as low as fifteen," Sutton said.

I squinted at him. "Really?"

"Yes, and at that price you'd be stealing my entire commission."

Now, I don't possess my sister's human-lie-detector ability, but my baloney meter is still pretty good. I gave Gilley the side-eye and he was looking at me the same way. Neither one of us was buying it.

So I wrinkled my nose and said, "We'll have to think about that, Jason."

Jason opened his mouth to perhaps come at us with another—better—offer, but he was interrupted by the sound of the door chime and two new patrons crossing the gallery's threshold.

Gilley gasped when he saw who it was.

My gaze landed on the large, heavyset man with a thick beard and matching eyebrows—so it took me a moment to switch my attention to his companion.

"Catherine!" Maks said, obviously surprised to see me.

"Oh! Well, hello there, Maks!" I said, flustered by his sudden appearance. "I didn't expect to see you here."

"Nor I you," he said.

I paid close attention to his mannerism and his expression, trying to detect if he was uncomfortable running into me, but he honestly seemed delighted.

"Hello, Gilley," Maks said.

Gilley gave a tiny curtsy. "Maks," he said.

Maks turned his attention back to me. "Are you here to buy some art?"

I glanced at Jason, who was looking intently at Maks's companion. "Maybe. I was intrigued by the Bilmes," I said, pointing to the lovely painting behind me. "But we'll have to think about it."

Maks nodded. "Very good. I was going to call you later and see if you wanted to have drinks with me this evening."

"Drinks?"

"Yes. A cocktail around six o'clock, if you're not otherwise busy?"

There was something in Maks's expression that seemed intent on letting me know he needed me to say yes.

"I think I can swing that," I said.

"Excellent," Maks said. "Text me later and I'll pick you up."

I smiled and nodded politely, but it was growing rather obvious to me that Maks was pointedly avoiding introducing me to his companion, and I started to wonder why.

Meanwhile, the man in question had walked over to the side, where he was speaking with Jason in low tones, and it was then that I noticed that Jason's entire demeanor had gone from oily slick salesman to terrified business owner.

And that's when it clicked. The companion was obviously from the "organization" and I was grateful that Maks had avoided introducing us. I was also aware that the longer I remained in Maks's company at the gallery, the more likely that was to become suspicious. "Well, Gilley and I really must be going," I said to Maks.

Gilley looked from me to Maks in confusion. "But weren't we going to—"

Taking Gilley by the arm again, I pulled him toward the door. "We'll need to hurry if we're going to meet our friends at the club on time," I said to him.

He finally got the hint and said, "Oh, yes! That's right. Time flies. Bye, Maks!"

Maks nodded, playing it very cool but I could've sworn he looked relieved.

"Who *was* that?" Gilley asked when we were safely a block away.

"The guy with Maks?"

"Yeah."

"That," I said, "was very likely the confirmation of a hunch."

Gilley turned to frown at me. "I'm lost."

"You know how I mentioned that galleries can be convenient places to launder money?"

"Yeah?"

"Well, I believe the guy who came in with Maks was . . . *connected* if you get my drift."

"Part of the mob," Gil said.

I nodded. "And did you see how terrified Jason Sutton was at the sight of him?"

"I did notice that he went pretty pale while they were talking."

We walked another block in silence and my mind was awhirl with theories. "Gil?" I said.

"What?"

"What if . . . ?"

"What if what?"

"Say you liked a house out this way and wanted to buy it, but it was out of your price range. Like, maybe way out of your price range. What's one way you could get the house to drop in price rather dramatically?"

Gilley sucked in a breath. "You *murder* someone inside the home!"

I nodded. He was following my train of thought. "But you can't murder the owners, because then the property would just end up in probate and that'd be at least a year to figure out, so you do the next best thing. You murder someone *else* in the home, like the real estate agent, and the owners are then so desperate to get rid of a house where a violent crime was committed that they're willing to lower the house by, let's say . . . twenty percent or more."

"I'd say you'd walk away the clear winner in the deal," Gilley said. "Especially if you got away with the murder."

"You certainly would."

"So you think that the Suttons hired Greta?"

"I think it's possible. Either them or maybe the head honcho of the organization hired her as a way to ingratiate the Suttons and make them loyal to him enough to move their gallery and allow him to funnel money through it."

Gilley shook his head. "I think the theory is amazing, but I can't help but think it's also kind of a big leap."

"Is it?" I asked. "I mean, hasn't the lead detective on the case been working it to nothing but dead ends for almost two years now? And isn't it also incredibly convenient that the victim you murder just so happens to be *that* lead detective's ex? And because of *that* connection, aren't you then ensuring that one of the only men in the area smart enough, dedicated enough, and true enough to his job would be totally distracted to the point of obsession for at least a few years trying to solve that murder, thus allowing *you and your associates* free run of the Hamptons?"

"My God," Gilley whispered, halting in his tracks to fully take in the theory. "If it's true, it's an absolutely *masterful* plan! Shepherd has been trying to find the link between the Chechen mafia and his wife's killing all these years, and he's the link, but indirectly!"

"Exactly," I said. My hands were shaking and my palms were sweaty. The genius, and cold calculation of the plot—if it were true—was enough to really, really rattle me.

"But how do we prove it?" Gilley asked next.

And that's where my quandary really began.

Chapter 7

After attending to other business for a few hours, we closed up the office, and Gilley and I headed to one of our favorite eateries so that we could sit, talk, and get some nourishment after having worked straight through lunch.

It was well after three by the time we arrived, we were both starved, and I had decided to bring Gilley more fully into what I knew—which was a risk, but I felt I needed to take it. As I had a great deal to tell him that might both scare and put him in danger, I felt it was best to confess all while breaking bread.

After being greeted warmly by the hostess, I asked that she seat us someplace where we could be given some privacy, hoping we'd be directed to a lovely booth at the back of the restaurant, away from prying ears, and I got my wish.

Once we were settled and the hostess had returned to the front of the restaurant, I leaned over and whispered to Gilley, "I have a few confessions to make."

Gilley took a sip of the water a busboy had set down for us. "Starting with the fact that Maks is wrapped up with the mob?"

"He's not so much wrapped up with them as he is quietly observing and taking notes, if you get my drift."

"He's an informant," Gilley said simply.

I didn't say a word. I felt so torn between revealing everything to Gilley, and simply giving him enough clues so that he'd figure it out on his own and I'd still be able to keep my promise to Maks. So, I focused on the menu.

"I *knew* it!" Gilley said after studying me.

"I can neither confirm nor deny your suspicions, my friend."

"You promised Maks not to say anything."

I set the menu down. "I promised myself to keep you out of danger."

"Danger?" he said, his eyes darting back and forth to look around the restaurant. He lowered his voice to a hoarse whisper. "We're in *danger*?"

"Hopefully not," I said.

"Hopefully?"

"Yes," I said, meeting his gaze. "This is tricky stuff, lumpkin."

Gil took another sip of water. "Wow, Cat. How did we get mixed up in all this?"

"Well, so far, I'm the only one who's really mixed up in it."

"You're in with them too?"

"No. I'm simply shaking hands with one of the good guys." Gilley's brow furrowed. So I dove into my purse and searched for something to write on. Finding an old receipt, I laid it on the table, fished around for a pen, then scribbled something quickly on the receipt.

I then folded the slip of paper, set it into my palm, reached for Gilley's hand, and when he shook it in confusion I made sure to set it firmly in his palm before taking back my own hand.

Gilley looked at his open palm and the bit of paper before he set it on the table and unfolded it to read it out loud. "This is a secret message."

When he looked at me again, I simply nodded, and then his brow lifted and he nearly shouted, "Ohmigod!"

"Shhh!" I hissed, looking around to make sure no one was glancing our way.

"Sorry," he whispered. "I just caught on to what you were saying. You're passing information on to that new client of yours, aren't you?"

I picked up my menu and began to read it again. "I can neither confirm nor deny your assumptions, Gilley."

"Whoa," Gilley said. "Cat, that's super dangerous, isn't it?"

"I doubt it," I said. "I mean, I'm assuming everyone is very, very careful to avoid suspicion."

"Still, I don't like it," Gilley said. "I mean, you're a mother. You have two sons to think about."

"And I do think about them, Gilley," I told him. "What I also think about is that there's a very, very bad man running around in my backyard, ordering the murders of innocent people."

"Like Lenny," Gilley said.

"Yes."

"But are we *sure* that's how it went down? I mean, speculating that Lenny was murdered so that the property she was showing would be affordable to two art dealers really is a stretch. And it's risky."

"True," I said. "But Boris Basayev takes risks for a living. This would've been just one more risk for him, and don't forget the part about tying up Shepherd in Lenny's murder investigation for years. That had to have been a pretty good incentive for hiring Greta to make that hit too."

"It's so cruel," Gilley said with a shudder.

At that moment our server stepped forward. "Are you cold, sir?" the young woman asked him.

Gilley smiled sweetly. "Only a little. Could you bring me some Earl Grey hot tea and the turkey club salad?"

"Of course," she said. "And for you, ma'am?"

"I'll have iced tea and the salmon fillet, please, with an extra side of the green beans and sweet potatoes."

Gilley's brow rose. "Hungry much?"

I looked up at the server and handed her our menus. "Thank you," I said, in a barely disguised dismissal. After she walked away I answered Gilley. "Remember my plans for tonight? I'm meeting Maks later for drinks, and I want to make sure I've got something substantial in my stomach to soak up the alcohol. I'll need my wits about me if I'm going to ask him about the Suttons."

"What're you going to say?"

"Well, for starters, I'm going to ask him if they're on the payroll."

"This is all so crazy," Gilley said, shaking his head.

"It is. But given Jason Sutton's reaction to the man who came into the gallery—which, for all we know *could* have been Basayev himself—I think we're onto a pretty good hunch."

"Do you think he'll tell you if the Suttons are working for Basayev?"

I considered that for a long moment. "I don't know. I hope he will, but he may want to shield me from knowing too much, and he may refuse to answer."

"Do you want me to do a little digging?"

"Yes," I said, laying a hand over his. "But be extra, extra careful, Gilley. It *can't* get back to either of the Suttons that we're looking into them."

"I'll be careful," he said. And then he played with his fork for a moment before asking, "Are we going to tell Shepherd any of this?"

"No," I said immediately. "We're not. We're not going to say anything to anyone until we've got some evidence, because, like you've already pointed out, this could be dangerous for everyone involved. Plus, Shepherd would definitely order us to stop investigating on our own."

"But *eventually* we'll tell him, right?"

"I hope so," I said.

"Do you think we should also talk to the other real estate agent?"

"Other agent?" I asked, blanking on the mention of another person.

"Sara Beth Sullivan. Isn't that a great name?" Gil said.

I shook my head. "Who the heck is Sara Beth Sullivan?"

"She was the agent of record on the sale of the house that the Suttons bought."

"Not Chanel?" I asked.

Gilley shook his head. "No. Chanel might've left town by the time the house sold. It went to a woman from the Realty Group."

"Huh," I said. "So, Sara Beth was either a legit referral, or she swooped in and scooped up the listing."

"Yep. And lucky for the old woman who owned the house, because what other agent would've wanted the listing where a fellow colleague was murdered?"

"Who indeed?" I said. "I definitely think we should talk to Sara Beth."

"What's our cover story, though?" Gilley asked. When I squinted at him he added, "How do we justify asking her about the sale of that house?"

"Um . . . let me think," I said, tapping my lip. Gilley was faster on his feet than I was at the moment.

"You could pose as a potential buyer," Gilley suggested. "You could say that you saw the house when we were cruising the neighborhoods, and you fell in love with it and wanted to know if it might come up for sale again in the future."

"I like that idea," I said. "But what if it gets back to Jason or Paul Sutton that someone is interested in their property? Or, what if they actually want to sell it?"

Gilley shrugged easily. "You changed your mind and found something else. No biggie. Happens all the time."

"All right. It's a plausible scenario, but I say we use it only if I don't get anywhere with Maks tonight."

Gilley smirked. "I for one am *really* hoping you get somewhere with Maks tonight." For emphasis, he bounced his brows.

I rolled my eyes, but I could also feel my cheeks heat. "Stop," I said, embarrassed.

"It *is* your third date, you know."

"Technically, it's the second-and-a-half date."

Gilley laughed. "Technicalities are for courtrooms, not for bedrooms."

"Still," I insisted, "don't you think it's a bit quick to move things to the next level?"

Gilley waved his hand dismissively. "I can only tell you what I'd do if a gorgeous biscuit of a man showed a keen interest in me, and that is to throw caution to the wind and take a romp in that bouncy house!"

I giggled. "Of course you'd sleep with him—"

"Duh."

"Because you're a whore."

Gilley held up his hand. "Guilty as charged."

"Seriously, though, there's no way I'm going to bounce in his house while all this mafia stuff is going on."

"Uh huh," Gilley said, in that incredibly annoying way that suggested he wasn't buying it. "You know what I think?"

I sighed. "The real question is: do I *want* to know what you think?"

"I think you're not going to get too physical with Maks because you still have feelings for Shepherd and you're worried that it'll feel like you're cheating."

My face filled with heat, even while I pretended to scoff and took a sip of water. "That's ridiculous," I said.

"Of course it is," Gilley replied, his voice dripping with sarcasm.

I played with my utensils while I searched for a new topic to distract Gilley away from Maks and Shepherd. "You know what I actually want to know?"

"What's the secret to juggling two men at once? Ask them both to the dance, if you get my drift." Gilley bounced his eyebrows again.

I laughed in spite of myself and then got back to my question. "Focus, Gilley. What I want to know is, how did you know all that stuff about Sasha Shkola? I had no idea you were into the modern art scene."

Gilley winked at me. "She was our neighbor when Michel and I lived in Manhattan."

"Really? I had no idea you lived next to an artist."

"Oh, yeah," Gilley said, waving his hand like it was nothing. "Sasha is a lovely girl, although she's *très recluse*, fully living that whole mad genius stereotype. We'd see her slinking about the hallways, paintbrush lodged in that tangle of hair and elbows and forearms covered in paint. We actually *did* have her over for dinner a few times because Michel felt sorry for her. The girl was so obsessed with her work that she almost never thought about eating."

"I wonder if she'd know anything about Jason and Paul Sutton?"

"I'll definitely ask her when I give her a call later on. She's going to be one of the resources I use to dig up info on the boys and their gallery."

"Good," I said. "But be discreet."

"I hardly need to with Sasha, Cat. Even if she did tell someone that I was picking her brain about the Suttons— which is unlikely given Sasha's introverted personality— it's easily explainable given the fact that Jason offered me his card and showed interest in having Sasha exhibit at his gallery."

"That's true," I said. "Sorry. I guess I'm being a little paranoid lately."

"Understandable," Gilley said, adding a soft smile.

Our food arrived and we ate in companionable silence. Afterward, I dropped Gilley at the office so that he could do some more digging while I headed home to change and get ready to meet Maks.

For our date, I chose a simple ensemble—a black pencil skirt, a beaded pearl shell, and a burgundy half coat with black velvet trim. For a little flair, I chose a tartan clutch and a pair of Jimmy Choo ankle boots with a shiny gold zipper.

Scooting back to the office, I caught Gilley on the way out. "You off?" I asked him as we practically bumped into each other at the door.

"Yes, I'm actually meeting Sasha for dinner!"

"She's coming all the way out here?"

"She is. Her girlfriend has a place in Noyack, so we're meeting in Sag Harbor for a little nosh."

"Excellent," I said. "Fill me in tomorrow?"

"I will if you will," Gilley said, dipping his chin.

I smiled and patted him on the back before singing, "Have a lovely evening!"

I headed into the office and returned e-mails until ten to six, which is when I sent a text to Maks that I was ready.

He didn't reply.

After ten minutes of glancing periodically at my phone, and receiving no reply, I started to get worried. Had something happened?

At six-oh-five I got up from my desk and walked over to the interior door, leading to the stairs and the upper suites. *Should I go up?* I wondered.

I looked at my phone again, waiting for the telltale bubbles to appear, showing that he'd at least read my message, but the screen below my text was noticeably blank.

I stepped away from the door and paced the room for another ten minutes, until, finally, at six-fifteen I moved through the door and up the stairs to the third floor. Approaching Maks's door, I could feel my heart pounding. Given the company he kept, I worried that something terrible had happened, and if it had, I couldn't help but wonder if I might now also be in danger.

As I was lifting my hand to knock, the door swung open and Maks started at the sight of me. "Catherine!" he said.

My breath had also caught at the sight of him, both in surprise and something else. Maks appeared to be . . . rumpled—as if he'd been wrestling with someone. I can't quite explain it other than his shirt and his blazer seemed to have been pulled violently in a way that left the fabric wrinkled and stretched in certain spots. There was also a thin cut and a bruise above his left eye.

"Maks," I said, my hand going reflexively to the spot on his forehead. "Are you all right?"

Maks laid his hand over mine and pulled it down to kiss it softly. "I knocked my head on the cabinet," he said easily. "And I'm sorry I'm late. I was caught on the phone and couldn't break free."

My heart was still racing and I was trembling ever so slightly. Maks squeezed my hand and squinted at me. "Are you all right, dear?"

I shook my head. "I thought . . . that something terrible might've happened to you."

Maks looked pained, and then I saw him glance back over his shoulder toward his open door. He turned back to me and very subtly shook his head, but then he said in an upbeat voice, "What could happen to me?"

I swallowed hard and tried to compose myself. I understood that Maks thought his office might have ears and I needed to be careful. "Um . . . well, you could've been hit by a bus or something."

Maks laughed lightly. "Ah, sweet Catherine. I always look both ways before crossing the street. Now come, let's get out of here and find a nice bar for our drink."

I waited while he locked up his office, and took the arm he offered me before we made our way downstairs.

Pausing at the back door to the parking lot, Maks said, "Why don't we both take our cars and drive separately? It's more convenient not to have to come back this way, don't you think?"

"Uh . . . okay," I said. I thought it was an odd request; after all, Maks did say that he'd meet me at the office and drive me over to the bar. If he'd wanted me to drive myself, he could've easily suggested we meet there. Still, I rolled with it and we parted in the parking lot to head to our separate cars, then I followed him to the end of Main Street to a bar called Trendy.

We got inside and I could tell the place lived up to its name. There was lots of leather and chrome, soft lighting, and the crowd was about fifteen years younger than either of us, but Maks still strolled in like he owned the place, and turned a few heads in the process.

I had to admit I quite enjoyed being on the arm of a man who was so handsome. My ex-husband was a fairly plain-looking man, but I hadn't fallen in love with his looks; I'd fallen in love with how kind and caring he'd been to me. At least in the beginning he was. But as the years progressed, he'd focused much less on me and much more on his golf game and the pro shop he ran at the country club (and, of course, on that bartender he'd taken up with).

To be fair, however, during much of our marriage, I'd probably focused a lot less on him, and mostly on my business too, which was why it'd been particularly hurtful to learn that, just at the point when I'd made an effort to divorce myself from my business to focus more on my family, my husband had chosen to divorce his family to focus more on his business.

"Catherine?" Maks asked. And I realized I'd been lost in thoughts about my ex.

"I'm sorry, what?"

"I asked if this was to your liking?" Maks said, and I then realized that he'd led me across the bar area to a cozy booth, set in the corner with a window to look out of.

"It's perfect," I said. "Sorry, I was a little distracted there for a minute."

Maks and I scooted into the booth, and he said, "Long day?"

"Of sorts. But it was a pleasant surprise running into you at the gallery."

"Yes," he said, smiling and tucking a lock of my hair behind my ear. "That was a nice chance encounter. I didn't know you were looking for art."

"Chez Cat could use a few pieces." (It didn't, but it was a good cover story.)

Maks nodded. "If you're looking for an honest deal, might I suggest a gallery that could be a better fit for you?"

I smiled slyly and was about to comment, but our server appeared ready to take our order. We each asked for a martini, a vodka martini for me and a gin martini for Maks.

After our server had gone, I said, "I got the sense when Jason Sutton was quoting me a price for that Daniel Bilmes painting that things weren't quite on the up-and-up."

"You'd do well to look somewhere else," Maks said, tracing my blazer collar with his finger. I rather loved that he wasn't afraid of subtle PDAs. Odd, too, how I never felt fondled or touched inappropriately. Tom used to get super handsy when he drank, and it always drove me nuts, but somehow Maks's touch never made me feel anything but a delicious shiver in parts best left to your imagination.

Still, I managed to keep my focus on getting information out of Maks. "Are you going to tell me how you *really* got that cut above your eye?"

Maks grinned. "Nicked myself shaving."

I laughed, but deep down it troubled me. "What about this?" I asked him, fiddling with his collar. It was then that I noticed he had a button missing.

"What?" he asked.

"Well, it almost looks like someone strong pulled you around by your collar. And a button is missing."

Maks patted at his clothing. "I snagged it on my coat earlier and pulled when I should've been more patient."

I sighed and at that moment our server appeared at our table again. While I waited for her to set down our drinks, I had time to consider that it really bothered me that Maks wouldn't tell me what'd happened to him because he'd clearly been in some sort of scuffle. And I only wanted to know because I worried about him and I didn't want him to be in danger. So, after the server left again, I pushed a little further.

"You know," I said next. "I read an article in *The Washington Post* about how the FBI had traced a money-laundering scheme to certain art galleries that were being used to wash money for organized crime."

"Mmmm?" Maks said, taking a sip of his drink and noticeably not making eye contact.

"I was wondering if Mr. Basayev might use the same tactic?"

"Why would you be wondering such a thing?" Maks asked.

His tone wasn't angry, more curious, so I felt okay about proceeding. "I think it's because I have a theory."

"A theory?"

"Yes. My theory, and it's purely speculative, goes like this: if I'm Boris Basayev, and I'm looking to do what I want in the Hamptons, without worrying about being investigated by the top detective in the town, and I'm also looking to funnel money through a gallery where I can sell very expensive artwork to wealthy clients, then I might *kill* two birds with one stone."

Maks's brow wrinkled, and I wasn't quite sure if he didn't follow me or if he was curious how I'd actually figured things out on my own.

I pressed on. "And the way to do that would be to hire someone to take out the detective's ex-wife, who just so happens to be a real estate agent, showing a home my gallery owners are interested in but can't afford, thus ensuring that the detective is swept up into an investigation that he'll most definitely become obsessed with, and allowing my gallery owners to purchase the house—possibly at a significant discount, giving them a reason to relocate their gallery from Manhattan to the Hamptons."

Maks was now staring at me in alarm, and I suddenly regretted telling him my theory. "Catherine," he said very softly.

"Yes?"

"Besides me, who else have you repeated your little theory to?"

I gulped. "Only Gilley."

Maks nodded ever so slightly. "Good. Make sure he's the *only* one besides me to hear of it, and make sure he also doesn't repeat it. To *anyone*. Do you understand?"

I bit my lip. Maks's tone was soft, but his eyes were deadly serious. "I've hit on it, haven't I? I've hit on the reason that Lenny Shepherd was murdered."

"Catherine," Maks said, his tone holding a hint of warning. "Please . . . forget this theory. And you should have *nothing* more to do with the Eastwater Gallery, do you understand?"

"I do," I said, sufficiently scared. "I'm sorry for even mentioning it."

Maks relaxed and wrapped my hand in his. Pulling it to his lips, he kissed it, and in that moment I felt him press something to my palm. When he set my hand down he smiled sweetly at me. "You're a brave woman. Like your sister."

Next to me, my phone, which was tucked inside my clutch, pinged with an incoming text. Maks set my hand back down on the table and said, "You have a text message. You should probably read it and put that away while you're at it."

I kept my fist closed, then reached over to my purse and opened the flap of the clutch. Depositing the flash drive inside, I then fished out my phone and looked at the display. There was a new text from a number I didn't recognize, and the text said,

It's Sam. Can we meet tomorrow at 3:00 p.m.? Also, it might be time to head home.

"I'm assuming I should reply to Sam's text in the affirmative, and then pretend to have a reason to leave?" I asked Maks. I had a feeling Sam's text meant more than confirming a meeting for the flash drive.

"Yes," Maks said. "Something's come up and I need to set up a meeting. I'm so sorry we couldn't spend more time together this evening. Being in your company is something I always look forward to."

I texted Sam a thumbs-up emoji, then set my phone back into my purse, and cupped Maks's face with my hand. "I like you, Maks. A great deal. But all this covert business scares the hell out of me."

"As well it should," he said seriously. "But, I promise you, it's not for much longer. We're very close to the end."

I took a deep breath and let it out slowly, attempting to settle my nerves. I then did something rather unexpected, and leaned in to give Maks a light kiss. His hand came up to cup my face, and against my lips he whispered, "Soon."

When he released me, I got out of the booth and left the restaurant, walking to my car with the unsettling feeling that I was being watched. And I realized that Maks had been quite deliberate about seating us next to the window.

Getting in my car, I forced myself not to look around, but as I pulled away from the curb, a car passed me going in the opposite direction, and I caught the driver tipping a pretend hat toward me.

I only caught a glimpse of the man, but I knew it was Sam, and I believe I shook all the way home.

Chapter 8

Gilley walked into Chez Kitty where I was sitting on the couch, wrapped in an afghan, watching the Hallmark Channel.

"Yikes," Gil said the moment he saw me. "It must be bad if you're doing more of the Hallmark Christmas thing."

He and I had watched literally *dozens* of Christmas movies together over the holidays, until we were well and truly tired of them, but this evening, when I got back to Chez Cat, I'd needed a bit of comfort to settle my frazzled nerves, so I'd headed to Chez Kitty and the comfort of Gilley's couch and fifty-two-inch flat screen.

"Are you tired?" I asked, hitting the mute button.

Gilley made his way over to the couch and sat down next to me. Lifting the edge of the afghan, he pulled it so that it covered both of us, and said, "No, I'm not tired. In fact, I'm glad you're here and we can talk."

"Good," I said. "Do you want to go first?"

"Duh, I always want to go first, but I'll defer to you. What happened with Maks?"

I told him everything . . . well, save the part about the flash drive. I still didn't feel like I could put Gilley in danger like that by confirming that I was passing on information to the FBI.

I did, however, confess the fact that Maks appeared to have been in some sort of altercation that he'd refused to tell me about.

"He's obviously trying to protect you," Gilley said. "Which is damn chivalrous if you ask me."

"I don't need chivalry," I said. "I need for Maks not to get into a kerfuffle that could get him killed."

"You don't know that it was a kerfuffle," Gilley said. "For all you know it could've been a wrestling match with a good friend that got a tiny bit out of hand."

"If it *were* that, then Maks would've told me, so that I didn't worry or obsess over it."

"Hmm, yeah. Good point. Still, he kind of confirmed our theory by not confirming our theory and telling you to stay away from the Eastwater and its owners."

"Speaking of which, did you have any luck with Sasha?"

"As a matter of fact, I did," Gilley said. "The second she heard the name she spit on the floor to dispel the evil that is . . . *the Suttons*."

"You and your dramatics."

"I'm not being dramatic," Gilley insisted. "She really *did* spit on the floor, Cat."

"So she's heard of them."

"Oh, yeah. Their reputation is hateful! They never pay their artists the full commission due, and lie about how much they sell the pieces for to further cheat the artists out of the money they're owed. There's also word going around that there may be a forged art piece or two showing up that hint back to the Suttons. Sasha said it's all just rumors, right now, but she's convinced they're capable of something like that."

"So she's a fan of theirs," I said with a smile.

"Big fan," Gilley agreed. *"Huge."*

Getting serious again, I asked, "How are they even still in business? Hasn't anyone investigated them for fraud?"

"What police department is going to investigate these guys for art fraud?" Gilley asked. "I mean, talk about low-hanging fruit. Shepherd wouldn't waste an afternoon looking into it, not when he's still working his ex-wife's murder."

"Which is *exactly* the point, isn't it?" I said.

"It would appear to be," Gilley said.

I then turned to him and gasped. "You didn't tell Sasha what we suspect about Lenny's murder, did you?"

Gil pulled his chin back in surprise. "What? No. The last thing I want is to get Sasha mixed up in any of this. No, I just gave her the heads-up that the Suttons were looking to get in touch with her about setting up an exhibit, and she said that she really hoped they'd call so she could tell them to eff the frick off, only she didn't use 'eff,' or 'frick,' if you get my drift."

"I do," I assured him.

A silence fell between us until Gilley asked, "What do we do now?"

"I was just thinking about that."

Another silence fell between us.

"What if we took all this to Shepherd?" Gilley said. "We could simply tell him our theory and let him follow the leads."

"We can't, Gil."

"Why the hell not? I mean, Cat, this is getting scary, right?"

"It is. Which is *exactly* why we can't take it to Shepherd. If he starts investigating, it could get either him or Maks killed. Maybe both."

"Oh, crap. I hadn't thought of that."

"I may have a resource, however," I said, suddenly lighting on the idea of telling all this to Sam.

Gilley looked at me curiously, but then he figured it out and said, "Your newest client."

I didn't confirm it, but I did say, "Adding a murder charge to the indictment might speed things up."

"And it would free us from pursuing this further."

I sighed. "I still think we should do a teensy bit more digging. If I'm going to take our theory to my other source, then we'll need something more than a hunch to offer him."

Gil frowned. "Sara Beth Sullivan, the Realtor who sold the Suttons the house?"

"Yes. Are you up for that?"

"I am if we're subtle."

"When are we ever subtle?"

"Truth. Still, maybe we can turn over a new leaf when we talk with Sara Beth."

I held my fist out for a bump. "Here's to subtlety."

Gilley tapped my fist with his own. "Kabloom," he said.

* * *

The next morning Gilley and I met up at the office early and sent out a message to the e-mail listed on Sara Beth's contact page. We were rewarded with a response only twenty minutes later. "She'd *love* to meet us," Gilley said.

"I bet," I replied. My message to Sara Beth had mentioned that I was interested in finding a home in the ten- to fifteen-million-dollar range.

"What time works for us?" he asked, pulling the keyboard on his desk closer, ready to email Sara Beth.

"The sooner the better. We've got to meet Willem at one for our beach outing, and then I've got my other client at three."

Gilley's brow arched. "Your *other* client is back so soon?"

I hated that he kept honing in on any mention—or nonmention—of Sam. I couldn't tell him anything, and I couldn't confirm anything, and this hinting at things was starting to fray my nerves. So I did the only sensible thing. I ignored his question and changed the topic.

"Where is Sara Beth's office?" I asked.

Gilley pursed his lips at my segue tactic, but he answered the question. "She's in downtown Apaquogue, so about twenty minutes from here.

"Ask if she can meet with us at ten," I said. It was only a little after nine, and that would leave Gilley and me plenty of time to get our story straight and head over there.

Gilley sent off the e-mail and we each got up to fetch a cup of tea. By the time we were seated back at his desk, Sara Beth's reply had come in. "She's cool with ten," Gil said.

"Perfect. Now, let's work on our story. . . ."

*   *   *

We arrived at Sara Beth's office at ten after ten. We'd had plenty of time to get there, but I wanted to be in the driver's seat, and showing up promptly would've sent the wrong message, I thought.

Gilley walked ahead of me as we entered the building, and I kept my sunglasses on while I stood in the lobby, ignoring everything and everyone around me while adopting an air of importance. For his part, Gilley played the role of stressed-out personal assistant to the T.

After Gilley had given our names, we were led to Sara Beth's office by the courteous receptionist. I continued to wear my sunglasses even after the introductions had been made and I'd sat down in one of the chairs facing Sara Beth's desk.

As for our unwitting Realtor, a statuesque brunette who dressed sharply right down to her Veronica Beard leopard-skin boots, she seemed to go with the flow of our energy with ease, and I had no doubt she'd handled many a client as pouty, self-important, and awful as I was pretending to be.

Folding her hands on her desk, Sara Beth eyed us keenly and said, "I understand that you're looking for a house, Ms. Cooper. What must-haves would you like to see in your new home?"

Without answering her I turned my head to Gilley and gave him one curt nod. Gilley then rushed to open up his messenger bag and extract a photo.

It was a heavily doctored photo of the murder house. Gilley had used Photoshop to give it a different paint job, trim, trees, and skyline. He'd also added a unique front door.

Overall it was quite different from the murder house,

but also, remarkably similar. "This is Ms. Cooper's former home near Boston," Gilley said. "In Brookline."

Brookline is one of *the* most exclusive neighborhoods in the Boston area. Tom and Gisele Brady had lived there, and I was hoping that Sara Beth knew that a house located in that town could easily fetch a similar price tag to any listing she might discover in Apaquogue.

Sara Beth leaned in to peer quizzically at the photo. Gilley handed it to her so that she could study it while he continued with the story we'd come up with. "Ms. Cooper simply *adores* that house's architecture, and she'd like you to find her one that looks and feels similar."

Sara Beth squinted at the photo, and a half smile formed on her lips. Her expression was one I was hoping for—it was the expression of recognition. "My goodness," she said. "You know, I had a listing not long ago that could've been this house's twin!"

I cocked my head and lowered my sunglasses slightly to look at her over the rims. "Oh?" I said. "Is that house still for sale?"

Sara Beth bit her lip. "No. I'm sorry. And, anyway, even if it were, I don't think it would've been something you'd be interested in."

"Really?" I said. And then I pointed to the photo in her hand. "I think I might be very interested. If you represented it, you must know the owners. Perhaps they'd like to put the house on the market again?"

Sara Beth shifted uncomfortably. "I understand your interest, Ms. Cooper, however, that property is a bit . . . stigmatized, and I'd hate to drum up some enthusiasm from the current owners without divulging to you, as required by law, about that property's history. You see, it was the site of someone passing away."

I took off my sunglasses and waved them at her. "So some old man died upstairs in bed. That doesn't bother me in the least."

Sara Beth set down the photo carefully and laced up her fingers again. "It's a little more than that, I'm afraid."

"What's a little more?" Gilley asked.

"Well, you see, a woman was actually . . . *murdered* in that house."

Gilley gasped dramatically, but I only frowned and put my sunglasses back on. "What happened *exactly*?" I asked, as if the circumstances would be the difference in my interest waning or holding steady.

Sara Beth shrugged slightly. "It was a terribly tragic event. A fellow Realtor was showing the home one afternoon about a year and a half ago, and someone entered and murdered her."

"Robbery gone wrong?" Gilley asked.

"No. At least, it didn't appear so."

"Jealous ex?" I asked next. I wanted her to be as forthcoming as possible so that we would seem justified in our more probing questions about the Suttons.

Meanwhile Sara Beth was shifting in her chair again. It was clear she was growing increasingly uncomfortable, but it was also clear that she was intimidated enough by my stature and bank account to answer our questions.

"It wouldn't seem so, no," she said. "The police never did solve the crime."

"Hmm," I said, and turned to look at Gilley, who only shrugged at me like he couldn't understand the senselessness either. "So the house sat for a long time afterward, I'm assuming?" I asked next.

"No," Sara Beth said. "It actually sold rather quickly once we . . . uh . . . put it back on the market."

"Really?" I said. "Who would buy such a stigmatized property?"

"A couple who had been interested in the house and hadn't been put off by the *exceptionally rare* act of violence."

"Did you know the Realtor who was murdered?" Gilley asked next.

Sara Beth inhaled deeply. "I did. She was a lovely woman."

"So she worked here with you, and you took over the sale?" I asked.

"No," Sara Beth said. "As a favor I took it over from the agent who'd been her partner. The poor woman was understandably too traumatized to show the property after the tragedy."

"So the people who bought it weren't your clients?" Gilley asked next.

Sara Beth shook her head. "No, they were actually also a referral from that same Realtor. They'd been interested in the property before, were planning on attending the open house, in fact, on the day of the murder. . . ." Sara Beth paused to shudder ever so slightly. "They were still looking for a home in that area when the house was put back on the market, and came to me directly, without representation."

I glanced quickly at Gilley. His stiffened posture told me that he realized Sara Beth had just confirmed our suspicions. "I bet they got a good deal on the home," I said. "With that kind of history it's a wonder it sold at all."

"They got a *very* good deal," Sara Beth confirmed, a bit chagrined, I thought. "It helped that it was a cash sale, but truly, they only paid half of the original list price."

My brow shot up. *"Half?"*

Sara Beth's hand went to play with the set of pearls around her neck. I think she knew she'd probably let slip a bit too much information. "Like I said, it was a very good deal, and the woman selling the home was happy to come away with what she could. I of course had to remain neutral in the deal as I represented both buyer and seller."

"The whole thing sounds simply *tragic*," Gilley said.

I nodded for emphasis, but I was too excited to sit there and play pretend much longer as all I wanted to do was talk to Gilley about what Sara Beth had revealed. "Thank you, Sara Beth, for that history. You're right, all of that makes the house you represented untenable for me, no matter how similar it is to my beloved house in Brookline." Getting to my feet, I added, "If you find a home similar to the one in the photo, do give us a call."

Sara Beth's expression turned to surprise and I didn't even wait for her to recover herself. Instead I turned and walked abruptly out of her office.

Behind me I heard Gilley say, "Good-bye. It was lovely meeting you. I'll take one of your cards, and do be in touch if you find anything, okay?"

"But . . . I don't even know how many bedrooms Ms. Cooper is thinking of," Sara Beth said rather desperately.

"Minimum of five," I called out over my shoulder, then hastened my steps to carry me farther away from her office. In truth, I wanted to run out of there, I was so excited that we'd seemed to hit pay dirt.

Gilley came hustling up behind me as we exited the building and made a beeline for the car. Hopping in, I didn't say a word until we were safely out of the parking lot. "Ohmigod!" I finally yelled.

"I know! I know!"

"*We were right!*" I shouted. "The Suttons totally targeted that house!"

"They did," Gilley said. "It feels so right, Cat."

"But we still need more to connect it all together, Gilley. We *need* to find Chanel. She can tell us if Jason and Paul contacted Lenny directly or came to Chanel right after Lenny was murdered. The timing of when they signed on with Lenny or Chanel might be important."

"Did you call her aunt again?"

"I did. She's not picking up. I'm guessing she has caller ID and she's dodging me."

Gilley sat silently for a minute, a determined look on his face, then he bent down, fished around in his messenger bag, and pulled up his tablet. He began tapping at it, and for the next ten minutes we drove in silence, until he did a fist pump and said, "Got her!"

"Chanel?"

"Yes!"

"Where is she?"

Gilley swiveled the tablet toward me, but I couldn't read it because I was driving. "Tell me what it says," I instructed.

"She's listing herself under her initials, C.J. Downey, and, Cat! Get a load of this! She's back here in the Hamptons!"

My jaw fell open. "She *is*?" How lucky was that?

"Yes! She's working out of an office in Amagansett, and she's only got one listing. Coming *soon*," he said, putting an emphasis of faux enthusiasm on the word.

"So she's *just* gotten back here," I said. "But Amagansett is a whole different market than what she used to work, correct?"

"It is. It's a good trip east of where her old office was."

"Hmm," I said. "It might be that she doesn't want to work in the same area because she's still so shaken by what happened to Lenny."

"Truthfully, I don't even know how you come back to work in the same field after something like that."

"Me either," I said, then I focused on the objective at hand. "Gilley, call and get us an appointment with Chanel, would you?"

"What's our story, this time?"

"It's the same one we gave to Sara Beth. We're looking to buy a large, expensive home, and want to take a look at her listing. She'll be more invested if she thinks we're interested in a home that'll give her the full commission."

"Okay," Gilley said. "But, Cat, can I make a suggestion about our approach with her?"

"Our approach? What's wrong with our approach?"

Gilley shrugged. "It's just that . . . the poor girl went through quite a trauma, right? She lost her partner and her business all in one fell swoop. Maybe we could come in a little softer with her. Build some trust, you know."

I thought about that for a moment and nodded. "You're absolutely right, but how do we do that exactly?"

"Maybe by showing up as two genuine people, and not as the wealthy heiress and her sniveling assistant, and actually *going* to her listing and getting to know her a little. You know . . . feel her out before we start throwing questions at her like, 'Do you know if your partner was murdered by two men who're laundering money for the mob?' Call me crazy, but that miiiiiiight freak her out after what she's been through."

"Yeah, okay," I said. "I actually like that suggestion. We'll do that."

I squeezed the steering wheel as I drove, excited that we really seemed to be on the trail of the right motive in Lenny's murder. "I can't wait to hand over all this information to—" I caught myself before I said Sam's name.

"To who?" Gilley asked, his face a perfect, innocent mask.

"My source," I finally said.

"Mmmhmmm," he replied. "Someday you're going to have to fill me in on all this"—Gilley paused to hold up air quotes—"source stuff."

"Someday I hope I can," I told him honestly.

"Cat?"

"Yes, Gilley?"

"Just be extra, extra careful."

"Lovey, I swear I'm doing my level best to be as careful as possible."

I could only hope that it was enough.

We met Willem on the beach at one o'clock. It was an absolutely stunning day, with clear skies, temps in the upper fifties, and a gentle breeze. "Ahhhh," Gilley said, getting out of the car and spreading his arms wide. "It *actually* feels like spring today!" With that he bounded down the beach toward the waves while I laughed at his antics and turned toward the grassy picnic area at the top of a hill.

After climbing all the way up, I sat down at one of the picnic tables, feeling tired all of the sudden, and I noted that I hadn't gotten a lot of sleep the past few nights. I'd been worried about too many things of late—all of them out of my control, but also all feeling like they were depending on me to set things straight.

As Gilley ran barefoot along the water I waited for any sign of Willem. As I looked around, I was delighted to see a hot air balloon in the distance, taking advantage of the warm temps, no doubt. Still, it had to be very cold in that basket, and I hoped the occupants were dressed warmly.

At last Willem's car pulled up next to mine, and out he got, looking wary but nicely dressed in casual khaki-colored slacks and a blue blazer. I waved to get his attention and he started coming up the hill toward me.

I smiled with contentment, because I knew there was nothing the curse could do to harm us way out here among all this open air and beautiful scenery.

"Hi, Willem!" I called.

He waved back and continued, rather laboriously, to walk steadily up the hill, and I was suddenly regretting the fact that I'd chosen to sit at the picnic table rather than wait for him on the beach.

Gilley had by now noticed Willem marching toward me, and he abandoned the sea to come up the hill as well.

As I sat waiting, I saw Gilley stop abruptly and look toward me. It was difficult to make out his facial expression, but he'd stopped so suddenly that it read to me like he was alarmed.

"What?" I whispered, as I continued to watch him. But Gilley didn't move. Instead, he simply looked toward me, his posture stiff and unchanged.

And then Willem also stopped, looking up toward me with a stiffened posture.

"What the devil?" I asked, beginning to look around, but nothing seemed out of place. I turned back toward the two men only to see them beginning to race up the hill toward me.

"Cat!" Gilley shrieked.

I got up from the picnic table. Now I was the one alarmed.

Willem began to wave his arm frantically, his short legs doing their very best to run up the hill.

Gilley overtook him and shrieked at me again. *"Cat! Move! Move, move, move!!!"*

I darted forward but then stopped. Was I supposed to go toward them? Or turn and run? And what the devil was I running from?

"Move, woman!" Gilley shrieked.

I dashed toward Gilley. It was the safest option, I thought, and just as I took maybe my tenth step, behind me there was a tremendous crash, and a horrific scream.

Chapter 9

I launched myself into Gilley's arms and we tumbled to the ground. He covered me as the world went dark, and I heard the flutter of fabric, ripping and tearing, all while a giant wave of hot air enveloped us.

I shrieked, not in pain, but in absolute terror, and Gilley squeaked too. At last some of the commotion subsided, and I heard Willem's voice calling out to us. "Catherine! Gilley! Are you hurt?"

Gilley got to his hands and knees, physically freeing me. "Crawl to freedom!" he said urgently.

I opened my eyes and looked around. The world had gone a strange, pastel shade of pinky blue, and I couldn't see any sign of the beach or the picnic table.

"What the hell happened?" I said.

Gilley pushed up on a large swath of silk fabric. "The hot air balloon. It crashed."

"Ohmigod!"

Gilley pointed to my right. "Crawl out that way."

I moved forward on my hands and knees, the deflated balloon heavier than it looked, and we finally made it out.

I was helped to my feet by Willem, who was sweating profusely and ashen-faced. "Oh, oh, oh!" he exclaimed. "I thought that thing was going to kill you!"

I wiped my hands and brushed off my knees, but my slacks were clearly ruined. "I'm fine, Willem," I said. But that was a lie. I was hardly fine. I was well and truly shaken.

Gilley got to his feet and surveyed the area. "Where're the people from the basket?" he asked.

Willem pointed to an area under a nearby tree. "There," he said.

I turned to look and saw a man, probably in his sixties, wearing a captain's hat and holding his left arm tightly to his chest, his face a mask of pain.

Next to him was a woman who was perhaps in her fifties, who looked a bit like she'd had her bell rung.

I sucked in a breath at the sight of them. "They're hurt!"

"Yes," Willem said, his voice shaky. "I think the pilot's shoulder is out of the socket. I've already called an ambulance, but I have to leave. Will you stay with them?"

"Leave?" Gilley and I said together.

"Where're you going?" I demanded.

Willem was already backing away. "It's the curse. I can't be here when the first responders arrive. Not after last time." With that, the poor man took off at a run.

"Gilley!" I said, pointing toward Willem. *"Do* something!"

"I'm not chasing him down," Gilley said quietly. "Uh uh. No way."

"Are you *kidding*?" I nearly screeched. And then I took a few steps in Willem's direction, but Gilley caught my arm, stopping me.

"Let him go, Cat."

I rounded on him. "None of this was his fault and you know it!"

"Maybe it wasn't. But even if the curse had nothing to do with any of this, right now he believes he's responsible, and until he calms down, what're you gonna say to change his mind?"

I opened my mouth to protest, but nothing came out. I really had to consider that Gilley was right. At least the part about not being able to change Willem's mind. I mean, what *could* I say?

So I let the poor man go, vowing to catch up with him later. Turning toward the two injured balloon passengers, I decided to try and give them any comfort I could until the first responders arrived.

As it turned out, we didn't have long to wait. The couple was taken away within minutes of the paramedics arriving and, to everyone's relief, they were able to guide the pilot's shoulder back into its socket. (It made the most *horrific* sound.) But otherwise, the pair appeared to have escaped with only a few bumps and bruises.

I overheard the pilot telling the first responders that the strangest gust of wind simply came out of nowhere, took him off course, and then his balloon began to rip. One of the responders suggested he was quite lucky to have escaped with his life.

Gilley and I then gave a statement to the responding patrol officer, and I shuddered when they finally moved the basket off the table where I'd been sitting right before the balloon crashed.

If Gilley hadn't waved me away from the area, no doubt I could've been seriously injured.

Around two, Gilley and I were finally able to get back in the car and leave the scene. We were mostly silent at first, which was more about both of us trying to process what the hell had happened at the beach than anything else.

"I was so certain the beach would've been a safe call," I muttered.

"Me too," Gilley said. "I still can't believe that, on a day when the beach is totally empty, not another soul in sight for miles and miles, a hot air balloon drops out of the sky and nearly kills you."

I glanced meaningfully at Gil. "Hey."

"What?"

"Thanks for saving my life back there."

"Don't mention it," he said modestly.

"Oh, I'm gonna mention it," I insisted. "And I'm gonna be grateful."

Gilley smiled in a way that suggested he was quite pleased with himself. "We heading back to the office?"

"We are."

"For your meeting with what's his name?"

"That's the plan. You'll need to make yourself scarce, though, Gil."

"Can't I just stay and hide?" Gilley asked.

"Ha! *Where?* It's a one-room office."

"I could hide in the closet."

We both looked at each other and burst out laughing. "Ahhh," Gil said. "I'm never hiding in the closet."

"Seriously. I mean, why start now?"

"Sistah, preach!" Gil said, snapping his fingers in a Z. "But really, why don't I get to be there?"

"Because my client would prefer to have some privacy."

Gilley scoffed. "Your *client*. Yeah, right."

"Gil," I said sharply.

"What?"

"I'm going to tell you something that I shouldn't, okay?"

Gilley was all ears. He leaned toward me and said, "I'm listening."

"You can't tell *anybody* that you suspect Sam isn't a legitimate client."

"What's that supposed to mean?"

"It means that you need to think of Sam as my *legitimate* client."

"Even though we both know that's not true?"

"Only one of us knows. The other merely suspects."

"Mmmmhmmm," Gil said, then he added a tisking sound.

"I'm serious."

Gilley sighed. "Fine. Your secret is safe with me. Drop me off at the cupcake shop. I've had a traumatic day and papa needs some buttercream."

I dropped Gil at the bakery and headed to my office, getting there with just enough time to hurry into the ladies' room and take a gander at my reflection.

Holding in the scream took effort.

I looked an absolute fright. I was dirty, disheveled, and my mascara had smeared.

Still, I managed to clean up and appear almost presentable, even though there was no hiding my ruined slacks.

Sam arrived right on time, and he paused in the doorway when he saw me. "Need I ask?" he said, coming forward while I stayed seated in my wing chair.

"Best if you don't."

"Alrighty," he said, taking a seat across from me. "We have a half hour before I can walk out of here today so that it won't look suspicious. What should we talk about, Catherine?"

"I have a topic," I said.

Sam made a *give it to me* motion with his hands.

"I'd like to know if you're privy to the fact that Boris Basayev ordered the hit on Lenny Shepherd?"

"This again?"

"Yes, *this* again," I snapped. I hadn't meant to be so curt. Perhaps it was all the excitement from earlier, or perhaps I was anticipating that Sam did know the details regarding Lenny's murder and he wasn't willing to be forthcoming with me.

"Why is this so important to you?" Sam asked me.

It was a good question. "I owe someone," I said. "Someone saved my life, and I feel like I owe him some relief from the torture of not knowing why Lenny was murdered."

"Shepherd," Sam said.

I didn't confirm his statement. I didn't need to. Instead, I offered him my theory. "I believe that Lenny was set up. I think that Boris Basayev wanted a new way to launder money somewhere away from the Big Apple, so he targeted the Suttons and their gallery, and lured them here with a promise of the cut from the profits if they relocated their gallery to the Hamptons. They could've come out here to look around at what homes were for sale, and afterward, suggested to Basayev that the prices were too high and they couldn't afford to make the move after all as, when Basayev found them, their gallery was struggling.

"So, Basayev found a listing under Lenny Shepherd, and figured he could kill two birds with one stone. He sent Greta to the home where Lenny was hosting an open house one Saturday in June, nearly two years ago now, and the Angel of Death murdered Lenny in cold blood. Greta made sure there were witnesses to see her exiting the property—she wanted her description to get back to the detective who would most certainly become obsessed with solving his ex-wife's murder. And Basayev would get to operate his little money-laundering scheme out here, unencumbered by thoughts of a nosy detective, who was now too distracted to pay the Suttons any attention."

Sam sat with his legs crossed and his hands folded in a relaxed position, patiently listening. His expression gave nothing away, although I made sure to focus all of my attention on it, hunting for any hint of recognition, or surprise, or even agreement. But his face and his eyes were a mask only of slight curiosity. There was nothing of an affirmation there for me.

When I was finished, he leaned forward and said, "That's a very interesting theory, Ms. Cooper, but I want to caution you about revealing it to your friend, the detective. The person you mentioned is still conducting business as usual, and he'll continue to do so for at least a little while longer. We can't assure your safety—or the detective's, if you get my drift—and any mention to the authorities of what you *think* may be going on, or what happened to Lenny Shepherd, would probably land you and the detective in the Atlantic, fifty miles offshore. And I'm not kidding."

I felt the color drain from my face. I believed him, and I suddenly felt very foolish. Still, it really bothered me that Sam might have some sort of proof or evidence that would tie all this together, and he was refusing to offer it up because he wanted Basayev on other charges.

It also occurred to me that Shepherd was beginning to close in on a motive himself, and he was closer to Basayev than I believed either Sam or Boris thought. How soon before he put it together like I had?

Sam continued to stare at me expectantly, and I hate to admit it, but I felt intimidated. "I understand," I said at last.

"Good," Sam replied. "Now how about—" Sam stopped midsentence and lifted out his phone, which I could just barely hear was buzzing. He put the phone to his ear with a crisp, "Dancer." There was a lengthy pause, during which Sam's gaze flickered to me. "Understood," he said. "I'll be there in ten."

"Is something wrong?" I asked, when he hung up.

"You could say that. I have to go."

Sam got up and so did I. "It's not Maks, is it?" I asked.

"Do you have the flash drive?" was his only reply.

"Yes. But if you want it you're going to have to be a little more forthcoming about Mr. Grinkov. Is he all right?"

"He's fine," Sam said, his voice softening just a fraction. "Walk me to the door and we'll shake hands again."

I followed him to the door where he turned to face me. I took his hand and pressed the flash drive into his palm. We shook hands and I let go. He casually put the hand holding the flash drive in his pocket, and tipped a pretend hat at me.

A moment later he was gone, and I was left to wonder what the heck had happened.

Fortunately, I didn't have long to wonder. My cell rang before Sam even made it to his car.

"Gilley?" I asked, seeing his name on the caller ID.

"Ohmigod, Cat! Did you hear?"

"Hear what?"

"The news!"

"What news?"

"The gallery owner—Jason Sutton . . ."

"What about him?"

"He's dead!"

My mouth dropped and for several seconds all I could hear was my own heart pounding in my ears. Gilley seemed to realize that it would take me a moment to let that sink in, because he was silent on the other end of the call.

"H-h-how?" I stammered.

"They found his car at the bottom of a lagoon. He was in the driver's seat."

"Suicide?"

"Maybe, I don't know."

"It was murder," I said, as if it were already a known fact. And then something else occurred to me. "How do you know all this, Gilley?"

"I'm watching it on the news. It was their lead story. His husband was shown on camera looking absolutely devastated."

"Or scared out of his mind," I said.

"Yeah. Or that."

"Are you still at the cupcake shop?"

"No. I'm next door getting a pedicure."

"Okay. I'm on my way to pick you up."

I hung up with Gilley but didn't head out the door right away. Instead I paced my office for a few minutes, thinking. Finally, I looked toward the inner office door and said, "To hell with it."

Marching forward, I pushed out of the door and nearly bumped right into Shepherd.

"Oh!" I said, as we almost collided. "Steve! I . . . What're you doing here?"

Shepherd looked annoyed. "Go back to your office, Ms. Cooper," he said formally. "I'm on official police business."

"In my building? I hope you have a warrant."

Shepherd held up a folded piece of paper. "As a matter of fact, I do." He then proceeded to walk past me and up the stairs.

I hesitated just a few seconds before I followed him.

He paused on the second-story landing to glare back at me. "I'm telling you to butt out, Catherine."

"And I'm telling *you* that as long as you're in *my* building I'll go where I want!" Something in my gut let me know *exactly* where Shepherd was going, and I'd be damned if I was going to make it easy on him.

"Fine," he said. "Have it your way." He then moved up the stairs at a faster pace than I could keep up with. Still, I managed to reach the third-floor landing only a little bit behind him.

Shepherd walked to Maks's office door and banged on it hard with his fist. "East Hampton P.D., Mr. Grinkov. Open up!"

I stood near the stairwell, watching Shepherd and dreading what I thought might be coming. The door to Maks's office suite opened, revealing the man I'd had drinks with the night before. However, he hardly looked like the same man.

Maks looked pale, and tired, as if he hadn't slept the night before. And yet he managed to remain calm in the face of one agitated cop. "What can I do for you, Detective?" he said.

"You can turn around and place your hands behind your back," Shepherd said, while also producing a set of handcuffs. "You're under arrest."

I stepped forward. "What're you arresting him for?"

"Butt. Out. Catherine," Shepherd snapped.

"I will not!"

Maks then got my attention. Holding up his hand in a calming gesture, he said, "It's all right, my dear. I'll be fine."

Maks then turned and placed his hands behind his back for Shepherd to cuff him, which he did, and I couldn't help but notice the satisfied smirk on his face as he clicked the steel bracelets closed. "Maks Grinkov," he said, taking out a card from his pocket to read from, "you are under arrest for the murder of Jason Sutton. You have the right to remain silent. . . ."

Shepherd read Maks all of his Miranda rights, while I stood helplessly by. Shepherd finished by saying, "Do you understand these rights as I have read them to you?"

"I do," Maks said. He then looked to me. "Catherine, would you please call Marcus for me?"

Marcus Brown was the best damn lawyer on the planet, and I should know because I'd retained him a little while back when I'd been in Maks's shoes.

"I'll call him," I assured him.

Shepherd sneered at me as he walked past with his

prisoner in front of him. "Glad to see you're looking out for your *boyfriend*," he muttered as the pair passed.

I let the comment go. Given the situation, Shepherd was going to think the worst, and I couldn't explain to him what was actually going on between Maks and me. And that wasn't simply because I didn't really know what was going on between Maks and me.

I followed the pair down the stairs and to the door, then watched as the detective put Maks in the back of his unmarked sedan. Shepherd never looked back; in fact, I rather thought he made a point to avoid looking at me altogether, but Maks did offer me a soft smile and a nod from the back of the car as it pulled away from the curb.

His reassurance in spite of being the one handcuffed and heading off to jail broke my heart a little.

The second Shepherd and Maks were out of sight I hurried into my office, sat at Gilley's desk, and placed a call to the attorney.

"Marcus Brown," he said crisply, answering the call before the third ring.

"Hello, Marcus, it's Catherine Cooper calling."

"Ms. Cooper," Marcus replied warmly. I smiled at the change in his tone. "What a surprise. How may I assist you, ma'am?"

Marcus had an office a few towns over in Sag Harbor. He had represented me a few months earlier when I'd been accused of murdering my neighbor. As a woman who'd run a multimillion-dollar business, and gone through a terribly contentious divorce, I'd had my fair share of legal representation, but none of those attorneys had ever held a candle to Marcus Brown, either in courteous manner, professionalism, or ability.

"I'm calling on behalf of a mutual friend of ours," I said.

The other end of the call was quiet, and I swear there was a note of tension there. "As in . . . ?"

"Mr. Grinkov," I said.

Through the connection I thought I heard the sharp sound of paper being turned over—like a sheet of legal pad being turned to a fresh sheet. "Talk to me," he said.

"I'm afraid I'm light on the details. A local gallery owner named Jason Sutton was found deceased in his car at the bottom of a lagoon somewhere in East Hampton. About five minutes after I heard the news, Detective Shepherd showed up at my office building and arrested Maks."

Marcus sighed. "Shepherd really likes to shoot first and ask questions later, doesn't he?"

"He is a tad overenthusiastic when it comes to making arrests," I admitted . . . mostly because, in my experience, it was true.

"Where are you now?" Marcus asked.

"I'm still at my office."

"Okay. It'll take about an hour to process Maks's paperwork once he reaches the station. And Shepherd's not dumb enough to question him until I show up. I'll leave here in thirty minutes and be there before five. If you can get word to Maks that I'm on my way, that'd be great."

"How would I do that?"

"By telling Shepherd, of course," Marcus said. "He'll pass the word on to Mr. Grinkov because he just won't be able to resist."

I realized he was right. Steve would pass that information on to Maks just to gauge his reaction. "I'll text Steve right away."

"Perfect. Thank you."

The moment I was off the phone with Marcus I texted Shepherd. After sending the text, I saw the little bubbles appear just below my message, but no reply ever came through. I tried not to feel disappointed—but I'd be lying if I said it didn't bother me.

Next I called Gilley as I was locking up the office. "Where are you?" he demanded. I realized I'd left him at the nail salon without updating him about what was going on.

"I'm on my way."

"You were on your way forty minutes ago!"

"Gilley," I said calmly, getting into my car. "Please don't be angry. There was a development."

"Uh oh, that sounds bad. What kind of development?"

"Shepherd arrested Maks for the murder of Jason Sutton."

Gilley audibly gasped. "No *way*!"

"Way."

"How did you find out?"

"It happened in front of me."

"No way!"

"Way."

"Why would Shepherd arrest *Maks* of all people?"

"Obviously, Shepherd believes he did it."

"You don't think this is just some way for your boyfriend to get back at your other boyfriend?"

I rolled my eyes and looked at my reflection in the rearview mirror. "Neither of them is my boyfriend."

"Have you told that to your boyfriends? Because, me thinks neither one of them got *that* memo."

"Would you stop?"

"Fiiiiine. But haven't you wondered if Shepherd is doing this just to be spiteful?"

I thought back to the patrol officer who'd harassed us the other night when Maks and I had gone to dinner. Shepherd had been behind that little stunt, but I didn't think he'd go so far as to arrest Maks without some pretty hard evidence. "He had a warrant, Gilley. That means it was signed by a judge, so Shepherd has something on Maks that he thinks is worthy of an arrest."

"That hardly holds water, Cat. I mean, he arrested you on pretty flimsy evidence."

He had a point there. "Still, I don't think Steve would do something so dumb. At least not twice."

"I wonder what he has on Maks to link him to Sutton's murder."

"I'm here," I said, without answering Gilley's question. I was double parked in front of the nail salon.

"Oh, so you are," Gil replied, then hung up the phone. He made his way out to my car and hopped in.

"Hey," he said.

"Hey," I replied, pulling away from the curb.

"So what do you think Shepherd has on Maks?"

"No idea. Whatever it is, Marcus will probably poke a lot of holes in it."

Gilley's interest piqued at the mention of the attorney. "Oooo," he said. "Is that tall, dark, *delicious* drink of water back on scene?"

"You know he's straight, right?"

Gilley wiggled his ring finger at me and his wedding band. "I'm just window shopping, sugar. No reason to worry over Marcus's *virtue*."

I gave Gilley some side-eye. "I wasn't really worried."

"Mmmmhmmm," Gilley said. "I could've had him if I'd wanted him."

"Keep telling yourself that," I said with a laugh. But then all humor left me when I thought about Maks, waiting for his attorney to show up and likely nervous that he'd been charged with murder. I too wondered what could possibly link him to Sutton's death. "Gil?" I said after a bit.

"Yeah?"

"Was there anything on the news about evidence left behind at Jason Sutton's crime scene? Something that might've hinted toward Maks being the killer?"

"You don't believe he's *really* the killer, do you?"

"No. Of course not." At least I didn't *think* he was the killer. "I mean, what could possibly have been his motive?"

"You know him better than I do," Gilley said.

"Which isn't as well as I should, apparently."

Gilley turned thoughtful and tapped his lip. "M.J. once gave me great advice."

"What's that?"

"She said that your first reaction to someone is almost always right. It's how we soften our memories of interactions with people over time that pollutes and clouds the picture."

"Hmmm. That's actually a really good observation."

"It is. So, I gotta ask. What was your first impression of Maks?"

"You mean like . . . ever?"

"Yes. The moment you two met, what was your immediate measure of the man?"

"Well . . ." I said, thinking. "I suppose it was an instant attraction, but also . . . maybe . . ."

"Yeah?"

I shrugged. "I don't know . . . a sort of ease. Being in his presence put me at ease, like I was safe in his company."

Gil nodded. "He's not the killer," he said. "No way would you have felt so comfortable around him so immediately if he were bad people."

"I agree," I said, pulling into the driveway at Chez Cat. Once I'd parked the car I looked at Gilley. "Now what?"

Gilley bounced his eyebrows. "How about I make you and me an early dinner and take your mind off your troubles."

"Count me in," I said with a sigh of relief.

Gilley headed over to Chez Kitty while I ducked into Chez Cat to change out of my ruined clothes and put on some comfortable loungewear. I then made my way over to Chez Kitty, let myself in and I plopped on the couch while he fussed in the kitchen.

Gil is an excellent cook, and I always marvel at his creativity. Tonight he was making a gorgeous-smelling pesto, with locally made pasta, roasted chicken, fresh tomatoes, and goat cheese. My stomach growled with impatience while I waited for him to bring it all together.

I also had a chance to contemplate the mysterious case of Jason Sutton's death. I had no doubt that he'd been murdered, and I also had very little doubt that the deed was done by someone in Boris Basayev's organization—but who and why?

And to that point, was Maks being set up by Basayev? Had the mafia kingpin identified Maks as an informant?

No, I thought. If that were the case, Maks *and* Jason would both be dead. Still, the fact that some evidence existed that had pointed the police so quickly to Maks meant that someone was trying to set him up to take the fall, and I had no real qualms about defending Maks on that front because I believed in his character, and I'd also been set up for a murder I hadn't committed, so I knew what that felt like.

So who had set Maks up to take the fall? An enemy in the organization, no doubt. But if it wasn't Basayev, then it was someone else capable of murder, and that thought made me shudder.

"Penny for your thoughts?" Gilley said, and I jumped, because he was practically standing right in front of me and I hadn't even noticed. "Whoa, sugar," Gil said, sitting down next to me to eye me with concern. "You look like you've seen a ghost. And I should know; I've seen plenty."

I put a hand to my chest and attempted a smile. "Oh, Gilley, I'm sorry. I was lost deep in thought."

"Care to share over dinner? It's ready and on the table."

I shook my head to clear it and stood up. "It smells amazing. Thank you for making it."

Gilley was clearly pleased by the praise. "Come," he said. "We'll eat a little nosh and talk about what's causing that furrow to your brow."

I rubbed my forehead self-consciously as I followed Gilley to the table. I gazed appreciatively at the bowl of pasta he'd prepared. It was a work of art. "This looks heavenly," I said.

Gilley swiveled back and forth. "Thank you. Now, sit, sit!"

We sat down and got settled, and then I took a bite and moaned. "Oh, my God."

"Good?"

I held up my hand and splayed my fingers. "Five stars, my friend. Five stars."

Gilley poured me a glass of chardonnay and shimmied his shoulders. I'd learned that there were two ways to Gilley's heart. One, flatter his outfit. Two, flatter his cooking. Do both, and you had a friend for life.

"All right," he said when I moaned again. "That's enough smoke up my ass. Now tell me; what dark thoughts were rattling around in that pretty head of yours?"

I sighed. "It's a very dark thought, Gil."

"So tell me about it. Maybe I can make it a little brighter."

I appreciated Gilley's enthusiasm, even though I knew there was no way for anyone to take the frightening feeling out of my mind. "I was just thinking that Maks was probably set up," I began.

"Duh," said Gil.

"Okay, so you already figured that out. But, what I keep wondering is who might've set him up?"

"We don't know any of the facts yet," Gil said. "It's impossible to speculate, Cat."

And I think that, more than anything, made me feel a little better. We *didn't* know any of the facts, so my leap from thinking that Maks couldn't have murdered Jason to Jason being murdered by someone who wanted to frame Maks was a huge leap. "You're so right, Gilley. I think I needed that reality check."

We spent the rest of dinner chatting about the events of the day. "I really should reach out to Willem and see how he's doing," I said.

"I tried calling him three times already," Gilley told

me. "He's not answering his phone or returning my calls."

"That's worrisome. Thank goodness the people in the balloon were okay. We need to make sure he knows that they're all right. I don't want him backing out of our plan."

"Wait, wait, wait," Gilley said, holding up his hand in a stop motion for emphasis. "You mean you're planning on taking him on *another* outing?"

"Of course," I said. "We knew pushing the curse would come with a few risks, and today's events were considerably more intense than I'd imagined, but I'm not about to give up on Willem. He needs us."

Gilley scowled. "Where could we possibly take him that *won't* have risks, Cat? I mean, a hot air balloon dropping out of the sky? Like, what the freak?!"

I sighed and forced myself to speak softly to Gilley, even though my patience was running thin. "Can you please find a place that'll have minimal risks?"

He scowled at me. "How about the moon? We could just load him into a rocket and keep our fingers crossed."

"Gil . . ."

"*Fine*, I'll look for something."

I was about to thank him when my cell rang. I got up to retrieve it. "It's Marcus," I said.

"Answer it!" Gilley encouraged when I hesitated.

"Hello, Marcus. Is Maks all right?" I said, after picking up the call.

"He's fine, Catherine. But I'm calling because we need you to come down and give a statement."

I stared at Gilley, my brow furrowed. He mouthed, *What?*

"You want me to come down and give a statement?" I repeated.

"Yes. Right away if you can."

"You mean like a character statement?" I was confused.

There was a pause on the other end of the call, but then Marcus said, "No. We need you to state that Mr. Grinkov was with you last evening."

"Oh!" I said. "Well, yes, of course. That's true."

I heard Marcus sigh in relief. "Excellent. You'll need to come down and give a sworn statement about that to provide Mr. Grinkov with an alibi. The police won't release him without it."

"I'll be right down," I said. "I just have to remember the time we were together, correct?" I was thinking that I'd left Maks at the bar at around seven, but it could've been later.

"Correct. He couldn't remember the specific time you two were together, but he knows that you two left your office building around six-thirty, and then you drove him in to work early this morning."

I blinked. "Come again?" I said.

"I'm sorry, what part didn't you hear?"

My mind was racing to catch up to what Marcus was telling me. "No, I heard you. I mean . . . yes. Yes, that's correct. I'll be right there, Marcus."

I hung up the phone and stared at Gilley. "What's happened?" he asked.

"It's Maks. He's asking me to lie."

"About what?"

"About where he was last night . . . into this morning."

Gilley got up and came over to me. "He needs an alibi?"

"Apparently."

"And you're going to give him one?"

I sighed. "Apparently."

Gilley closed his eyes as if he was thinking about how to break some bad news to me. When he opened them again he looked at me very seriously and said, "Maks is accused of murder. That's a felony and, I'm no lawyer, but lying to police about his whereabouts might also be a felony. So, I have to ask, are you absolutely *sure* you want to do this, Cat?"

I tucked the phone away in my purse and moved over to retrieve my coat. "Of course I don't *want* to do this, Gilley, but what choice do I have?"

"You could tell the truth," he said simply.

I bowed my head and pinched the bridge of my nose. A headache was starting to form from all of this stress. "Maks was there for me when I needed someone to believe I didn't kill Heather Holland. I think I owe him this favor."

Gilley stepped forward to reach for my hand. Squeezing it to get my attention, he said, "I know you think you do, Cat, but this will get you mixed up in something that's pretty scary."

"I'm already mixed up in it," I muttered.

"What's that mean?"

I sighed. "It means that my mind is made up and I'm going to help Maks by covering for him."

Gilley nodded. "Okay. But be prepared to look Shepherd in the eye and tell him that Maks was with you last night. All night."

I felt my stomach muscles clench. "Dammit," I whispered. "I hadn't thought of that."

"Are you changing your mind?"

I shook my head. "No. But someday I hope I can explain all this to Shepherd."

"Me too, sugar. Do you want me to come with you? For moral support?"

I did want Gilley to come, but I also knew that Shepherd might then want to grill Gilley about whether or not he'd seen me with Maks last night and this morning, and I couldn't allow Gilley to be tempted to commit perjury too.

"No. Thank you, Gilley. I'll be fine."

Gil hugged me. "I'll whip up some dessert that'll be ready for you when you get back."

I offered him a lopsided smile. "No nuts in the brownies, okay?"

Gilley put a hand to his chest. "Perish the thought."

I kissed him on the cheek and set off, ready to commit a very real, very serious crime.

Chapter 10

Marcus met me at the door of the East Hampton P.D. "Thanks for coming so quickly," he said, escorting me through the lobby. "Detective Shepherd is waiting to take your statement."

"Of course," I said. "Is there any chance I can see Maks first?"

Marcus eyed me sideways. "No. I'm afraid I can't allow it."

"*You* can't allow it?" I said.

"Your conversation would be open to being recorded by the police, Ms. Cooper. I can't allow Maks to say anything on record that might further implicate him in this crime."

I understood immediately. "Yes," I said. "Yes, of course. I'll just give my statement then."

We headed through a corridor and made our way to familiar territory—one of two interrogation rooms, in front
of which a stoic, blank-faced Steve Shepherd now stood.

"*Ms.* Cooper," he sneered when we stopped in front of
him.

"Hello, Detective," I said just as formally.

No one said anything for an awkward few moments,
but I could feel the tension radiating off Shepherd. He
was angry, that much was obvious, and I had no doubt
that, mixed in with the apparent jealousy that my statement was about to justify, was also a real anger that I was
about to blow his case. Shepherd opened the door to the
interrogation room. "After you," he said.

Marcus and I filed in and sat down, and Shepherd
closed the door and brought a file with him to the table.
As he sat down I could feel my heart rate tick up, but I did
my best to appear calm.

"Mr. Grinkov has given us an accounting of his where-
abouts last night, and I need to confirm the details with
you."

"Of course," I said, hating that I'd have to look him in
the eye when I lied.

"Okay," he said. "Why don't you tell me about your
evening with him last night."

"Well," I said, trying to think of what details Maks
might've divulged to Shepherd during the interrogation.
"I'm not especially comfortable telling you every minor
detail of our date, Detective," I said, as a way to both stall
and be as vague as possible, and with a pang in my heart
I noticed that his neck went a slight shade of crimson.
"What I can say is that Maks and I went out for drinks,
one thing led to another, and we ended up back at my
house. And then we went in to the office this morning to-

gether, and that's the last time I saw him until you showed up to arrest him."

Shepherd's finger tapped at the desk, and it was impossible to tell if he believed me or not. "Who drove?" he said.

My brow furrowed. "Who drove?"

"Yeah. It's a simple question, Catherine. Who drove the two of you to your house from the bar?"

I resisted the urge to shift in my seat—a clear body language signal that I'd be lying, and instead my memory honed in on what Marcus had said to me on the phone earlier—that I'd driven Maks in to work this morning, which meant that he needed me to say that we took my car. Knowing Maks, however, I felt that, even though we'd taken my car, he probably would've said that he drove, and this was why Shepherd was asking specifically about who drove home from the bar. Crossing my fingers that I was getting the story right, I said, "Well, as Maks probably already told you, we drove separately to the bar, and then over the course of a few drinks, I'd felt the alcohol hit me, and I asked Maks to drive my car back to Chez Cat."

Shepherd frowned, but in a way that suggested he was disappointed that I'd answered the question the right way for Maks. But then he looked into his folder and produced a receipt, which he showed me. "See, this is the part that doesn't make sense to me," he began, as I took in the receipt, which was for only two cocktails. "You felt impaired after *one* drink, Catherine?"

I smiled pleasantly to show Shepherd he wasn't going to rattle me. "I know it may seem odd, but I'd had very little to eat all day and I'd also had a very stressful afternoon on top of that, and as I'm only five-foot one and one hundred and five pounds, Detective, a normal-sized martini, for me, can often pack a wallop."

For the first time since I'd sat down, Shepherd regarded me skeptically. "You forget; you and I have been out to dinner, and we've thrown back a few."

This time it was my cheeks that felt the heat of embarrassment, and out of the corner of my eye I swear I saw Marcus arch an eyebrow. Still, I had a counterpoint that I hated to use, but I felt like Maks needed his alibi to be iron-clad. "That's true; we have gone out and shared a few, but if I recall, both of those occasions involved a substantial amount of food spread over a few hours. Maks and I didn't linger at the bar. I . . . I was anxious to get . . . home."

"Why were you anxious to get . . . ?" Shepherd began, and I arched my own eyebrow at him. He stopped mid-sentence and dropped his gaze, that same crimson color returning to his neck.

I felt terrible in that moment, both for lying to him and for allowing him to think that I'd made some kind of a choice—when I hadn't. And even if I had, I would never want to hurt Shepherd by blurting it out like that. The man could be an absolutely insufferable horse's ass, but he'd also saved my life and had opened up to me in a way that I knew was especially difficult for him.

Shepherd pulled the receipt back to the folder and traded it for a piece of paper that read, "Witness Statement." He then shoved a pen across the table, got up, and turned to the door. "Write it all down, Ms. Cooper," he said, and then he simply left.

After the door closed, Marcus put away his legal pad, which he'd extracted from his messenger bag when we'd sat down. I simply stared at the paper and pen on the table, fighting the water forming in my eyes.

"Are you all right?" Marcus asked, after a moment.

"Fine," I said hoarsely. Then I swallowed hard, pulled the paper forward, and began to write out my statement.

When I was done, I handed it to Marcus, who looked it over and nodded. He then got up and moved to the door. Poking his head out into the hallway, he spoke to someone who said something back, and then he pulled his head in again. "We can go," he said to me.

I stood and picked up the statement. "What do I do with this?"

"Leave it on the table," he said softly.

I held on to the statement for a moment of hesitation. I wasn't officially committing a crime until I walked out that door and left the statement behind.

"Something wrong?" Marcus asked.

"No," I said, adopting a smile and setting the statement down. "Let the chips fall where they land," I muttered, and moved out into the hallway.

Marcus offered me a curious look as I passed him, but he didn't otherwise comment.

Instead he walked me to the front entrance, where I paused and turned toward him, because I still had so many questions. "What evidence did they have linking Maks to Jason Sutton's murder, anyway, Marcus?"

"I'll let Maks explain," he said.

I frowned, but Marcus added, "If I took the time to explain, I'd have to bill you, Ms. Cooper."

"Ah. I forgot. Marcus Brown is always on the clock." But I put a hand on his arm to let him know that I still thought of him as a friend.

He rewarded me with a beautiful smile. "Have a good night, Catherine," he said, and went back inside.

I drove home in a frustrated fog. I'd learned nothing, other than Maks hadn't wanted to place himself at his house the night before, or . . . if I really thought about it . . . near his car. That was a curious detail, and I wondered how it would all play out.

When I got to Chez Kitty, Gilley was waiting up for me. I couldn't help but notice as I set down my purse that he'd consumed a quarter of a pan of brownies and a half gallon of milk. "Thank the baby Jesus you're finally home!" he said. "Tell me everything."

"There's really nothing to tell," I said, moving to the cupboard to fetch a dessert plate. "I lied, and I have no idea why I needed to."

"Yikes," Gilley said. "So no one told you what evidence they have against Maks?"

"Marcus said he'd have to charge me a billable hour to take me through it."

"Ha! Marcus—ever the professional," Gilley giggled. "So, did you actually lie to Shepherd's *face*?"

I took a bite of brownie, and while I was chewing I lifted the glass of milk I'd just poured in the air in a toast motion. "I did indeed."

"Whoa," Gilley said. "Was it hard?"

"Yes, and I feel so guilty. It sucked, Gilley. It sucked big, rotten, stinky, ostrich eggs."

Gilley pulled his chin back. "You sound like your sister."

I shrugged. "We're cut from the same cloth. I just work

at stifling my inner trucker mouth, while she lets that freak flag fly free."

Gilley smirked. "How'd Shepherd take it?"

I shoved more of the brownie into my mouth. "He was hurt," I said bluntly, because I knew it to be the truth.

"Damn, girl. Shepherd got his feelings hurt? That would be hard to see."

"It felt like kicking a stray dog," I confessed. "And I hated it."

Gilley took the now empty plate from my hand and walked to the counter, where he cut me off another big piece of brownie. "I should've made a double batch," he said, bringing it back to me.

"Thanks," I said, taking up the second piece. "It's even more terrible because I can't really talk to anyone about any of this . . . Well, at least not to anyone but you, and even you I can't tell everything to."

"Yeah, why is that?"

I shook my head. "I just can't, Gil."

"It has to do with your new secret client, right?"

I shoved a giant piece of brownie into my mouth and muttered in the affirmative incoherently. No way could I ever be quoted for that.

"Mmmhmmm. Say, though, does your new client know the latest about what's going on with Maks?"

I set down the rest of the brownie I was preparing to shove into my mouth. "I don't know," I said, blinking. "I mean, I assume so. But maybe I should text him?"

"Ah ha!" Gilley said, getting up to point at me. "I *knew* it!"

"Dammit!" I swore, something I so rarely do. "Gilley, you need to *chill*!"

Gilley fell theatrically onto the couch. "Relax," he said. "Who would I tell? And *what* could I tell them? Only my suspicions, really."

I let go of my tense posture and walked over to the couch, where I sank down onto it too. "I just don't want you overly involved. This is tricky and dangerous business, and even I feel like I'm now caught in this web of lies and deceit."

"So, maybe text your *client* and let him know what's happened," Gil said.

I nodded and got up to retrieve my phone. Scrolling down the messages, I found the one from Sam and sent him a text that simply said: **Do you know about our friend?**

Within fifteen seconds I received the reply. **Yes.**

Nothing beyond that, just yes, and that was incredibly dissatisfying, but I figured it was all Sam was going to say on the subject.

"He knows," I told Gil.

"What'd he have to say about it?"

"Nothing. As in, literally nothing."

"So we're locked out of the information?"

"It looks that way—" At that moment there was a soft knock on the door. I smiled at Gil. "That'll be Maks," I said. "I'm sure he's come to explain."

I walked to the door, stopping by the mirror next to it to check my smile for brownie (all clear), and pulled on the handle with relish. "I'm so glad to see you!" I said, but came up short.

Standing in front of me wasn't Maks, but Shepherd. He looked truly taken aback by my statement. "Why?" he asked curtly.

Gilley came to stand next to me. "Ah, Detective!" he

said. "So good of you to drop by. Cat's happy you're here to save her from having to polish off the rest of the brownies I made. Won't you come in?"

Shepherd looked from me to Gilley and back again, as if he didn't quite know what to do with the invitation. I stood back from the door and made a sweeping motion. "Yes, please come in, Steve. The brownies are still warm and gooey."

Shepherd wiped his feet on the doormat and entered Chez Kitty. He looked around as if expecting the decor to be different than the last time he'd seen it, but nothing about Chez Kitty had been changed.

Meanwhile, Gilley and I both hustled to the kitchen to get the detective a plate of brownies and some milk. My hand was shaking slightly as I poured his beverage, and my mind was racing to come up with a theory about why he was here. I couldn't think of a single reason other than he wanted to arrest me for perjury, but then, why hadn't he already done that?

I then had to consider that maybe he was drawing it out simply to torture me for fibbing about spending the night with Maks.

We all sat down at the table, and Shepherd shrugged out of his coat. Gilley placed the brownie and milk in front of him, then we both eyed Shepherd expectantly.

"I can't eat if you're gonna stare at me like that," he said.

"Sorry," I said. "It's just, we're both a little surprised to see you."

Pausing the hand that held the brownie that'd been about to enter his mouth, Shepherd turned his head to the door, then he made a snorting sound. "Of course," he said. "You were expecting your boyfriend to show up."

I tugged at the collar of my sweater. "Not at all," I said. "I knew it was you."

Shepherd lifted the brownie a little in my direction before taking a big bite. "Sure you did."

"So what brings you by, Detective?" Gilley asked before the tension got too intense.

"Well . . ." Shepherd said, wiping his hands on a napkin as he chewed, but then he paused to say, "Ohmigod, that's good."

Gilley puffed his chest out. "I put a little peanut butter in the batter instead of nuts."

Shepherd nodded. "Anyway, like I was saying, I'm here because I wanted to ask Catherine . . . off the record, why she lied."

I sucked in a breath and stared at Shepherd. "What makes you think I lied?"

Shepherd took another bite of the brownie. "Don't worry, it's nothing I can prove. It's just that you told the same story Maks did, in general. His story gave lots of details while your story was super vague. The facts match, but the story doesn't feel like the truth to me."

"I've given you my sworn statement," I said quietly.

"And I've told you I'm here off the record."

"Like I should believe that," I scoffed. "You'll remember that you once pulled me down to the station in handcuffs over a broken punch bowl."

"A broken punch bowl and twenty witnesses that all saw and heard you threaten a murder victim."

"Still, that was a flimsy arrest and you know it."

Shepherd sighed and stared at the table. Then he lifted his gaze to mine and I was able to see my friend behind the cop façade. "Catherine," he said gently. "Come on. Talk to me."

I glanced at Gilley and he shrugged. "I think he's telling the truth, Cat. I think you can talk to him off the record here."

"Fine," I said, relieved to tell Steve the truth and undo some of the hurt I'd no doubt caused him. "Maks and I parted at the bar, but I told you differently only because I know Maks didn't kill Jason Sutton."

"And how do you know that?"

"Because I believe I know who did."

Shepherd did a double take. "Come again?"

"I think it was a hit. A *professional* hit." I wanted Shepherd to get the hint of what I was implying.

"Of course it was a professional hit," he said, surprising me.

"Wait, so you *know* about Jason Sutton and his connection to Boris Basayev?"

"Of course I know about Jason Sutton and his connection to Boris Basayev!" Shepherd yelled. "Why do you think I arrested Boris's right-hand man?!"

"Hey, hey, hey!" Gilley said in a singsong voice, like a teacher out on the playground when the little kids start yelling at each other. "Let's use our inside voices, please."

Shepherd glared hard at Gilley.

Gil sank down in his chair a bit. "Or, you know, never mind."

I was frowning at Shepherd, who then turned that hard glare on me. "Maks isn't who you think he is," I said.

"Oh?" he snapped. "So, he isn't the guy who buys an assassin dinner right after she's shot up a coffee shop and me in the process? Or the guy seen all over town entertaining known Chechen mafia members? Or the guy who was seen by *six* witnesses, roughing up Jason Sutton yesterday in the parking lot of the gallery? Or the guy whose car was seen speeding away from the lagoon where Sutton was found this morning, shot through the head, neck, and torso?"

Gilley curled his lip in distaste. "Wow. Someone really wanted him to die."

"No, Gilley," Shepherd said softly. "Not *some*one. Maks Grinkov."

"But why?" I said. "Why would Maks want to kill Jason Sutton?"

"I don't know, Catherine, maybe he's the new hit man for Basayev, or maybe Sutton sold him a crappy painting, or maybe just because it was a Thursday and Grinkov felt like murdering someone new this week. Who knows and who cares? The point is that I had that bastard dead to rights until you came in and screwed me. And because I had him dead to rights, I knew that I could eventually get him to flip on Basayev and maybe, just *maybe* get him to tell me the truth about why Lenny was murdered."

"Steve, I—"

"Save it!" he barked, shoving back violently from the table and getting to his feet. Wadding up his napkin, he threw it onto his empty plate. "Thanks for the brownie, Gilley. I'll see myself out."

Shepherd grabbed his coat and moved to the door while Gilley and I stared with wide eyes both at each other and Shepherd's retreating form. Neither of us called out to him, because neither of us quite knew what to say. A moment later, Shepherd was through the door, slamming it hard on his way out.

"Well," Gilley said into the stunned silence that followed. "That escalated quickly."

* * *

I wandered back over to Chez Cat right around eleven, feeling mentally beaten and frustrated. I'd texted Maks a simple inquiry about how he was doing, and he'd not texted back. And even though it'd only been a few hours, it really bothered me that he hadn't reached out to even say thank you, or that he was okay but exhausted, or swamped, or whatever the hell he *actually* was.

And the look that Shepherd had given me as he'd stood up from the table at Chez Kitty . . . it'd be a long time before I'd be able to forget that look or forgive myself for invoking it.

I went through my evening ritual, getting ready for bed, but I didn't know if I'd be able to sleep. Coming out of the bathroom, I stared at my big, beautiful bed, with its silk sheets, fluffy pillows, and inviting duvet, and all I wanted to do was head back over to Chez Kitty and curl up on the couch, because I simply didn't want to be alone tonight.

But poor Gilley had been asleep on his feet when I'd left him, and I hated to disturb him yet again.

So I wandered downstairs to the bar and poured myself a glass of brandy. I felt like, if I could only take the edge off, I might be able to settle down.

As I was heading back upstairs, there was a soft knock on the door. Hope blossomed in my chest. Maybe Gilley couldn't sleep either?

I hurried to the door and looked through the peephole, gasping when I saw who was standing on the other side. Turning the dead bolt and pulling open the door, I greeted Maks with a cool look. "Hello, stranger."

Maks picked up on my barely veiled anger immediately. "I'm so sorry," he began. "I couldn't text you back."

"Oh?" I said. "Tied up, were you?"

"May I come in?"

"It's late, Maks."

"Yes," he replied, and said nothing more. He'd let me decide.

I inhaled deeply and let it out very slowly, trying to cool my own hurt feelings, and frustration at hurting someone close to me as well. When I felt a bit calmer, I simply stepped aside.

Maks came forward and lifted the brandy from my hand with gentle fingers. He took a sip, then placed it back in my hand and moved into my foyer.

I closed the door, locking it again, and turned to face him. When I did, my breath caught anew. There was the most incredibly delicious smoldering look on Maks's face. Immediately I felt my pulse quicken and he closed the distance between us like a shot, enveloping me in an embrace that was both commanding and fluid. His lips descended on mine like molten metal, and I sank into the feel and the smell and the passion of his embrace with an ease that surprised me.

Our kiss was charged and hungry, and the connection was nearly primordial. Maks kissed me with a hungry passion and then he lifted me into his arms and carried me upstairs, where all thoughts of regret, or guilt, or common sense fled the stage and I was left willingly vulnerable and ready for the taking.

Chapter 11

Hours later I propped my elbow on the pillow, placed my head onto my palm and stared at Maks in the soft glow of the full moon streaming in from the window. It struck me in that moment that this was like something out of a movie, and everything about having him here next to me felt both comfortable and foreign at the same time.

Maks smiled at me and reached up to tuck a strand of hair behind my ear. "What's going on in that gorgeous head of yours?" he asked.

"I was thinking this is all a bit surreal," I confessed.

Maks cocked his head. "It is?"

"Yes. I . . . you're the only man I've . . . uh . . . *entertained* in my bedroom since my husband. And I was with him for nearly two decades."

Maks chuckled. "If it's any consolation, I was *quite* entertained."

I felt my cheeks heat. "Saying, 'had sex with' just takes the romance out of it, you know?"

He nodded. "I do. But I can't imagine anything taking the romance out of what just happened between us, Catherine."

I fiddled with the bedsheet. "It was pretty great, wasn't it?"

"It was *fantastic*."

It was my turn to chuckle and then I sighed contentedly. "What brought you over here anyway? I mean, I'm sure you didn't come by just to carry me upstairs and have your way with me . . . or did you?"

Maks rolled onto his back and stretched. "No, no. I didn't come here expecting anything. But when you opened that door and I saw how beautiful you were in the glow of the moonlight and your robe . . . well . . . can you blame me?"

I reached out and traced his biceps with my index finger. He was gorgeously well defined and in incredible shape for a man in his midforties. "So why *did* you come here?"

"Well . . . I wanted to thank you, and I wanted to explain what happened."

A small area of tension that I'd been carrying with me ever since I'd been pulled into Maks's arrest eased. I'd been worried he'd try to avoid explaining things to me, and it was a great relief to hear that he wanted to set the record straight. "I'm listening," I said.

Maks rolled onto his side and mirrored my posture. "I needed to be seen with you," he said.

"You did?" What did that even mean?

"Yes," Maks continued. "I'm very good at reading

people, Catherine. Not nearly as well as your sister, but she's in a league of her own—"

"True," I said.

"But I'm still very, very good at picking up subtleties that other people miss. It makes me a very good poker player, and it's the reason I've managed to remain alive even though I swim with the sharks, so to speak."

"Okay," I said. "So who was it that you needed to read?"

"Boris," he said bluntly. "Basayev has been off lately. He's a suspicious man by nature, and because of that, he's very structured and habitual. He gets up at the same time every day. He eats the same thing for breakfast every single day, et cetera, et cetera, but lately, his routine has been off. Not by much, but enough to send a few of my alarm bells ringing."

"You think he's on to you."

"I do. Which is why I needed to see you, to establish an alibi, not for the police, but for Basayev. I suspected that he's been having me watched."

I gulped. That was a terrifying prospect.

"So, he's watching you and you needed me to be your alibi for Basayev's people, which means that something took place after I left you at the bar, right?"

"Yes," Maks said. "I needed to meet someone, and I couldn't be seen with him."

"Who?"

"I can't tell you, and I'm sorry for that, but I can't."

"Is your mysterious meeting something that's going on the next flash drive?"

"It is."

"Did you have anything to do with Sutton's murder?"

I asked next. If Maks was putting some of his cards on the table, I thought I might as well ask him to play his cards faceup.

"No," he said.

I studied him in the glow of the moonlight, waiting to feel or sense that he was lying.

"I swear," he insisted.

"I believe you."

Maks audibly sighed in relief. "Good. Your trust is important to me."

"I trust you, Maks, but I also wish you'd be more revealing to me. If I'm getting sucked into this, even tangentially, I deserve to know what you're involved in."

Maks seemed to consider that for a moment, and then he spoke so quietly I had to lean toward him a little just to hear him. "Jason was skimming the books," he said. "I knew it because I had a source who revealed it to me, but I hadn't told Boris about it, even though he suspected that's what was going on. The day we saw you in the gallery, Boris tried to feel Jason out, get a sense of whether to trust him or not. I couldn't get a read on if he believed Jason or not, but later I went back and confronted Jason, and told him to put the money back. He stuck to his guns and wouldn't admit that he was skimming. We got into an argument over it in the parking lot, and Jason took a swing at me—"

"That cut above your eye," I said, gently stroking the spot on Maks's forehead.

"Yes," he said, reaching up to take my hand and hold it in his own.

"What happened to Jason?"

"He got more than a cut above his eye."

"Ouch."

"That's what he said."

I let out a surprised laugh, but quickly stifled it. This was hardly a laughing matter. "Then what?"

"Then I left to meet you, we went to the bar, we had our drink, I gave you the flash drive, you left and I exited quietly out the back to meet my contact, but I didn't take my car. I walked to where we'd agreed to meet. My source and I spoke, it was brief, but when I went back to retrieve my car, it was gone."

"Gone?"

"Stolen."

"Someone stole your car?" I gasped.

"Yes."

"Wow. Did you report it?"

"I did. But not until the next morning."

"Why?"

"Because I couldn't take the chance that someone knew I'd walked out of the bar and around to the parking area only to leave my car there and walk somewhere else, then return an hour later and report my car being stolen."

"Ahhh, there would've been a gap in the timeline."

"Yes."

"How did you get home?"

"Sam sent me an Uber."

"How did Sam know you needed an Uber?"

"Boris's people aren't the only ones keeping tabs on me," Maks said.

"Didn't Sam's people see who took your car?"

"No. They were too busy following me to my contact's location. It was probably one of Basayev's people anyway. Somehow they discovered that I'd gone somewhere and they took my car to teach me a lesson."

"The murderer used it when he killed Sutton."

"I believe so, yes."

I took all of what he was saying in, and a shudder traveled up my spine. This cloak and dagger stuff was seriously scary. It took me a moment to work up the courage to ask my next question. "Now that you've been given an alibi, will Basayev try to kill you?"

"He might," Maks said.

I stared at him in shock, and felt tears sting my eyes. "I don't want you to die," I whispered.

Maks reached up to cup my chin. "Then I'll try to avoid it. But another reason I'm here, Catherine, is because this is getting too risky to continue to include you."

"What does that mean?"

"It means I'm going to have to find another way to get Sam what he needs. I'm not going to put you in the middle anymore. It's too dangerous."

My heart began to pound. On the one hand I felt like I was being dumped, but on the other hand, I felt relieved not to have to insert myself into the middle of an undercover sting to catch a ruthless and deadly mafia kingpin. "So, we're not going to see each other anymore?" I asked, hating the squeak that snuck into my voice.

"No, my sweet. At least, not for a little while."

I swallowed hard and fought back the tears, which were so stupid anyway. I mean, Maks and I weren't in love, and we'd only gone out, what? Two and a half times? It was ridiculous to get emotional over this new development, and yet, I couldn't stop the tears from falling.

Maks looked at me with such sympathy, and he gently wiped away the tears with his thumb. "I'm so sorry," he said, then pulled me to him and held me close. "I never wanted to hurt you."

I shook my head. "You haven't. A lot of this is simply that I'm worried for you."

"I'm a little worried for me too," he admitted.

And that did nothing to ease my anxiety. Then I thought of Shepherd, and how he wasn't going to let Maks go so easily. "Maks?" I said.

"Yes?"

"I need to ask you something. It's really important, and I need an honest answer."

Maks pulled his chin down to look at me intently. "If I can answer it, I will."

I nodded. I understood he was bound by some sort of oath or code to keep certain things top secret. "Did Boris order the hit on Lenny Shepherd?"

Maks hesitated a moment before he answered. "You genuinely like Shepherd, don't you?"

"I honestly do." Maks wasn't the only one putting all his cards on the table.

Maks sighed, and there was perhaps a wee note of disappointment in the sound. "I don't know, Catherine. And that's the truth. I don't know if Boris ordered the hit or not. He's never told me, but I do know that he benefitted from her murder—significantly—if that helps."

I breathed out the breath I'd been holding. I'd been afraid that Maks was keeping that secret from me. "It does, thank you," I said, even though it really didn't.

I wished I could've taken something to Shepherd, some token or peace offering to show him that I really did have his best interests at heart, but now, with this confession from Maks, I was still back at square one.

I reached out and took Maks's hand. "Do we really have to avoid each other from now on?"

He pulled my hand to his lips and kissed my knuckles.

"Do as you normally would, my sweet. I'll be the one who will make himself scarce."

"But how will I know if something happens to you?"

Maks smiled sadly. "I've already made it clear to Sam that, should anything happen to me, he's to let you know, so that you don't think I've simply abandoned you."

"So, all we get is tonight?"

Maks kissed my knuckles again. "All we have is the next hour," he said. "I'll have to go soon."

My gaze lingered on his face for a long time. I wanted to imprint this night and his physical presence in a way that would make it seem like it was only yesterday, no matter how far from now I tried to recall it. And then, when I felt like I'd sealed the memory and all its details into my mind, I moved over to lay on top of him. "If we only have an hour, let's at least make the best of it."

And we did.

The next morning Gilley popped over for coffee . . . uninvited. "Gooooood morning, sugar!" he sang, waltzing into my kitchen like he'd gotten a good night's sleep. And then he took one look at me and said, "Ohmigod! What *happened*?"

I was so alarmed I craned my neck to look over my shoulder. "What?" I said.

"No, Cat," Gilley said, calling my attention back to him. "What happened to *you*?"

Self-consciously I put a hand to my hair and realized I must look a mess, what with all the early morning . . . *gymnastics*. "Why? I'm fine," I said lamely.

Gilley's left eyebrow arched. "I'd say you were more than fine. . . . So, who was it?"

"Who was what?" I asked. I kind of knew exactly what Gilley was getting at; however, I was also trying to stall and come up with a reasonable explanation for why I looked like a rumpled, tired, hot mess with a healthy afterglow.

Gilley propped his elbows onto my kitchen island. "Come on, Cat. Dish!"

"There's nothing to dish," I said mildly, then picked up the carafe of French pressed. "Coffee?"

Gilley moved to my cupboard and took down a mug. "I'd love a cup. And the truth."

I sighed. "Fine. It was Maks."

Gilley clapped his hands together. "I *knew* it!"

I rolled my eyes. "It was no big deal."

Gilley snorted out a dismissive sound. "Yeah, right."

"It wasn't."

"It so was. Even if you don't want to admit it. So tell me . . . how was your first time back on that horse since . . . what? You and Tom got divorced two years ago, so . . ."

"Three years," I said.

"Yikes! My God, Cat, I think I'd *explode.*"

"You'd be fine," I told him, feeling embarrassed and exposed but trying also to appear like it was no big deal.

"No," Gil insisted. "I'd explode."

"Fine. You'd explode. The point is that I didn't, and everything is fine."

My eyes misted and my voice cracked. I turned away from Gil and pretended to wipe down the island.

"Oh, my," Gilley said, setting his mug down and hurrying over to hug me around the waist. "Was he mean to you, or something?"

I shook my head. "No. He was the exact opposite of

that. He was courteous, honest, kind, and . . . shall we say, generous where it counted."

"Sounds amazing. But if it was so great, why are you crying? Don't you want to see him again?"

"Oh, yes," I said. "I do. But things are super complicated between us and Maks has a great deal of work coming up, so I don't think we'll be seeing each other. As often. We won't be seeing each other as often. . . ."

I stopped because my voice hitched. I turned away from Gilley and wiped the tears away from my eyes. I was simply so worried about him. I didn't know how he'd get more information to Sam without my help. And without my help, I worried that the next method would be far riskier to Maks.

Gilley wrapped an arm around my shoulders. "Sugar," he said with sympathy, and added a small tisk. "I had no idea your feelings for Maks were so strong."

"I just don't want to see him get hurt," I blurted out before I had a chance to catch myself.

Gilley's eyes narrowed. "Hurt? You mean, emotionally or physically?"

I shook my head. I was done lying to Gilley, so I settled for something in the middle. "Either."

Gilley left my side and retreated to a bar stool at the island. I wiped my eyes and turned to look at him, and was surprised to find him looking cross. "What?" I asked.

Gilley shook his head. "I wish you'd be straight with me."

"How am I not being straight with you?"

"You don't want Maks *physically* hurt? That says he's in over his head. And by that I don't mean he's in over his head emotionally with you. But I can't help you *or* him without knowing the full scoop. It's up to you if you want to tell me, or keep it to yourself, but I think that together we can figure something out. Just sayin'."

I drew in a deep breath, held it, then let it out. Gilley was right. "Maks is an informant," I whispered. "He's been providing information about Basayev to the FBI."

"Duh," Gil replied.

I came over to the island and sat down next to Gilley. "Maks was also set up to take the fall for Sutton's murder."

"Double duh."

I sighed. "Okay, how about you tell me what you *don't* know."

"I don't know how we should help him. Or Shepherd. But I *do* know that, if we could prove that Basayev murdered Lenny, it might speed things along for both men and keep them out of danger, don't you think?"

My eyes widened. "Ohmigod, Gilley!" I said. "That's *it*!"

Gilley took a demure sip of his coffee. "This ain't my first rodeo, sugar. Or my first murder."

I was too busy following the thread to reply to Gilley's sharp reasoning. Instead, I laid out the case for making the case. "If we can provide proof to the FBI that Basayev ordered the hit on Lenny to provide Jason and his husband a cheap space to live here in the Hamptons while they laundered money through the gallery, then both the FBI and the E.H.P.D. will have to work together, which gives more security to both Maks and Shepherd."

"The question is how do we prove it without drawing the attention of a very dangerous mafia boss?" Gilley said.

"Yes. That is the conundrum. But I think I have a way to work the back channels and at least give Shepherd a direct line to follow."

"You're talking about Chanel, aren't you?"

"Yes. And we've got to speak to her."

Gilley whipped out his phone and checked the time. "Nine-seventeen. The realty office where she works should be open." He placed a call and I waited anxiously while he tapped his finger on the countertop, but then he sat up straighter and said, "Well, hello, Freesia, it *is* a lovely day! I'm the personal assistant to someone who's interested in seeing some listings, and I was looking at your company's Web site for a good agent to match for my employer's . . . shall we say, aesthetic. . . ." Gilley dropped his voice and added, "She likes pretty people, you know? You know.

"Anytoodlehoo, I happened upon the gorgeous photo of one C.J. Downey and—what's that? Oh, I did *not* know she was a former model!" Gilley chuckled like he and Freesia were best chums. "But I can see how she would've been. That girl is stunning, and I think she'd be a good fit for my employer, who just can't be seen with any uggos, you feel me?"

I rolled my eyes and glared at Gilley. He was laying it on pretty thick here, and painting me up to be a shallow snob. He ignored me and continued his conversation with Freesia. "So is it possible for you to set us up with an appointment with C.J.? Or do we need to contact her directly?"

I was now tapping my finger on the countertop, waiting to hear what Freesia said.

"You can set up the appointment? Perfection! What's that? She goes by Chanel not C.J.? Got it. Okay, so we're free this afternoon—could Chanel make that work? If she can't, there is another Realtor from Saunders and Associates—what's that? You can definitely make that work?

Wonderful! Okay, pencil us in for one o'clock. And make a note that we'll want to see listings in the fifteen- to twenty-million range."

Gilley gave me the thumbs-up. I nodded enthusiastically. "Hmmm?" Gil said next. "The name? Ha! Oh, yes, I forgot. It's Gillespie, first name Catherine, and I'm Gilley. Yes. We'll see you soon. Ta-ta!"

After he hung up I said, "Why'd you combine our names?"

"I don't want it getting back to either Shepherd or Max that Catherine Cooper is sticking her nose into Lenny's murder case by interviewing her ex-partner. And, your name is more well-known than mine, so combining it just seemed like the thing to do. Plus, we don't need Chanel looking up Catherine Cooper on social media and realizing that it's the same Catherine Cooper who was almost murdered by the Angel of Death."

I pointed at Gil. "Good thinking." But then I had another thought. "What if Chanel tries to look me up on social media and can't find a Catherine Gillespie?"

Gilley reached over the island to where my laptop was resting. Pulling it to him, he lifted the lid, cracked his knuckles, and said, "Leave it to me."

At one o'clock Gilley and I strolled into the real estate offices of Bennett and Bennett. We were both dressed to kill. Gilley in a slick black suit with tan shoes and a bow tie, and me—sans shades this time—in a cream knit sweater, with a big (faux) fur-lined cowl neck, and matching suede pants with cocoa leather boots. Oh, and I'd also brought out the big guns—my dusky rose-pink Hermès Birkin was dangling off one elbow, which helped position to eye

level the four-carat pink sapphire ring crested in dia-
monds that Tom had given me on our fourteenth wedding
anniversary.

We looked the part.

"Hello," Gilley said, walking right up to the receptionist. I guessed she was the Freesia he'd been talking to earlier.

"Hello, and welcome to Bennett and Bennett," she
said warmly. "You must be Gilley."

Gilley smiled and dipped his chin, clearly pleased that
she was savvy enough to greet him so personally. "In the
flesh," he said. "And you must be Freesia?"

"Yes I am," she said, offering her hand over the countertop. She then came around to the lobby and pointed to a
door. "Mr. Gilley, Ms. Gillespie, won't you please follow
me to Chanel's office?"

We followed Freesia down a wide, carpet-lined corridor, passing various artworks lining the walls. I took note
that all of the art featured the same subject, a house, but
the styles of the different artists were quite varied. The
effect was subtle, but nice; home was interpreted as
something different by everyone, yet made of the same,
somewhat basic, structure. This agency clearly had its act
together, and paid attention to the details.

I'd think about using them in the future if I was ever
inclined to purchase another piece of property here in the
Hamptons.

Around a corner at the end of the corridor was a small
office, its door open. Sitting behind a desk was a lovely-
looking woman with red hair, full lips, and the lithe figure
of a ballerina or a model. She stood as we approached and
I liked her style. She was dressed simply, in a blue dress
with white crisscross, pencil-thin lines. The dress was

very retro, but the rest of her, from her hair to her subtle makeup, was chic and modern. She was a gorgeous creature, and there was a moment where I was glad that I'd dressed up a bit.

"Chanel," Freesia said when she reached the doorway. "This is Mr. Gilley and Ms. Gillespie. Your one o'clock."

Chanel smiled, but there was something about it that didn't quite touch her eyes. And that's when I noticed that her hands were plastered to her sides.

I'd once had an assistant who was terrified of me. Okay, so most of my assistants had lived in some kind of fear of me, but the one that Chanel reminded me of was a young girl in her early twenties who was terrified of most things.

I'd learned late in her employment with me that a few years earlier, she'd been asleep in her apartment when she woke up to find a man on top of her, attempting to rape her. She'd managed to fight him off, flee the apartment and seek help, but she'd confessed to my office manager that it'd left her with a pretty good case of PTSD.

She used to plant her hands at her sides whenever she was on the verge of a panic attack, and it was because I'd had that experience with her that I understood that Chanel was inwardly fighting a terrible battle.

Of course it didn't help that Freesia was standing in the doorway with narrowed eyes and the flat-lipped frown of the judgmental. I had no doubt Freesia was the little spy in this agency and would report any misstep by Chanel to one or both of the Bennetts. It made me rethink my earlier approval of the agency.

So, I lowered the Birkin and walked into Chanel's office to look around at the simple but elegant work space that Chanel had created for herself. "This is lovely," I said gently. And then I made eye contact with Freesia, whose own eyes had widened slightly, and I nodded to her in a way that told her I approved of Chanel.

Freesia bowed ever so slightly and turned away. I waited until she was a few feet down the hallway before turning back to Chanel. "Hello, Chanel, I'm Catherine. Most of my friends call me Cat, but you may address me any way that feels comfortable to you."

Chanel blinked, as if she hadn't been expecting anything but major attitude from me. It took her a moment to even acknowledge that I'd spoken.

I filled the awkward silence by waving toward the two guest chairs in front of her desk. "Would it be all right if we sat down?"

"Y-y-yes," she stammered. "Of course. Please sit."

Gilley had taken the cue from me and he moved to the chair, sitting down in a relaxed manner while he also looked about and nodded.

As I sat down I saw Chanel's hands come away from her dress, and there was a slight easing of her shoulders. She sat down too. "May I . . . may I offer you something to drink? Tea? Coffee? Water?"

"I'm fine," I told her. "But thank you." Gilley nodded, indicating he was also fine.

Chanel's fingers fluttered on the desktop. She didn't seem to quite know what to do with them. "Freesia said you were looking for a new home," she began.

"I am," I said.

"And are you also looking to list?"

"No."

Chanel pulled the keyboard to her computer close. "Can you describe to me your ideal home, Ms. . . . . Cat . . . therine?"

I grinned at her to show her that I truly was comfortable with any version of my name that she wanted to use. "Well, I want a view, of course. And an infinity pool and a large deck. I don't need a large lot; all that maintenance is a chore to manage, but I'd appreciate a place to dine al fresco.

"The architecture should be something midcentury modern, with lots of light, and large open spaces to display my art. I don't like multiple stories . . . oh, but a wine cellar would be nice. I also don't like too many bedrooms, no more than three, but of course an enormous master suite is a must, with a sauna and workout room. I'd prefer something on a bluff if you can find it. I want to see the ocean from every window and I'd like to feel as if I'm at the helm of a ship."

I was trying to describe something that would be very difficult to find in the Hamptons. Most of the homes here were the typical and traditional large beachfront houses, with big lots and a more colonial style. And almost nothing was ever available in the higher latitudes, because most of East Hampton was at sea level.

My effort wasn't based on having Chanel run around in circles, so much as it was an effort to have her take us around East Hampton in search of something close enough, which would take time and allow us to tease out any information she might have on the connection between the Suttons and Lenny.

And, as I'd already abandoned the direct approach, I felt like this was the best way to accomplish that. After all, Chanel was obviously still so traumatized by her partner's murder that she was struggling professionally. I mean, they don't put agents who're crushing it in a tiny back office of the firm. And something of the way Freesia had looked at Chanel—there was an almost unspoken, "Don't blow this" look in her eyes that told me that the pretty redhead was on thin ice at Bennett and Bennett.

I hated that I wasn't *actually* going to use Chanel, and I vowed to do two things after we got the information we needed from her. I'd write to the head of this agency and let them know how pleased I'd been to work with her, and I'd recommend her to anyone I could.

I was having all of these thoughts when I finally noticed that Chanel had stopped typing and was looking at me with her mouth agape. "I think I have the absolute perfect home for you to look at, Catherine."

"You do?" Gilley and I both said. He'd obviously taken note of the hard to find home that I'd described.

"Yes," she said, somewhat shocked. "I . . . I just got this listing yesterday, and I haven't had a chance to even post it to MLS yet, but it's *exactly* what you're describing. . . . Oh, but it's an East Hampton zip code. It's right on the boarder of Amagansett, though, if you had your heart set on living here."

I looked at Gilley and he looked at me. We were both stunned. Turning back to Chanel, who was expecting us to be thrilled, I said, "I'm not at all concerned with the zip code, and it sounds very intriguing. When can we see it?"

"Well, I'll just need to text the owner and make sure we can get in. . . ."

Chanel reached into a drawer and lifted out her phone. She tapped at the screen and her brow furrowed and a look of distress came over her.

"Is something wrong?" Gilley asked softly.

Chanel shook her head, but her fingers began to tremble. Something on her phone was upsetting her. She tapped at the screen and the worry in her face intensified. Finally, she said, "My grandaunt's dogs got out of her yard. I'm so sorry, but would it be all right if I respond to this text?"

"Of course," I said, and I turned to Gilley with a knowing look. I still hadn't quite forgiven Chanel's grandaunt for dodging me, but perhaps I could understand now given how nervous and anxious Chanel was. Her elderly relative was obviously only trying to protect her.

We waited for Chanel to send her text, then she focused back on us. "There. Where were we?"

Oh, dear, I thought. The poor girl really was a bit of a mess. "You were going to text the owner," Gilley said gently.

Chanel's face turned crimson. "Oh! Yes. Let me just do that."

We waited patiently while Chanel's fingers tapped at the screen, but I noticed that she kept hitting the backspace button, likely because her fingers were still trembling a bit. At last she put the phone down and said, "The property is just down from the marina, but it's on the north side, so there's not much traffic or noise that makes its way up the bluff."

"Perfect," I said, working to appear ever so interested.

Chanel's phone buzzed slightly and she picked it up. "We can get in after four-thirty, so would five o'clock work for you?"

"Five works just fine," I said.

Chanel seemed relieved. "Great. Let's meet here at quarter to."

"It's a date," Gilley said, getting up to shake her hand.

I followed suit and I was surprised at how cold her fingers were.

We then left her, smiling broadly at Freesia on the way out.

When we got to the car, Gilley said, "Wow. She spooks easily."

"Can you blame her?"

"I suppose not. Still, how're we going to get a word out of her, Cat? The girl nearly curled up into a fetal position when she got a text from her grandaunt."

And then I had an idea, and I couldn't believe it'd taken me this long to think of it. "We'll invite her to dinner."

"We'll what now?"

"We'll go, we'll see this property—and I *am* a little curious to see this property. . . ."

"Me too, right?"

"Right. And since we're going to this showing at dinnertime, we can segue into inviting her out to dine with us."

"I love it! But what if she turns us down?"

"We'll throw on the charm," I said. "And we'll rave about the house. She won't want to blow the sale. Trust me, she'll come out to eat with us."

"You're right about her not wanting to blow the sale. The poor love. It's probably her only listing."

"Even if it is, she still stands to make a pretty penny off a sale in the Hamptons."

"That I'll remind you she's not going to be making from us."

I shrugged. "I'll throw her some business."

"From who?"

I sighed. "I have contacts. I'm sure one of my friends might be interested in a vacation home out this way."

"Good," Gilley said. "I'm glad you're doing that. I was getting ready to feel good and guilty."

"Me too. Glad we'll be avoiding it."

Gilley sighed. "Wouldn't it be great if we got Chanel to connect the Suttons to Lenny's murder? She could be the key to all of this."

"She could. And I bet it's an angle that Shepherd hasn't looked at yet."

"How do you know he hasn't looked at it yet?"

"Well, because, the last time he and I went out to eat, he revealed a lot of what he'd already investigated to me about Lenny's murder. He never once mentioned the Suttons, and if they're as big a lead as I think they are, I think he would've told me."

Gilley grinned. "We make awesome detectives, you know?"

"We do," I said smugly. "Here we've been on the case only a few days and look at all the progress we've made."

"We deserve a medal."

"Or a piece of cheesecake."

Gilley swiveled in his seat. "I definitely think we deserve cheesecake."

I nodded. "Then it's settled. Instead of going back to the office, we'll head over to Carmen's for a treat!"

I moved over one lane and got into the left-hand turn lane to make a U-turn. It wouldn't be the only time that day I'd catch myself heading in the wrong direction.

Chapter 12

We arrived back at Bennett and Bennett at four forty-five sharp. Chanel met us in the lobby and I was glad to see there was no sign of Freesia. Chanel carried her laptop and a tablet, and her Louis Vuitton purse was set in the crook of her arm.

My keen eye went to the purse—what can I say? I'm a purse connoisseur—and I noticed it was scuffed and slightly worn at the handle and the corners, but otherwise well maintained.

I had a feeling that Chanel had either purchased the bag secondhand or she'd had it for quite some time. Her shoes were also high-end, but not from anyone's recent spring line. They'd seen a few seasons, I thought.

Still, she maintained the aura of fitting into the Hamptons' success scene fairly well. It took money to live here—a lot of money—and those without did the best they could not to call attention to their disposable income, or lack thereof.

And I wasn't being judgy of sweet Chanel, only curious about the fact that I had a sneaking suspicion that she was struggling financially, and doing her level best to hide it.

"Would you like to follow me or ride in my car?" she asked us, and she then waved toward the parking lot where a silver Mercedes was parked. Again I couldn't help but notice that the Mercedes was at least ten years old.

"We can ride with you," I said. "That way we can get to know a little more about each other."

Chanel shoved a smile onto her lips, but I could see that she was uncomfortable. "Terrific," she said. "This way . . ."

We followed her to her car, and Gilley got into the backseat while I got in the front and buckled up. As soon as we were under way, Gilley leaned in over the space between us and said, "So! Tell us about yourself, Chanel."

Chanel's grip on the steering wheel tightened. "There's not much to tell really," she said easily. I had a feeling she'd used that line quite often for how readily it rolled off her tongue.

But Gilley wasn't about to let her wiggle out of his subtle interrogation. "There's always stuff to tell. Have you worked at Bennett and Bennett long?"

"Oh, no. Not long," she said. "But I've had my license for six years."

"Where'd you work before Bennett and Bennett?" I asked.

"Um, I worked for another agency that has since been dissolved."

"That had to be hard," Gilley said. "It's tough to imagine an agency going belly up in this market, though. I mean, everyone I know is looking for a house in the Hamptons."

Chanel eyed Gilley in her rearview mirror, and for the first time I saw the nervous façade relax and a bit of humor crept into her smile. "Really? Can you send them all my way?"

Gilley chuckled. "Aren't you adorable! Of course I will, sugar. But tell us about this other agency. How long were you there?"

Chanel shifted in her seat, and the humor left her expression. "I was there two years, until it dissolved and I left to take care of my grandmother in Connecticut for a while. I've only recently come back to the Hamptons."

"Awww. Aren't you precious! Taking care of your granny is such a good sacrifice. Was it her dogs that got out of the yard?" Gilley asked.

"No, those belong to my grandaunt. She was my grandmother's sister."

"Was?" Gilley said.

Chanel swallowed hard. "Yes. My grandmother passed away just a few months ago."

"Oh," I said, turning to Chanel. "I'm so sorry, dear."

"Thank you," Chanel said, pushing a smile to her lips, but I could see that her eyes misted a bit, the poor thing.

"What made you come back to the Hamptons?" Gilley said next. "The real estate market in Connecticut must be fairly lucrative too, no?"

Chanel licked her lips. "I'm not licensed in Connecticut, and I would've had to go back to real estate school to get licensed there. It seemed more reasonable to come back here where I am licensed and know the market better."

Ahhhhh, I thought. Now I understood the source of Chanel's financial struggle. She probably hadn't worked since she'd moved to Connecticut and had come back here when her savings ran out. Plus, I also knew that real estate school was expensive—I'd looked into it before settling on my new career as a life coach—so Chanel had probably made the difficult choice to leave her grandaunt's house in favor of simply renewing her New York real estate license, which would've been much less expensive.

We chatted a little more about Chanel's life in the Hamptons, but she really wasn't very forthcoming. And I'm almost ashamed to admit that I was hoping that, after she showed us this listing and we took her out to dinner, we could get a drink or two into her so that she'd relax her guard a little.

Neither Gilley nor I dared to approach the topic of Lenny or the Suttons given Chanel's current demeanor.

We arrived at the home she wanted to show us, and I had to say, I was impressed.

The road leading up to the house was private; it even had a gate that required a code at the base of a steep hill. We wound up the hill, but there were no other homes or driveways visible, which somewhat surprised me—it took a *lot* of money to have a private road put in in this part of town.

When we crested the hill we zigzagged through a snakelike drive to the front door of an Asian-inspired midcentury modern home with lots of teak, dark trim, and floor-to-ceiling windows. The place was gorgeous, like something right out of an architectural magazine, and I was somewhat glad I hadn't seen it prior to building Chez Cat, because I might've been sorely tempted to snatch this home up in a hot second, even though it no doubt would've eaten up a substantial portion of my liquid assets.

We exited Chanel's car and Gilley and I stood in front of the house, admiring it while Chanel walked to the front door and punched in a code on the door handle to get it to unlock—which was a handy way to avoid putting an ugly lockbox on the gorgeous front door.

Once she'd unlocked it, Chanel held the door for us as we moved forward and past her into a large, open section that served as a sort of seating area and living space. It was sparsely decorated, with only two suede chairs, dyed a sea green.

The walls were bright white, and the floor was a bleached pine. Lining the walls were a series of impressive contemporary art pieces that were a bit harsh for my taste, but the owner clearly enjoyed dropping a pretty penny on art.

The one piece I liked—especially even—was a bright orange sculpture that was at least five feet tall and set in the middle of the room under a skylight. I walked around the piece admiring its soft, flowing curves while Gilley took in the paintings and Chanel stood near the door allowing Gilley and me to walk in a circle around the room, admiring the art, the flow of the space, and the lighting.

I was a little sad that the day had turned overcast and light was quickly escaping the landscape, so we wouldn't be able to see the house in full daylight as I assumed it was truly meant to be taken in.

When we'd had our fill I nodded to Chanel, who walked us to the hallway leading to the back of the house, but we stopped short of making it all the way there when we ducked into the kitchen, which was sleek and modern and not at all my taste.

I wrinkled my nose at it even, and Chanel said, "It wouldn't take much to turn it into something more to your liking, Catherine."

"True," I said with a sigh, then remembered that I was supposed to pretend to love this home, so I brightened and gave her an extra, "True."

We then moved back into the corridor and walked behind Chanel as she led us to the rear of the house, which mirrored the front in that it was an enormous room with floor-to-ceiling windows, and the view was absolutely spectacular. Even in the gloom of the day and the late afternoon we could still clearly make out the ocean, which was rolling and undulating angrily, as if an impending storm was driving big waves toward shore.

Chanel stopped a few feet into the room, and Gilley and I stepped around her to walk toward the windows, both of us drawn to the motion of the sea.

And I really had to give it up to Chanel, because when I'd described wanting a house that made me feel like I was on the helm of a ship, I never actually imagined that a house like that would exist—until now.

Gil and I stood at the windows and I could feel myself swaying slightly, as if the ship itself were rocking and rolling with each undulation. "Wow," Gil said, then turned away from the windows. "I'm a little seasick!"

I laughed lightly. I don't get motion sickness. "I think it's marvelous." And I meant it. The house had no backyard. Instead, the half we were standing in jutted out over the bluff's edge, and as the seas pounded the rocks below, you could literally feel the reverberation through your toes. But rather than feeling scary, I found it quite exhilarating. And it was amazing to see the ocean, angry and feral today, build large waves, swelling up like faceless sea monsters, growing nearly to eye level before they raced toward us like a giant train, ready to pummel us into oblivion, only to suddenly and nearly unexpectedly deflate under us and crash into the rocks below. It was mesmerizing. "This is so incredible, Gilley. You're missing it!"

In response, Gilley's hand reached out and leeched onto my arm. I laughed again and tore my eyes away to look at him and try to talk him down from his motion sickness, but when my gaze landed on him, I was shocked to see that he'd doubled over, was seeming to hyperventilate, and had turned quite pale. "Oh, dear, Gilley. Is it really that bad?"

Gil shook his head, then waved his free hand out in front of himself, gesturing oddly.

"Gilley?" I said, moving closer to him. "Honey, are you all right?" But Gilley kept sort of waving his arm and shaking his head. I bent down. "Gil?" I said, peering closely at him. "Are you in crisis? What's happening?"

"Duh . . . duh . . . duh . . ." he said, staring listlessly out in front of himself.

"What? What?" I bent low and cupped his face to turn it toward me. "Do you need help? Should I call nine-one-one?"

Gilley nodded and I let go to search through my purse for my phone. "Chanel!" I called. "Chanel! I can't find my phone! Something's wrong with Gilley!"

Behind me I heard the unmistakable sound of an outgoing call, and then the line was picked up. "Nine-one-one dispatch, what's your emergency?"

Chanel's voice, trembling with emotion and barely above a whisper, said, "Yes, hello, I'm at four-two-seven-one Gull's Point Ridge. There's been . . . there's been . . . he's been . . . *murdered*."

My mind hitched on her last word, and I abandoned my purse to finally, really look at Gilley's posture. I realized too late that he wasn't so much waving his arm out in front of him, as he was pointing to something behind me. That's when I craned my neck to look over my shoulder and saw a man, lying on his back, and previously hidden from our view by the couch. A pool of blood encircled his head, and the rest . . . well, let's just say that the rest was simply too gruesome to describe.

After swallowing hard, I grabbed Gilley by the arm. He straightened, and finally spat out, "Duh . . . duh . . . dead! He's dead!"

Meanwhile Chanel had stopped speaking to the dispatcher and was instead in a state of shock. Something about where she was looking made me also glance in that direction, and I realized that she was no longer staring at the man on the floor, but at something above the fireplace. Still holding on to Gilley's arm, I took a few steps toward Chanel so I could see what she was staring at. And that's when I saw that a large mirror, hanging above the fireplace, had something written on it. Across the mirror, in beautiful, loopy script written in hot pink lipstick, were the words:

Welcome home, my sweet!

My gaze went from the cryptic message to the man on the floor, who'd obviously pissed off either a lover or a wife, and that's when my breath *really* caught.

Even with the distracting gaping hole in his forehead, I still recognized the man from when I'd seen him at the Suttons' gallery. He'd been there with Maks which is how I knew that the man lying dead on the floor was Basayev.

I then looked around the gorgeous digs with fresh perspective. The furnishings, the artwork, the kitchen—all of it had a heavy, masculine feel. It suited a crime boss.

And then my gaze landed on Chanel. She was still staring dully into space, her face pale, her body stiff and trembling, and the phone still clutched in her hand. I could hear the 911 dispatcher attempting to get her attention. "Ma'am? Ma'am? Are you there? Ma'am, first responders are on the way. Can you speak to me?"

I went into motion, grabbing Chanel by the arm with my free hand while shouting, "Dispatch, send help!" And then I hurried all of us out the door.

Shepherd was one of the last to arrive. It disappointed me to see him showing up so late, and I can't exactly say why, but it almost felt like he'd let me down by turning up thirty minutes after the first patrol officer had arrived.

By then I'd already given my statement, as had Gilley, as had Chanel. We'd been told to wait to speak to the detective, which was why the three of us remained at the scene. I stood near the two of them while Gilley hugged himself and Chanel mirrored his posture. The cold of the evening was beginning to settle in, and while I too shivered under my sweater, I refused to adopt any other posture than irritated impatience, which was why my arms were merely crossed.

Meanwhile a team of patrol officers, crime scene techs, and the medical examiner moved about with calm efficiency, giving the grisly scene a somewhat distorted perspective.

I watched Shepherd closely as he headed first to the patrol officer, who spoke to him at length. Not once did he turn in our direction, even though the officer pointed toward us three times. That told me that Shepherd *knew* that I was here and was decisively *not* looking at me. And that made me angry.

Shepherd nodded at the responding officer after a lengthy exchange, and then a man in a dark windbreaker with the acronym M.E. on the back approached. He joined Shepherd and the responding officer, who nodded to both men, then walked away, leaving the medical examiner and Shepherd to talk.

Shepherd took out a small notebook, and the M.E. did most of the talking while Shepherd simply nodded and scribbled, and then the M.E. took something out of his pocket and held it up so Shepherd could see.

I squinted and saw that the object was a gold necklace with what appeared to be a charm dangling from it. Shepherd reached into his own pocket and extracted one black glove, which he quickly donned, and then he took the necklace and placed it into a plastic evidence bag, which he'd also pulled out of his pocket.

As the M.E. continued, Shepherd pocketed the charm. You didn't have to be a trained detective to come to the conclusion that the necklace had been worn by the woman who'd scrawled the sinister message on the mirror before murdering Basayev.

My guess was that there'd been a little bit of a struggle between Basayev and either his lover or his wife, and perhaps during the struggle Basayev had yanked the necklace free, while she'd gotten off one fatal shot. No doubt Shepherd would attempt to trace the woman through the necklace.

After the M.E. finished filling Shepherd in, the pair headed toward the front door and disappeared inside.

I sighed heavily and it truly took everything I had not to go marching inside and give Shepherd a piece of my mind. After all, we'd been standing outside in the increasing cold for over thirty minutes and hadn't even been allowed to wait in Chanel's car where we could warm up.

"Where's he going?" Gilley asked, his teeth chattering as Shepherd followed the M.E. inside and out of sight. I knew what he meant. He wanted Shepherd to come talk to us so that we could get the hell out of there. Neither he nor I had worn a coat, and poor Chanel had nothing more to cover her thin self than a light raincoat over her dress.

"This is ridiculous," I snapped after another fifteen minutes when Shepherd hadn't appeared or called for us to meet him inside. "Come on," I said to Chanel and Gilley while I turned to walk toward Chanel's car.

"Where're you going?" she asked.

"To warm up in your car."

"We were told to wait here."

I turned back to her. "We were *advised*," I said. "Only advised. We're not under arrest, we're witnesses, and as such, we can go where we please. And if the East Hampton P.D. has a problem with that, then they may take it up with my attorney."

Gilley's expression transformed from one of misery to relief and he leapt to his feet to follow after me, but

Chanel remained seated on the boulder she'd been sharing with Gilley. "Hold on," she said, and reached into her purse. She withdrew a set of keys and tossed them to me. "You two warm up. I'm going to stay put."

I nodded to her, took the keys, and we moved to Chanel's car. Sliding into the driver's side while Gilley got into the passenger seat, I started the engine and the Mercedes quickly warmed up. We waited silently, watching the first responders busy themselves collecting evidence, brushing for fingerprints, and foraging for any clue they could find. After fifteen more minutes with no sign of Shepherd, I fished around once again in my purse, hunting for my phone, and this time I easily found it zipped into a side pocket. Once it was free of the pocket, I began to tap and swipe at the screen.

"Whatcha doin'?" Gil asked.

"Making arrangements."

"For pizza?" he said hopefully. And that's when I heard his stomach rumble.

"No. But great suggestion." I closed the app I'd been tapping on and moved to another. After I was finished, I set the phone back in the pocket of my purse and concentrated on breathing deeply to calm my mounting anger.

Meanwhile my gaze flickered to Chanel again and again. She was shivering all over, and yet no one paid her any attention. I thought about going to her to try and insert some reason into her frightened mind, but I had a feeling any lecture I gave would fall on deaf ears. If she wasn't willing to disobey orders when she was clearly miserable, I doubted I'd be able to sway her.

Another eighteen minutes went by, and my phone pinged. I looked at Gilley. "Time to go."

"What? Time to go? Where?"

I turned off the engine and got out of the car. Gilley followed after me. I moved to Chanel and handed her the keys. She looked at me in bewilderment, as if confused by why I'd left her car.

"I called for a limo. We're heading home," I told her. "The car is two minutes away."

"You are? But they told us to wait to speak to the detective."

"You wait, dear. Gilley and I are leaving. But do tell Detective Shepherd that if he wants to speak to me, he knows where to find me."

With that I turned on my heel and began to head down the drive in the direction of approaching headlights. A patrol officer, set up at the base of the drive, held his hand up to stop the car, but I called out to him. "He's here for us."

The officer turned to me as I approached. "Did the detective speak to you?"

I merely smiled and said, "Several times."

The officer looked skeptical. "He say you could go?"

I glared at him with the full volume of my practiced, successful-businesswoman authority, and snapped, "Would I be leaving if he hadn't?"

The cop frowned, but he finally relented with a curt nod. I strode forward without looking back, and heard Gilley quickstep behind me.

We got to the limo and the driver hurried to put the car in park, jump out, and hold the door open for us. Gilley got in first and I scooted in after him. The limo smelled like pizza and Gilley made a squeaking sound of delight.

Perched on the seat was a box of pizza from our favorite pan pie place, and Gil wasted no time tucking into a slice. I was hungry, but I was also still angry, and my attention was directed toward the house and Chanel.

Our limo driver craned his neck and began to back up. The driveway didn't really allow for a turnaround unless you got closer to the house, and as the drive was filled with cop cars and such, our poor driver was going to have to find a place somewhere on the road to turn around, which would be a task given the length of the limo.

We made it about ten feet when behind us a pair of headlights lit up the backseat.

"Damn," our limo driver muttered.

I looked behind us, but all I could see were headlights. For a moment, neither car moved, and then, suddenly, the car behind us honked. "Where does he want me to go?" the limo driver snapped.

The patrolman who'd grilled me about leaving, looked annoyed, and he went to the car where he spoke to the driver. Sighing with impatience, I focused on the house again, and that's when I saw that Shepherd had come out of the house and was now standing with Chanel. "Drat," I whispered. Shepherd would no doubt order us out of the limo so that he could question us, and I'd bet he wouldn't even invite us inside out of the cold, but as I watched Shepherd for any signs that he was interested in where Gilley and I had gotten to, he surprised me when he reached for Chanel's shoulders and pulled her into a hug. He then cupped the back of her head protectively and rested his cheek on her hair.

My breath caught as I watched them. I mean, obviously Chanel would know Shepherd—she'd been his ex-wife's partner, and hugging her after not seeing her in so long was probably not so unusual, but there was something about their embrace.

Something familiar.

Something special.

Something intimate.

It bothered me.

Like . . . it *bothered* me.

I was jolted away from focusing on the intimacy of their embrace when the patrol officer knocked on the limo's window and our driver lowered it to speak to him.

"You'll have to pull forward and let him pass, then I'll guide you into a turnaround."

"Thanks," said our driver.

The limo moved forward at the officer's direction, and the other car began to pass. My attention shifted to the car passing by, and I sucked in another breath when I realized that Sam was behind the wheel. He turned to look in our direction as he passed, and our eyes met. He did *not* look happy.

Our car made a hard left, and I switched my attention back to Shepherd and Chanel.

The detective still had his arms around her, but he was leading her to his car. They got in as the limo made its three-point turn and began heading out of the drive, head-first. I turned in my seat and stared out the back window, watching Chanel and Shepherd get into his car.

"Cat," Gilley said, and I realized that he'd spoken my name at least once before.

I sat forward again. "What?"

Gilley cocked his head. "What's going on with you?"

"Nothing."

Gilley swiveled in his seat, still holding on to his piece of pizza. He looked out the back window too, but he didn't seem to notice what I had. "Oh, look. Shepherd finally saved Chanel from the cold."

"Yes," I said. "Hopefully, she'll be able to head home soon. This day has been quite eventful."

Gilley shoved a giant bite of pizza into his mouth. "Mofwging gidding."

I eyed him crossly. "Really, Gilley. Language."

He snorted a laugh with a mouth full of food. "Yoonderstdwat?"

I lowered my lids and looked at him dully. "Yes, I understood that. I have tween sons, you know."

Gil chewed some more. "Srry."

"It's fine," I sighed. "Sorry I was so cross. I just want to get home and wait for Shepherd to appear. Because you know he's going to."

Gilley swallowed hard, but instead of commenting he took another giant bite of pizza. I was beginning to regret tagging it onto the limo ride. Still, he nodded while he chewed. At last, when he'd swallowed again, he said, "He's definitely gonna show up and give us a lecture. Sometimes I think he does that just so he can see you."

I felt myself blush. "Why do you say that?"

"Cuz, duh, Cat. He's totally into you."

"Oh, I think he might not be now that he knows Maks is in the picture."

"Are you kidding?" Gil said, pausing the next bite of pizza headed to his mouth so that he could stare slack-jawed at me. "That's only got him even *more* interested in you."

"Come on," I said.

But Gilley nodded. "It's true. You know how these hetero men are. They gotta win their woman and beat their chest and take out their dingle-dangle for a pissing contest in the snow."

"Lovely visual."

He shrugged. "It's a gift."

Gil went back to gobbling down the pizza while I sat moodily in the backseat, irritated and upset far beyond what I should've been. And while Gilley believed that Shepherd was actually even more interested in me than he had been before Maks and I became something of an item, I had my doubts.

He'd played Cool Hand Luke with me before, but there was something different now. Something about the way he'd showed up to the crime scene and had made an effort *not* to look at me genuinely bothered me.

And then he'd also never once looked in our direction as the limo was exiting the scene. I would've expected that the hotheaded detective would've been livid that we were leaving without speaking to him, but he'd never even once shown that he was remotely interested in what Gilley and I were doing at yet another crime scene. Instead he'd focused all of his attention on Chanel.

Which again had me wondering about their relationship. I hadn't realized how close they were.

With a sigh I decided to put all judgments aside and simply wait for Shepherd to show up at Chez Kitty and give us a piece of his mind. I rolled my eyes when I imagined the tongue-lashing we'd endure, and then I had to roll my eyes again when I realized that I was actually looking forward to it.

Chapter 13

I woke up the next morning curled up on Gilley's couch with an afghan tucked around me. Sitting up abruptly, I realized that a thin stream of daylight was creeping in through the blinds, and this truly put me out of sorts because, for a long, foggy moment, I couldn't understand how it could be morning when Shepherd hadn't even come over yet.

And then I realized that it was morning, and Shepherd had never swung by.

I felt like I wanted to cry.

Swiveling sideways, I glanced over at the clock on the far wall. It read five forty-five. Laying back down on the couch, I pulled the afghan over my head and dabbed at my eyes. The waterworks were a surprise. I hadn't imagined I'd ever feel so hurt that Detective Steve Shepherd was ignoring me, but the truth was that there was this lingering energy hovering above me that insisted that Steve Shepherd and I were officially dunzos.

And I couldn't account for the sudden and drastic change, but something had definitely shifted between us, and his behavior the night before was only an example of how it would be between us from now on . . . namely awkward and uncomfortable.

So I had myself a good pity party. And by the time I was done, it was going on six-twenty. Dabbing my eyes one final time, I got up, shuffled to the kitchen, and threw a pod into the Keurig.

While I was waiting for the coffee to brew, I opened up the fridge and extracted a yogurt. Gilley and I had similar palates, and I was over here as much as I was at my house, so it was easy to grocery shop for the both of us and always have something I'd like to eat on hand.

"Don't tell me *that's* breakfast," I heard Gilley say.

I turned to see that he'd shuffled out of his bedroom and was propped against the wall of the hallway, eyeing me with disapproval.

"I'm not all that hungry."

Gilley pushed off from the wall and made his way over to me. Snatching the yogurt out of my hands, he said, "By my count you had less than one piece of pizza last night, so even though you don't have a big appetite this morning, your body needs a meal, Cat, not a snack."

"I might've had more pizza if you'd left me some," I said. I was feeling a little snarky because I was still nursing hurt feelings over Steve's apparent dismissal of me.

"Oh, please. I offered you a slice at least every mile on the way home."

I sighed and moved over to the Keurig to retrieve my coffee. I didn't really feel like talking, and I was considering simply taking my mug and heading over to Chez Cat, but then Gilley said, "Shepherd's a jerk."

My chin lifted and I looked at Gil. Waiting to see if he'd expand on that.

"I mean, what is this all about anyway?"

"What is what all about?" I asked him.

"This . . . ditching us."

I was surprised that Gilley seemed a little hurt too. "I don't know," I said. Because I didn't.

Gilley shook his head in disapproval. "Like, he should've been over here before the limo was even out of your driveway, right?"

I shrugged and moved to the table to sit down. "Or at least over here before nine."

Gilley eyed me with sympathy. "What time did you finally pack it in?"

"Midnight. You were right to head to bed at ten."

"Girl, I could barely keep my eyes open. Yesterday was a *day*!"

"It was. I think I'm still tired."

Gilley pursed his lips sympathetically. "Sugar, you sit and drink your coffee. I'm gonna make us some breakfast and then we're going to focus on something fun, okay?"

"Like what?"

"I don't know. Maybe we could go into the city for a day, hmm? A nice stroll through Central Park might be nice."

"Oh, Gilley, that does sound wonderful, but I think we're supposed to get rain."

"We are?" he asked. "I haven't seen the news in days. How about you turn on the TV while I whip us up a frittata?"

I smiled a little, which was pretty encouraging given

how blue I'd been just a few minutes before. "You always know how to lift my spirits."

"Frittatas lift everyone's spirits."

I moved to the couch and plopped down, reaching for the remote. Flipping on the television, I surfed the channel selection until I landed on the morning news. I then watched dully while, behind me, Gilley got out pans, and ingredients, and began to cook.

Very soon Chez Kitty filled with the aroma of sautéed potatoes. Right around the time that Gilley was pulling together his egg, mushroom, spinach, cheese, and potato concoction, the top of the hour hit and, with it, the morning's lead story.

Which was about the murder of Boris Basayev.

"So that *was* Basayev from last night!" Gilley called out, as I sat forward to watch the screen intently.

"Gilley, shhh!" I hissed. "They've made an arrest and I want to hear who did it!"

"My money's on the wife. Or maybe the lover. The chick with the bright pink lipstick did it."

"And we've just confirmed that the name of the suspect in custody this morning is Chanel Downey, a twenty-eight-year-old real estate agent from Amagansett," the reporter said.

I dropped my jaw and the remote.

Behind me something clattered to the floor. Gilley was as stunned as I was.

"What the . . . *what?*" Gilley cried. Then he rushed over to the couch, picked up the remote, and cranked up the volume.

"We've also learned that Downey was the real estate agent of record on the listing for the murder victim's house, which was for sale. Police have not yet identified a

motive in the case but we'll keep on this story and provide more details as they come."

Gilley muted the TV and we both turned to look at
each other.

"Now I know why Shepherd didn't come by last
night," I said.

"Yeah, because he was throwing another innocent
woman in jail!" Gilley threw the remote back on the
couch and stomped off to the kitchen. "What is *with* that
guy anyway? I mean, you know she didn't do it, right?"
he asked me.

"Of course she didn't do it!" I confirmed. I'd seen the
look on her face when I'd finally noticed Basayev's body,
and *no way* was that an act. "I can't even imagine what
that fool is thinking!" I added. "Shepherd has gone off the
deep end."

"And, meanwhile, the *real* killer is out there, somewhere, gloating," Gilley said, waving his hand toward the
front door.

I crossed my arms and stood up. Then I began to pace,
something I do when I'm supremely agitated. "Why
would Shepherd suspect Chanel?" I asked, not really in-
tending Gilley to answer.

He did anyway. "She was at the scene—which we
know from experience is the only thing he needs to make
an arrest, but more importantly to Shepherd, I think, is
that it was her listing, which meant she had access via the
code to the door."

"Yeah, but what's the motive? I mean, why would
Chanel kill her client? Especially if she had any suspicion
that Basayev was a mafia kingpin?"

Gilley looked up from the stove. "*Did* she know he
was a mafia kingpin?"

I shrugged. I had no idea, but then I thought of something and it gave me pause. "We suspect that the hit on Lenny was ordered by Basayev. What if Chanel murdered him out of revenge, and used us to cover it up?"

Gilley frowned. "Damn. That would make a good motive."

I felt disappointed too. Chanel had seemed so lovely. It felt wrong to believe her capable of murder. After thinking on it, however, I had to shake my head. "I'm not buying it, though."

"Me neither," Gilley said. "It just feels off."

"It does. Her reaction at the scene was genuine, Gil. I'm sure of it."

"But Shepherd wasn't there with us to see her reaction. Maybe he started grilling her and she cracked under the pressure and said something that made him think she did it."

I scowled. "He *is* insufferable. And I bet she doesn't even have anyone to represent her, the poor thing. She covered it well, but I suspect she's hurting financially."

"The purse, shoes, and car?" Gil asked. "All from past seasons . . . long ago?"

"You picked up on those too?"

"Please," Gil said. "What do you take me for? An amateur?"

I smiled. "I should know better."

"You should," he agreed. Then he got back to the topic at hand. "So, are we going to help Chanel?"

I moved over to the counter where my purse sat. Fishing through the contents, I lifted out my phone and held it up. "It's early, so I'll just leave a voice mail for Marcus and let him know I'm sending him a check for a retainer."

Gilley poked at the sautéing spinach. "You're a good woman, Catherine Cooper."

I dialed Marcus's number and was surprised when he answered. "Good morning, Catherine. What can I do for you?"

"Oh! Marcus," I said, giggling nervously. "I didn't think you'd pick up. It's quite early."

"Yes, which means there's trouble. What's happened?"

I filled him in on the details to the best of my ability. When I was done telling him about the night before and Chanel's arrest, I added, "I'd like to pay you to represent her, Marcus. And if bond has been set for her, I'd like to post that too."

"Are you sure you want to do that?" he asked me—and that surprised me.

"Pay for you to represent her? Or post her bond?"

"Both," he said simply. "This could get expensive."

I tapped the counter with my finger, thinking. . . . "Yes. I'm sure. She's innocent, Marcus. I *know* it."

"Good. I just wanted to make sure you were all in. Her bond hearing will probably be set for first thing this morning. I'll text you when and if her bond gets set. Meet me at the courthouse with your checkbook and we'll go from there."

Marcus hung up and I let out a sigh of relief. Gilley closed the oven door on the frittata and turned to me. "All good?"

"All good," I said with a satisfied smile.

Three hours later I got a text from Marcus. Chanel's bond was set at two hundred thousand dollars. "Yikes," Gilley said, peering over my shoulder to read the text.

"I only have to put up ten percent of that," I said, pointing to the next line in Marcus's text.

"Yeah, but still. Twenty grand isn't chump change."

"No, but if it'll keep an innocent woman out of jail, I'm willing to do it. Plus, I'll get it back once she's exonerated."

"Her attorney's fees could pile up too," Gilley said. "Cat, are you *sure* you want to do this?"

I sighed. "What's the alternative, Gilley? She doesn't strike me as someone who can afford an attorney, and her only listing is a crime scene. Her choices are probably to go with a public defender or represent herself, and neither of those two choices are likely to keep her out of jail."

"Okay, Cat," Gil said. "But before you retain Marcus for a lengthy murder trial, maybe hear him out for the evidence Shepherd has against her. I mean, there could be something we don't know about going on."

"That's a fair point, Gilley. And I will," I promised. "Now, are you coming with me to the courthouse? Or staying here?"

"I'm coming," Gil said eagerly.

We drove to the courthouse and met Marcus in the grand lobby. He pulled us aside to talk privately. "Shepherd's pulled the trigger early again," he said, and using air quotes, he added, "The 'evidence' against Ms. Downey is so circumstantial and so flimsy I'm surprised the judge didn't throw it out immediately."

"What *is* the evidence, Marcus?"

"A tube of lipstick used to write a message on the mirror at the house that had Ms. Downey's prints and DNA on it. It was discovered at the scene. Also the fact that she had access to the house and knew the victim's schedule."

"That's *it*?" Gilley asked.

"That's it," Marcus said, shaking his head like he couldn't believe it either.

My mind went to something else that I'd seen recovered the night before. "Was there any mention of a necklace, Marcus?"

"A necklace?"

"Yes. A gold necklace with a charm?"

"No," Marcus said. "Should there have been?"

"I saw the M.E. hand Shepherd a necklace with a charm on it, and Shepherd put it into an evidence bag. It made me think that maybe Mr. Basayev was either clutching it or it'd been near the victim when the M.E. examined him."

"Hmmm," Marcus said. "Interesting that I didn't see any reference to it. I'll make a point of asking the prosecution to list it in their exculpatory evidence. If it didn't belong to Ms. Downey, then we open the door for other suspects and reasonable doubt. Either way I should be able to get this case tossed out without a lot of effort."

I breathed a sigh of relief. "Good," I said. Then I handed Marcus two checks, one for his retainer and one for Chanel's bond. "How soon will she be released?"

Marcus took the checks. "I'll have her out by lunchtime. You two get on with your day, and I'll make sure to let her know that you're covering all the expenses. I'd expect a call of appreciation right around noon."

I smiled, and felt better about forking over so much money on behalf of a relative stranger. I was doing a good thing. The right thing, and it felt pretty darn great. "Excellent. Thank you, Marcus."

* * *

We left the courthouse and got into the car, with Gilley at the wheel. "Have we heard back from Willem?" I asked.

"Not a peep. I've left him half a dozen voice mails, but he's not responding."

I frowned. I was torn between letting Willem be or pestering him until he at least answered our call. What I couldn't really allow, however, was the thought that we'd put him in an even worse mindset than he'd been in when he'd so bravely reached out to me at the office. I had to convince him that the curse could be overcome, because in my heart, I simply refused to believe otherwise.

"Gil?"

"Yes?"

"Do we know where Willem lives?"

"You mean, can I obtain his address in two winks and a shake from a lamb's tail? Yes, Cat. Yes, I can."

"Good. Pull over and look up his address."

Gilley pulled into a doughnut shop parking lot, turning to me with a grin.

"It's like you planned that," I said with an eye roll.

"Sometimes, life just works out," he said, with a bounce of his brow.

"Fine. I'll get you a treat while you look up the address."

"Don't forget the sprinkles!" Gilley called as I got out of the car.

A few minutes later I was back with a coffee and chocolate-covered doughnut (with sprinkles) for Gil, and a hot tea for myself. "Did you find the address?"

"Does the Easter Bunny like eggs?"

I handed Gilley the doughnut. "How far away is he?"

Gilley had already taken a bite, and as his mouth was

full and I was looking at him like, *Don't you dare answer me with your mouth full and spray me with doughnut crumbs,* he opted to point to his left and splay out five fingers, twice.

"Ten minutes west of here. Good," I said. Then I pointed in that direction myself. "Tally-ho, my friend."

Almost exactly ten minutes later we arrived at the address Gilley had found for Willem. "Wow," Gil said, when we paused in front of the massive, castle-like structure. "That's some house!"

"Willem's granny is loaded," I said, impressed not just by the sheer size of the place, which was probably double the square footage of my own home, but also by the immaculate care of the grounds. It took serious money to maintain a home like that—I somewhat knew from experience.

"Shall we?" I asked, motioning toward the driveway.

"We shall," Gilley said.

We pulled into the drive and parked near the front door. As we got out and approached the door, it was opened by a woman in a crisp white suit with carefully coifed ash-blond hair and a chin held at a slightly haughty elevation. "*May* I help you?" she asked, stepping out onto the top step.

I adopted a friendly smile. "Hello," I said. "I'm Catherine Cooper and this is my associate, Gilley Gillespie. We're here to ask after Willem. Is he home?"

"What is it that you want with him, exactly?"

I couldn't quite figure out who this woman was, but she was clearly the home's gatekeeper. She stood in front of the door, guarding it with a thin frame but formidable attitude.

"Well," I said, turning to Gilley, who looked put on

the spot. "We want to make sure that he's all right, of course."

The woman's brow furrowed suspiciously. "Why wouldn't Mr. Entwistle be all right?"

"Because of the other day," I said. I was purposely holding back details, hoping the woman's suspicion would be over-ridden by her curiosity.

"Could you be more specific?" she asked, and there was an impatient cast to her posture.

"Well, there was an accident involving a hot air balloon, and Willem was quite affected by it. No one was hurt, thank goodness, but as his life coach I did want to check in and just make sure he wasn't still suffering adversely from the incident."

The woman blinked. Slowly. "His . . . *life* coach?"

It was my turn to hold my chin a little higher. "Yes. His life coach."

The woman looked me up and down, her eyes assessing, before her gaze drifted briefly to Gilley's car. A Lexus LS. We, and it, apparently passed the muster. "Come into the foyer, I'll see if he'll come talk to you."

We followed behind the woman through the door to an enormous open foyer that faced twin staircases. Above us was a dome ceiling and a fresco that could've been painted by one of the great Renaissance artisans.

And speaking of Renaissance artisans, a little deeper into the foyer was a lit painting, secured behind thick glass, that I swear was a Sandro Botticelli original (I minored in art history).

And if I was correct and that *was* a Botticelli, then Willem's granny didn't just have money. She had *power*.

As the gatekeeper began to walk away from us, I heard an elderly voice call out, "Who was at the door, Nancy?"

Nancy moved in the direction of the voice, disappearing into a room just behind the staircase. "It's two people here for Willem, ma'am," she said. I had no doubt she thought she was far enough away from us that we wouldn't be able to hear her, however, the acoustics in the circular foyer were so good that we could probably hear half the house from where we stood.

"Here for Willem?"

"Yes, ma'am."

"Who would be here for Willem?"

"A woman who claims to be his *life coach*, and her companion," Nancy said, the disdain for my profession leaking into her speech.

"His what?"

"Life coach."

"Willem has a life coach?"

"Perhaps. I'm going to check with him, but I'll also alert Anthony that he may need to escort the pair off the property."

"I want to meet this woman," the elderly voice said.

Gilley and I exchanged looks. No doubt the voice belonged to Willem's grandmother, and perhaps I could win her over and she could help convince Willem that he should give coming out with us another try.

"Are you sure, ma'am?" Nancy asked.

"Of course I'm sure. Now, be a dear and wheel me out to them."

Gilley and I straightened and out came Nancy, pushing a wheelchair that held a tiny woman. Not a dwarf like Willem, but tiny and frail all the same. I pegged her to be at least in her early to mideighties, dressed in a gorgeous green plaid tartan skirt with a black turtleneck, pearl earrings, and wispy white hair, wound in a bun at the top of her head. She grinned when she saw us. "Hello," she sang.

"Hello," Gilley said.

"Hello, ma'am," I said, dipping my head demurely.

"I'm Julia Entwistle," she said, as Nancy wheeled her to a stop in front of us. "Welcome to my home."

I bent forward and held out my hand to her. She grasped it in hers and I think she might've even tried to squeeze it a bit, but she was clearly frail and her touch remained light. "Lovely to meet you, Mrs. Entwistle. I'm Catherine Cooper, and this is my associate, Gilley Gillespie. We're here to see Willem."

"So I heard," she said. "Please tell me, when did my grandson get himself a life coach?"

"About a week ago, ma'am," I said. "Willem told me that he's taking your advice to heart and working up the courage to get out into the world, beginning with a visit to my office."

Julia's brow arched in surprise. "He went to your office?"

"Yes, he certainly did."

Her brow lowered. "What disaster struck while he was there?"

I'll admit that it was my turn to be surprised. And I was about to lie to her so as not to cause even more alarm, but then I thought that lying to her would only make her distrust me, and I couldn't have that.

"We had a tiny fire on the third floor of my office building. But it was truly nothing. Just a toaster that overheated."

"Uh huh," Julia said, with a knowing nod. "I figured. Anything else?"

I bit my lip. "There may have been a very minor incident involving a hot air balloon at the beach."

Julia barked out a laugh—a big sound coming from such a tiny woman. "You coaxed him to the beach?" she asked, almost as if she'd caught on to that tidbit after the fact.

"We did. Unfortunately, it wasn't for long. He'd practically just arrived when a hot air balloon ripped and came hurtling down toward us."

"Anyone hurt?"

"A few bumps and bruises but nothing serious."

Julia exhaled in relief. "And now you're here to talk him into going out again, I suppose?"

"We are," I said, almost feeling guilty about it.

"Good," she said. "Good." And then she patted Nancy's hand, which was still on the handle of the wheelchair, and said, "Nancy, if you would please fetch my grandson. Tell him I need to see him in the foyer."

"Yes, ma'am," Nancy said, not looking especially pleased that she was being asked to play fetch.

Once she'd walked off, Julia leaned forward and said, "Now, tell me everything!"

I laughed lightly. Julia was delightful, but there was no way I was breaching my client's trust. Even if it was her grandson.

"Mrs. Entwistle, I can only tell you that Willem has come to me seeking guidance on helping him get out into the world—something I know you encouraged him to do."

Julia frowned. "What was your name again?"

"Catherine. Catherine Cooper."

She brightened. "I know you! You were that woman they accused of murdering Heather Holland."

I could feel my cheeks redden, and my smile tightened. "I was completely exonerated."

Julia laughed. "Well, of course you were. I saw the aftermath of the coffee shop. Dreadful conclusion to the whole mess, wasn't it?"

"It was an especially difficult day," I admitted.

"Yes, yes. Well, it shows you have pluck. And, if you're going to help my grandson, you'll need a fair share of that."

It was my turn to frown. "Honestly, I find Willem to be a lovely young man."

"Isn't he though?" she said, and that's when I understood that she hadn't been talking about Willem's personality.

"So, you also believe in this curse? That it's real, I mean?" I asked.

"Certainly I do!" she said. "But then, I've known Willem his entire life. Do you know that when he first came to live here a sinkhole swallowed up my entire tennis court and the Olympic-sized swimming pool? And that was just that morning. In the afternoon a fierce windstorm blew in and knocked down a two-hundred-year-old oak tree right onto the west end of the house, causing major structural damage."

"Oh, my," I said.

Gilley audibly gulped. "Yikes," he whispered.

"Yikes is quite right. It was an absolutely dreadful day. But I loved my grandson more than I feared the curse attached to him, and I refused to send him back to that awful mother of his. So I stuck it out, and we were able to fill in the sinkhole and rebuild the tennis court and pool, and fix all the damage from the tree, and nothing else happened after that day, so I figured the curse had its limits. But for Willem, it's been a torturous life. Everywhere he goes something dreadful always seems to happen, so for the past fifteen years he's barely left the house.

"And none of this is his fault, mind you. His mother was the culprit, and if her son has to pay the price, then so be it as far as she's concerned. Another reason for me to rue the day *she* was born."

Wow, I thought. There was obviously no love lost between Julia and the other Mrs. Entwistle.

"The point is that I know from Willem the curse can be broken; you simply need to keep bringing it to new locations and let it exhaust itself."

"That's been our strategy," I admitted. "The hard part has been getting your grandson to cooperate."

Footsteps approached from the corridor where Nancy had ventured. Julia looked quickly over her shoulder, then back at me. "Not to worry. If we both gang up on him, I think we can get Willem to agree to another outing."

I was about to reply when Willem and Nancy appeared from the corridor. Willem paused slightly when he saw me, and his curious expression turned down in a frown.

I completely understood, of course, and I felt for him, but I was also there to help him, and he was a mission I wasn't about to give up on. "Hello, Willem," I said once he'd reached his grandmother's side.

"Ms. Cooper," he said with little to no warmth. "Gran, I see you've met my life coach."

Julia reached for and took her grandson's hand. "I have, my sweet boy, and I'm so proud of you!"

Willem seemed surprised. "Proud?"

"Yes, yes!" she said. "You took my advice but clearly felt the task was quite daunting, and turned to a professional to get the job done. You've made me immensely proud, and I sit in awe of your courage!"

I had to press my lips together to avoid the huge smile tugging at my lips. Julia wasn't going to strong-arm Willem into giving me and my method another go; she was going to charm him.

And to my relief, the technique seemed to be working. Willem blushed and dipped his chin. "Thank you," he said softly. "But you should know it's not going well."

"On the contrary!" she remarked. "I hear that you went to the beach again The *beach*, Willem! How many summers have we sat together at the pool and dreamed of you actually swimming in the ocean? Oh, I knew we should've stayed after that one dreadful attempt to go there. But your grandfather was the one driving and he wasn't having any of it that day. . . ."

Julia shook her head at the memory, but she wore a grin, as if it somehow delighted her.

Willem, however, was looking chagrined. "Did you hear about the balloon?"

Julia waved her hand dismissively. "No one was seriously injured now, were they?"

Willem looked to me, and I shook my head. "Just a few minor bumps and bruises, and a thrilling story to share with friends and family."

"But it could've been much worse," Willem insisted. "Gran, I'm a menace to society."

Julia patted his hand. "Nonsense! You're a lovely boy who's been afflicted by a curse I'm positive we can beat, Willem. We simply need to continue to stress it, tire it out, and allow it to release you."

"But what if it never grows tired?" Willem asked.

"If it never grows tired, you've still expanded your

world by venturing out into it and surviving whatever this nasty bit of magic can throw at you. After all, we survived your arrival and within a day the curse had calmed down and allowed you to live here peacefully all these years. I believe that it's already thrown the worst it can offer at you, and you're probably safe to venture back to the beach."

"And to my office," I added.

Beside me Gilley squeaked and subtly shook his head. I ignored both him *and* the urge to slap him.

Julia squeezed her grandson's hand. "I'm going to ask you to be brave again, my darling. I'm going to ask you to go on another adventure with Catherine and her associate, Mr. . . . ?"

"Gilley," Gil said with a smile. "No Mr. Just Gilley."

"Gilley," Julia repeated with a nod and a smile to Gil before turning back to her grandson. "They'll look out for you, and afterward, you'll have one more place that will expand your world."

Willem turned almost hopeful eyes to me, and I nodded encouragingly.

"Please, Willem?" I said. "It would mean a great deal to me if you'd trust us and allow us to help you."

Willem seemed to consider that for a moment, and I thought it was interesting that he never once looked to Nancy for her opinion or encouragement, and given the skeptical scowl on the woman's face, it was easy to see where she came down on the idea.

"Where would we go?" Willem asked softly.

I looked at Gilley, hoping he'd done his homework and could suggest a safe spot. He didn't let me down. "How about a farm?" he said.

Willem brightened. "A farm?"

"Yeah," Gil said. "There's a small family farm in Amagansett that raises alpacas, sells seasonal fruits and vegetables, and has a lovely country store of alpaca wool products. I've seen all the photos and the farm is big, open, and no hot air balloons in sight." Gilley added a smile to that last part.

Willem grinned too. I think it was the first time I'd seen the man smile, and it was glorious. "All right," he said. "But if anything terrible happens—"

"You'll come home, spend a day feeling miserable, and then go right back out into that world, Willem," said his grandmother. "The only way to break this curse is to drive it nuts before it does the same to you."

And that, it appeared, was that.

Chapter 14

"You're sure about this alpaca farm?" I asked Gilley as we walked out into the daylight again.

"It seemed the safest place for him besides the beach," Gil replied.

"Are alpacas dangerous?"

"Are you kidding?" he asked me, then read my expression. "You're not kidding. Okay, so, alpacas are adorable, Cat. They're basically big, fluffy Muppets."

"How big?"

Gil held his hand above his head at almost full extension. "The biggest are about yea high."

My eyes widened. "That's tall."

Gilley lowered his hand to his waist. "You only think that because you're this tall."

"Short jokes? Really?" I said. "I'll remind you, Gilley

Gillespie, that on the topic of below average height, you'd be living in a house made almost entirely of glass."

Gilley chuckled good naturedly. "Speaking of glass houses, we'll be driving right by Basayev's house on our way to the farm today."

"We will?"

"Yep. The alpaca farm and the murder house are basically neighbors."

"Huh," I said. "I don't remember any barnyard smells when we were there."

"You were too distracted by the dead guy on the floor."

"Indeed," I agreed. And then I glanced at my watch. "Chanel should be released at any moment."

"I still can't believe Shepherd arrested her."

"I can," I said, and the thought infuriated me. But it also frustrated me too. Shepherd could be an impulsive horse's ass. But there was a side of him, hidden behind the shield of defensiveness he put out to the rest of the world, that was good, and decent, and earnest, and surprisingly charming. The mix was dichotomous, both annoying and alluring. Sometimes, I didn't know if I was angry with Shepherd or angry with myself for being so invested and interested in him.

With a sigh I said, "I wonder how long Willem will be."

"He said he needed to change," Gil reminded me. "From what I've seen of him, Willem's a dapper dresser. It'll take him a bit."

I looked down at myself. I was hardly dressed to visit an alpaca farm, but at least I was wearing boots and black pants that were easily sent to the dry cleaners should any dirt, hay, fur, or dust settle into the fabric.

Gilley was better dressed in jeans and a gorgeous butter-soft black leather jacket, with a gray and burgundy plaid scarf. I touched his sleeve. "You look rather dapper your-self, my friend."

Gilley beamed "Thanks for noticing."

Finally, Willem appeared. He wore jeans as well, with a thick army-green sweater, and black boots. He was such a handsome man overall, with a striking face and a sin-cere expression. His size was definitely the first thing you noticed about him, however, it was also the first thing you forgot once you got to know him. And I genuinely liked him. He simply gave off a lovely, inquisitive, easily accessible vibe. I wanted very much to help break him out of this self-imposed prison, because he was the kind of man who should have lots of friends and be having lots of adventures.

Stopping in front of our car, he said, "Would you mind if we took my car? I tend to get motion sick if I'm not driving."

"Of course," I said immediately, but Gilley cocked an eyebrow, and I refused to acknowledge the somewhat shameful concern I knew we both had about how Willem would manage not just reaching the pedals, but seeing above the steering wheel.

Willem smiled, and a little of the worry I'd seen in his eyes when he first appeared relaxed. "Thank you. My car is over here."

We followed behind him around the corner of the house to a six-bay garage. Willem pulled out a small re-mote and one of the bay doors lifted, revealing a silver-blue Range Rover that sparkled with shine.

"Nice," Gilley said, nodding in approval.

Willem grinned. "It's supercharged. I had it delivered yesterday, so this is a good excuse to break it in."

Now I understood why Willem had somewhat easily

given in to our suggestion for another excursion. He was itching to drive his new toy.

"You're into cars?" Gilley asked.

In answer, Willem pulled out his remote again and tapped it a few more times. All of the bay doors began to open, revealing a dazzling range of vehicles, two per bay. Several of them were vintage. All of them sparkled as if they'd just come off the showroom floor.

And, I'm no car expert, but I would've appraised the value of Willem's car collection to be somewhere in the low millions.

"Impressive," I said.

Willem beamed again. But then his expression turned sad. "I can't really drive them anywhere. Mostly just around the grounds, but they're still my passion."

I looked at him sincerely and said, "Willem, I'm going to make it my mission to help you crack this curse so that you can take any one of these cars out anytime you want."

Willem pressed his lips together, in a doubtful grimace that belied his reply. "That would be really nice, Catherine."

"Shall we?" I asked.

We approached the car and I immediately got into the backseat, motioning to Gilley to sit up front. "You know the way," I said to him. "Help navigate, would you?"

"Of course," Gilley said eagerly. Whenever there was more than just the two of us, Gil always seemed to relegate himself to the backseat, so this was a nice treat for him.

We set off and what I noticed immediately was that Willem had obviously had the Range Rover fit with a custom seat and pedals adjusted for his specific height. And I will admit to breathing a tiny sigh of relief.

While Gilley and Willem chatted amiably, I enjoyed the passing scenery. Even though the day was overcast, and a hint of rain was in the air, it was still a nice, mild day, and signs of spring were everywhere.

As we neared the ocean, the wind picked up. Gilley looked over his shoulder at me and said, "Did you hear about the big storm coming to our shores?"

"No," I said, feeling a touch of foreboding. "How big and when?"

"Big. Like, nor'easter big. And it'll be here the day after tomorrow."

I winced. The boys were set to head off on their spring break vacation with their father the next morning, and I hoped they didn't encounter any weather issues. They'd all be flying out of LaGuardia. I'd have to start paying attention to the weather.

While I was worrying over impending storms, Willem said, "Did you hear that a man was murdered up there?"

I looked up and realized he was pointing to the road leading up to Basayev's home. There was still a Bennett and Bennett for sale sign out front too.

"Would you believe we were the ones who found the body?" Gilley said to Willem.

Willem stared at Gilley in shock. "No!"

"Yes," Gilley replied. And then he proceeded to tell Willem all about the harrowing ordeal—leaving out the components about Basayev being a mafia kingpin, and us posing as buyers to try and get information out of Lenny Shepherd's old partner that could've helped us nail Basayev for the murder.

"Whoa," Willem said, when Gilley had finished (rather smugly, I might add). "That's insane!"

"Yeah, but would you also believe that it wasn't even

worthy of making it onto my honorable mentions for some of the craziest stuff that I've seen?"

Willem's eyes widened again. "What else have you seen?"

For the next ten minutes, Gilley gave Willem a short list of the crazy, weird, disturbing, deadly, but above all, terrifying things he'd encountered when he was a ghost-buster touring the world with M.J. and Heath for their cable ghostbusting TV show.

Of course, I'd heard all the stories before, but every time Gilley told someone about his "honorable mentions" I could feel the hair rise along my neck and arms.

Willem was so impressed that by the end of Gilley's list of horrors, all he could do was stare at Gilley with mouth agape. "Good God, man," Willem whispered. "I had no idea you've lived such an *amazing* life!"

Gilley puffed himself up in his seat, so pleased I thought he might float out the window. "It's been inter-esting," he said. I smirked, but was pleasantly pleased that Willem and Gilley were getting on so well. A little bromance would be good for the two of them—especially since Michel had been away so much of late, and I worried that Gilley was lonelier than he was letting on.

We arrived at the alpaca farm just a short time later. Willem parked and we got out and approached a little booth set up at the front gate. The booth had a call button, which I depressed, and within a few seconds a woman's voice came through the speaker. "Yes?"

"Hello. We're here to walk the grounds and pet the al-pacas," Gilley said.

"Great!" she said merrily. "I'll be right down to let you in."

We waited by the gate, and peering through it we

could see a large herd of what looked like a cross between a dog and a long-necked goat. Within a few moments, a woman emerged from the barn, waved to us, and moved over to a four-wheeler. She came down to the gate by way of a dirt road, and after dismounting from the four-wheeler, ambled over to meet us.

Dressed in a green and blue flannel shirt, jeans, and riding boots, she wore her silver hair short, and there were laugh lines and crinkles at the corners of her eyes. It told me she spent a majority of her time either smiling or laughing, and that made me instantly like her.

"Well, hello!" she said, as she came to the gate with a key for the padlock. "I'm Audra. Welcome to Paccadilly Farms!"

We were all charmed by her bright disposition—well, at least Gilley and I were. Willem wore a forced smile and I noticed that he'd occasionally lick his lips nervously. I could also see that he was trembling ever so slightly.

He'd been so brave on the drive over, but I suspected now that he was here and faced with another possible incident from the curse, he was worried about what harm might come of it.

But, looking around at the wide open setting, and the adorable creatures at the end of the paddock, it was hard to imagine that any harm could be done.

Still, as I walked through the gate, I *did* keep an eye on the barn, making sure there were no signs of smoke to be had.

"Shall we meet the herd?" Audra asked.

Gilley nodded earnestly, and even Willem seemed to relax a bit at the mention of getting to pet these exotic creatures.

As we walked toward the herd, Audra gave us an education on alpacas. "I've had this herd for about fifteen years, and we started out with Studly, over there in the paddock across from the barn."

I looked and saw a much smaller group of alpacas curious about our arrival, pressing against the bars of their paddock adjoining the one we were in. "He's with all the other males," Audra said. "You've gotta keep the boys and the girls apart, otherwise it's just an ongoing orgy and the parents get upset. Of course the kids are delighted and they giggle and laugh, but in the Hamptons it's like the natural order of things is unseemly or something." Audra added a shake of her head.

Gilley and I chuckled and the tension in Willem's smile eased.

"Now, we're coming up on shearing season," she continued. "The herd's a little long in the coat, as you can tell, and we're going to be taking off their winter coats next weekend—unless that storm roars in and blows my plans to pieces with it. There's nothing worse than trying to shear a soggy alpaca, take it from me."

I smiled again. I genuinely liked this woman.

"Anyway, you're free to pet and cuddle them. They're a really friendly bunch, and most of my females are pregnant right now, so they're happy just to lay around and get fat."

As we got closer I couldn't help but ask, "Do they ever bite?"

Audra shook her head. "They're incapable of it. They only have bottom teeth and a hard pallet up top. You're more likely to get nuzzled by them than anything else. They like people and they're very personable."

Audra then looked down at my feet, where I was also looking, to make sure I didn't step on any "land mines."

"No need to watch yourself," she said. When I eyed her curiously, she added, "Alpacas have a communal dung hill. See that mound way over there?" she said.

I looked and there indeed was a big pile of poo.

"That's the community toilet. We sell the poop for a pretty penny around here. People love to use alpaca waste as fertilizer because they get less weeds in their gardens. It's great stuff."

By now we were close to the herd and I slowed my gait. It wasn't that I was necessarily afraid of them, but they were larger up close than I'd thought, and that made me a teensy bit wary.

Gilley and Willem, however, held no such reservations. They stepped forward and were quickly surrounded by white, gray, black, and rosy brown fluffy Muppet creatures.

Willem was sent to giggling delightedly when several alpacas began nuzzling his shirt, probably looking for treats.

Audra moved over to Willem and offered him a small baggie that had an assortment of apples, carrots, and broccoli stalks in it. "There," she said. "Feed them that."

Willem took the baggie and began to dole out the treats. His expression made my heart swell and tears glisten my eyes. His face was filled with wonder and delight, and I was both thrilled for him and heartbroken for this man who'd lived most of his adult life shut away in a big house with no access to simple but wonderful experiences like this.

Gilley caught my eye just then, and he nodded. We'd done a good thing bringing Willem here.

We spent about twenty minutes mingling with the herd, and I found them to be a bit magical myself. Their coats were incredibly soft and plush, and they had a split lip that kept trying to part the buttons on my shirt. It was impossible to stand amid a herd like this and be in a bad mood.

Audra disappeared at one point, but soon she reappeared with more treats for us to share with the herd. After handing a treat bag to Gilley, and one to me, she said, "Let me know when you'd like to see the store. I've got a sale on all my winter sweaters right now. All sizes, all colors."

I perked up and handed Gilley my baggie. I was always in the market for clothing for the boys, who were growing at a rapid rate. "Any in navy blue?" I asked. The boys were only allowed to wear navy blue sweaters on their campus as their uniform code was strictly enforced.

"A bunch," she said. "This way."

I began following behind Audra, listening to the sounds of Gilley's delighted giggles, which sent me giggling as well. Gil has the most infectious laugh.

I also allowed myself a small sigh of relief. So far, nothing bad had happened and there wasn't even a hint of disaster in the air.

Of course, that was the moment that all hell broke loose.

As we neared the building that was marked "Paccadilly Store," there was a screeching of tires, and out on the road a car with what appeared to be a distracted driver overcorrected and launched itself directly into the corner of fencing for both paddocks. As Audra and I stared in stunned silence, the car came to a stop just inside the female alpacas' enclosure, sending the herd nervously in circles around Gilley and Willem.

I realized that I'd reflexively reached out to grab Audra's arm, but as the car door opened and a man got out who seemed no worse for wear, I let out the small breath I'd been holding. "Oh, thank God," I whispered. "He's all right."

But Audra hardly seemed relieved. Her gaze went from him over to the gaping hole between the two enclosures and the smaller herd of males who were moving toward it with increasing speed. "Oh, *shit!*" she exclaimed.

Before we knew it a dozen male alpacas were streaming into the enclosure with the females, who were now even more animated by the appearance of the males, and Gilley and Willem were stuck within their midst being bumped and pushed around.

Audra's hand went to her forehead; it was as if she didn't quite know what to do. And then I saw her look toward her four-wheeler and she began to run toward it.

Meanwhile the first of the male alpacas had reached the females, and he began to try to mount anything that moved. Some of the females immediately laid down, but several more simply began spitting.

"Gilley! Willem!" I yelled. "Get out of there!"

But they were surrounded and there was a flurry of chaotic movement as they both did their best to fight their way out of what was quickly becoming an alpaca orgy. Several males lay down next to the females and they began to go to town, while other males clung to the backs of the spitting and spinning females and little alpacas simply tried to move out of the way.

Willem managed at that point to break free, and he

came dashing toward me as fast as his small legs could carry him. I was torn between trying to help him to safety outside the paddock or going in for Gilley, who was totally overwhelmed.

Willem was closer to me, and with a growl I climbed up on the paddock's poles and reached out for his hand. He grabbed on and I pulled as hard as I could, getting him up and over to safety.

I then looked for Gilley, hearing him begin to shriek, and saw that one of the male alpacas had become *very* excited and was propped up on Gilley's back. "Get him off me! Get him off me!" Gilley shrieked.

He darted forward trying to lose the alpaca, only to run right into a female who then spit into his face, covering Gilley with chunks of the treats he'd been offering her only moments before. "Oh, my God!" I shouted. "Gilley!"

But poor Gil was apparently blinded, and he covered his eyes and simply stumbled this way and that, still trying to shake the determined male alpaca on his back.

I watched the whole thing in horror, not knowing what to do. If I went into that pen, I didn't know if I could get out, and just when I was seriously considering it because I couldn't stand to see Gilley in such distress, Audra appeared on her four-wheeler, charging into the fray, scattering many of her alpacas to save Gilley.

With strength and agility that belied her appearance, Audra reached down, grabbed Gilley by the back of the collar, and hauled him into the seat next to her. She then gunned the engine and roared over to us.

I got up on the paddock poles again, reached down to help Gilley, who was still shouting, "I'm blind! I'm blind!" over the railing. He landed with a thud on the ground and promptly lay down on his back. "And I've been *defiled*!"

Audra looked at Willem and said, "In the barn! Get me all of the harnesses on the pegboard!" She then hit the gas and shot out toward the herd.

Willem took off toward the barn while I crouched down beside Gilley, digging through my purse to pull out a small packet of tissue and a bottle of water that I always carry with me. Carefully, I wiped away the mess on his face and gently poured the water around his eyes. Gilley blinked and took up the tissue to help remove the rest of the sticky mess.

Meanwhile, Audra was racing around the paddock, shooing some of the males away from the females. Willem came out of the barn, loaded down with harnesses, and he raced over to the fencing and began to climb up the poles. I almost moved to help him, but he managed to get up and over, in spite of the short length of his legs, and then he was off racing again toward Audra.

Once he reached her she grabbed a few of the harnesses, pointed to several of the male alpacas, and mimed how to put on the harness. She then pointed to a section of fence, and I understood that they were going to round up all the males and tie them to the fence until Audra could attend to the broken section near the road.

I got close to Gilley, handed him the water, and said, "I'm going to go help Willem and Audra. Will you be okay here?"

"I've already been defiled, Cat, what else could possibly happen to me?"

I bit my lip, as Gilley blinked his bloodshot eyes and poured more water on his face. "Wait," he said. "Don't answer that. Just go help them."

It took us about twenty minutes to round up all the alpacas and get the females into a third, much smaller paddock, and the males into the barn.

Once Audra had locked the males in, the sound of their distress calls filled the air. "They hate being locked up like that," she said, brushing off the dust and grime that'd been kicked up as we all raced around to corral the herd. "Nothing I can do about it at the moment. My boys don't get back from their jobs until six, and that'll be the soonest I can get that fence fixed."

Out on the road, a tow truck had appeared, along with a patrol officer. He came up through the paddock and met with Audra while Willem and I made our way over to Gilley, who was seated against the fence post. I squatted down next to him. "Hey," I said, brushing some of his tousled hair to the side. "How're you doing?"

Gilley made a sweeping motion down his front. "How do I *look* like I'm doing?"

Willem came to stand next to Gilley too. I was shocked to see actual tears in his eyes. "This is all my fault," he whispered.

Gilley's face fell and his anger instantly dissipated. "It's not," he said. "Willem, it's not."

Willem looked toward the road, and the car that was being hoisted onto the tow truck. "That's not a fluke," he said, pointing to the gaping hole in the fence. "That's the curse."

I stood up and reached out for Willem's hand. "Hey," I said, struggling to find any kind of a silver lining or even an encouraging word to say. The afternoon had started off so beautifully—and ended in chaos and disaster. Still, no one had been hurt. Well, Gilley's ego might've suffered a severe blow, but he'd recover. I decided to lead with that.

"So we got a few bumps and bruises, Willem. We're all okay, and even the driver's okay. No alpacas were hurt—"

Gilley interrupted with a bark of laughter. "*They* had a good time, I assure you. That one over there even looks like she could use a cigarette."

We looked over at the dopey-eyed female who I *swear to God* was wearing a postcoitus grin the size of Texas.

And that made me giggle. And then I began to laugh. And then I couldn't stop laughing. And soon, Willem also began to laugh, and finally, Gilley joined in too.

So we left the farm a little worse for wear, but having survived yet another encounter with Willem's curse.

Which was what I call progress.

Later, when Gilley and I arrived back at Chez Cat, I invited him over for dinner and the use of my master bath to get the lingering scent of horny alpaca off him.

Gilley has long admired my master bathroom, with its immense shower stall, eight shower heads, and adjoining sauna.

Meanwhile, I used one of the other six bathrooms to quickly clean up and change. Then I headed into the kitchen and began to prepare a meal for us.

I decided that one of my favorite pasta recipes was called for—Gilley definitely needed some comfort food after his tryst with Mr. Studly, the poor dear. And while I prepared it I thought about Willem and wondered if it was wise to continue to push the boundaries of this curse.

With that in mind I placed a call to Heath. I was quite relieved when he picked up the call. "Cat?" he said. "How are you?"

"I'm good, Heath, thank you, but I do have quite a lot to share with you. Do you have a moment?"

Over the course of the next twenty minutes, while I prepared a delicious, decadent sauce for the pasta, made with bourbon, cream, Baileys, and Kahlúa, served over al-dente linguini with chicken and sweet English peas, I explained everything that'd happened to us since Willem became my client.

Heath did a fairly good job stifling his laughter when I described what'd happened to Gilley that afternoon, but he grew serious when I begged the question, "Is it safe to continue to push Willem to go out into the world? I mean, am I putting anyone's life at risk?"

"That's a very good question, Cat, and, unfortunately, it's not one that I can easily answer. The energy I picked up around Willem didn't feel deadly, *but* it did feel deter-mined. It wants to cause mayhem, and it may, and I do mean *may* want some sort of a sacrifice to satisfy its appetite."

I felt my blood run cold. "Sacrifice? You mean . . . like *human* sacrifice?"

Heath sighed. "Maybe."

I gulped. "Well, it's not getting one!" I said defiantly. But then I tried to reason with Heath's assessment. "If it'd wanted a human sacrifice, Heath, wouldn't it have gotten one by now? I mean, Willem is in his midthirties, and although he almost never leaves his home, he still *has* ventured out, to school, and his grandmother's home, and my office. And no one was seriously injured in any of those instances."

"I hear you, Cat, but I feel it's still necessary to warn you that just because the curse didn't *feel* powerful to me, doesn't mean it can't, at times, be quite powerful. Enough to cause some real damage. So all I'm saying is . . . tread lightly."

I paused the stirring of the bubbling sauce I was making to stare out into space, and the memory of Willem's delighted face as he reached out to pet the alpacas for the first time was all I could see in my mind's eye. "I don't want to stop trying to help him," I whispered.

"Then don't," Heath said. "Hell, M.J. and I have tackled far more destructive curses in our time, and we survived. Even Gilley came through those scenarios intact."

And that gave me courage.

I thanked Heath, hung up, and got back to cooking. Right around the time Gilley appeared looking flushed with heat but very relaxed in my extra fluffy white bathrobe, I glanced at my watch and realized something. "Huh," I said.

"What?"

"Well, it's almost seven, and I never heard from Chanel."

"Did you check your phone? Maybe there's a voice mail."

I lifted the phone and checked all the calls, smirking when I saw two missed calls from Shepherd. "Can you believe Shepherd called me?" I said. "Twice!"

"He probably just wanted to yell at you for springing his number one suspect."

I rolled my eyes. "Of course that's what he wanted. So glad I didn't give him the satisfaction of picking up the line. Meanwhile, there isn't a single missed call, text, or voice mail from Chanel."

"Maybe she needed to go home and take a nap," Gilley suggested. "I doubt she slept at all in that jail cell."

"Good point. I'll bet that's exactly it."

Still, something bothered me about the fact that Chanel hadn't even sent me a text to say thank you. . . . After all, I'd bailed her out of jail and I'd gotten her the best attorney money could buy.

With that in mind I set Gilley's plate in front of him (waiting for him to take a bite, moan appreciatively, and give me a twin thumbs-up) before I placed a call to Marcus.

"Catherine," Marcus said before I'd heard the phone even ring. "How is my favorite client this evening?"

I laughed and could feel a blush touch my cheeks. "Your favorite, huh? I bet you say that to all your clients."

"Only the ones who fork over such generous retainers. To what do I owe the pleasure of your call?"

"Well, I just want to double check and make sure that Chanel was processed out of jail without any issues."

There was a slight hesitation on the other end of the call. "Yes. She was processed out this morning at eleven-thirty. I personally arranged for her car to be released from the tow lot and gave her cab fare to get there. Didn't she tell you all that when she called you?"

It was my turn to be silent for a moment. "No, Marcus. She never called me."

There was another pause, then, "I'm sorry for the confusion, but I had a lengthy conversation with Ms. Downey and told her all about your generosity. She was anxious to call and thank you. I personally texted her your contact information."

I felt a chill run through me. "Marcus . . . you don't think something's happened to her, do you?"

He blew out a heavy sigh. "I hope not. The lot would be closed right now, but I'll call them first thing in the morning to see if she picked up her car."

I hung up the phone and stared at Gilley. "Something bad has happened to Chanel, hasn't it?" he said.

"I don't know, Gilley. But Marcus insisted that she was anxious to call me, and she never did."

"Did he give her the right phone number?"

"He says he texted her my contact info, which means he probably just shared it with her, so it all would've been accurate."

I began to pace the kitchen, wondering what might've happened to her. And then I had an idea. Sorting through my phone, I found the number I'd called in Connecticut for Chanel's grandaunt, and tried it again.

It rang twice and was picked up. "Hello?" said a male voice.

I was so surprised by the male voice on the other end of the call that I was thrown into a confused silence. And then my brain began to work again, and I was about to speak when the voice said, "Hello? Who's calling?"

My brow furrowed. *"Shepherd?"* I said.

"Catherine?" he replied.

"What are you doing answering Miranda Downey's phone?"

"What're *you* doing calling it?"

In the background I heard several other voices. It almost sounded like there was a party going on. "I'm . . . I'm looking for Chanel."

"So am I!" he barked. "No thanks to *you,* I might add."

"What's that supposed to mean?" I snapped. I'd had quite enough of Shepherd's flinty attitude of late.

"It means . . ." Shepherd's voice trailed off with a sigh. "Listen, I need to talk to you, but I'm gonna be late here. Any chance you'll be up around midnight?"

"Are you kidding?" He wanted to talk to me at midnight? What the heck was going on?

"No. I'm not kidding. It might even be later, Catherine, but I'll try and get there by then."

"Wait, you're coming over?"

"I have to talk to you," Shepherd insisted, and I realized that he'd lowered his voice and the sounds in the background weren't nearly as distinct anymore. "It's important."

I shook my head, and Gilley was looking at me oddly, but I finally offered him an exasperated sigh. "Fine," I said. "I'm at the main house. I'll try and wait up for you."

"Take a nap," he said. "I'll text you when I'm outside your door."

I could tell that he was about to hang up, so I called out to him and asked, "Wait! Steve, just answer me this: where is Miranda and why is she letting you answer her phone?"

"Miranda's dead, Catherine. She's been murdered."

Chapter 15

I sat at the counter while Gilley fussed over me. "Here, Cat, drink this."

I stared down with little interest at the cup of tea he'd made me. Still, I lifted it into my hands and felt the warmth from the mug breathe a little life into my cold fingers, and that sort of brought me out of the deep mental rabbit hole I'd traveled down.

"Ready to talk about it?" Gilley asked.

I took an unsteady sip of the tea. It was a little sweeter than I was expecting, but it helped. "Chanel's grandaunt is dead. She's been . . . murdered."

Gilley sucked in a breath. "No!"

I nodded.

Gilley took up the chair next to me, pushing his dinner plate to the side. "How?" he asked.

"I don't know. That's all Shepherd would say."

"Chanel . . . ?" Gilley said.

I shook my head. "He didn't say if she was there or not, but I suspect she is. He probably heard about Miranda's murder and hightailed it over to New Canaan, thinking Chanel had something to do with it, knowing him."

Gilley frowned. "That girl wouldn't hurt a fly, much less her grandauntie!"

"I know, Gil, but it *is* Shepherd we're talking about. Arresting people for things they had no hand in is his calling card."

"But he's coming here? Tonight?"

"Yes. But not until around midnight. He's in Connecticut, so he's at least two and a half hours away."

Gil eyed the clock. It was quarter to eight. "He's not coming here to arrest you, is he?"

I smirked. "Let's hope not, but make sure you have Marcus's info handy, just in case."

Gilley reached out and rubbed my arm. "Do you want me to stay here tonight?"

I sighed wearily. I felt like all the air had been let out of me. "No, lovey. I think we both need a little rest, and if we're together we'll just chat each other into exhaustion. You head to Chez Kitty. I'll clean up here, then get a few hours of sleep before Shepherd shows up."

Gilley popped off the bar stool. "You cooked, I'll clean up," he said, then promptly set about fussing in the kitchen. Before storing the leftover pasta, he heated a small plate of it for me and set it in front of me. "I know you're not hungry, but this was too good not to sample, sugar," he said.

I smiled and gamely swirled some pasta around my

fork while moody thoughts tumbled inside my head like hyperactive children.

At around nine Gilley left me tucked into an afghan on the sofa in the family room off the kitchen. I fell almost immediately to sleep, but was awakened just a short time later by loud knocking.

Bolting upright, I shook my head to clear it and padded to the door to peer into the peephole. Shepherd stood on my front step, looking much worse for wear.

"You got here sooner than I expected," I said.

Shepherd's brow furrowed. "It's quarter past midnight," he said. "I'm fifteen minutes late."

My eyes widened and I looked to my wrist, but I'd already taken off my watch. "It's after midnight?" It felt like I'd only closed my eyes and he'd knocked.

"Can I come in?" he asked, and I realized he was still standing on my front step. Behind him a drizzling rain had begun and it was a cold night.

"Yes, I'm sorry," I said, stepping out of the way. We walked through the foyer, me leading the way to the kitchen. "Did you want some coffee? Or tea?"

"Do you have anything decaffeinated? And I'd prefer tea if you have it."

"I do. I'll make you a cup."

Shepherd sat at the counter and we didn't speak while I turned on the stove and got a cup and tea bag ready. And then I had another thought and went to the fridge, removing the Tupperware of leftover pasta. I heated Shepherd up a plate of that in the microwave, and both his dinner and the tea were ready at the same time.

Without a word I set him a place at the counter, and offered him the food and drink.

He closed his eyes for a moment and inhaled the aroma of the pasta. "Damn, that smells good."

I came around to sit next to him. "I figure that if I feed you, you're less likely to arrest me."

Shepherd took a bite of pasta, closing his eyes again with pleasure. "Why would I arrest you?"

"Isn't that what you *do*, Detective? You arrest people who're obviously innocent all the time."

"Are you referring to yourself, or Chanel?" he asked, without looking at me while he tucked into more pasta.

"Both."

Shepherd chewed thoughtfully, took a sip of his tea, and said, "You really do have a way of throwing a monkey wrench into things, don't you?"

"*Me?* What did *I* do?"

"You set Chanel Downcy free."

I threw my hands up in exasperation. *"She didn't do it!"*

"Of course she didn't," he said softly.

I blinked. "Wait. What?"

"I know she didn't murder Basayev."

"Then why'd you arrest her?"

"To keep her safe."

"From who?"

"Don't you mean *whom*?"

"Don't even *think* about playing coy with me, Detective. It's after midnight, I've had quite the day, and I'm willing to entertain this late-night chat only so far."

Shepherd nodded with a sigh, but then he polished off the final bite of pasta, wiped his mouth, and pushed his plate away. Turning to me, he said, "The biggest crime boss this side of Manhattan is murdered in his love nest, and all the evidence points to his real estate agent. If I hadn't arrested her, she would've been dead before yesterday morning."

I put a hand to my mouth. "Oh, my God . . . I hadn't thought of that."

"I know. And instead of coming to me for an explanation, you send your slick city lawyer over to get her bonded out of the isolation cell I'd personally put her in. And now she's gone."

I felt the blood drain from my face, and then I felt dizzy and light-headed. "She's . . . she's . . . *dead*?"

"What? No. She's not dead. At least, not that I know of. She's gone off-grid, and now that her grandaunt is dead, I have no way of tracking her down."

"Who murdered Miranda?" I asked next.

Shepherd shook his head. "Don't know. She was killed with a single shot to the forehead, so someone got up close and personal. They murdered her and set her dogs free, which is how the New Canaan P.D. discovered her. A neighbor captured all four dogs and put a note on Miranda's door that she'd found them roaming the neighborhood—apparently this is a pretty common thing. The dogs are escape artists, according to the neighbor.

"Anyway, when Miranda didn't come over to retrieve the dogs, the neighbor got worried. She sent a text to Chanel, but then Chanel never showed up—"

"Because you'd arrested her," I interrupted.

Shepherd dipped his chin in acknowledgment and continued. "And when she couldn't get ahold of Chanel, the neighbor called police to do a wellness check on Miranda."

"How did you get involved?" I asked, thinking it was odd for the New Canaan police to reach out to Shepherd.

"I arrived just after they discovered the body. I was

headed there to see if Chanel was hiding out at the only relative she has close by."

"So who killed Miranda? Someone looking for revenge against Chanel for killing Basayev?"

Shepherd shook his head. "That's the part that's creepy," he said. "Miranda was murdered at least seventy-two hours ago. Well before Basayev."

Again the blood drained from my face. I'd called Miranda just about three nights ago. There'd been a knock at the door when I'd called. Had that been . . . the killer?

"Where . . . where was her body found?" I asked.

"Front hall," Shepherd said, stifling a yawn. He was so tired he didn't seem to notice my distress. "Right in front of the door. It's like she answered the door, took one step back, then blamo. Lights out. Poor old woman never had a chance."

I looked at Shepherd, wondering if I should tell him, and decided I probably needed to. "I called Miranda three days ago. She and I chatted for only a moment before she said she had to go because someone was knocking on her door."

It was Shepherd's turn to stare at me in shock. "What time?"

"It was around ten in the morning."

He nodded. "That fits with the timeline. Did she say anything about who was at the door? Or even give you any kind of a description?"

"No. She simply said to call her back because she had to answer the door."

"Damn," Shepherd said. "I'd really like to know who'd kill an old woman in cold blood like that."

"Do you think her murder could in some way be connected to Chanel?"

"I want to say that it's a random fluke, a robbery gone wrong, but my gut says that somebody came looking for Chanel and shot Miranda so there wouldn't be any witnesses."

I shuddered. It was all so cold blooded.

Shepherd then seemed to focus on me. "Hey, what were you doing calling Miranda Downey anyway? And for that matter, what were you doing touring Boris Basayev's house when I know for a fact that you're not looking to move out of this place?"

I squared my shoulders, putting up a little bravado in the face of being called out for my investigative shenanigans. "How do you know I'm not thinking of moving? Maybe I'd like a change of scenery."

Shepherd dipped his chin to look at me with half-lidded eyes. He wasn't buying it.

I sighed and dropped the bravado. "Fine. I called Miranda looking for Chanel. I learned that she was Lenny's partner, and I wanted to talk to her about the clients she passed on to Sara Beth Sullivan."

Shepherd cocked his head. "Sara Beth Sullivan? What's she or Chanel's clients got to do with anything?"

"The clients in question were Jason and Paul Sutton."

Shepherd's face lit with recognition. "I'm listening."

"Gilley and I did a little snooping, and we discovered that the house where Lenny was murdered had been listed for *considerably* more than it eventually sold for. After Lenny was murdered, the price dropped in half. The people who bought that house were the Suttons, and they paid cash."

Shepherd scratched his head. He looked like he was trying to keep up, but was having trouble. So I backed up a bit. "Gil and I formed a theory," I said. "And our theory goes like this: Basayev is looking to launder money out here in the Hamptons, away from prying eyes in the city. And through what business could he do that very effectively without raising a lot of suspicion but an art gallery?"

Shepherd nodded as he was following along.

I continued. "Basayev decides to recruit the Suttons; they've been struggling with their gallery in Manhattan, and they need a place to relocate it to, but they've fallen on hard times and they can't afford the housing prices out here. They connect with Chanel, who may or may not have shown them a listing or two, but then they stumble onto the listing that Lenny has, and they want that house, but they can't afford it.

"So they report back to Basayev that they're in if he can get them a deal on the house. Basayev learns that Lenny is *your* ex-wife, and he thinks that he can kill two birds with one stone. In ordering a hit on Lenny, he knows that East Hampton's top detective will likely become obsessed with finding out who murdered her, and get so distracted by solving that crime that he'll overlook some others. He also knows that any house where there's a murder becomes stigmatized, and sure enough the owner of the house that the Suttons purchased—the house where Lenny was killed—did in fact accept a half-priced offer because the owner was so worried she wouldn't get another one for months or maybe even years."

Shepherd's jaw dropped. I could see that the theory that Lenny was murdered as a way to lower the value of the house she was showing, while simultaneously entrenching him into a murder investigation that would most certainly become an obsession, had never occurred to him.

"Holy shit," he whispered.

As a mother, I've always tried to mind my language, but in this case, I couldn't agree more.

Shepherd got up and walked a few steps on shaky legs. He looked as if he might crumple to the floor, in fact. I hurried to his side and guided him to the couch. "It's diabolical!" he said.

"It is," I agreed. "And it makes sense, right?"

Shepherd nodded dully, his gaze staring off into space and his mouth still agape. "I had all the pieces, all this time, but I could never put them together to form a coherent theory. I mean, I suspected Basayev was behind Lenny's murder, but I could never figure out why. He wasn't somebody I would've messed with. I would've left him to the Feds."

"But you didn't," I said. "You were investigating Tony Holland's murder, remember?"

Shepherd closed his eyes, as if he now understood. "Yes," he said.

My former neighbor, Heather Holland, who'd also been murdered, had been married to a man who'd laundered money through his construction firm for Basayev. When Tony Holland began skimming some off the top, Basayev put a hit out on him, and Greta did the deed. That was Shepherd's first Angel of Death investigation. And, it was the reason, I suspected, that Boris had eyed Shepherd as an annoyance to be dealt with.

"It's so clear," he said, shaking his head. "Why didn't I see it?"

I put my hand over his. "Sometimes, when we're too close to things, we can't see the whole picture."

Shepherd looked up at me, his expression a mixture of emotions, from gratitude, to regret, and even something else. Something that made my pulse quicken. I could feel the chemistry between us charging, like a current running down a wire. Without realizing it, I leaned forward, and so did Shepherd.

And then our lips hovered over each other, and I could feel his breath against my skin. The pulse of the current strengthened, and I closed my eyes against its power.

I felt Shepherd's hand come up to cup the side of my jaw, and then his lips touched mine, and it was such a delicate, gentle movement. It completely belied the personality of the man I'd come to know.

I leaned in another few centimeters, desiring more, but Shepherd only brushed my lips again with his, drawing out the moment, luring me forward to the cliff's edge. And then, when I thought I couldn't stand another second of our lips not pressed tightly together, he swept me into his arms and unleashed all of his desire.

I tumbled forward off the cliff with an eagerness that surprised me. And what surprised me even more was the man who unveiled himself in that moment.

I'd never even fathomed that underneath that gruff, irritating, moody, petulant exterior, Shepherd could hold such a deep and *glorious* sensuality. He kissed, and stroked, and moved with a rhythm and a touch that did things to me that I couldn't even put into words if I tried. He led me to a well of desire that I'd never even known existed, and there he offered me cup after cup of its sweet water, and I drank until my thirst was good and satisfied.

Much later, I led him to my bedroom, and drank long and deep one more time for good measure.

* * *

Shepherd left just before dawn. I'd barely been aware that he was up and moving, but I did feel his lips softly kiss my cheek, and his fingers stroke my hair, before hearing the front door gently close. I drifted back to sleep for another two hours and dreamed of him. Of us.

The smell of coffee woke me again, and I rolled over, squinting in the daylight streaming in through the windows. I sniffed the air tentatively. Yep. Someone was brewing coffee in the kitchen.

And then the smell of bacon wafted to my nose. And what smelled like French toast.

With a jolt, I realized that Gilley was downstairs, cooking breakfast, which wasn't at all alarming until I remembered that most of my clothing was littering the floor of the adjoining family room, *and* I remembered the state of the family room after Shepherd and I had finished our . . . workout.

"Son of a . . . !" I hissed, scrambling out of bed and racing to the bathroom to quickly grab a robe.

Gilley had taken my big white fluffy robe, so I was left with the silk kimono. I didn't even pause to look at myself in the mirror, too intent on getting downstairs and recovering my clothing while Gilley was turned toward the stove.

"Maybe he hasn't seen it," I whispered, hustling down the stairs with my fingers crossed.

Rounding into the kitchen, however, all my hopes to keep last night's adventures with Shepherd a secret flew out the window when Gilley greeted me over a mug of coffee with an overly enthusiastic, "Well! *Gooooood* morning!"

My gaze flicked to the family room. It was neat as a pin. Then it drifted to the pile of clothing, neatly folded— à la Marie Kondo style—on the countertop.

Heat rose up from my chest, enveloped my neck, then traveled to engulf my entire head.

"Gilley," I said, greeting him tersely.

"Catherine," Gilley replied, his tone so giddy I wanted to sock him.

I cleared my throat, lifted my chin, and walked over to the pile of clothing. "Thank you for straightening up the family room. I was . . . ahh . . . decluttering last night when I had a pretty intense hot flash. I've been getting those, you know. Perimenopause setting in . . . probably."

Gilley nodded with wide, innocent eyes. "Decluttering, hmm?"

I pulled at the collar on my robe. At that moment I probably looked like I was having a hot flash.

"Yes," I said, sticking to my guns.

"Huh," Gil said. "I can only imagine how lively a time *that* must've been. I found your thong hanging off the bookshelf."

I closed my eyes, absorbing the enormity of my embarrassment. But Gilley wasn't through having a bit of fun at my expense. When I opened my eyes again, he turned sideways and said, "Hey, Cat, does your underwear spark joy in your life?"

Turning the other way and adopting a breathy, falsetto voice, he said, "Why no, Detective Shepherd. It doesn't!"

Turning back, Gilley laid out his hand as if asking for something to be handed over and then he switched again where, pretending to be me, he shimmied out of a pair of pretend underwear, handed it over to himself, took up the dish towel, twirled that above his head, and said, "If it doesn't spark joy in your life, then set it freeeeeeeeee!"

The dish towel launched into the air and it fell with a plop onto the island.

Turning to me, and rather proud of himself, Gilley curtsied and grinned from ear to ear.

I made sure to glare extra meanly at him. "*This* coming from a guy who just went allllll the bases with an alpaca. . . ."

Gil's hands found his hips and he screeched, *"What Mr. Studly and I shared was sacred! Sacred!"*

I rolled my eyes. "Fine," I said, irritated that he was making such a big deal out of my tryst with Shepherd. "You caught me. Shepherd was here and we sparked some joy together. Happy?"

"That depends," Gilley said, smoothly setting a fresh cup of coffee in front of me. "Are *you* happy, Cat?"

I sighed. The ruse was up and I lowered my shoulders back to neutral. Picking up the coffee, I let the moment of silence play out for a bit before I muttered, "Yes. Quite."

Gilley giggled and turned back to the stove. "Speaking of quite, you've had quite the love life lately, haven't you? Two beautiful men desiring you all in one week. How're you going to manage?"

"Oh, God," I said. "I completely forgot about Maks!"

Gilley eyed me over his shoulder. "Huh," he said. "Shepherd was *that* good?"

In answer I simply melted onto the countertop, laying my face against the cool marble.

"Wow," Gilley said. "I never would've guessed."

Lifting myself back to a sitting position, I nodded. "Me either, but oh, my God, Gilley. What that man *did* to me . . ."

Gilley toasted me with his coffee mug. "Good for you, sugar."

I giggled. "It was. It really, really was good for me."

Over breakfast I caught Gilley up on Miranda's murder, and how I'd finally told Shepherd about our theory of the motive behind the hit on Lenny.

"How'd he take it?" Gilley asked when I got to that part.

"Stunned," I said. "But he agreed that it was the most likely scenario."

"The real question now is, who killed Sutton and Basayev, and why?"

I stared at Gil. "Why would we be concerned with them? Clearly someone within their organization was behind their murders. I mean, it's very likely just a power grab."

"But why frame Chanel?" Gilley asked. "I mean, if I'm looking to move up in the organization, and I want to take out the big boss, I'm not going to pin it on some poor twentysomething real estate agent. I'm going to make sure that everyone knows it was me, and strike some fear into the heart of any of his loyalists."

I tapped the countertop with my finger. "That is a very good point, Gilley."

"And the other question is: what does Chanel have to do with all this? I mean, yes, she was representing Basayev in the selling of his home, but why her? Why did he choose Chanel out of all the real estate agents in the Hamptons? After all, that was probably her only listing, Cat. She'd just arrived back in the area, she was clearly treading water financially, and her agency only offered her what was probably a converted broom closet to work out of. So why hire Chanel when Basayev could've hired one of the Bennetts and been better represented?"

I bit my lip. Gilley was making some very valid points and asking some truly puzzling questions. My mind began whirring, trying to fill in the dots. "You know," I said, "when I look at all these dots, all these murders that don't necessarily appear to be easily connected together, the one person they all have in common is Chanel."

Gilley nodded. "And, since yesterday, she's in the wind, and you're out two-hundred big ones if we don't find her."

I gulped. I hadn't even thought of the fact that, if Chanel had truly gone into hiding, the twenty thousand dollars I'd put up as 10 percent of her bond would quickly turn into two hundred thousand plus whatever Marcus's bill would be.

And while I was more than financially comfortable, I wasn't at all comfortable with the idea of losing almost a quarter million dollars to someone who'd simply decided to skip town.

So I turned to my phone and immediately called Marcus. "Catherine," he said smoothly. "Have you heard from Ms. Downey?"

"No, Marcus, I haven't. Which is why I'm calling. I have reason to suspect that Chanel has skipped town, and I need to understand what my obligation is should she not show up for trial."

"You know, when you called me last night and said that you hadn't heard from her, I was afraid of that. So, maybe I can offer you some hope, because I know you must be thinking that you're going to be out the two hundred large, right?"

"I'm terribly worried about that scenario, yes."

"Well, I could move forward with a motion for dismissal. The evidence against Ms. Downey is so flimsy and circumstantial that it wouldn't last two days at trial. Shepherd only has the fact that Ms. Downey had access to the house and her lipstick to tie her to the crime. I told her to jot a note for me on my legal pad that included all of the same letters used in the message on the mirror, and not one of the letters matched the writing on the mirror, so I'm confident she wasn't the person who murdered Basayev, and whoever it was must've discovered her lipstick lying on the ground after it fell out of her purse, or something, and used it to shock or surprise Basayev when he came home that day.

"The M.E.'s report talks about the fact that Basayev was murdered in front of that mirror, so it's likely he went into his living room, saw the message, moved forward to inspect it, and was shot by the intruder when they stepped out of the shadows."

"That does sound like a likely scenario," I said. "And I've had things fall out of my purse before. Your theory rings very true, Marcus."

"I'm glad you like it," Marcus said, and I could hear the bit of humor in his voice. "More importantly, I can't see a judge refusing to toss the case out on those two flimsy pieces of evidence, and Chanel doesn't necessarily have to be present at that pretrial hearing. I could come up with a simple excuse to have her absent. As long as I can get the judge to agree the arrest was bogus, you won't forfeit your bond, or have to fork over the rest."

I blew out a sigh. "Phew!" I said, giving a thumbs-up to Gilley, who was leaning in to hear the conversation.

I was about to thank Marcus for his time when I

thought of something else. It bubbled up from my memory banks and, even though I was fairly certain Shepherd wouldn't aggressively pursue the case against Chanel, I wanted to be extra sure that there were no more evidentiary surprises to be had. "Marcus?"

"Yes?"

"What about the necklace discovered at the scene?"

"You know, I haven't heard back from the D.A. about that. It's time to go right to the source. I'll call Dr. Beauperthy now."

"The medical examiner?"

"Yes. If the locket was purposely held back as exculpatory evidence, it'll help our case even more. I'll let you know what I find out," he said, and clicked off the phone.

After setting my cell down, I looked at Gilley, who was looking back at me expectantly. "What necklace?" he asked.

"The medical examiner came out to greet Shepherd when he first arrived on scene at Basayev's house. I saw the exchange between the two men, but I couldn't hear what they were saying. Anyway, the M.E. handed Shepherd a gold necklace with what I think was a heart-shaped charm. I assumed that Basayev probably pulled it off the woman who murdered him right before she pulled the trigger."

"So, Shepherd withheld it on purpose?"

"He wanted to put Chanel safely behind bars where Basayev's people couldn't get to her. I didn't know any of that before I set her free, which is why she took off, obviously. But I could see why Shepherd would withhold evidence that would link Basayev's murder to another woman. He just wanted to keep Chanel safe."

Gilley winced. "And now, by mentioning the necklace to Marcus, you're likely getting Shepherd in hot water."

I sucked in a breath. "Oh, no! Gilley, you're right!"

I picked my phone back up and dialed Marcus's number, but it went to voice mail. Then I called Shepherd, but his phone also went straight to voice mail, and I had a bad feeling that I'd started some trouble. I knocked my forehead with the phone. "Why did I have to mention it to Marcus?"

"You weren't thinking," Gilley said, reaching up to grab my arm to stop the pounding I was giving myself. "But it's okay, Cat. Shepherd's used to landing in hot water. I'm sure he'll talk himself out of it, and he'll have to drop the charges against Chanel, which will save you not only the two hundred thousand, but additional attorney's fees as well."

I brightened. "You know, you're so right. Thank you, Gilley."

"You're welcome. Now, why don't you go take a shower and get ready for the day while I clean up the breakfast dishes."

"I have to wait for Marcus to call me back," I said.

Gilley took my phone. "If he calls, I'll answer, I promise. Now, shoo! Go enjoy a nice hot shower."

With a sigh I headed upstairs, pausing at the doorways of both of the boys' rooms, sighing wistfully. I missed them and I vowed to reach out with a call later on in the day.

Then I made my way to my bedroom and fished through my closet for something appropriate to wear. I owned a dazzling red sweater with a deep V-neck that always made me feel sexy, and since I was feeling that already, I thought that donning it would be appropriate. Next, I selected a pair of black knit pants, and some booties.

I didn't know if I'd see Shepherd again today, but I was secretly hoping I would.

After making the bed, I dragged myself toward the shower, feeling sluggish after a night with very little sleep and a whole lot of . . . um . . . calisthenics. (Ahem.)

So, perhaps I was a bit distracted when I walked into the master bath, flipped on the light, looked in the mirror, and screamed.

Chapter 16

Gilley entered the bathroom clutching the handle of a cutting board, held aloft like a bat. "What's the matter?!" he gasped.

I pointed at my reflection. "Why didn't you tell me I looked . . . ?"

Gilley lowered the cutting board, and a smirk replaced the look of alarm he'd entered with. "Tousled? Disheveled? Like you'd been properly rolled in the hay?"

Mascara had smudged the area under my eyes, my lips were bright red—as if they'd been burned, and speaking of burn, Shepherd's five o'clock shadow had given me quite the burn all around my chin, my neck . . . and, oh, God . . . my bosom . . . not to mention the *gigantic* hickey on my neck. But all of that paled in comparison to the hot mess happening on top of my head.

My hair, which I now kept long, is especially fine, so

it's constantly susceptible to becoming unruly and tangled. In other words, last night's romp had been more than a little catastrophic to its appearance.

The more I stared at my reflection, the more I could see a resemblance between me and Animal, the Muppet. I buried my face in my hands. "I'm humiliated," I moaned.

Gilley chuckled lightly. "Oh, Cat, don't be. I'm just glad that Stella got her groove back. Now hop in the shower, put some balm on that rash, and meet me downstairs. Marcus just called back with some news."

Gilley turned to leave but I caught his sleeve. "What? What news?"

"Shower," he ordered. "Then news."

And the irritating schmuck flounced out of the room.

Twenty minutes later I was back downstairs, wearing a towel wound round my hair turban style, a black turtleneck that hid all the beard burn, and roomy boyfriend jeans that I opted for instead of the tighter knit pants because my face and chest weren't the only things left with a little burn on them. (Ahem!)

I found Gilley on the sofa, watching HGTV.

Moving over to the remote, I clicked the mute button and stood in front of Gilley with my hands on my hips. "Tell me."

"Marcus confirmed that the M.E. found the necklace on Basayev. He says he gave it to Shepherd and told him where he found it. Then Marcus called the D.A. again and raised some hell, but the D.A. insisted that the evidence report they got from Shepherd didn't include the necklace. Now the D.A.'s office is super uptight about it, and they vowed to get to the bottom of it."

I frowned. "Why would Shepherd withhold evidence from the D.A.? I mean, even if the necklace didn't belong to Chanel, I'm sure the D.A.'s office would've proceeded given the lipstick and easy access Chanel had to the property, along with the knowledge of Basayev's schedule. The necklace could've been explained later."

Gilley shrugged. "Beats me. But maybe he forgot about it?"

I tapped my lip. "Maybe," I said. But that would've been unusual for Shepherd. With a shrug myself, I turned and headed back upstairs to blow-dry my hair, which took very little time as it was nearly dry from wearing the towel, all the while thinking about that necklace.

There was something not quite right about it, and I couldn't put my finger on it.

While I was straightening up the bathroom, I heard someone knocking on the front door. I came to the landing overlooking the first floor just as Gilley approached the door. "Pssst!" I said, to get Gilley's attention. "See who it is first!"

I was wary about who might be showing up at the house unannounced, remembering the circumstances of Miranda's murder.

Gilley peered through the peephole and turned to me. "It's Shepherd," he said quietly.

"Oh?" I replied, my voice going up an octave. This would be a pleasant surprise.

"He doesn't look happy," Gilley said.

"Oh," I said, my voice going down two octaves. Maybe this wouldn't be so pleasant after all.

"Well, let him in," I said, moving to the stairs.

As I descended the steps, Shepherd breezed into the foyer looking mad enough to spit. It was particularly hurtful, I think because I was still floating on air from

our night together, and to see him like this, so clearly irritated, was a bit of a blow to the ego.

"Detective," I said cordially.

"*Why* did you have to mention the necklace" he nearly
shouted at me.

I pulled my chin back in shock. Gilley also appeared
quite surprised by Shepherd's outburst.

"Dude," he said sternly. "What the fffff—?"

"Hey," I warned.

"—flamingo?"

Shepherd rounded on me. "Nobody but the M.E. and I
knew about the necklace, Catherine. Nobody saw it, nobody mentioned it, nobody needed to know about it until
you came along and raised the alarm and now my ass is
on thin ice and I have *no choice* but to put it into evidence!"

I crossed my arms and glared at him. How *dare* he
come into my home and start yelling at me for something
that was completely his fault. "I was looking out for
Chanel's best interests," I growled.

"How is *that* looking out for her best interests?" he demanded.

I lowered my arms and balled my fists. This man was
intolerable! "If the necklace was found on Basayev, and
it doesn't belong to her, then wouldn't it completely ex-
onerate her?"

Shepherd ran a hand down the front of his face. I noticed that he hadn't shaved, but at least he'd showered and
changed clothes from the day before. With a long, measured sigh, he said, "Did it ever occur to you that maybe
the necklace *does* belong to her? Huh? Did that ever cross
your mind, Catherine Cooper, super sleuth?"

His lip was curled up in a snarl as he spoke, which

would've set me on edge if not for what he'd just confessed.

"What do you mean it belongs to her?"

"Just what I said. The necklace belongs to Chanel. I was trying to keep it off the evidence list so I could drop the case at a later date when I knew she'd be safe. But now you've come along and completely ruined it. Now I *have* to put it into evidence."

I put a hand to my mouth. But then I thought of something. "How do you know that the necklace belongs to Chanel? I mean, I never saw her wearing it. And Marcus never mentioned that Chanel had told you about a necklace found at the scene, something she certainly would've confessed to her attorney if she knew the police had confiscated it as evidence."

Shepherd put his hands on his hips, his head shaking back and forth slightly, and I was shocked to see him at an apparent loss for words.

"Steve," I said firmly "How do you know the necklace belongs to Chanel?"

Shepherd was suddenly avoiding eye contact with me. "I just do," he said.

And then a ripple of something distasteful traveled up my spine. There was something in his expression, something I recognized because I'd seen it before on the face of my ex-husband.

It was the expression of a married man facing his wife who's just discovered evidence of an affair. It was the mask of guilt I'd seen on Tom's face right before he told me he wanted a divorce because he was in love with another woman.

And then the memory of Shepherd embracing Chanel at the scene came flooding back to me. And the fact that he'd made a point to avoid acknowledging any of us when he'd first arrived on scene and we were all standing together. And the fact that he'd never come to find me and take my witness statement the night of the murder.

It all added up now.

And I felt profoundly betrayed.

"You know it belongs to her because *you* gave it to her," I whispered.

Shepherd's gaze flickered to me. He didn't say anything, but then he seemed to read my expression and the tension in his shoulders let go. "It was a long time ago, Catherine."

"Well, would you look at the time," Gilley said. His voice made me jump. I'd nearly forgotten that he was even in the room. "I need to go call Michel before he heads to bed. Cat, I'll catch up with you later."

Gilley passed Shepherd on his way out the door, and I heard him make a tisking sound as he went. He was disappointed in Shepherd too.

"Chanel was the reason your marriage broke up, isn't she?" I asked after Gilley left. My eyes misted a bit, and I couldn't really say why the knowledge that Shepherd had been unfaithful to Lenny was so personally hurtful to me . . . but it was.

"No," Shepherd said, hanging his head. "Not completely."

"What does that mean?"

Shepherd lifted his chin and stared at me. And for maybe only the third or fourth time, I saw his guard go down, and that vulnerable side of him appeared in his eyes. "Lenny and I had been having issues. I was working long hours investigating the Tony Holland case, and she was launching this new agency. We were spending less and less time together, and neither of us seemed to mind it. But then I took a step back from the case, because I realized what it was going to cost me, and I tried to reach out to Lenny and let her know that I wanted to be a more involved partner . . ."

"And?"

Shepherd sighed. "And, she didn't want me to be more involved. She was on this independent kick, I guess, and she felt that I was holding her back or something. So, I turned to a friend, who knew Lenny almost as well as I did, and who could give me some perspective about where Lenny was coming from."

"Chanel," I said.

"Yeah. Chanel."

"How long did it go on?"

"Six months or so. But it wasn't much of an affair. Just two people struggling with their relationships who found a little comfort with each other."

"Chanel was also married?" I asked.

Shepherd shook his head. "No. She was seeing someone who was controlling and jealous, and who she was really ready to quit, but she didn't know how to do it without it becoming a big thing. I told her I could help her if he started any trouble, but she said she could handle it, so I let it be. She would only refer to the guy in third person too, like she didn't want me to know who it was, which I guess I could understand. She'd always just call him the IO."

"IO? What's that stand for?"

The corner of Shepherd's mouth quirked, and he raised his hands to make air quotes. "The insignificant other. Anyway, he was the reason she left town after Lenny died. Chanel was pretty destroyed by what'd happened to Len—we all were—and she couldn't cope with a jealous and controlling boyfriend on top of grieving for one of her closest friends, so one day she sent me a text and said, 'I'm outta here,' and I didn't see her again until the other night."

I tugged at the neck of my sweater. I was incredibly uncomfortable hearing about Shepherd's affair, because it hit too close to home, but I was also really curious, and I couldn't seem to hold back asking him the one thing I needed to know, which, ironically, was the same question I'd asked Tom when he'd confessed his affair to me. "Did you love her?" I asked.

Shepherd looked me in the eye, which I could tell was a bit of a struggle for him, because he was clearly ashamed of what he'd done, and it was something Tom had never given me when faced with that same, simple inquiry. "I wasn't in love with Chanel," he said, "but I cared about her. The way you care about a friend who was there for you when you really needed them. And that's why I gave her the necklace, Catherine. I wanted her to know that she'd meant something to me. Because she had."

In that moment, I, myself, wondered what I meant to Shepherd. I was his friend, for certain; I felt confident in that. But what had last night meant? Was I relegated to a status similar to Chanel? Or was I a more serious endeavor, like Lenny had been?

Those were all the questions I really wanted to ask him, but knew that I couldn't, so I simply stood there, tugging on my sweater, wondering what to say next.

For his part, Shepherd was looking at me in a way that seemed to ask for forgiveness, which was ludicrous of course. He'd betrayed his wife, not me.

And yet, I couldn't shake the feeling that I'd been the one he'd cheated on. And I couldn't simply decide to feel differently.

I wasn't a mind reader, but I swore that Shepherd understood, and his expression seemed pained. "Listen," he said softly as he took a step closer to me, and that current that'd been so present only hours before reignited with intensity.

But I didn't want to get lost in that current again. At least not yet. So I backed up a fraction, and he stopped his advance. "What . . . what was Chanel's necklace doing at the scene?" I asked, relieved to have something else to focus on and distract us from our current path.

Shepherd dropped his gaze to the floor and shook his head slightly, but he answered me. "Basayev was wearing it."

"Wait . . . he was . . . *wearing* the necklace?"

Shepherd made a sound like a humorless laugh. "Yeah, if you can believe it."

"What'd Chanel say about *that*?"

"She said she'd left her necklace behind when she made a run for it a year ago. She has no idea how it ended up on Basayev."

"Do you believe her?"

Shepherd nodded, but he also shrugged. "Chanel never lied to me. That's something that I liked about her. She was a straight shooter. If she didn't want to tell me the whole truth, she'd be a little vague, or change the subject, but overall she was always honest."

"But she lied to Lenny," I insisted. "I mean, here she was, having an affair with her husband, and pretending to be her friend and business partner too."

Shepherd shrugged in acknowledgment. "That's true. But why would Chanel tie herself to Basayev's murder by putting her own necklace around his neck—one that she knew I'd definitely recognize?"

Shepherd made a very good point there. And then I thought of another angle. "Could it have been her ex?"

"He's who I thought of," Shepherd admitted. "If she left the necklace behind, he could've had access to it."

"So he kills Basayev and frames Chanel for the murder out of revenge?"

"I've seen people murdered for a lot less."

"Would he have known *who* he was murdering?"

"Hard to say," Shepherd said. "If he did, he wanted Chanel dead too, because no way would the mob let that stand."

"Did Chanel say anything to you about this guy's identity?"

"No," Shepherd said. "She shut down, almost completely, when I told her about the necklace and the lipstick. I think she went into a state of shock, and I was hoping to get her to come out of it by keeping her nearby in the only safe place I could legally put her, but then you sprung her out of jail and now she's in the wind."

"And her grandaunt is dead too. Murdered by the same guy?"

"Probably," Shepherd said sadly.

"It means this guy is playing for keeps, Steve."

"It does."

"Let's hope he doesn't find out about your affair with Chanel."

Shepherd winced, and I could tell that maybe I'd pushed it just a hair too far. He cleared his throat and glanced at his watch. "I gotta get back," he said. "The captain wasn't done chewing me out for withholding evidence. I don't think he's buying the 'I forgot' defense."

"I'm sorry about that," I said, because I was.

Shepherd shrugged again, and turned to leave. I followed him to the door, feeling like there was so much between us that had been left unsaid, and as lengthy and revealing as our conversation just now had been, it hadn't been the *real* conversation we could've had.

Shepherd opened the door, and I could see that it was raining now in earnest. I was about to offer him an umbrella when he turned to me, stepped in close, and held my head gently as he peered into my eyes. "I know you feel lied to," he said softly. "I know that you might even feel betrayed, but if I can look past whatever's going on with you and Grinkov, maybe you can look past whatever happened between me and Chanel."

My eyes widened, as the full weight of his words settled into my chest like a lead fist. My God, I'd been such a hypocrite! I opened my mouth to attempt an apology, but Shepherd stopped me by grazing my lips with his own again, then pressing his forehead to mine for a brief moment while that current between us charged up to new voltage, and I reached up my own hands to cover his.

But then he abruptly released me to turn and walk out into the rain.

And I was left wanting more.

After Shepherd exited my drive, I grabbed an umbrella and scurried over to Chez Kitty.

Coming through the door shaking the umbrella, I found Gilley deep in conversation on his cell.

"Mmmhmm," he said. "I understand. Yes. Yes, that's true, but I still think it's premature. I know, I was there. . . ."

Seeing me, Gilley covered the microphone with his finger and whispered, "It's Willem."

"Really?" I whispered back. "Is he okay?"

Gilley shook his head and then lifted his hand from the microphone. "Willem, Cat's just arrived here at the office. Let me put her on, okay? Just a moment while I transfer the call."

Gilley clicked the mute button and thrust his phone at me. "He wants to quit."

I took the phone. "Quit? Quit what?"

"Us."

"What? Why?"

"He's decided to let the curse win. He says he's lived nearly thirty-five years at his grandmother's estate, what's another forty more?"

"That's ridiculous," I said, clicking the mute button again. "Willem? Hello, it's Catherine. What's this non-sense I hear that you want to quit?"

"It's nothing personal, Catherine, I swear. Both you and Gilley have been great. But I'm worried that we're pushing too hard, and the next time someone really will get hurt. I couldn't live with that on my conscience."

I sat down and tried to think of something, anything to convince Willem to hang in there. "But don't you also think we're very close to breaking the curse?" I asked him. "Willem, this thing can't keep offering up disasters at this rate, and I believe my friend Heath when he says that the best way to break the curse is to push it to its lim-its. If we keep finding these wide open spaces for you to explore, then the curse has to work that much harder to cause trouble, and if we keep going I just *know* we can send it packing once and for all."

But Willem was not to be persuaded. "Catherine, I'm

very sorry, but I just can't risk it. What if one of you had been seriously hurt? Or Audra? Or even one of the al-pacas? It would kill me if an innocent creature was hurt because of me."

"Well, then we won't go anywhere near furry creatures or people," I said, and the moment I said it I knew how ridiculous it sounded. Where would that have been, exactly? The moon?

For his part, Willem seemed to overlook it. "You're very kind to want to help me but my decision is final."

My shoulders sagged. I could tell there was no argument I could make that would convince him. With a sad sigh I said, "Well, I suppose I'll have to honor your wishes, Willem, but I want you to know that, should you change your mind at any point in the future, Gilley and I will be there for you, all right?"

"Thank you," Willem said simply, but there was a small hitch in his voice, and it just about broke my heart to hear it.

After hanging up I looked sadly at Gilley, who stared back in sympathy. "Oh, puddin', it's been a *day*, hasn't it?"

"And it's not even lunchtime," I sighed.

Gilley came over to wrap his arm around my shoulders and squeeze. "What happened with Shepherd?"

"He had an affair with Chanel," I said, stating the most important part of the story.

Gilley backed his chin up. "No!"

"Yes." I sighed again. It still stung to think of the fact that Shepherd had cheated on Lenny.

Gilley understood. "That hits a little too close to home, huh?"

"A bit. But he also called me out for my relationship with Maks, and I know it sort of makes me a hypocrite to feel disappointed with Shepherd when I've been romantic with two men—"

"In the same week!" Gil interrupted. I cocked a warning eyebrow at Gilley, but he just grinned at me, lifting his hands high in celebration. "Congratulations!"

"Who am I turning into?" I said wearily, moving to the sofa.

Gilley came to sit as well and he took up my hand. "You are who you've always been, Cat. And that's what both these men find so attractive, which is why you should take both suitors seriously. Tom never fully appreciated your strong, independent side. In fact, he was threatened by it, but both Maks and Shepherd seem to find that one of your more desirable traits. So the only thing you need to decide—and mind you, you don't even have to decide that now—is who do you want to continue seeing?"

I looked at Gilley and grateful tears formed in my eyes. Sometimes, he was so wise it was surprising. Of course, he also sprinkled these wisdoms with lots of ill-timed, not-so-perfect comments, but I had a little of that same trait myself, so I didn't feel right to judge.

"Thank you, Gilley."

He patted my hand. "Anytime. Now! Tell me what else Shepherd said about Chanel and that necklace."

I filled Gilley in on the entirety of the conversation, and when I was done, Gil seemed good and puzzled. "So, our new working theory is that Chanel's ex murdered Basayev and is trying to frame her for murder?"

"Yes," I said. "I guess so."

"Wow," Gilley said. "That's a profoundly stupid move, given who Basayev was."

"But it almost makes sense, doesn't it? I mean, the

only two people who would've had the gall to kill a mafia kingpin would've been either someone who knew exactly who he was, and was trying to make a power grab, or someone who *didn't* know who he was—perhaps thought only that he was some rich guy trying to sell his house—and that made him the perfect target for the framing of Chanel."

"Who does Shepherd think it was?"

"He didn't specifically point to any theories."

Gilley got up and paced for a bit, tapping his finger to his lip. I smiled, because that was typically my signature move. "This is all so complicated," he said. "And it doesn't explain Jason Sutton's murder."

"Maybe they're not connected," I said.

"The only way to know for sure is if the same gun was used. What do the ballistics say?" Gilley asked me.

I shrugged. I had no idea.

"If you asked Shepherd, would he tell you?"

"Doubtful. You know how he bristles when I try to insert myself into his investigations."

Gilley lowered his finger and looked at me with a wicked glint in his eye. "There *is* a way to find out, you know. . . ."

"We are *not* hacking into his computer!" I said immediately. Sometimes it shocked me how willing Gilley was to break privacy laws.

"Relax," he said calmly. "I didn't have anything like that in mind."

"Then what *did* you have in mind?"

"Well," he said, and I could tell he was trying to figure out how to break it to me gently. "Do you trust me?"

"No."

Gil leveled his eyes at me. "Cat," he said.

I sighed. "I trust you with my life, Gilley, but I don't trust that you won't do something that could land the two of us in prison."

He laughed. "Fair. But this won't land anyone back in jail. At most, it's a misdemeanor, and we'd face a fine."

"How much of a fine?"

"More than a traffic ticket, less than it'd cost to hire Marcus for a murder trial." I hesitated, and Gilley added, "Listen, we need to know if Basayev's murder is connected with Jason Sutton's, because if they're not, then we know we're probably dealing with a jealous ex who wants to ruin Chanel's life, but if they are, then that's a whole new can of worms, and Chanel could be in *real* danger."

"She's already in *real* danger," I said. "Her grandaunt was murdered."

"Oooh, that's another reason why we should call the crime lab," Gilley said.

"Wait, *we're* calling the crime lab?"

"Yes."

"Why would they give *us* any information in an ongoing police investigation?"

"Because they'll think the call is coming from Shepherd," Gilley said.

My brow furrowed. "How're you going to pull that off? You don't have access to his phone and you don't sound anything like Steve Shepherd, Gilley."

Gilley cleared his throat and said, "Catherine, you need to butt out of my investigation!"

My eyes widened. Shepherd had a distinct voice. It held a note of smoky rumble and low undertones and Gilley had just mimicked it nearly flawlessly.

Gilley bounced his brows. "I've been practicing. I

thought it might come in handy someday. And to your other question, it's an insanely easy thing to piggyback my number onto any phone number I want. The caller ID on the other end of the line would register as Shepherd's cell when I call the crime lab."

My palms began to sweat. "Oh, God," I said. "You really want to do this?"

Gilley wiggled his phone. "I'm ready when you are."

I got up to pace, tapping my lip just like Gil had done not five minutes before. I needed to think this through. After only two times back and forth, traversing the room, I decided it was too risky and turned back to Gilley, who was putting his phone to his ear. "Julio? Detective Shepherd," he said tersely as the call was picked up.

Blood drained from my face and my heart started to hammer hard in my chest. He'd made the executive decision to go through with it. He'd called the crime lab.

"Is the ballistics report back on the Basayev case?" There was a pause, then, "If I got that e-mail, do you think I'd be calling? Just read me the damn report!"

Although he sounded spookily like an irritated Shepherd, Gilley was grinning at me and holding a thumbs-up like he was having the time of his life. "Mmmhmm," he said. "Yep . . . yep . . . okay, and what did the ballistics on the Sutton case show in comparison? . . . Same caliber? . . . Mmmhmm, mmm-hmm . . . same grooves . . . yep . . . so you're certain the two bullets were fired from the same gun? Good. One more thing. Have you reached out to New Canaan P.D. like I asked to get that ballistics report yet? . . . What the hell do you mean I didn't order you to do that? Julio, I *definitely* ordered that first thing this morning! . . . Well, get on it! I'll call you back in twenty to get those results."

With that Gilley clicked off the phone and his grin was ear to ear. "That was fun," he said, with a squeaky laugh.

I sank onto the sofa, my hand over my heart. "Good God, Gilley. You're going to give me a heart attack one of these days!"

He snickered. "*That* got your heart racing? Jeez, Cat, remind me never to divulge the stuff I don't tell you about."

I gulped. "Not. Helping."

He chuckled. "I'm kidding."

"Good," I said.

"Mostly," Gilley added. I glared at him. "*Any*way, the good news is that now we know that Sutton's murder and Basayev's murder are connected."

I stared out into space, truly puzzled. "So, it was more than likely someone in their organization who murdered both men."

"Yes," Gilley said.

"But what does any of it have to do with Chanel?" I wondered.

"Well, maybe Chanel's ex is also in the organization," Gilley said simply.

My breath caught. "Ohmigod, Gilley," I whispered. *"Of course!"* I got up to pace again too. "It would explain how Chanel got Basayev's listing. She probably floated in those circles when she was dating this guy."

"Did Shepherd ever tell you his name?" Gilley asked.

"No. In fact, he said that Chanel was careful not to mention it. She merely referred to him as her IO."

"IO?"

"Insignificant other."

"Ooo, that's clever."

"And telling," I said. "If he in fact was someone

within that crime family, then you could see how being left by his girlfriend would be a big blow to his ego."

Gilley nodded. "So what we really need to do is track down who Chanel's ex might've been."

"Yes," I said. "But how would we even do that?"

"Well, maybe you could go to Maks and ask him?" Gilley suggested. "I mean, he's connected to all those players, right? And he might even have met or have seen Chanel with someone high up in the organization, right?"

I hadn't seen Maks since our night together. I didn't even know if he was still going to his office regularly . . . but I could check.

Still, the thought of seeing him made my pulse quicken, not from desire, but from guilt given the previous night's . . . *sparking joy* adventures with Shepherd.

"What's with that look?" Gilley asked me.

I shook my head. "What look?"

"The look of guilt you'd wear if you had actually cheated on Maks."

"Didn't I?"

Gilley rolled his eyes. "Cat, you're not exclusive with Maks. And you're not exclusive with Shepherd. My God, woman, you've only had a tiny tryst with both of them, and so what if it's in the same week. That's hardly cheating."

"It feels like cheating, though, Gilley."

"Well, for someone who was married for as long as you were, it probably would, but for everyone else who's been single in the past decade, it's not a big deal. You have nothing to feel guilty about. Besides, the three of you are all adults; I'm sure no one expects anyone to be quite so serious yet."

"Really?" I asked.

"Really," Gilley said. "Now, go find that gorgeous hunka man and ask him about Chanel. I'll stay here and try another route to ferret out this ex-boyfriend of hers."

"What other route?"

"Social media, of course," Gilley said.

I pointed at him. "You know, that might help us track her down too, Gilley. She's obviously gone into hiding. Maybe you'll pull up something that can lead us to her location."

"I can try," he said.

I left Gilley and drove to the office. It took me twice as long as normal to arrive at my building due to the weather. It was starting to get a little treacherous outside, with all the wind and rain.

Hurrying inside, I hustled first to my office to flip on the lights and make it look like I was in residence, and then I deposited my coat, umbrella, and purse before locking the inner office door again to make my way upstairs.

Pausing on the second-floor landing, I saw Dr. Strickland—the dentist—locking up.

"Hello, Doctor," I said when he turned away from the door.

He jumped slightly. "Catherine," he said, recovering himself. "I was just leaving. The storm's getting bad out there, and we've had nothing but cancellations, so I thought I'd take the rest of the day off to hunker down."

"Good choice," I said as he began to pass me.

He nodded. "Don't stay here too long yourself," he suggested. "I hear some trees are starting to come down and the roads are only getting worse."

"I won't. You take care and drive safe."

He waved over his shoulder and was gone.

Looking down the hallway, I noticed the darkened

door of the other suite and remembered the absence of cars in the parking lot. I suddenly wondered if it'd been a fool's errand to come into the office at all this morning.

Still, I had to check just to be sure, so I continued up the stairs to the third floor, which was very quiet.

Moving to Maks's door, I tried the handle first, but it was locked. I knocked anyway, but no one came to the door. With a sigh I abandoned the locked door and headed back downstairs to sit in my office for a few minutes and think of what to do next.

With some reservation, I pulled out my cell and sent Maks a text that I needed to talk to him. It was urgent.

And then I busied myself with a game of solitaire for an hour, my gaze flicking every few seconds to the phone, but there was no response from Maks.

Staring moodily out the window, I knew I needed to get back home before the storm got even worse, but an idea kept niggling at me, and try as I might I couldn't let it go.

I didn't know where Maks lived, so there was no heading to his home to confront him, but I could access his office with the master key and look for a clue or two as to where I might find him.

After one last glance at my phone, I acted on that impulse and reached into Gilley's desk for the master key ring.

Hurrying out the door and up the stairs before I could change my mind, I approached Maks's door again, my heart racing. By this time, I was quite certain that I was the only one left in the building. I'd seen my first-floor tenant walk out shortly after Dr. Strickland, so I knew there wouldn't be any curious eyes to see me enter Maks's locked office, but I was still shaking with nerves because I'm usually a fairly upstanding citizen who doesn't go around entering private spaces she hasn't been invited into.

Then I thought back a few months to a similar excursion and had to concede that I might be making this a habit. Still, I pressed forward, entered the key into the lock, turned the handle, and let myself in.

The space wasn't very surprising, or exciting. It was neat and orderly with an open area at the entrance and two offices off the central lobby—which held a seating area, a Turkish rug, and a fake plant.

The lights were all off, and I kept them that way, even though, with the wind howling eerily outside, I really wanted to turn them on and help settle my nerves.

Plus, it was quite dark in the interior given the storm. I settled for using my phone as a flashlight and shined the light around, looking for anything that might indicate where I could find Maks.

Making my way out of the seating area and over to his office, I peered in at his desk. There was no desktop computer—he probably carried a laptop with him—and there was nothing on his desk, no mail carried in from home that might have given me a clue as to where he lived.

Knowing it'd been a long shot but still frustrated that I wasn't finding any leads to follow, I began to make my way out, but stopped at the closed door to the second office. "Might as well be thorough," I whispered, trying the handle. It opened easily, and what was hidden behind the door sent a jolt of shock straight down to my toes.

Chapter 17

Stepping forward into the room, I walked over to the canvases and stared down at the dozen or so paintings laid up against the far wall.

The room was empty save for the artwork, which had been packed in brown paper but was all exposed now, facing outward. One painting in particular drew my attention—the Bilmes painting I'd been so drawn to at the Suttons' gallery was center stage among the pieces.

I touched the top of the canvas, but then withdrew my hand quickly. These pieces had all been at the gallery, I was certain of it. But what were they doing here? Why did Maks have them tucked away like this?

And then another thought formed in my mind. A tiny seed that implanted itself into my head and sprouted the first leaves of doubt. I stepped back from the canvases and frowned. I didn't know what they had to do with anything, but I did know they likely came from the Suttons' gallery on the day Jason Sutton was murdered, and that bothered me.

A lot.

So I closed the door and traced my way quickly out of Maks's office, locking the door behind me as I went.

From there, I couldn't seem to get to my office quickly enough. I wanted to leave the building immediately, get home, and tell Gilley what I'd found. Together maybe we could come up with a reason why Maks would have those paintings in his office, a reason that would help spray that little plant of doubt in my mind with some weed killer.

But when I approached the door to my office, I found it open. And what was even more troubling . . . someone was inside, rummaging around.

I stopped short and put a hand to my chest. I'd locked the door when I went upstairs—I was certain of that. And I knew I'd done that, because as I was locking the door, I'd had the thought that it was a silly thing to do because the building was clearly empty, and *no one* was going to just come strolling in on a day like today, but I'd had my Birkin stowed in Gilley's desk, and that was a purse I never took chances with.

Gripping my phone, I wondered if I should call the police, as I was certain there was an intruder in my office, but then I took one look out the window and knew the East Hampton P.D. had far more urgent matters to attend to than my Birkin.

But I couldn't just walk away. The nerve of some would-be thief, taking advantage of the cover of the storm to prey upon local businesses . . . Well, it made me *mad.*

So I used that anger, and a bit of theater when I rounded the corner and shouted, *"Freeze, dirtbag!"*

There was an ear-piercing shriek, and something came flying across the room at me. I ducked in the nick of time and avoided getting hit in the face by the missile.

"Gilley!" I yelled. *"What the hell are you doing!"*

"Cat!" he yelled at the same time. *"What the hell are you doing!"*

We both glared at each other, our hands on our hearts, adopting identical expressions of shock and anger. "I asked you first!" I snapped.

Gil wiped his forehead with his fingers. "I've broken out into a cold sweat! You scared me half to death!"

"What are you doing here? And why are you rummaging around in . . . your desk?" I realized how stupid I sounded, but adrenaline was still coursing through my veins.

"I was looking for some extra batteries," Gilley said, walking toward me. He bent down near my feet and scooped up what I now saw was a remote. "Please don't be broken," he whispered to it as he turned it over to inspect.

"Why are you here?" I asked again. "You shouldn't be out here in this weather."

Gilley, having finished his exam of the remote, popped open the back lid for the battery compartment and began changing the batteries. "My projector was here. And you were here. And I had a whole presentation to show you."

"A presentation?"

"Yes."

"Are you kidding?"

"No."

I stared at him rather speechless. I couldn't understand what he was even talking about. So I simply waved to him to show me.

He motioned me over to his desk and cut the lights. I could see his projector was set up on his desk, and it was currently casting an image across the room to the far wall. The image was of a woman with long black hair, olive skin, and gorgeous olive green eyes.

"Who's that?" I asked.

"Lenny Shepherd," Gil said.

I stiffened. I didn't really know what I'd expected Lenny to look like. Shepherd was a good-looking man, so I knew he would've attracted someone at least his equal, but Lenny Shepherd was breathtaking. "Whoa," I whispered.

"She was stunning, right?"

"Yes," I agreed. "She was." Without realizing it I wrapped my arms around myself, feeling a bit self-conscious. I'd inherited most of my looks from my mother—who'd once been a stunning beauty and Veronica Lake look-alike, right down to the peekaboo hairstyle from her high school senior picture.

So, while I was fairly confident and comfortable with my looks, even I knew that I was no match for someone like Lenny, who held an exotic, natural beauty.

"Why are we looking at Lenny?" I asked, hoping Gilley would get to the point quickly, as the wind outside was howling so loudly I had to raise my voice just to be heard.

"Because I told you I was going to dig into Chanel's social media accounts, but that girl isn't even on Instagram, so I had to go back to known associates and I came across Lenny's account." Gilley pressed the remote and another photo came up. It was Lenny and Chanel out at a club, dancing together and having a great time.

I wondered if Lenny ever suspected that the other woman Shepherd was seeing was her good friend and business partner. And I wondered if the photo was taken at the time that Shepherd was having his affair with Chanel.

For her part, Chanel seemed to be having a glorious time. She was holding on to Lenny's arm and smiling genuinely at her friend.

It was quite obvious to me that Chanel cared about Lenny, and I wondered that someone with that much affection for another could still betray them so deeply.

Gilley switched to another photo, and this one made me sit up and take notice. Chanel and Lenny were at the same club, but in the background was a figure I recognized. Boris Basayev.

"Whoa," I said, pointing at the screen.

"Yep," Gilley said. "It's this photo that made me wonder if Lenny knew Boris. He's not looking at the girls, but he's there. Present. So they obviously floated in the same circles. I checked all the rest of Lenny's Instagram photos, but there wasn't any other image of her out with Chanel, or any other connection to Boris, but then I got an idea and began to research Boris's social media accounts, and wouldn't you know, the Chechen kingpin *loved* to party, and documented all of it.

Gilley changed to the next several images, which all featured Boris aboard a beautiful yacht, then out at a nightclub, then at a strip joint, then next to a private jet, and finally, driving a Bentley.

"He really did like to live large, didn't he?"

"He sure did. And I've spared you the worst of it. There's even a picture of him sitting on a golden toilet."

"Ick," I said. "So gauche."

"Right? Anyway, amid the dozens and dozens of photos, I came across this series, which was at a party on his yacht taken about two years ago. . . ."

Gilley flashed to an image of a group of people all toasting the photographer with glasses of champagne. Boris was there, and over to the right was Chanel. I sucked in a breath and pointed at the screen. "She knew Boris socially!"

"Yes. Now look again," Gilley said.

I turned back to the screen and focused on the image. Standing behind Chanel, his face partially hidden by shadow, was a man with his arm snaked around her middle, in a sort of possessive hug. Her right arm was raised and her hand was cupping his face in a familiar and loving manner. His face was one I knew well. Intimately in fact. I sucked in another breath. "Oh . . . my . . . God!" I whispered.

"Yep," Gilley said. "It's why I had to race through the rain to come down here and show you. Maks and Chanel were an item. I think he might've been the IO."

My heart began to pound hard in my chest. I could feel the bite of betrayal on the back of my neck, and I almost didn't know where to look. Gilley switched to the next image, which again showed the same boisterous crowd, but Chanel and Maks were in the back of the group, huddled together intimately.

"Maybe they were just hanging out at this one party, though," I said weakly.

"It wasn't just this one party," Gilley said, hitting the button on the remote to project another image of Chanel and Maks, sitting together cozily in front of a bonfire with Basayev and others. And then there was a photo of the two of them hanging out on a sailboat, with Basayev at the helm and no one else around.

A mist of tears formed in my eyes. Maks had lied to me or, if not outright lied to me, he'd definitely purposely withheld the fact that he'd had a relationship with the partner of Lenny Shepherd, a woman whose death I'd told him I was actively trying to solve.

And then my mind began to swirl around all the other connections that started to add up. He'd asked me to lie to Shepherd and provide an alibi for the night that Jason Sutton had been murdered. A murder where Maks's car had been spotted leaving the crime scene . . .

"Cat?" Gilley asked.

I shook my head. I'd been lost in thought. Dark thought. "I have to show you something," I said.

"What?"

Without explaining I grabbed Gilley by the hand and led him to the door, but then I stopped, looked over my shoulder at his desk, and retraced my steps to grab my Birkin. After locking up the office I motioned for him to follow me up the stairs.

As we climbed the steps, the hallway lights flickered. The storm outside was getting worse by the second, but I couldn't focus on that right now.

We made our way up to the third floor and I inserted my master key into the lock on Maks's door, letting us inside again. Flipping the switch, I lit up the interior because, by now, it was quite dark outside, which meant it was equally gloomy on the inside.

"Why are we in here?" Gilley whispered.

"Follow me," I said, heading straight to the second office where I'd seen the paintings. Opening that door, I flipped on that light and the room lit up as well, exposing the dozens of art pieces lining the walls.

Gilley walked into the center of the room and looked all around, his mouth ajar. "What does this mean?" he finally asked me.

I shook my head and shrugged. "I don't know. But, Gil, look at this!" Moving over to the painting, I lifted it and turned it toward him. "Seem familiar?"

"We saw that in the Suttons' gallery, right?"

"Almost," I said. "It's a close rendition, but not the exact painting we saw. Bilmes's work all looks very familiar, but there're nuances and differences in each piece, which is why it surprised me to find . . ."

I let the sentence dangle while I turned back to the row of paintings and pulled out the other painting signed by the same artist, which was a complete match to the one I already held. ". . . *this*."

Gilley blinked, and his gaze traveled back and forth between the two. "I don't see a difference."

"Of course not. Because they're identical."

"I don't get it."

"Do you remember how Sasha told you that the word on the street is that the Suttons are selling fake copies of some artists' works?"

Gilley pointed to the two paintings. "Those are fake?"

"I think at least one of them is. Hear me out: Maks goes back and forth between here and Canada. What if he's in a partnership with Jason and Paul Sutton to ferry copies of pieces that'd sold here to a gallery in Canada? The art world is small, but it's made up of individual markets that don't always cross paths. The Hamptons–L.A.–New York City paths might merge into one, but would be unlikely to mingle with the Toronto–Quebec markets.

Maks and the Suttons could pass off originals in both places with ease, and only pay the artist for one commission."

"Sounds like a lot of work," Gilley said.

"It could be, but it could also potentially be quite profitable."

"So what's your point?"

"My point is that maybe Maks and the Suttons had some kind of side hustle, and Basayev found out about it and wasn't happy."

"So how does Chanel fit into this?"

I set down the paintings and began to pace, working it out as I went. "Okay, so if I'm Maks and I'm sticking close to Basayev, and he somehow finds out that the Suttons are making copies of expensive art and selling them in Canada, and he ventures to the gallery to confront Jason Sutton—"

Gilley gasped. "Yes! Remember how nervous Jason was when Basayev entered?"

"I do," I said meaningfully. "And I also remember the cut above Maks's eye that showed up the night he and I had drinks. The night he also asked me to lie to Shepherd about where he was for the duration of the evening."

"Yes!" Gilley said.

"Anyway, say Maks is worried that Jason's going to rat him out to Basayev, so he takes care of Sutton, and *then* he also takes care of Basayev *and* gets revenge on his ex—Chanel—by leaving all that evidence linking her to the crime!"

"My God," Gilley said softly. "It's so wickedly evil!"

"Right?" I agreed.

I then gasped as I began to put more of the puzzle pieces together. "Ohmigod," I said. "Maks *knew* Greta!

They were having dinner together the night Shepherd got shot!"

Gilley put a fist to his mouth. "*He* ordered the hit on Lenny! It makes total sense! By ordering the hit on Lenny, he would've secured the Suttons' loyalty by providing them a price on a house in the Hamptons they couldn't refuse, *and* curried favor with Basayev by tying up Shepherd in the investigation into his ex-wife's murder!"

I could feel myself turn cold and clammy almost instantly, and a violent shiver rattled my entire frame. "Oh, God," I said breathlessly. "I slept with a psychopath!"

Gilley and I stared at each other for a good ten seconds, absorbing all the terrible realizations as they seemed to explode like small grenades in both our minds. I opened my mouth to suggest that we needed to call Shepherd immediately when my phone rang.

It startled both of us and I dropped the phone onto the floor, where it landed faceup, clearly showing the name of the caller on the screen.

Gilley gasped so loud it sounded like a stifled scream. *"It's Maks!"*

I grabbed Gilley's arm, clinging to him like a scared creature, staring down at a snake on the floor. "What do we do?" I said, my voice shaking in fear.

"*Don't* answer it!"

We waited through the rings . . . five in total . . . until the call finally went to voice mail. Tentatively I picked up the phone and stared at the screen, waiting to see if Maks would leave a voice mail.

Instead, a text appeared and the sound of it coming in made both Gilley and I jump again. But that was far less of a fright than the actual text from Maks:

Why r u in my office?

I dropped the phone again with a loud gasp of my own. Immediately, Gilley and I looked all around the room, finally spotting the camera in the far corner.

"What do we do?" Gilley whispered.

A surge of adrenaline coursed through me and I picked up the phone angrily. I tapped out a text of my own and sent it angrily on its way.

We KNOW what you've been up to, you LIAR!

I held the phone with shaking hands while Gilley pressed himself close to me, and we each stared at the screen.

Stay there. I'm on my way. I'll explain it all.

Gilley squeaked. "What do we do now?"

My posture was so stiff and tense that it hurt. I wanted to flee but I didn't think it'd be wise to dash out of the room and run for our lives. Instead, I turned my head away from the camera and told Gilley, "We have to play it cool as long as he's watching us. Follow my lead." Lifting my face to the camera again, I glared at it, but then added a shrug and held up my thumb. Gilley mimicked my posture, and then we exited the room and Maks's office at a nice, leisurely pace. Once we hit the stairs, of course, we raced down them at breakneck speed. Gilley led by a lot of stairs, so it was a surprise to find him at the first-floor landing, pulling himself back into the hallway and up one step toward me.

"What?" I asked, panting. "Come on, Gil! Let's get our things and get the heck outta here!"

"There's a man knocking on the door!" Gilley whispered.

I froze and leaned over Gilley's shoulder to listen.

Sure enough, I could hear faint knocking. "Is that Maks?" I asked softly.

Gilley shook his head. "No! It's some guy—tall, thin, bland, forgettable. . . ."

I moved around Gilley to take a very quick peek through the inner glass door. Sam stood outside in the pelting rain and wind. He was peering through the glass of my office, looking around for signs of life.

Pulling my head back quickly before he could spot me, I said in a hissy whisper, "It's Sam!"

"Who's Sam?" Gilley replied, also in a hissy whisper.

"My client, remember? The FBI operative that I was passing information to from Maks."

"You never confirmed nor denied that's what he was about."

"Well, that's what he was about!"

"So maybe he can help us. If he's a Fed, he can protect us from Maks!"

I put a hand to my mouth. "What if he's not though?"

"Not what?"

"What if he's not a Fed! What if he's just some guy working with Maks to make it look like Maks is a good guy, when he's really this very, very bad man?!"

"Did he ever show you his badge?" Gilley asked. "Or identify himself in any way?"

I shook my head.

"Oh, crap," Gil said. "We're doomed!"

I inched forward again and took another peek. "He's walking away from the door!" I whispered. "We just have to wait for him to go, then we'll need to grab our stuff and get the hell outta here!"

"Okay," Gilley said, but then he pointed to the door

right in front of us. "In case he's coming around to try this entrance, that door is locked, right?"

I gripped Gilley by the arm. I didn't think it was. Lurching forward, I turned the dead bolt. Five seconds later someone outside tried the handle.

Ohmigod! Gilley mouthed.

I put a finger to my lips—I was so afraid Gilley would let out one of his famous terrified squeaks.

The rattling to the handle stopped and we both breathed a sigh of relief, until there came a strange clicking sound on the lock and it began to wiggle.

My eyes widened. So did Gilley's. *He's picking the lock!* Gilley mouthed.

I bit my lip. We had to get out of there! My gaze flicked to the hallway behind us which led to the parking lot, but if we exited there Sam might see us before we could make it to the car. The best chance at avoiding him seeing us was by exiting the front of the building through my office. Pointing to the office, I mouthed, *Through that door!* and Gilley nodded.

Hustling over to the locked interior door, I inserted my key and got us inside the office, locking it again after we made it. "Come on!" I said, my voice just above a whisper.

Grabbing Gilley by the arm, I pulled him to the door at the street entrance, but as we got close to the exit, he started to pull back. "Wait! My laptop! My projector!"

"No time!" I told him firmly.

"My keys!"

"We'll take my car!"

Unlocking the door to the street, I grabbed Gilley again and shoved him out into the pouring rain. Locking the door one last time, I hunched stiffly against the wind and rain, then ran with Gil to the side of the building away from Sam. We ducked low behind the half wall that separated the parking lot of my building from an alley, where we both crouched low and peered over the wall. Sure enough we caught a glimpse of Sam entering the building after picking the lock.

"Come on!" Gilley whispered loudly, and we made a break for the car.

As fast as we could hustle inside, we did, and I started the engine, flipped on the lights, and clicked the windshield wipers onto full blast.

As the water cleared from the windshield a figure came into view standing right in front of my sedan.

Gilley and I both sucked in a breath as an angry Sam pointed something dark at us.

"GUN!" Gilley screamed.

Muscling back the gear shift, I stomped down on the accelerator and we rocketed backward, then I pulled hard on the wheel. We spun in a tire-screeching one-eighty until I hit the brakes, threw the car into drive, and stomped on the accelerator again. We bulleted out of the parking lot, jumping the curb and fishtailing our way out onto the street.

Luckily, there was absolutely no traffic in sight, otherwise, we'd probably be dead.

Wasting no time, I gunned the engine and we raced forward, both of us soaked to the skin and shaking like leaves. "Is he coming after us?" I asked. The rain and the wind were making it impossible to see out the rearview window.

Gilley ducked his chin to look out the passenger side mirror. "I don't see him!" he said. "But he could be coming anytime!"

"Ohmigod, ohmigod, ohmigod!" I cried, gripping the wheel until my knuckles were white. "What do we do?"

Gilley turned to me with a sudden idea. "Call Shepherd! He'll know what to do!"

I nodded. "Grab my phone! It's in my purse!"

Gilley got my phone out, punched in the security code (it had always annoyed me that he knew my code, until that moment that is . . .), and scrolled through my contacts. "Got it!" he said, tapping the screen. He then put the phone to my ear.

"Shepherd!" the detective barked.

"It's Cat!" I said, weaving around a fallen traffic sign and refusing to slow down. "I'm with Gilley and we're in trouble!"

"What kind of trouble?"

"The kind that's trying to kill us!"

"What?!" Shepherd barked. "Where are you?"

"Fleeing my office!"

"Dammit," he swore. "I'm on the other side of town! Can you get to the East Hampton P.D.?"

I was about to answer yes when a memory drifted up to my mind—the memory of Sam, driving past the limo I'd ordered for Gilley and me to take us home from the crime scene on the day that Basayev had been murdered.

A terrible thought occurred to me and I followed the thread all the way to a wince-worthy conclusion. "That's a negative, Detective!" I said. No way was I gonna walk into a trap with anyone I didn't know or trust. And right now the *only* two people I trusted were Gilley and Shepherd.

Shepherd growled. "I'm almost to my destination. . . . Can you come to me?"

"Where are you?"

"I'm headed to Basayev's house. I'll be there in five minutes."

I wanted to ask him why he was going to the mafia boss's house, but I'd have to save that for later. Right now all of my attention needed to be devoted to simply navigating the streets in this weather. "We'll come to you," I said, then I nodded quickly at Gilley and he hung up the phone.

"We're going back to the murder house?" Gilley asked. I looked over quickly and noticed that he looked as pale and frightened as I felt.

"Yes," I said bluntly.

"Why aren't we headed to the police station?"

"Because Sam was at Basayev's crime scene. He pulled up as we were leaving."

"So?"

"So that means he's very likely a Fed."

"I still don't get why that makes seeking help from the East Hampton P.D. a bad idea."

"If Sam's a Fed, and he pulled a gun on us and tried to shoot us, then he's probably a dirty Fed. And if he's a dirty Fed, he could walk right into the East Hampton P.D., claim we'd committed some sort of federal crime, take us into custody, and there wouldn't be a damn thing anyone at the E.H.P.D. could do about it."

"Oh, *God*!" Gilley exclaimed. "You're right!"

I nodded. I knew it. "Shepherd's the only one who'd believe us, and I know he'll shelter us. We've got to get to him."

"You keep driving," Gilley said. "I'll navigate."

Chapter 18

It took us only fifteen minutes to reach the drive leading up to Basayev's house, which was an incredible personal achievement given the state of the raging storm outside.

I'd driven like a madwoman, weaving in and out of felled trees, racing over downed power lines, and refusing to stop for any light that wasn't redder than Rudolf's nose.

I simply couldn't take the risk that Sam had managed to catch up to us or had somehow trailed the path of our flight.

As we headed up the hill toward the house on the cliff, Gilley and I were silent and the car was filled with incredible tension. I just wanted to be in Shepherd's company again, to feel that protective energy he emitted and know that a guy with some power and a great deal of willpower was looking out for me.

Shepherd's car was in the drive in front of the house, and I parked as close as I could get to it before Gilley and I both bolted for the front door.

The house was eerily dark, but then again, so was half of the island. The storm was raging so hard the surf sounded like a demolition derby.

Gilley reached the door first, and he tried the handle. It was unlocked and we walked right in. "Steve?" I called out.

But no one answered.

"Shepherd?" I called louder.

Silence.

I glanced at Gilley. He took a step closer to me, wariness once again a part of his expression.

I walked past the art collection and deeper into the interior of the house, with Gilley practically glued to my side.

We found Shepherd on the floor in the kitchen, a large pool of blood enveloping his head and spreading out across the floor.

I cried out when I saw him and dropped to his side.

Gilley eased down beside me. "Is he . . . ?" he said, his voice quavering.

I laid a gentle hand on the back of Shepherd's head, my chest so tight I found it difficult to breathe. "Please . . ." I whispered to him as my eyes flooded with tears. So much meaning went into that word, and my mind filled with all the unsaid things that followed.

Please don't be dead!

Please don't be too hurt to recover.

Please don't leave me.

Please don't go like this, before I had a chance to tell you who really murdered Lenny.

Slowly, and with a shaking hand, I moved my fingers to the side of his neck and pressed down, searching for a pulse.

When I couldn't locate one I pulled my hand back and crumpled forward, choking on a sob.

Gilley laid an arm across my back, and as I cried I could hear the sounds of his sniffles.

"Catherine," said a voice.

My breath caught. Gilley audibly gasped and dropped his phone, otherwise we were both frozen by the sound.

Slowly I turned to look behind me. Maks stood there in the darkened kitchen, a gun in his hand and an expression that was impossible to read. I shrank against his presence, and Gilley leaned hard against me too.

"Is he dead?" Maks asked. His voice flat, uncaring.

My lips trembled too much for me to speak, and I simply nodded. The acknowledgment hurt my heart more than I could say, and I regretted every second I made Shepherd feel bad after he confessed to me about his affair with Chanel.

"Sam said you fled the office," Maks continued.

My gaze went from his face to his gun, and back again.

"How . . . how did you find us?"

"It was fairly easy," Maks said. "Given what you saw in my office, I figured you'd go to Shepherd, so I had Sam call the E.H.P.D. and find out where the detective was."

More tears leaked out of my eyes when I realized that I was the one Maks was really trying to stop. He'd obviously gotten here before us, shot Shepherd, and had been lying in wait for us. If not for the fact that I'd run away from Sam and sought Shepherd out, he'd be alive right now. I was as responsible for his murder as Maks was.

And then my mind went to my boys, and my heart broke anew. They'd be without a mother after tonight, and that seemed so wrong. It went against every parenting instinct I had. So I pleaded with Maks for the sake of my sons. "My boys . . ." I began, my voice trembling so much that I wasn't even sure that Maks could understand me. "They . . . they need me."

A sort of quirk formed on Maks's mouth, and it hit me how cold blooded he really was. He thought it was funny that I was pleading for my life. And there was no mercy in his eyes.

"We won't say a word!" Gilley tried. He was unwilling to give up. I didn't know who Maks was going to shoot first between us, and I didn't know if I wanted it to be me or Gilley, because I could no more watch him die than die in front of him and leave my sons.

"You won't say a word?" Maks repeated.

Gilley shook his head vigorously. "I swear! Maks, if you let us live, we won't say a single word to anyone! And Shepherd's dead, so who would we tell?"

Maks stared at Gilley for a long time, and then he came forward and dropped down in front of us, no doubt to get a better shot at us lest we try to dart past him and run. I grabbed Gilley and he grabbed me. We'd die together.

Maks raised his hand and I closed my eyes tight. I didn't want to see it coming.

And then I felt something cool against my temple and my breath caught, and Gilley's posture stiffened anew.

"Why would you think I'd hurt you?" Maks whispered.

Tears streamed down my cheeks, and a sob escaped my lips. He was toying with me, drawing it out. The bastard.

"Catherine," Maks said. "Open your eyes."

I shook my head and gripped Gilley tighter. He sobbed too.

And then I heard something like a clunk on the wood floor and felt Maks's presence get up and step back from me.

I waited tensely for several seconds, but nothing happened, and I couldn't decide if Maks was simply waiting for me to open my eyes and shoot me, or . . . if something else was going on.

Finally, I took a chance and peeked out one eye, opening it, then closing it quickly again. But I hadn't really seen anything other than Maks standing at the kitchen island, arms crossed, staring at me.

So I peeked again. Maks held the same posture as before.

After several more moments I finally took a bigger risk and opened my eyes fully. Maks continued to stand there, patiently waiting for me to look at him. So I did, but he didn't say anything.

"What's happening?" Gilley asked in a shaky whisper. "Is he going to shoot us?"

Maks nodded and I bit my lip as fresh tears formed in my eyes. He *was* going to kill us.

But then I realized that Maks wasn't nodding in agreement. He was nodding toward me. Or, toward the floor in front of me.

I looked down and there was the gun he'd been hold-ing. It was lying on the floor right in front of me.

I tried to speak, but only a hoarse sort of choked sound came out. I cleared my throat and tried again. "Is this some kind of a trick?"

"No trick," Maks said. "The gun is loaded, ready to shoot."

I stared at the gun again. "So if I pick it up, you'll shoot me with your *other* gun?" I couldn't figure out Maks's game, but I was a little relieved that he was allowing us to stall.

Maks uncrossed his arms and held open his rain-stained blazer. For good measure he even took it off and set it on the kitchen island. "I'm unarmed," he said. "If you wanted to shoot me, you could."

I stared at him. Then at the gun. Then at him again, and with both eyes glued to the man, I felt around for the gun until my hand had hold of the handle.

It was cold against my fingers, and heavier than I'd ex-pected. I confess, I've never held a gun before. My sister knows how to shoot—she supposedly even owns a gun—but for me, they've always been terrifying weapons of destruction. I hated the touch of the thing, and I hated that Maks had even brought it here to tempt me into using it.

Which I wouldn't.

At least, I didn't think I would.

"Why did you give me this?" I asked Maks.

"To make you feel safe."

"You think giving me a *gun* will make me feel safe?"

"No. I think giving you *my* gun will make you feel safe."

"Why are you arguing with him?" Gilley whispered. "Just point that thing at him and if he moves, *shoot!*"

I ignored Gilley and continued to hold the gun with the barrel pointed at the floor. "Why did you come here, Maks, if not to kill us?"

Maks breathed in deeply, as if what I said had insulted him in some way. "I came to explain to you about the artwork."

"We know about the artwork!" Gilley snapped. "You and Sutton were in business together!"

Maks shrugged. "Yes. That's correct."

"Ah-ha!" Gilley said, pointing at him. "See? He admitted it, Cat! You're justified if you want to shoot him."

Again, I ignored Gilley and stared angrily at Maks. The betrayals all cut so deep, I decided to unpack them. "No one's seen or heard from Chanel since her release. Did you kill her too, Maks?"

He squinted at me. "Of course I didn't."

"So she's hiding from you too, huh?"

"I suspect she's hiding from everyone. Most especially her ex, who's responsible for all of this." Maks nodded toward Shepherd, but I couldn't glance at him, because I was certain I'd lose it emotionally all over again.

"We know, Maks," I said to him. Raw anger was now coursing through me.

"You know what?"

"That *you're* her IO. Her insignificant other. The guy she's really hiding from."

Maks's mouth opened slightly and I swear to God he let out what sounded like a small laugh. "You've got it all wrong, Catherine. All wrong."

A tiny seed of doubt crept into my mind. But then I remembered that Maks was a master at deception. He'd lied to my sister—a world-renowned psychic who could detect a liar a mile away—and gotten away with it. Some-how . . .

Damn. That tiny seed of doubt sprouted roots.

So I challenged him. "How exactly have I gotten it all wrong, Maks?"

"I wasn't Chanel's lover."

"We saw the photos on Basayev's Instagram!" Gilley yelled, bolstering our argument. "You and Chanel at a party. You and Chanel on Basayev's yacht. You two were obviously a thing!"

"Why would you conclude that from a few photos?" Maks asked.

"Because on that yacht you three were the only ones there!" I yelled. We were all getting a little emotional. "You and Chanel looked super cozy together," I sneered.

Maks's gaze flicked between me and Gilley, then back again. "You're forgetting about the photographer," he said. "The one who, I guarantee, was *never* in any of the photos taken. Chanel's lover, who I unwittingly intro-duced her to and have sincerely regretted ever since."

I stared at Maks. It'd never occurred to me that the camera phone being used in the photos was being held by someone, and I couldn't believe how dumb it was to not have considered the person behind the camera—the one who wasn't in any of the photos.

"Who was behind the camera?" I asked, almost afraid to hear the answer.

"Me," said a voice from the corridor.

All three of us stiffened. I knew that voice. I'd heard it in my nightmares for months.

"Oh, God!" Gilley squeaked. He recognized it too. "We're all dead!"

The Angel of Death stepped into the kitchen, holding a gun with a silencer attached. Although, she needn't have bothered—the crash from the surf outside as the storm raged was enough to drown out a cannon.

"Hello, Catherine," Greta said, looking at me with a snarky smile. "We meet again."

Seeing Greta again, holding a gun pointing at me, brought back a wave of fear that gripped my rib cage like a python. For a long, tense moment I didn't think I was going to be able to inhale a single breath, but then Maks made the smallest of moves toward me and Greta shifted the angle of the gun over to him.

"Ah-ah, Maksie. Leave the gun be. It's quite safe in Catherine's hands. No chance of it going off, you know."

My gaze dropped to the gun in my hand, and without even thinking about it I pivoted it in my palm, lifted my rib cage, which allowed that first, deep breath of air, and shot Greta.

It all happened so fast that, as the pungent odor of the discharged gun in my hand filled the room, everyone stared at me as if to say, "Did that just happen?"

And then Greta sank down to her knees, her hand going to an expanding red stain just above her hip. "You *shot* me!"

I started to tremble so violently that I dropped the gun. Greta raised hers to my face when there was a blur of movement as Maks dove for his gun on the floor.

Almost in slow motion I saw Greta change the angle of her arm a fraction before she fired. Maks hit the floor and grunted, but he did manage to grab hold of his gun before rolling into me and Gilley.

We toppled over and panic caused both of us to scramble away from everybody holding a gun.

Gilley gained his feet first, and he grabbed my arm, pulling me out of the kitchen into the hallway leading to the back of the house. There was an exchange of gunfire in the kitchen, and we ducked low, moving behind the sofa.

And then Maks appeared out of the kitchen, both of his arms dangling oddly as he ducked low and shuffled to us. Before he dropped down next to us, I saw that his left arm was bleeding so badly that his sleeve and hand were completely covered in blood. And then I saw another wound to his right shoulder, which left his right hand limp and barely able to hold the weapon in his hand.

He leaned over on his knees, sweat now coating his forehead, and the gun fell onto the floor in front of him. "We have to get to the bedroom!" he panted.

"She's still alive?" Gilley asked him, his eyes wide with panic.

Maks nodded, his breathing labored. He nodded toward the bedroom and Gilley and I helped him to his feet, causing him to grunt in pain again.

We'd taken three steps when Maks looked over his shoulder and said, "My gun!"

Gilley and I exchanged a look that debated going back for the gun or continuing to move to the bedroom, where, hopefully we could lock the door against Greta and make a frantic call to the police.

Gil pressed his lips together with determination and began to turn back for Maks's weapon when a vase on the table next to us exploded into a million pieces, pelting us with shards of glass.

I cried out as I felt the sting of tiny shards, slicing open my cheek, but I also reacted reflexively by pulling Maks closer and ducking quickly down the hallway.

Gilley abandoned his effort to retrieve Maks's gun and we rushed into the master bedroom, where I fell to the floor with Maks while Gilley slammed the door shut and locked it. He then looked frantically around the room for something to put against the door to secure it, but the room was quite utilitarian—only the platform bed and armoire counted as furniture, and I doubted he and I could move either—especially the armoire, which was very large and looked very heavy.

"The mattress!" Gilley said, pointing to the king bed.

I thought he had to be kidding, but we had to try something. I rushed to one side while he rounded the bed on the other.

"Stop," Maks said, his voice straining with effort.

I looked over at him and saw that the wood floor under his arm had already collected an alarmingly large pool of blood, and it was then that I realized Maks's wound was far more serious than I'd originally thought. Greta's bullet had hit an artery.

"He's bleeding out! Gilley, give me your belt!" I yelled at Gilley, abandoning the bed to rush to Maks's side again. Gilley came down next to me and pulled on his belt to loosen it from around his waist.

Maks collapsed from his seated position onto the floor to lie on his side, his breathing shallow and his complexion growing paler by the second. "Panic . . . room," he said.

"Shhhh," I told him, hurrying to find a point above the vicious-looking wound on his arm where I could secure a tourniquet. "We're trying not to panic, Maks. Just hold still for a moment."

Maks's eyes rolled up in his head, and he fought to stay conscious. "No," he whispered. I pulled tight on the belt, my hands finding it difficult to grip the leather as I trembled in fear. Still, I managed and wound the leather around his arm again, looping it over itself and working to secure it so that it would stem the flow of blood.

Maks winced and shook with each pull on the belt, and I hated that I was hurting him, but I kept at it because otherwise, he'd die within a matter of minutes. Meanwhile Gilley was staring at Maks as if trying to work something out.

And then I realized that Maks was pointing to a corner of the room, and Gilley was turning his head from Maks to the corner and back again. Gilley then got up and hurried to the corner, where he laid his hand on the wall, which was wallpapered with a print of deep teal and small gold squares.

Gilley gasped. "There's a door here!" he whispered.

I secured the belt as tightly as I could and watched Maks's wound for any further evidence that it was still the source of so much blood loss, but his fingers began to turn blue and I knew I'd secured it well. I then turned my attention to his other wound, which was also bleeding but not nearly as profusely. Yanking a discarded towel off the small bench at the base of Basayev's bed, I pushed it onto Maks's shoulder and he grunted and moaned in pain.

More than anything, this seemed to revive him slightly, and he stared at me with intensity. "Get . . . into . . . the panic . . . room," he panted.

I glanced toward Gilley, who was still running his hand along the seal of the hidden door.

"How?" I asked Maks.

Maks's eyes rolled up again, and I knew he was losing consciousness, so, without any other choice, I pushed down on his shoulder again and he moaned but came back to me. "I'm so sorry, Maks, but *how* do we get into that room?"

Maks nudged his chin toward the Nest thermostat on the wall next to the bed. "Ninety . . . eight . . . degrees," he said so softly I could barely hear him.

"Gilley!" I called, but then lowered my voice to just above a whisper. "Set the thermostat to ninety-eight degrees!"

Gilley looked at me in confusion, but I motioned to the thermostat sternly and he seemed to catch on. He left the wall and began to head toward the thermostat when a series of shots exploded through the bedroom door.

Gil dove for cover and I laid down and pulled Maks out of the line of fire. When the shots stopped, the area near the handle was riddled with bullets, but the door held . . . barely.

And then Greta began to kick on the door. It was a fairly feeble sound at first, suggesting the wound I'd given her was taking its toll, but she was a determined bitch and I knew she wouldn't stop until at least one of us was dead.

I lifted my head to look toward Gilley, who'd disappeared behind the other side of the bed. "Gil!" I cried. "You have to do it now!"

To my relief, Gilley's head popped up, his eyes wide and panic-stricken, but still he found the courage to crawl up onto the bed, make his way across the mattress, and reach up for the thermostat. After he moved the rotating dial to ninety-eight degrees, the Nest's face suddenly turned from red to green and there was a *whoosh* sound across the room.

The hidden door slid to the side and revealed a small

room with three blank walls and one made completely of glass, mirroring the design of the wall facing the ocean in the living room.

It dawned on me then that this was the hidden space between the fireplace and the outside wall that linked the bedroom with the living area.

And huddled in the far corner, sitting on a thin mattress on the floor with her knees pulled up to her chest, was Chanel. She was staring at us with the terror of a cornered little fawn.

Meanwhile Greta continued to kick at the door, and the first sound of it giving way reached my ears. "Help me!" I yelled to both Gilley and Chanel as I got to my knees and tried to pull Maks to the doorway.

Gilley reached me and lifted Maks under the arms. Maks cried out, his eyes rolling back into his head one final time, and he went limply into unconsciousness. Neither Gilley nor I paused in our effort to get him into the panic room, because along with the sounds of the door beginning to give way, there was a barely detectible beep coming from the Nest thermostat. One glance in that direction and I saw that the temperature setting had counted down from ninety-eight to twenty-one and I realized that the dial was giving us roughly thirty seconds and counting before it would close the door again and either shut us in, or lock us out.

"Hurry!" I urged. Gil pulled Maks, and I moved to his middle, lifting him around the waist.

Somehow we managed to get Maks through the doorway with just three seconds to spare, but in those three seconds we saw the door finally burst open, and a sweaty, bloody, *enraged* Greta appeared. She lifted her hand as the waves and surf crashed against the rocks below us, sending shudders through the floorboards, and the door closed as she got off three more shots.

Gilley and I collapsed onto the floor, but I quickly looked at him to make sure he wasn't injured. "Are you okay?" I asked.

"No!" he yelled.

I sat up to check on him and it appeared he wasn't hurt, just shaken. I then looked to Chanel, who hadn't moved from her spot in the corner and appeared to be in a state of shock as she stared listlessly out in front of her, but otherwise she didn't look injured.

I then focused on Maks, who was so pale, I thought at first that he might be dead. Putting my head down onto his chest, I listened and was rewarded to hear his heart still beating, albeit far too weakly.

"We need to get him to a hospital," I said. "Gilley, call the police!"

Gilley patted his jacket and then his hand went to the inside of his jacket to fish around in the pocket, but suddenly his eyes widened and he pulled his hand out to slap the side of his face. "I dropped my phone in the kitchen!" he said. "When we first saw Shepherd, I pulled it out to call nine-one-one, but dropped it as soon as Maks showed up."

I looked down at myself. My phone was in my Birkin, which was also in the kitchen on the floor, next to Shepherd's body.

Wincing at the memory of realizing my friend and lover was dead, I sucked in a steadying breath. I would mourn Shepherd after we got out of this mess. "My phone's in my purse, which is also in the kitchen," I said.

"You can use mine," Chanel said. Gilley and I turned to her. She'd obviously snapped out of whatever shock she'd been in, and was holding her phone out to us. "It won't matter though," she said as Gilley got up to retrieve her phone. "She'll find a way in."

Just then a particularly large wave crashed against the rocks below us and the entire house shook to an alarming degree. I glanced out the window at the oncoming waves and felt the first twinges of foreboding weave their way through the tapestry of emotions coursing through me since entering this horrible house.

"Gilley," I said.

"Yeah?" he replied, taking Chanel's phone from her.

"Tell them to hurry!"

Chapter 19

Moving over to Chanel's bed, I pointed to a sheet. "Can I have that? I need to make Maks comfortable."

Chanel got up from the bed. "I'll help you move him."

While Gilley called the police, Chanel and I moved Maks to her bed. I had a chance then to look around and realized she'd been staying here for quite some time. There was a stack of paperbacks, and snacks, and extra batteries for the lantern next to her lone mattress, along with a case of bottled water.

"How long have you been here?" I asked her.

"Two weeks."

My eyes widened. "Two weeks?"

She nodded. "Boris was unloading assets, getting ready to flee back to Chechnya for a while. He knew the Feds were closing in. He found me at my grandaunt's and told me he didn't want to pay over a point and a half to sell his house in the Hamptons. He knew that if I listed it, he'd only have to pay the agency the one and a half percent, because I'd work for free."

"You would?" I said.

Chanel eyed me with a wisdom born from experience. "*Nobody* said no to Boris."

"Ah," I said. I understood. "And in exchange for your taking on the listing, he let you stay here?"

"Yep. And as you can see he provided all the luxuries. . . ." Chanel made a sweeping motion with her hand, and I frowned. Boris had been an obvious ass. "Still, I figured it was safe to come back, and if I'd sold this place, I could've continued on with the agency and tried to get a few more listings."

"You were running out of money," I said.

Chanel nodded. "My grandaunt was generous to allow me to stay rent free for the past two years, but I had expenses I couldn't ask her to cover. I needed to work."

"Guys?" Gilley said, interrupting us. When we turned to him, he said, "I can't get a signal."

My jaw dropped. "What do you mean you can't get a signal?"

Gilley pointed to the wall of windows, and the waves that seemed to have grown even larger from only moments ago. "The storm must've taken down a cell tower or something. Chanel's got no bars."

Chanel made an impatient sound. "Stupid cell company!" she growled, taking the phone from Gilley's hand. "I had to go with the cheapest carrier, and cell service around here is always spotty, but I never thought their service would go out altogether!"

"What do we do?" I asked, hoping Gilley had an idea.

And I'd take *any* idea at that moment because our options—especially where Maks was concerned—were quite limited.

"I don't know," he admitted.

We fell into silence, because we all knew that there was very little hope of saving Maks now, much less ourselves. Greta wouldn't let us remain hidden for long. I believed Chanel when she said that the Angel of Death would find her way in.

"Why is she after you?" I asked Chanel. Maybe there was something we could use to convince Greta to let us live.

"Because I left her," Chanel said simply. "Greta wouldn't have let that go for long."

"How could you even date her, though?" Gilley asked. "I mean, the woman *kills* for a living!"

Chanel nodded. "Would you believe that for the longest time I didn't know? Maks didn't either. Boris used to call Greta his personal accountant. I thought she worked with numbers, and that's why Maks befriended her, I think. I was always suspicious of Maks. I thought he was an informant, but of course I never said anything. By the time I found out what Greta really was, I was in way too deep."

"Why did Greta kill Lenny?" I asked next. That was a question I wanted to know the answer to more than anything.

Chanel bit her lip and tears formed in her eyes. "Greta suspected I was having an affair and she was right. Shortly after he and I stopped seeing each other, I began wearing a necklace that Steve had given to me. Greta noticed, but she didn't let on that she'd noticed. She secretly worked to hunt down the jewelry store it came from and then she broke in to their accounting office and stole their receipts. She discovered that Shepherd's credit card had been used to pay for it and she started to put what she thought was two and two together. But she was off about which of the Shepherds I'd been cheating on her with.

"She assumed that, because I was into her, the person I was having an affair with had to be a woman. She thought I was sleeping with Lenny, and she assumed that Lenny had used her husband's credit card to buy me the necklace. Since I was also working with Lenny, Greta assumed she was a threat to our relationship, so she eliminated the threat."

I put a hand to my mouth. "She killed Lenny because she thought she was having an affair with you?"

Chanel nodded. "Yes," she said in a choked whisper. "I never told Steve, but that's why Lenny died."

"But the Suttons . . ." Gilley said.

"Greta knew they were trying to find a house here in the Hamptons and that they were going to launder money for Boris. She was the one who went to Boris and told him that she'd just cleared the way to have the gallery owners move here—and she'd also just tied up Hampton's lead detective in a case he'd never solve."

"She was the mastermind behind it all," I said.

Chanel sniffled, wiping a tear that had slid down her cheek. "She was. She confessed it all to me, probably to punish me. She didn't kill me then, but she might as well have. She murdered one of my closest friends and business partner, and still expected me to take on the Suttons as clients. Cold doesn't even begin to describe Greta. She's subzero."

I wondered if Chanel knew about her grandaunt's murder. She hadn't mentioned it, and I didn't feel brave enough to bring it up to her. Or to tell her about Shepherd's body out in the kitchen.

"Did you know we were here?" I asked her, trying to ferret out what she knew about our arrival—and Shepherd's.

"Not you specifically, but I knew someone was in the house. The storm started getting bad and I was thinking about leaving when I heard somebody at the front door. I'd just made it into this room when I heard Greta's voice and a shot ring out. I'm assuming one of Boris's henchmen came here looking for treasure and arrived right around the same time that Greta figured out where I'd been hiding. Unfortunate for him, but that's what he gets for looting the boss's house."

Gilley and I exchanged a look. So, Chanel *didn't* know that the person who'd come here and had gotten shot by Greta was Shepherd. Gilley subtly shook his head. I agreed. No way were we going to tell her.

At that moment another huge wave rattled the house, and the three of us looked out the windows at the terrifying sea. It was like something out of the movie *The Perfect Storm*. The crests of the waves were at least thirty to forty feet high and the bottom of the window was wet with ocean spray.

I didn't know then if I was more nervous about Greta gaining access to this room or the increasing violence of the storm. Either way it felt like we were sitting ducks.

"We have to do something," Gilley said.

"I'm all ears," I told him. I was open to any idea. Gilley looked at the other three walls, which were solid except for what appeared to be the only exit out. "Chanel, how do you get out of here?" he asked her.

She pointed to a green button on the wall. "You punch that."

Gilley looked at me, and there was a sort of resigned sadness in his eyes. "She can't shoot all three of us if we rush her, can she?"

"She's a trained assassin," I said. "She probably could."

"She's a *wounded* assassin," he corrected. "And she could very well be unconscious right now from all the blood loss." For emphasis he looked to Maks.

I weighed the thought of staying here and hoping the authorities eventually showed up, looking for Shepherd, against the likelihood that, if the three of us opened the door and rushed out of here, Greta might only shoot one or two of us as we fled.

My mind drifted to Matt and Mike, and my heart broke for a future where I wouldn't be alive to see them grow into men.

But then something came to mind that gave me some courage. My sister—Abby—had once predicted that I'd own property in Hawaii. Just a year ago she'd said she'd had a very clear vision of visiting me on the island of Kauai, where I had a lovely vacation home on the southeast side of the island. She said she also saw the boys there, but they were in their early twenties so she knew it was at least a decade away.

I realized that if Abby had seen me vacationing in Hawaii when the boys were in their twenties, then I must be fated to make it through this day.

Still, I felt my chest tighten at the thought that Gilley and Chanel had no such assurances.

Another wave hit the rocks below the house with

tremendous force, and the entire structure reverberated, and then something else sounded and shook the house.

It almost sounded like the snapping of wood, but it was sharper, and louder, and the whole house creaked and strained.

We looked at each other, realizing there was no way we could stay in this room and survive, but there might still be a chance for us beyond the door.

"Well," I said. "We don't seem to have much choice. We have to go."

Gilley pointed to Maks, and I felt my fists clench with frustration. We couldn't leave him in this room alone either. I motioned to Gilley. We'd carry him out between us.

Chanel moved over to my side and said, "Let me. I'm taller."

I moved out of Chanel's way and over to the green button on the side of the door. Gilley and Chanel had a tentative hold on Maks, each gripping an arm and the waistband of his jeans. His body sagged between them.

"Get him clear of the house, then set him down and run," I whispered to them. "We can't carry him to safety beyond the front door."

Gilley nodded. "Got it. Now get us out of here, Cat."

I moved over to the nightstand and picked up Chanel's lantern. It was the only weapon in the room. I was going to launch it at Greta, create a diversion, and pray the three of us could skirt around her and out the door.

My heart pounded in my chest as the surf pounded against the rocks. With a final nod from Gilley, I punched the green button and the door slid open.

Across the room Greta hovered near the thermostat, turning it this way and that. She held herself nearly double, her body coated in sweat. She turned as the door

opened, obviously surprised. Gilley and Chanel ducked
low with Maks and tried to run, but their effort was more
of a fast shuffle. The second they were clear of the door I
stepped through and hurtled the lamp toward Greta with
all my might.

Her arm came up and deflected the lantern to the side,
and she screamed in pain as her arm connected with the
heavy plastic object.

The second the lantern struck its mark, I bolted, ready
to race after Chanel and Gilley, but something flew past
me and struck the wall. A glance to the side showed me it
was a knife. Greta was armed with more than a gun, it
seemed.

Gilley and Chanel made it out of the room, but I
slipped on the pool of blood on the floor from Maks's
wound. I went down, tried to scramble up, but went down
again.

Greta came at me with another knife and barred teeth,
beating me to the door. Changing course, my arms and
legs moving in any and every direction, I tried to get
away from the arc of the knife as she brought it down in
my direction. She nearly sliced me open twice as she too
slipped in the blood.

I backed away from Greta, my gaze darting between
her and the door where Gilley, Chanel, and Maks had escaped, trying to find an angle I could move that would
take me to them, but Greta was too quick for me. Even
critically wounded she was a formidable opponent.

She and I both gained our footing at the same moment,
she, hovering in the doorway, and me backing away toward the windows.

"It's *over*, Greta!" I yelled at her.

"Oh, it's *far* from over, Catherine," she growled.

A wave struck the rocks below the house with tremendous force and the whole house didn't just shake, it dropped several inches. I lost my footing again and went down, but so did Greta.

Several of the windows broke, and a cold forceful wind entered the room, whipping our hair and pulling at our clothing. All I wanted to do was make it out of that room, but Greta continued to block the way.

And then, a lone figure appeared in the doorway. He was small, but he was carrying what looked like a police baton. "Catherine!" he shouted to me.

"Willem!" I cried.

Greta turned and raised her arm, lashing out at poor Willem. He got the baton up in the nick of time, blocking the blow, but Greta held tight to the knife. She lunged again, but Willem was still quicker, and he dodged out of the way with only a fraction of space between him and the knife.

I realized that Greta would likely win their battle unless I did something, so I used the only weapon I could find, which was the lantern again. I bent, picked it up just as Greta lunged toward poor Willem a final time. Flinging the lantern with all my might, I watched as it connected to Greta's back and she went down to the floor.

"Run!" I screamed at Willem, and I charged toward the door.

Leaping over Greta as she rolled to her side, I was just about out the door when yet another wave crashed into the rocks below the house. There was a tremendous *snap* and more windows exploded outward.

I fell to the floor yet again, and so did Willem. He was only inches from me, and he crawled on his belly to my side. "Come on!" he yelled above the sound of crashing surf, wind, and the raging storm. "We've got to get out of here!"

I clung to him and pushed against the wall to try and gain a purchase. The floor of the house had given way by several feet, and I realized the entire structure of the house was about to fall away onto the rocks below.

With Willem's help I managed to get to my knees, and then to my feet, and he pulled and coaxed me to the door.

Behind me there was a terrible shriek, and I glanced one last time over my shoulder only to find Greta had slipped on the wet floor and slid down toward the far wall. As I looked she was clinging to the armoire, which was also beginning to slip down the increasingly steep slope of the floor. A wave as big as any I'd ever seen in my life was beginning to roll straight for us. We had maybe ten seconds to make it out of the house.

"Goooooooo!" I screamed to Willem, but he held my hand tight and pulled me forward with a strength that belied his stature. Fueled by panic, we cleared the bedroom, then the living room, and raced down the hall toward the open front door.

As we passed the kitchen, my head turned when I thought about Shepherd. I didn't want his body to be lost to the ocean when it took the house, but I knew I'd have to leave him behind because there wasn't time.

We raced past the kitchen so fast that he wasn't in view, which might've been a blessing, because I'd no doubt take that image of his prone body, lying there on the floor, with me to my grave.

Behind us more snapping and glass breaking reverberated through the collapsing structure, and I truly didn't know if Willem and I would make it, but with only three feet to go, Willem pulled hard on my hand and whipped me through the front door, diving out himself right after me.

We landed in a tumble on the front drive, the cement tearing into my clothing and skin, and pounding my bones as hard as the surf had pounded the house's under-pinnings.

As I curled myself into a ball from pain and fear, I heard a tremendous series of cracks and crashes, one final scream, and then only the sound of the howling wind, pelting rain, and raging sea. . . .

Chapter 20

A hand landed on my shoulder. In a dense series of chaotic, life-threatening, earth-shattering moments, that's the one I remembered the clearest. Or maybe I just remembered the feeling of that warm hand on my person, letting me know I was alive, that I'd survived, that some-one was there with me to offer me some comfort from all that I'd witnessed and experienced in just the past half hour.

Lifting my face from its cradled position in my arms, I looked up, blinking through the rain, and sucked in a breath.

"Hey," Shepherd said. "You okay?"

I sat up, wincing the whole way. "How . . . how're you . . . I thought you were . . ."

The detective—who had squatted down next to me—put a hand to his head where a nasty gash had grazed his temple right down to the bone. "The Angel of Death isn't the great shot she thinks she is," he said.

I reached up too and put a hand on the side of his cheek. Tears formed in my eyes and streamed down my face, joining the rain. All that pent-up emotion came tumbling out and Shepherd seemed moved by it. He opened his arms wide and pulled me close to him, encircling me with strong, supportive arms. "Shhhhh," he whispered. "It's okay. It's all okay."

Somewhere in the distance came the sound of sirens, loud enough to be heard just above the raging sea. Wind and rain pelted us, but I still felt safe cradled against Shepherd.

A long time passed, and there was no doubt quite a bit of movement was going on all around me. I heard the crunch of footsteps, and the words of first responders, and the work from paramedics who were tending to Maks.

I finally pulled my head away from Shepherd's chest just in time to see Maks loaded into the ambulance, an oxygen mask on his face and an IV hooked to his arm. And then I saw Gilley and Chanel, each huddled under a blanket, also staring with concern toward Maks.

As the ambulance left the drive, its lights on and siren blaring, my attention went to two figures across the drive, staring down into the abyss where once had been a house. Willem was talking with a man in an FBI jacket, and I realized it was Sam.

"How you doin'?" Shepherd asked me again.

"Cold," I said, shivering against him.

He pulled me to my feet slowly and carefully and walked me over to the bay of another ambulance. "Can we take a look at that wound now, Detective?" an impatient paramedic asked.

"Sure," Shepherd said. "As long as you look her over first."

"I'm fine," I said, but I was gently eased out of Shepherd's arms anyway.

When the paramedic pulled on my arm I cried out. He eyed me with one cocked eyebrow, raised the sleeve on my right arm, and said, "Could be broken."

My wrist was swollen and turning an unflattering shade of purple. While Shepherd was attended to, my wrist was wrapped very gingerly in an Ace bandage and my entire arm put into a sling. They wanted to take us both to the hospital, and Shepherd began to decline, but I said, "I'll go if he'll go."

He frowned, knowing he could hardly turn the paramedics down now. "That's some dirty pool, there, lady."

"You clearly need stitches and you lost an awful lot of blood, Detective."

"I'm fine, and there's too much to wrap up here," he insisted, but he didn't look fine. He looked pale, and exhausted, and in need of a little TLC.

Gilley came over to the open bay of the ambulance. "Nice to find him alive after being declared dead, huh?"

Shepherd cocked an eyebrow at Gilley, and I was quick to explain. "When we entered the house we found you on the floor in the kitchen in a pool of blood. I felt for a pulse and couldn't find one."

"You gotta press directly on the carotid artery," the paramedic explained. "It can be a lot harder to find than people think."

"So it would seem," I said, smiling at Shepherd. There were no words for how happy and relieved I felt at the sight of him alive.

The ambulance took us to the hospital, but Shepherd

insisted they not use the lights or siren. Once there, he was sent for an MRI and then stitches, and my wrist was X-rayed and set in a cast. I had a hairline fracture to the right radius and would have to wear a cast for six weeks.

I found Gilley in the waiting room, still huddled in his blanket. He too looked exhausted but anxious to learn that I was okay.

"Is there any word on Maks?" I asked after he'd given me a gingerly hug.

Gilley nodded. "He was taken into surgery two hours ago. We won't know anything more for a while."

"Chanel?"

"She's okay. She and that FBI agent were talking when I left to come here."

Sam would want to talk to Chanel at length, I imagined. "How's Willem?" I asked next.

"You mean the hero of the hour?"

I cocked my head, not understanding.

Gilley explained. "I accidentally hit Willem's number on my phone when Maks entered the kitchen. I had no idea my phone had dialed his number until he told me about it later. He said he listened to most of what went on, thinking it was some sort of drama you and I were putting on to convince him to come out of his house. But then he heard gunshots, and he heard Maks hit the floor and moan in pain. He hopped in his Range Rover and braved the storm all the way to Basayev's house."

"How'd he even know where to go?"

"I asked him the same thing, and he said that he knew where we were the minute Maks mentioned Sam telling him to find Shepherd at Boris Basayev's house. Willem's a news junkie—the local news is his only window into the community, and remember, he even mentioned to us on the way to the alpaca farm that he'd heard that a murder had taken place here."

I nodded. I did remember that.

"Anyway," Gilley continued, "Willem drove like a bat outta hell to get here, and he found Shepherd just coming to on the kitchen floor but still really out of it. He was going to call nine-one-one right there, but then he heard gunshots from the bedroom, and he had to be very careful to sneak Shepherd out of the house without drawing Greta's attention.

"When he got Shepherd safely out of the house and behind his car, he called nine-one-one. Dispatch told him they'd do what they could but it might be a while because they were fielding nine-one-one calls from everywhere in the area due to the storm. So, he sat tight with Shepherd for a bit, and he said he had his hands full with the detective because Shepherd kept trying to get up to go into the house and rescue us, but the man could barely keep his head up without collapsing."

"Concussion," I assumed. One of the paramedics had found an egg-sized lump and another, smaller gash on the back of Shepherd's head. He thought that when Greta's bullet had grazed Shepherd, the detective had fallen backward from the recoil and hit his head on the kitchen island, which then pitched him forward again and he'd knocked his head a second time on the floor when he landed.

"That's why there was so much blood on the floor," I added. "Shepherd had bled from not just one spot, but two."

Gilley nodded. "For sure," he said. "So Willem finally convinced Shepherd to stay put while he went inside to see what he could do. Greta had taken Shepherd's gun, so

Willem had only the baton from Shepherd's car as a
weapon."

"No mace? No spare gun somewhere?" I asked.

"You watch too many cop shows," Gil said. "I'm surprised that Shepherd was even carrying the baton."

"Well, it *is* East Hampton. Shepherd probably didn't
think he'd need much of a backup for his police issued
handgun."

"Truth," Gil said. "Anyway, where was I?"

"Willem was approaching the house."

"Yes, yes," Gilley said. "So he gets inside and *boom!*
That first wave hits and he hears one of the support
beams give way."

My eyes widened. "The curse . . ."

"For sure it was the curse," Gilley said.

I shook my head in wonder. "I'm surprised Willem
didn't run."

"He's super brave," Gilley said. "And you know the
rest, except Willem told me that when the two of you
came through that doorway as the house collapsed behind
you . . . which, I know you didn't *see,* Cat, but I swear it
was like something straight out of an action flick. . . ."

I shuddered. "I felt it collapsing under my feet, Gilley.
I know it was an epic thing to watch."

"Yes, and one that Willem swears helped lift the curse
from him. He says that as he went through the doorway it
was like a heavy coat he'd always worn got pulled right
off him. When he landed, he knew something had
changed. He thinks the house and Greta took the curse
over that cliff."

I put a hand to my mouth. "Heath had suggested that
the curse might need a sacrifice in order to be lifted."

"Well, the Angel of Death would be a pretty good sacrifice."

I nodded. "She would indeed."

At that moment a figure entered the waiting room and Gilley and I glanced up to see Sam standing there, looking around. Spotting us, he came over and sat down across from us. "How're you doing, Ms. Cooper?"

I lifted my cast. "I'll mend," I said curtly.

His brow furrowed. "You mad at me?"

"Yes," I snapped. "But I tend to get upset with people who point a gun at me."

Sam seemed taken aback. "Gun? I never pointed a gun at you."

"Yes you did!" I insisted. "As we were backing out of the parking space you pointed your gun right at us."

Sam began to laugh, but then he sobered quickly when both Gilley and I glared hard at him and crossed our arms.

Holding up his hand in surrender, he said, "Let me show you." Reaching behind him, he pulled up a small walkie-talkie. "I was using this because the storm took out a cell tower and I couldn't get service. It just happened to be in my hand when I was ordering you to stop."

"Oh," Gilley and I said together, and we both uncrossed our arms.

"Well, it looked like a gun," I said, still a little grumpy.

"I would never point a gun at you, Ms. Cooper, or you, Mr. Gillespie, without a damn good reason." Switching topics, Sam looked around again and said, "Is there any word on Grinkov?"

"He's in surgery," Gilley said.

"Care to fill us in on what *exactly* was going on with

your little operation?" I asked. I wasn't certain that Sam would tell us, but now that Basayev *and* the Angel of Death were dead, I thought maybe he'd clue us in on a few details.

Sam seemed to agree. "I suppose I owe you that. Let's see, where should I start?"

"Start with Lenny," I said. I wanted Sam to understand that her life had meant something. He might've been after a big fish when he tried to bring down Basayev, but Lenny Shepherd had meant something to the world, and her life was worth an acknowledgment of that.

Sam dipped his chin in a show of respect. He got it. "Okay. As I'm now aware of the full story after having talked with Ms. Downey, let's start with her.

"But first a little background might be in order. Chanel met Boris when she represented him as the buyer's agent for the plot of land where he built that house. As a side note, Paul Sutton was the architect who designed it. That's how Maks knew about the panic room; Paul told him about it and how to get into it back when we were getting ready to move in to arrest Basayev because Paul knew Boris would've headed there at the first sign of trouble.

"Anyway, Paul was a better artist than he was architect—"

"Obviously," Gilley interrupted. We both looked at him. "I mean . . . his house *did* fall into the ocean."

"True," said Sam. "Mostly, Paul was a troubled alcoholic in a miserable relationship with an abusive husband. He wanted out of his marriage and he wanted to get away from Jason's mafia connections, so he started a side hustle where he'd see what was selling through the gallery, then mimic the styles of that artist and get the paintings to Maks, who would pretend to sell them in Toronto and split the commissions with Jason.

"It's how we were able to nail him for fraud, and get him to flip to our side."

My jaw dropped. "Paul was your source? Your informant?"

"He was," Sam said. "But he was unreliable in many ways due to the alcoholism, which put Maks in a precarious situation that started to fall apart when Boris found out about the counterfeit paintings. He thought that Jason was the one who'd orchestrated the scheme, and the day you two were at the gallery, Boris nearly killed Jason, but Maks was able to talk Boris down. But then Maks went back to the gallery to try to smooth things over with Jason, because Maks was worried Jason was going to go home and kill Paul. Their talk didn't go so well, and things got heated."

"The cut above his eye," I said.

Sam nodded. "Anyway, when Jason was found dead, we all thought Boris had ordered the hit, but we couldn't figure out why Boris would frame Maks unless he was onto him. That's why Maks had to lay low for a few days, to figure out what Boris might know."

"*Did* Boris kill Jason?" Gilley asked.

Sam shook his head. "No, that was Greta. She must've been in the area, observing things for a while. We believe she murdered Jason because she figured out he was working for Boris and she wanted to mess around with Boris as revenge for not paying her when Heather Holland was murdered.

"We know she killed Boris as a message to Chanel and to frame her for the crime, which would put her life in jeopardy with the mob, but we think an additional side motive would've been to get further revenge on the guy who jilted her out of her contract money."

I shuddered when I thought about how close I'd come to being one of the people listed in Greta's body count.

"Anyway," Sam continued, "Maks figured out it was Greta when Boris showed up dead. He knew the fact that Chanel was set up to take the fall would throw the whole organization into chaos. Nobody was gonna believe that Chanel killed Boris. She'd been a jilted lover or something. It was well known that Chanel was gay, and she'd sidestepped Boris's advances before. So the real killer was somebody the family was actively trying to find. I don't think anybody but Maks suspected it was Greta."

"But Chanel knew," I said.

"She did. She recognized the handwriting on the mirror, and knew her former lover was coming after her. And now you also know why Lenny was murdered."

"We do," I said. "Chanel told us when we were all in the panic room together."

Sam nodded. "It was Greta who also insisted that Boris have the Suttons seek out Chanel for the listing on the house where Lenny was murdered."

"Why?" I asked, horrified by Greta's cruelty.

Sam shrugged. "It was another twist of the knife," he said. "She wanted Chanel to suffer for cheating on her, and what better way to do that than to kill her lover and force her to represent the two men eager to benefit from that murder."

"Whoa," Gilley said. "It stuns me that Chanel found the courage to leave Greta."

"Maks helped her," Sam said. "He knew that Chanel was miserable in her relationship with Greta, but at the time, he didn't realize that Greta was the Angel of Death. He thought Greta was Boris's personal accountant, which is why he introduced Chanel to Greta in the first place. He was hoping to befriend her, and flip her too."

"What would Chanel know?"

"Well, she was living with Greta, so if there was accounting information nearby, Chanel could've gotten it. But Maks realized she'd make a terrible informant given how timid and meek she was. He felt bad for getting her involved with Boris's crowd, so he helped her leave Greta by letting her know about a trip Boris was taking to Chechnya where Greta was going along. While they were away, two things happened: a powerful family member died of a sudden heart attack, from which Boris moved up the chain of command, and Chanel escaped to her grandaunt's house in Connecticut."

"I'm shocked that Greta didn't hunt Chanel down then and kill her," Gilley said.

"Again, that was because of Maks," Sam said. "The minute he knew that Chanel was safe in Connecticut, he called Boris and told him that he had some intel that Chanel was being looked at by the FBI as someone they might want to turn into an informant. Maks had taken it upon himself to move Chanel out of the area to eliminate her as a possible leak, and then Boris told Greta that if she took up with Chanel again, there would be no further contracts coming her way."

"Which protected Chanel. At least for a while," I said.

"Yes. Anyway, we still didn't put it together that Greta was the Angel of Death until she tried to kill you, Catherine." Sam said.

"Which surprises me," I told him.

Sam shrugged. "Greta was a master of disguises. Anytime she interacted with Maks, she was dressed very professionally, and all the descriptions of the Angel of Death had her in these wild outfits. We were too slow to connect the dots."

I sighed. It was all so depressing. "What will happen to Chanel now?"

Sam shook his head. "There's quite a lot we could charge her with—obstruction, lying to a federal officer, conspiracy . . . but we all know that Chanel wouldn't have been in the position to lie to us if Maks hadn't set her up with Greta in the first place, so I'm recommending that we move on and let her be. She's no longer relevant to our investigation."

"Where is she now?" Gilley asked.

"She's with Detective Shepherd's sister," he said. "I had to inform her that Greta murdered her grandaunt. Chanel took it pretty hard, and the only friend she has still in the area is Sunny D'Angelo."

I nodded in approval. "Sunny will take good care of Chanel," I said. "I'm glad you got her to someone who'll look after her."

Sam put his hands on his knees and stood up. "Now you know all of it," he said. "And I'm gonna try and find out how Maks is doing."

Sam walked away and Gilley and I leaned against each other, both of us exhausted.

"You two aren't falling asleep here, are you?" a voice said. We looked up and Shepherd stood in the entry of the waiting room, a large white patch covering the wound at his temple.

"We're hoping to hear something about Maks," I said.

Shepherd came forward. "I just asked. He's out of surgery. It went well."

I let out a huge sigh of relief and Gilley wrapped his arms around my shoulders, giving them a squeeze. "Thank God," he said. Looking at me, he added, "Can we go home now? I'm dead on my feet, Cat."

"We can," I said, taking up his hand and squeezing it.

"Can I come?" Shepherd asked softly. "I'd . . . prefer not to be alone tonight."

Gilley and I looked at him in shock, then Gilley turned to me expectantly.

"Of course," I said, feeling a flush touch my cheeks. "We can all commune at Chez Cat. I'll have Sebastian preheat the oven, and I'll throw in a frozen pizza for dinner and then we can get some rest."

The tension in Shepherd's shoulders relaxed and he smiled shyly at me.

Without another word, we left the hospital together.

Chapter 21

It was nearly ten days later before I was allowed to see Maks. His recovery was very difficult given not just how much blood he'd lost and how close he'd come to dying, but because of an infection that'd set in shortly after he got out of surgery. It was very touch and go for a few days, and I worried anxiously over his health until I called my sister, caught her up on most of the events, and told her about Maks.

She'd assured me that Maks would be fine, but she'd also said that any thoughts of romance with him would soon be dashed. That led to a series of questions about the *other* romantic interest in my life . . . but more on that in a minute.

Anyway, I was finally given the all-clear by a kindly nurse at the hospital to visit Maks the next day, and after staying up late that night to prepare something special for him, I wasted no time getting over to the hospital to see him the next morning.

"Hey there," I said, entering his darkened room on tip-toe.

He stirred in the bed and smiled weakly at me. "Catherine," he said, my name rolling off his lips like a soft rumble of far-off thunder. "I've been waiting for you."

I came to sit next to his bed and brushed the hair back from his forehead. Even lying weak and unshaven in a hospital bed, he was still sexy. "How're you feeling?"

"Fantastic," he said, his voice coarse and barely above a whisper.

I smiled. "I'll bet." Reaching down, I pulled a large container out of a warming bag and set it on the rolling dinner tray. "I won't stay long, but I wanted to bring you this. I know you must be tired, so if you want me to store it somewhere, I can do that for you."

"I'm tired of this bed," he said, peering at the container. "What did you bring me?"

I lifted the lid and allowed the smell to waft out. Maks bent forward and sniffed. "You made me beef Wellington?" he said.

I grinned. "As promised."

Maks chuckled, but it was a weak sound and it worried me. "Ahhh, delightful," he said. Then he lifted both arms slightly, which seemed to take significant effort and caused him some pain. "Cutting into that might be a challenge for me, though."

I pulled the container close and used the fork and knife I brought to cut the food. "Would you like me to feed you?" I asked.

"Very much," he said.

I offered him the first bite and watched happily as he

chewed it and rolled his eyes up in pleasure. "That's amazing," he said.

I fed him a few more pieces, but then paused when he lay his head back on the pillow and sighed as if exhausted. Putting the cover back on the container, I said, "I should go."

Maks limply reached for my hand. "Don't go just yet," he said. "Catch me up on everything that I missed."

"You haven't heard the story yet?"

"Bits and pieces," he said. "Greta's dead, yes?"

"Yes, she's in the category of *very* dead, actually."

"Chanel?"

I grinned again. "She's good. She was heartbroken after the loss of her grandaunt, but lately she's been in the company of someone who's taking very good care of her. Together they've been doing a lot of exploring and sampling all the best restaurants in the area."

Max eyed me curiously. "A new suitor?"

"Definitely."

"Who?"

"One of my clients. I don't know that you ever met him. His name is Willem Entwistle. He's a lovely young man. He saved our lives, you know."

"The dwarf?"

"Little person, and yes."

Max let out a wheezy chuckle. "Good for Chanel," he said.

"Good for Willem. They actually make a terrific couple. And, according to Willem's Instagram, they just bought an alpaca together."

"An alpaca?" Maks said. "You're joking."

"Nope."

"Well, if alpacas are involved, it *must* be serious."

"I think it could be," I said with a giggle.

"How's Gilley?"

I looked at my watch. "I suspect he's much better right about now."

"Why?"

"Because I booked him a flight to Marrakesh to visit his husband. He should be deplaning right about . . . now."

"You're a good friend, Catherine."

I smiled. "I'm glad you think so."

Then I caught Maks up on the rest of what'd happened, from right after he'd passed out to the ten days since he'd entered the hospital.

"I miss all the good stuff," he said when I'd finished.

I put his hand to my cheek and felt tears sting my eyes. "I'm so glad you're still with us, you know."

He pulled my hand feebly to his lips and kissed it, and we simply enjoyed the sweet moment between us for a bit in silence. And then Maks said, "I'll need to get back to Toronto soon."

"Toronto? You're leaving?"

Maks nodded. "As soon as I can walk out of here I'll have to go home and explain what happened."

"What do you mean? Explain to whom?"

"Mikhail Magomedov."

"That sounds like a made up name."

He smiled. "It's real. I swear."

"Okay, so who is this Mikhail Magomedov and why does he need explaining to?"

"He's the new head of the organization," Maks said simply.

I shook my head a little. "Wait . . . you're still dealing with these mafia people?"

"It's my job, Catherine."

"But . . . why hasn't Sam and his cronies brought these guys in? I mean, don't they have everything they need now that you've turned Paul Sutton in to an informant?"

"Paul has gone missing," Maks said.

"What do you mean he's gone missing?"

"Sam got word to me this morning. Paul has either fled or someone within the organization figured out he's a liability and took care of him."

"You mean . . . he may be *dead*?"

"Yes."

I was aghast. I'd thought for sure that now that Basayev and Greta were both out of the picture Maks would be able to stop this whole mafia informant thing. "So, you're going to continue to work undercover."

"I am," he said. "I'm going to take credit for killing Greta, which should help cement me as a trusted member of the organization and allow me access to even more information."

"Which will also ratchet up the danger," I said.

"Perhaps," he said noncommittally.

"No," I said, setting his hand down on the bedsheet.

"No, what?"

I closed my eyes for a long moment, and when I opened them I looked directly at Maks. "No, I can't be involved with anyone who does what you do, Maks."

Maks winced and didn't say anything. He simply waited me out.

I sighed and dropped my gaze to the bedsheet. "I have two boys. They need their mother. If we were to see each other romantically, who's to say that some member of that organization wouldn't suspect you as an informant and make *you* disappear, and me along with you?"

Maks nodded. "Of course you're right," he said. "But . . .
I'll miss you, Catherine."

I put my hand over his, and brought my gaze to his
face again. "Promise me you won't get killed," I said.

"I promise to do my best to stay alive," was all he
would commit to.

It would have to be good enough.

I left Maks a short time later, a bit sad, but also relieved.

I'd probably also already decided that, between Maks
and Shepherd, as vexing as Shepherd could be, I was
likely better off with him as a romantic partner than Maks.

Speaking of which . . .

"Well, hello, pretty lady," Shepherd said when I
stepped out of the car to join him for a picnic by the beach
where I'd nearly been taken out by a hot air balloon.

"Hello yourself," I told him. Pointing to the spread on
the picnic table, I added, "This is nice."

"Made it myself," he said, taking the plastic cover off
two take-out orders that were clearly from Cittanuova's
Italian restaurant. I laughed and rolled my eyes.

"How's Maks?" Shepherd asked next as he handed me
one of the dishes and a fork.

"Good. Still recovering, but good."

Shepherd nodded and dug into his pasta. I felt for him,
because I knew he was itching to ask me if I was going to
start seeing Maks again. I decided to put him out of his
misery.

"Maks is leaving for Toronto as soon as he recovers," I
said.

Shepherd paused the energetic stabbing of his food. "Oh,
yeah?" he asked so casually you'd have really thought he
didn't especially care.

"Yes. I don't think we'll be seeing a lot of each other from now on."

A tiny quirk to the corners of Shepherd's lips appeared. "You don't say?"

"And I know it's still very early in this thing between us, Steve, but I just wanted you to know that I don't plan on seeing anyone else besides you as long as we're an item."

Still playing it cool, Shepherd simply nodded. "Have you forgiven me yet?" he asked, and his question took me by surprise.

"Forgiven you?"

Shepherd stopped poking at his pasta and looked up at me. "For not telling you about Chanel."

I sighed. "What went on between you and Chanel isn't any of my business. Plus, it was all in the past. Just promise me that if you decide to see me exclusively, that you'll tell me, and that you won't break that promise as long as we're together."

"That's a fair ask," he said, and went back to poking at his pasta.

The moment felt awkward and I found myself doing more poking than eating too. A long silence played out between us and I started to regret bringing up the topic.

"Hey, Catherine?"

"Yeah?"

"I'd like to see you exclusively, and I promise that, as long as we're together, it'll be just you and me. That sound okay to you?"

A slow grin inched its way onto my lips. "Yeah, Steve. That sounds okay to me."

"Good," he said.

And it was.